1988

University of St. Francis
GEN 823.912 N554j
C0-AJY-784
3 0301 00090285 4

Joyce's *Ulysses*

Joyce's *Ulysses*

The Larger Perspective

Edited by
Robert D. Newman and Weldon Thornton

Newark: University of Delaware Press
London and Toronto: Associated University Presses

LIBRARY
College of St. Francis
JOLIET, ILLINOIS

© 1987 by Associated University Presses, Inc.

Associated University Presses
440 Forsgate Drive
Cranbury, NJ 08512

Associated University Presses
25 Sicilian Avenue
London WC1A 2QH, England

Associated University Presses
2133 Royal Windsor Drive
Unit 1
Mississauga, Ontario
Canada L5J 1K5

The paper used in this publication meets the requirements of the American National Standard for Permanence of Paper for Printed Library Materials Z39.48-1984.

Library of Congress Cataloging-in-Publication Data

Joyce's Ulysses.

Includes bibliographies.
1. Joyce, James, 1882–1941. Ulysses. I. Newman, Robert D., 1951– . II. Thornton, Weldon.
PR6019.09U6595 1987 823′.912 86-40399
ISBN 0-87413-316-5 (alk. paper)

Printed in the United States of America

823.912
N554j

Contents

128,719

Notes on Contributors

MICHAEL H. BEGNAL, Professor of English and Comparative Literature at the Pennsylvania State University, has published widely on modern and contemporary literature, including two books on *Finnegans Wake*.

ZACK BOWEN, Professor and Chairman of the Department of English at the University of Miami, is the author of numerous books and articles on Joyce, Mary Lavin, Padraic Colum, and other modern British authors. These include *Musical Allusions in the Works of James Joyce: Early Poetry Through Ulysses* (1974) and *A Companion to Joyce Studies* (1984), coedited with James Carens.

SHELDON BRIVIC, Associate Professor of English at Temple University, is the author of *Joyce Between Freud and Jung* (1980) and *Joyce the Creator* (1985). He is now finishing a novel, *Stealing,* and his next book will be a Lacanian study, tentatively entitled *The Subject of Joyce*.

MICHAEL PATRICK GILLESPIE, Associate Professor of English at Marquette University, has published *Inverted Volumes Improperly Arranged: James Joyce and his Trieste Library* (1983) and a number of essays on modern writers.

ELLIOTT GOSE, Professor of English at the University of British Columbia, Vancouver, is the author of *The Transformation Process in Joyce's* Ulysses (1980) and *The World of the Irish Wonder Tale* (1985).

CHERYL HERR, Associate Professor of English at the University of Iowa, is the author of several articles on Joyce and of *Joyce's Anatomy of Culture* (1986). She is currently working on an edition of unpublished Irish historical melodramas, and on a cycle of interdisciplinary essays about semiotics and spatiality.

RICHARD M. KAIN, Professor Emeritus at the University of Louisville, is the author and editor of a great many books and articles on Joyce and on the Irish Literary Renaissance.

KAREN LAWRENCE, Associate Professor and Chairperson in the English Department at the University of Utah, has written numerous articles on Joyce, in addition to her book *The Odyssey of Style in Ulysses* (1981). She co-authored *The McGraw-Hill Guide to English Literature* (1985) and is currently working on a book on issues of gender, language, and authority in travel novels.

PATRICK A. MCCARTHY, Professor of English and Director of Graduate Studies in English at the University of Miami, is the author of *The Riddles of Finnegans Wake* (1980), *Olaf Stapledon* (1982), and of numerous articles. He has recently edited *Critical Essays on Samuel Beckett* (1986) and is now writing a book on *Ulysses* for Twayne Publishers.

JAMES MADDOX, Professor of English at George Washington University, also teaches frequently at the Bread Loaf School of English. He is the author of *Joyce's Ulysses and the Assault Upon Character* (1978), as well as articles on Joyce, Samuel Richardson, and Defoe. He is now completing a book on Richardson and the English novel.

ROBERT D. NEWMAN, Assistant Professor of English at Texas A&M University, is the author of *Understanding Thomas Pynchon* (1986) and of several articles on modern and contemporary literature. He is currently writing a book on Joyce and the Hermetic tradition and is coediting a volume of essays entitled *Postmodern Humanism*.

JOHN HENRY RALEIGH, Professor of English at the University of California, Berkeley, is the author of *Matthew Arnold and American Culture (1957), The Plays of Eugene O'Neill* (1965), *Time, Place, and Idea: Essays on the Novel* (1968), *The Chronicles of Leopold and Molly Bloom: Ulysses as Narrative* (1978), and of some fifty articles.

STANLEY SULTAN, Professor of English at Clark University, has published books on Joyce, Yeats, Eliot, and Synge. His most recent book is a novel, *RABBI: A Tale of the Waning Year* (1977). His essay in this volume is based upon the final chapter of *Eliot, Joyce, and Company* (1987).

WELDON THORNTON, Professor of English at the University of North Carolina at Chapel Hill, is the author of books on Joyce and Synge and of articles on a number of modern British and American writers. He is currently working on a book on the roots of modernism, entitled *Beware of What You Wish for: Modernism as Western Aspiration*.

G. J. WATSON, Senior Lecturer at the University of Aberdeen, is a graduate of Queen's University, Belfast, and of Oxford University. His publications include *Irish Identity and the Literary Revival* (1979) and *Drama: An Introduction* (1983), as well as numerous articles on Irish literature. He is currently writing *Irish Literature Since 1800* for the Longman Literature in English series.

Preface

Over the past several decades, criticism of Joyce's works—and particularly of *Ulysses*—has developed an impressive diversity of approaches, including some that deal with such presumably fundamental questions as whether *Ulysses* be a novel at all, whether Joyce has abandoned "representation" as an artistic aim, and whether the critic should presume to seek determinate "meanings" in the text. These approaches raise questions not only about whether *Ulysses* presents its meanings and values through the traditional novelistic modes of character, plot, imagery, and tone, but about whether the book proposes any values at all. And to critics of this persuasion, it begs the very questions that we should be debating if we presume that *Ulysses* is a novel, or if we presume that we can give the term *novel* sufficient definition to justify our using it in critical discussions.

To other critics, however, these questions and claims about *Ulysses* run the risk of depriving us of the affective and connotative richness that reading the novel should provide. We seem in danger of coming to regard *Ulysses* not as one of the finest and richest novels ever written, but as a compendium of techniques, or as a philosophical (or anti-philosophical) treatise. And while the term *novel* may not be capable of formal definition, it still seems the most appropriate term for the discussion of *Ulysses,* in its assumption that the book is primarily a *narrative* about *characters.*

Among the many critical issues that these divergent perspectives upon *Ulysses* raise is a question that has troubled the Western mind at least from the time of Socrates—namely, whether we can have meaningful knowledge of anything if we cannot give a formal account of how we know it. Socrates challenges Euthyphro as to whether he has any real knowledge of piety, if he cannot provide for a formal definition of piety and give a foolproof "effective procedure" for recognizing it. (The example and some of the language here are indebted to Hubert L. Dreyfus's *What Computers Can't Do* [1979].) The analogous question for the literary critic is whether we can make any meaningful statements about a "novel" if we cannot agree upon a definition and upon a formalized program for analyzing such a thing. But if literary criticism took seriously this line of thinking, it should abandon all further discussions of literary texts—whether "novel" or "poetry" or "drama"—until it has agreed upon a formal definition not only of these terms, but of "literature" itself. Many of us—including the contributors to this volume—are simply not prepared to do that.

This willingness to assume that *Ulysses* can be approached as a novel should not be taken to indicate that the essays within this volume exemplify any critical school or program. Beyond the very general "program" implied by the title of this collection—i.e., a concern to pursue a wholistic or "novelistic" approach to *Ulysses*—it would be inaccurate to say that there is any articulated critical position common to all of these essays. The editors of a collection such as this have, broadly speaking, two choices—to develop a specific rationale for their volume and then require the contributors to conform to that rationale; or to propose a more general perspective and permit the contributors considerable leeway in pursuing it. We have taken the latter approach, in the belief that the value of such a collection resides more firmly in the quality of the individual essays than in a neatly articulated rationale. And we believe that this decision will be applauded by anyone who reads through these quite varied and distinctive essays.

Since there is no procrustean rationale, there was likewise no prescription to the contributors as to how broad or narrow their *point d' appui* for viewing the novel might be. Some of these essays propose a broad overview of the text, while others approach it in terms of one theme or technique. Some are brief and suggestive; others are longer and more comprehensive of their topics. Similarly, there is no neat plan of arrangement to the contents of the volume, beyond some juxtaposition of essays that are similar in scope and approach, and a complementary aim to encourage some fruitful contrasts of perspective as the volume proceeds. And while there was no attempt on our part to impose any overall design, the reader of these essays will discover among them many instances of complementariness.

The first two essays—those of Cheryl Herr and G. J. Watson—both pursue broad, overarching issues about the novel. Herr's "Art and Life, Nature and Culture, *Ulysses*" provides an appropriate entry to the volume by its exploration of the various ways in which reading *Ulysses* requires us constantly to move back and forth between the received categories of "art" and of "life," of "nature" and of "culture," thus causing us to understand, even to experience, how inextricably intertwined these categories are. Watson's "The Politics of *Ulysses*" also takes an overview, exploring the broadly "political" implications of *Ulysses* to show that the novel both implicitly and explicitly challenges the simplistic, monocular vision of the sacred march of Irish history that was a received feature of the nationalist imagination of the time.

Patrick A. McCarthy's "*Ulysses* and the Printed Page" focuses much more sharply on one aspect of *Ulysses*—its various uses of the medium of the printed page—but does so in order to show how Joyce uses the rich possibilities of the medium of print only to expose it as one more convention, one more artificial and inexact means of approximating reality.

Richard M. Kain's reminiscence testifies to the ways that *Ulysses* can, over the course of several decades of one's living with the text, become part of the fabric of one's experience, and thus reminds us that our relationship with the literary texts that we value is not abstract and theoretical.

Karen Lawrence's "Paternity, the Legal Fiction" deals succinctly with the broad theme of paternity (and its complement, maternity) to show how Joyce in *Ulysses* questions the singleness and authority of authorship and the corollary idea of the originality of the author as the source of his own language.

John Henry Raleigh's "*Ulysses:* Trinitarian and Catholic" is an impressive and detailed exploration of relationships among the central characters, arguing that the "meaning" of *Ulysses* is the whole of *Ulysses,* and that the most important meaning-constituents in the mighty labyrinth are the central characters themselves. Michael Patrick Gillespie's "Redrawing the Artist as a Young Man" also assumes the basic importance of the characters to the meanings of *Ulysses* and discusses in considerable detail the growth of Stephen Dedalus from *Portrait* to *Ulysses,* showing how this growth reflects Joyce's own progressive understanding of what is involved in an individual's development.

James Maddox's "Mockery in *Ulysses*" skillfully uses the theme of mockery and the idea of a rivalry among modes of discourse in the novel as a basis for demonstrating that *Ulysses'* two main subjects—its novelistic concern with character and plot on the one hand and its metanovelistic concern with styles on the other—are in fact integrally related aspects of Joyce's larger purposes in the novel.

Zack Bowen's "*Ulysses* as a Comic Novel" takes an overview of the novel to propose that Joyce's perspective is ultimately that of comic affirmation—a depiction of a world in which nothing is resolved, because Joyce's purpose is not to propose solutions to life's problems and dilemmas, but to celebrate the vitality of the ongoing struggle.

Robert D. Newman's "*Transformatio Coniunctionis:* Alchemy in *Ulysses*" uses the perspectives of alchemy and of Jung's ideas on individuation to show Joyce's sympathy with the hermetic mode of thought and to reveal how these perspectives contribute to the unified psychological design of the novel. A complementary psychological approach is offered by Sheldon Brivic's "The Other of *Ulysses.*" Brivic draws upon the Freudian concept of the superego (as elaborated by Lacan) to discuss the complex relationships among the psyches of the various characters of the novel and an underlying "mind of the text"—a psychic substrate deriving from Joyce himself that provides an "other" to stand over against and complement the personalities of each of the characters in the novel.

As its title indicates, Elliott Gose's "The Coincidence of Contraries as Theme and Technique in *Ulysses*" demonstrates the pervasiveness in *Ulysses* of the Brunonian principle of the coincidence of contraries. As Gose shows, this principle manifests itself, as technique and as theme, in virtually every facet of *Ulysses,* thus providing one of the most persistent bases of its complex unity.

Michael H. Begnal's "Art and History: Stephen's Mirror and Parnell's Silk Hat" uses the responses to art and to history of Bloom and Stephen as a basis for arguing the superiority of Bloom's reactions, because while Stephen regards art and history as abstract categories, Bloom handles them as lookingglasses that reflect a meaningful image of himself.

Weldon Thornton's "Voices and Values in *Ulysses*" returns to the vexed question of the meaning of the various voices in *Ulysses* to argue that Joyce's style in the opening episodes of the novel is in some respect "normative," and that the voices of the later episodes represent perspectives that Joyce wishes to expose as somehow distortive or insufficient, illustrating these claims through a discussion of the theme of idolatry in Oxen of the Sun.

Stanley Sultan's comprehensive "The Adventures of *Ulysses* in Our World" offers the fullest discussion of the critical context out of which the various views of *Ulysses* alluded to earlier in this Preface arose. After showing his awareness and even his appreciation of the various anti-novelistic approaches that have been taken to *Ulysses* in recent years, Sultan reaffirms the primacy of the novelistic aspects of the work, thus providing an appropriate conclusion to a volume of essays devoted to exploring and extolling *Ulysses* as one of the greatest and richest novels in our literary tradition.

Robert D. Newman
Weldon Thornton

Acknowledgments

Permission to quote from *Ulysses: A Critical and Synoptic Edition,* published by Garland Publishing, New York, was obtained from Random House, Inc., New York, and the Bodley Head, London.

Thanks to the Department of English and the College of Liberal Arts of Texas A&M University for providing funds that helped to offset the costs of permission fees and editorial work.

Abbreviations Used in the Text

CW — James Joyce. *The Critical Writings of James Joyce,* ed. Ellsworth Mason and Richard Ellmann. New York: Viking Press, 1959.

D — James Joyce. *Dubliners,* ed. Robert Scholes in consultation with Richard Ellmann. New York: Viking Press, 1967.
James Joyce. *Dubliners: Text, Criticism, and Notes,* ed. Robert Scholes and A. Walton Litz. New York: Viking Press, 1969.

FW — James Joyce. *Finnegans Wake*. New York: Viking Press, 1939; London: Faber and Faber, 1939. (Both editions have the same pagination.)

JJI — Richard Ellman. *James Joyce*. New York: Oxford University Press, 1959.

JJII — Richard Ellman. *James Joyce*. Revised edition. New York: Oxford University Press, 1982.

JJA — *The James Joyce Archive,* ed. Michael Groden et al. New York and London: Garland Publishing, 1978

Letters I, II, III — James Joyce. *The Letters of James Joyce*. Vol. I, ed. Stuart Gilbert. New York: Viking Press, 1957 (reissued with corrections, 1966). Vols. II and III, ed. Richard Ellmann. New York: Viking Press, 1966.

P — James Joyce. *A Portrait of the Artist as a Young Man*. The definitive text corrected from the Dublin Holograph by Chester G. Anderson and edited by Richard Ellmann. New York: Viking Press, 1964.
James Joyce. *A Portrait of the Artist as a Young Man: Text, Criticism, and Notes,* ed. Chester G. Anderson. New York: Viking Press, 1968.

SH — James Joyce. *Stephen Hero,* ed. John J. Slocum and Herbert Cahoon. New York: New Directions, 1944, 1963.

SL — James Joyce. *Selected Letters of James Joyce,* ed. Richard Ellmann. New York: Viking Press, 1975.

U — James Joyce. *Ulysses: A Critical and Synoptic Edition,* ed.

Hans Walter Gabler et al. New York and London: Garland Publishing, 1984.

James Joyce. *Ulysses.* New York: Random House, 1986. (Reference to both of these editions is by episode and line number, as called for in the *Critical and Synoptic Edition,* 1903–4.)

Joyce's *Ulysses*

Art and Life, Nature and Culture, *Ulysses*

CHERYL HERR

> It was life but was it fair? It was free but was it art?
> (*FW,* 94.9–10)

In a reflex from its own energy, *Ulysses* has moved its readers down many critical paths. In the early 1920s Valery Larbaud and company sought the clue to *Ulysses* in the work's Odyssean and other schematic structures. During the New Critical heyday, the key was thought by some to be, among other things, the one that Bloom leaves behind him and seeks all day along alley and, yes, quay. Readers fruitfully charted images and triangulated motifs in order to reveal the designs-upon-designs upon which the meaning of the work was assumed to rest. More recently we have seen a poststructuralist concern with disembodying voice and locating *aporiae,* with reflexivity and the self-consciousness of Joyce's fiction. And in recent work, Freud / Lacan and Marx have begun to receive articulation with Joyce's writing. The fact is that Joyce's great narrative has made the critical enterprise into a simulacrum of the travels of the legendary Wandering Jew whose footsore angst Leopold Bloom emulates and whose worldweariness formed an unmistakable part of Joyce's own experience of Europe between the two wars. Legend composing art composing life composing art composing response to life and art—something like this vacillating sequence maps out a territory that is not contained within the covers of the "usylessly unreadable Blue Book of Eccles" (*FW,* 179.26–27). What I propose to offer here is not a compact reading of the narrative but a positioning of it; I want to identify the key to *Ulysses* not with a theme nor even with the roads along which the narrative has guided us but with what the narrative does, not with the action in the work but with the work enacted on the borderline between art and life.

I chart my course in this way partly because, like the literalist preachers of my youth, I have discovered that Joyce's synoptic scripture, as the author knew, interacts alchemically with life. Like most if not all great works of art, *Ulysses* changes with the reader[1] and unlike many merely interesting pieces of literature, keeps pace with (or perhaps even paces) the reader's experience of life. At first, the reader finds in *Ulysses* the grand themes of Western literature: the son's search for the father, the father's search for the child he can never truly know to be his offspring, the artist's struggle for recognition and cash, the quest for romantic love, the often unsatisfying domestication of that love, the acceptance of death, the human battle with betrayal and despair. Visiting Ireland, the same reader may become convinced that the narrative must be understood in context; it is a book about a writer's vexed relationship to a land plagued with poverty, dominated by an oppressive foreign government, and hostile to its own prophets. Later, our reader may tire of travel or politics and turn to aesthetics. By his new lights, *Ulysses* becomes a multiply reflexive work; style is the subject as well as the medium of this meta-fiction. Or the work may turn forward another of its prismatic faces and lure him into a study of metaphysics, theosophy, epistemology, psychoanalysis, or syntax. In contrast, the philosophical and psychological colors may fade along with the technical and archetypal, casting into relief the personal dimension of the work. Hence, it may dawn on our representative reader that *Ulysses* is *really* about the effort to return home and the difficulties of getting there, or it may seem that the novel centers on whether Bloom, at day's end, will go upstairs and join his unfaithful Penelope in bed.

But I do not want to be misunderstood as merely voicing the platitude that *Ulysses* is a great and various fiction that grows with the reader. Rather than view Joyce's first epic as being about the topics and ideas traditionally put forward as explaining or unlocking the work, it seems more enlightening altogether to view such material as the stuff through which Joyce posed his challenge to the received relationship of art and life. Without a doubt, that confrontation is in *Ulysses* raised to a power higher than is characteristic of any other work canonized in most American colleges and universities. The challenge emerges from the fact that the narrative is a masterpiece of semiotic pseudo-comprehensiveness; it is a model of cultural processes and materials. And it is the nature of this model, what it encompasses and what it marginalizes or excludes, that occupies me when I consider not this or that aspect of *Ulysses* but the work as a tenuous and vexing whole. Certainly, a margin—in addition to being a popular spot in critical discourse today—is the appropriate area for examination when studying the whole, not least because it defines a dialectical relationship between what is inside and what is regarded as external. As I read it, *Ulysses* calls into being a boundary that it challenges in order to reveal the formulaic nature of both life and art—and to evoke something not contained by the specific formulae it repeats. That "something" I will later label, in echo of Fredric Jameson's work, the "cultural unconscious" of *Ulysses;* it is the complex nostalgia that the work's probing of both mind and society centers on.

But first, to underscore the peculiar relationship of *ars* and *vita* that *Ulysses* explores, I must recur to a day not long ago that I spent in the National Library of Ireland. While doing some research into Irish censorship, I ran across an open letter written in 1885 by a Mr. Frederick J. Gregg to the *Dublin University Review*. Mr. Gregg claimed to have overheard an attendant at the National Library tell a reader "that Walt Whitman's poems had been suppressed." Gregg asked about this matter and was informed that the librarian, William Archer, had in fact banned or withheld the volume from circulation. Gregg then proceeded to defend *Leaves of Grass* as a great book, which he found, despite the objections of some critics, not "indelicate." In fact, he calculated that only eighty of its 9,000 lines could be considered objectionable.[2] In a letter of response printed the following month, Archer denied having suppressed Whitman, but what caught my eye in this controversy was the cited address of the open-minded Gregg: 6, Eccles Street, Dublin. Delighted at the possibility that Gregg was Leopold Bloom's next-door neighbor, I was playfully pulled at once in two directions. First, I wanted to check Thom's Directory to see how long Mr. Gregg had resided on Eccles Street; was he there in 1903 when the Blooms "moved in"?[3] At the same time, I thought of the ironies of Stephen Dedalus's disappointing conversation with the intelligentsia at the National Library. Whether or not Archer's defense was any more accurate than Gregg's accusation, it is woefully appropriate that after having his place at the Tower usurped by Haines, Stephen should find no better reception in the library than was apparently accorded to Whitman. In another corner of my mind, I wondered in which room of the current library the conversation of Stephen, Mulligan, A.E., Eglinton, Best, and company "took place." Clearly, there are problems involved in such speculation, not the least of which is punctuation; are double quotation marks (like those I've used above) the appropriate markers for verbs that refer to the projected-as-real actions of Joyce's characters? A similar difficulty plagued Richard Best, who, having been absorbed into the world of *Ulysses,* felt that he had to defend his status as a nonfictional person.[4] He had to fight against the quotation marks that forever surrounded his name once it was used in *Ulysses.*

At this point in the history of *Ulysses* criticism, it is not necessary to document in detail the curious effect that the novel creates from its reference to an overwhelming number of details from the real Dublin. Nor need we linger long over the book's own oblique comments upon its narrative practice. It may be sufficient to note that Scylla and Charybdis, the episode in which Stephen devotes extensive theoretical ingenuity to elaborating his theory that Shakespeare wrote his life into his art, begins with words that comically highlight the literary uses of life:

Urbane, to comfort them, the quaker librarian purred:
—And we have, have we not, those priceless pages of *Wilhelm Meister.* A great poet on a great brother poet. A hestitating soul taking arms against a sea of troubles, torn by conflicting doubts, as one sees in real life.
He came a step a sinkapace forward on neatsleather creaking and a step backward a sinkapace on the solemn floor.
A noiseless attendant setting open the door but slightly made him a noiseless beck.
—Directly, said he, creaking to go, albeit lingering. The beautiful ineffectual dreamer who comes to grief against hard facts. One always feels that Goethe's judgments are so true. True in the larger analysis.
Twicreakingly analysis he corantoed off. (*U,* 9.1–12)

The librarian measures art by its echoing of "real life," but his words and actions as *Ulysses* presents them echo the works he has read and are narrated to us in a self-consciously artificial style. In the brief passage quoted above, we find not only that the librarian's romantic notion of literary truth relies on Goethe but also that the texture of his "life" blends phrases from *Wilhelm Meister's Apprenticeship, Hamlet, Twelfth Night, Julius Ceasar,* and the *Essays in Criticism: Second Series* of Matthew Arnold.[5] Clearly figuring the process by which texts make our reality, Joyce continually quotes both other works and his own, extending the reflexive gesture of his fiction to include all of the life that the tradition of Western fiction has created.

The significance of Joyce's varied and insistent mingling of art and life is not exhausted when we merely cite his idiosyncratic attachment in the narrative to the facts of his experience of Dublin. At least two aspects of *Ulysses* come to mind as germane to our understanding of this narrative practice. The first is Joyce's well-advertised narrative "innovation" in *Ulysses*—one that attracted much of the initial attention to the text. I refer to Joyce's use of the interior monologue and stream-of-consciousness techniques. A second relevant matter is the rough adherence of the book's design to the encyclopedic schemata that Joyce circulated to Carlo Linati, Stuart Gilbert, and Herbert Gorman. I want to discuss here the persistence with which *Ulysses* looks and moves in both directions—interior and schematic—at once. With its attention to the supposed workings of the mind and the revelation of the inner identity of Western man, the stream-of-consciousness technique appeals to our sense of what is natural—to the life, particularly the unconscious life, that we seem to share. With its attention to many of the categories by which the Westen world knows itself, this schematic book directs us toward a concept of culture, toward the domain of art. Life and art, nature and culture—on these grand dichotomies *Ulysses* is constructed, and to the exploration of these oppositions as such the fiction is dedicated. From this process of assertion and challenge, which describes what *Ulysses* does at its margins, comes, I believe, the force of the narrative for a surprisingly diverse community of readers.

Stream of Consciousness: "Nature It Is" (*U*, 18.1563)?

Arthur Power tells us of an intriguing conversation in which Joyce maintained that *Ulysses* explored parts of the psyche that had never before been treated in fiction; "the modern theme," Joyce argued, "is the subterranean forces, those hidden tides which govern everything and run humanity counter to the apparent flood: those poisonous subtleties which envelop the soul, the ascending fumes of sex."[6] The means of this revelation have long been discussed,[7] the techniques employed by Joyce including third-person narration attuned to the speech mannerisms and thought patterns of the character under attention, direct dialogue, interior monologue, and seeming transcription of thoughts in sentence or fragment form. There's no question that Joyce's approximation of the flow of consciousness, although dependent on at least fragments of words, represents a significant experimental attempt to portray the movements of the mind; hence, quite early in the presentations of Stephen, Bloom, and Molly, the narrative begins to employ this crucial modernist technique. By the fourth page of the book, we find ourselves eased from narration per se into Stephen's first fully presented thought, "As he and others see me. Who chose this face for me? This dogsbody to rid of vermin. It asks me too" (*U*, 1.136–37). Elegaic, measured, rhetorical—these few comments introduce us to Stephen's mind and set the tone for much of his moody self-assessment on 16 June 1904. Similarly, by the eleventh line of Calypso, the episode in which we meet Leopold Bloom, we find fragments of directly "reported" thought punctuating the third-person narration:

> Another slice of bread and butter: three, four: right. She didn't like her plate full. Right. He turned from the tray, lifted the kettle off the hob and set it sideways on the fire. It sat there, dull and squat, its spout stuck out. Cup of tea soon. Good. Mouth dry. (*U*, 4.11–14)

Likewise, from the first word of Penelope, Molly may be regarded as speaking, or rather thinking, her mind.

In one sense, then, *Ulysses* constantly and with ever-greater fervor moves us close to life not only by signaling about certain word-units, "These are an individual's most personal thoughts," but also by directing those thoughts toward a wide range of topics, including many subjects obviously unsuitable for polite conversation in Joyce's Dublin. For instance, Bloom recalls his love-making with Molly on Howth and ponders Milly's budding sexuality; he thinks that he might masturbate in the bath; he considers Gerty's serviceable underwear. Stephen rejects both the corpse-chewing God of his imagination and the ghost of his mother; he broods over his social usurpation by medicine man and conqueror; he probes the mysteries of sex and birth. Molly thinks of Boylan, Bloom, Mulvey, Stephen, Rudy, Milly, and a host of other people; she appreciates her soft thighs and firm breasts; she remembers with joy various sexual experiences; she declares her belief in her own powers of seduction. *Ulysses* asks us to view these passages as reporting the kinds of things that most real people think even if they do not always say them, and readers generally go along with the game, many of them marveling, as Carl Jung did, at Joyce's psychological acumen. That is, the narrative asks for our tacit agreement that the art of *Ulysses* mirrors life.

But in addition, we are asked to agree that life is like art, that our own thoughts emerge just as spontaneously as those of Joyce's characters not out of a void of preverbal desire but out of the fictive discourses and received ideas among and through which we live. Consider Stephen as he walks along Sandymount Strand: freed from friends and foes alike, he occupies himself with speculations on God, fatherhood, consubstantiality, aesthetics, sensation, women, language, library slips, and his own rotting teeth. Although Nestor ends with the supposed comment of a supposed omniscient narrator ("On his wise shoulders through the checkerwork of leaves the sun flung spangles, dancing coins" [*U,* 2.448–49]), Proteus begins by confronting us immediately with the language of Stephen's thoughts: "Ineluctable modality of the visible: at least that if no more, thought through my eyes. Signatures of all things I am here to read . . ." (*U,* 3.1–2). The entire first paragraph presents part of Stephen's somber-witty meditation on vision, knowledge, and the reality of the external world. From these thoughts, we learn that the young Dubliner, supposed by Homeric design to be in search of his father / Father, is wondering how he'll know him if he meets him, with the emphasis on *how*. The process of knowing and the perils of that process occupy Stephen's interior experience as he defines for himself the bottom line of cognitive possibility ("at least that if no more, thought through my eyes") and accepts the challenge of living as he sees it (not to be able to say with Mr Deasy *"I paid my way"* [*U,* 2.251] but to read the "Signatures of all things"). Stephen's thoughts here, as Weldon Thornton, John Killham, Hugh Kenner, and others have documented,[8] are mainly derived from philosophic or mystic masters like Aristotle, Aquinas, and Boehme. The precision and inventiveness with which Stephen weaves together bits and pieces from their texts are his own, of course, but it is the implied presence of such texts that structures his thinking.

Possibly Stephen's awareness of the claustrophic hovering of Western cultural tradition both outside and within his mind accounts in part for his nostalgic search for a non-received language of gesture. As he drunkenly describes the project to Lynch in Circe, he wants to transcend derivation from intermediary texts and to speak the "structural rhythm" of things. To create or use such a "universal language" would be to find "the gift of tongues rendering visible not the lay sense but the first entelechy" (*U,* 15.106–7). Hours after his walk on the strand, Stephen returns to the question of the visible and his hope that he can both read the language of nature and learn to speak it. Alas, Stephen's illustrative gestures allude to "the loaf and jug of bread or wine in Omar" (*U,* 15.117); *The Rubaiyat* is for the moment the dominant work, although not the only one giving contextual significance to Stephen's gestures. One of the things that Joyce's insistent alluding makes clear is that thinking, the streaming of consciousness, the content of interior monologue, the very shape of the self are woven from the materials of one's culture. *Fair Tyrants* joins *The Odyssey* and a host of other books in accounting for the contours of individual experience in the narrative; such works insure that whatever the stream of consciousness accomplishes in terms of artistic technique, it does not provide even the shadow of an access to a mythical human nature within or behind or beyond or above those informing texts. The art that seems to bring us closer to life seems to show us that art constitutes life and that nature as we can know it is always only culture. This conclusion, though familiar enough in contemporary thought, had its own radical charm in Joyce's day; it clearly fascinated Joyce enough for him to devote years to charting its implications.

A similar point might be made in our consideration of Molly's thoughts as they are rendered in Penelope. Even without knowing Joyce's famous description of her chapter as "perfectly sane full amoral fertilisable untrustworthy engaging shrew limited prudent indifferent 'Weib,' "[9] readers would have identified Molly with nature. Her ready acceptance of sexual difference and of different sexualities, her flowing speech and overt desiring, her maternity and menstruation, all mark Molly's Gea-Tellus status and distinguish her from the more intellectual Stephen and Bloom. This assessment of Molly recurs throughout Joyce criticism. And yet, however fundamentally unreflective she may appear to be, Molly's "thoughts" exhibit as much of the reflexive quality of language as do Stephen's. For example, the almost continuous pressure of syntactic ambiguity in her monologue ("the german Emperor is it yes imagine Im him think of him can you feel him trying to make a whore of me" [*U,* 18.95–96]) urges on

128719
College of St. Francis Library
Joliet, Illinois

the reader the constructedness of that prose and its attention to itself as language. Similarly, the eight "sentences" of Penelope and the "8 big poppies because mine was the 8th" (*U,* 18.329–30), like her reference to other books that have Mollys in them, nudge the reader into seeing *Ulysses* as a world of ambiguous and constantly shifting signs.[10] Like the Circe episode, which pretends to be a descent into the unconscious but constantly cycles out into the comedy of received ideas, Penelope paints the mind almost exclusively as the site on which convention and cliché register. And yet, perhaps because of Molly's own enthusiastic embracing of the natural ("God of heaven theres nothing like nature" [*U,* 18.1558–59]), or because of the convention by which women are construed to be closer to nature than men,[11] readers have often coded her as the Flesh or Nature or Life that Stephen must embrace before he can become an artist. Elaine Unkeless directly attacks this view in her recent essay, "The Conventional Molly Bloom," in which she argues that Joyce's portrait mostly restricts Molly to "preconceived ideas of the way a woman thinks and behaves."[12] Hence, our response to Molly as Earth Mother is based on our conventional notions of what constitutes naturalness. Drawing that artificial nature into the text, Molly's interior monologue is not unshaped thought but idea and self-image structured by society. The episode conveys at best a nostalgia for primal authenticity voiced from within the heart of culture. This voice echoes Stephen's sense that the "self" is "ineluctably preconditioned to become" what it is (*U,* 15.2120–21); such conditioning, as we see it in *Ulysses,* is largely social.

The ersatz quality of nature in *Ulysses* is perhaps most pointedly conveyed when Joyce's Dubliners go on or think about going on holiday outside of Dublin. Miss Kennedy and Miss Douce vacation at a seaside of music-hall clichés; Bloom recalls a "High School excursion" (*U,* 15.3308) to the falls at Poulaphouca, the most typical of tourist day-trips from the city. In Eumaeus, the narrative portrays Bloom as pompously and hilariously holding forth on the value of such trips; "the man in the street," he feels, "merited a radical change of *venue* after the grind of city life in the summertime for choice when Dame Nature is at her spectacular best constituting nothing short of a new lease of life." Bloom cites Poulaphouca, Wicklow, "the wilds of Donegal," and Howth as suitable spots in which to become attuned to nature (*U,* 16.551, 552–54, 557). Similarly, Simon Dedalus seems able to conceive of nothing farther outside Dublin than the fifty-mile-away Mourne mountains: "—By Jove, he mused, I often wanted to see the Mourne mountains" (*U,* 11.219). Significantly, in Sirens that wish becomes part of the linguistic play of that extraordinarily reflexive episode: he speaks and drinks with "faraway mourning mountain eye" (*U,* 11.273).

Even when *Ulysses* deals with animals, natural behavior is subsumed by cultural vision. Consider Bloom's conversation with his cat.

> —Milk for the pussens, he said.
> —Mrkgnao! the cat cried.
> They call them stupid. They understand what we say better than we understand them. She understands all she wants to. Vindictive too. Cruel. Her nature. Curious mice never squeal. Seem to like it. Wonder what I look like to her. Height of a tower? No, she can jump me.
> —Afraid of the chickens she is, he said mockingly. Afraid of the chookchooks. I never saw such a stupid pussens as the pussens.
> —Mrkrgnao! the cat said loudly.
> She blinked up out of her avid shameclosing eyes, mewing plaintively and long, showing him her milkwhite teeth. He watched the dark eyeslits narrowing with greed till her eyes were green stones. Then he went to the dresser, took the jug Hanlon's milkman had just filled for him, poured warmbubbled milk on a saucer and set it slowly on the floor.
> —Gurrhr! she cried, running to lap.
> He watched the bristles shining wirily in the weak light as she tipped three times and licked lightly. Wonder is it true if you clip them they can't mouse after. Why? They shine in the dark, perhaps, the tips. Or kind of feelers in the dark, perhaps. (*U,* 4.24–42)

Bloom's early morning interchange with Molly parallels this scene. Molly's twice-repeated "Poldy" and insistence that he hurry with the tea are forms of mild anxious, aggressive purring. Bloom "calmly" gazes at Molly's "large soft bubs, sloping within her nightdress like a shegoat's udder" (*U,* 4.304–5), much as he observes the cat's whiskers and sheen: "Mr Bloom watched curiously, kindly the lithe black form. Clean to see: the gloss of her sleek hide, the white button under the butt of her tail, the green flashing eyes" (*U,* 4.21–23). Molly drinks her tea with a degree of self-absorption also found in the milk-lapping "pussens." Of course, the cat does not question Bloom on the meaning of metempsychosis, but the narrative does suggest that the feline and the female share a quality that the book is working hard to capture.

Again, many readers have taken this kind of connection at face value and have asserted that Molly is not only artless; she is nature itself. But we need only recur to the description of the cat to be aware of the non-objective rendering of experience in *Ulysses.* On the one hand, it is the subjective Bloom who sees cruelty as natural to a cat and masochism as natural to mice. On the other hand, for the narrative to portray a cat as having "avid shameclosing eyes" that are "narrowing with greed" is not even to pretend to a neutral description; animal "nature" is indistinguishable from imposed interpretation. To be sure, there is much about cats that

Bloom does not know: he is unsure of how he looks from the cat's perspective; he thinks its feelers might "shine in the dark." But to observe these gaps in his knowledge, especially the latter, is only to recognize that this modern Odysseus has merely blundered about in his culture's encyclopedia of texts and has emerged from his brief schooling with his facts awry. Bloom's view of what is natural and his quest to understand the essence of things lead only to conventional wisdom and comically fractured received ideas.

In portraying the unreflective and animal, the text undoes our belief in the natural by circling us back to the social and to a language that purposefully confuses nature and culture. Despite the narrative's evident desire to uncover "subterranean forces" in the mind, the presentation of minds in progress remains a combination of old materials in new ways. In general, the primal unconscious mind, unknowable in words, is evoked—only to be blocked or even denied by the strategies, styles, and content of the fiction. And yet, there is the occasional exception to this statement. For example, Stephen's description of the self, which I mentioned above (the "self" is "ineluctably preconditioned to become" what it is), suggests a contradiction—that the self is culturally conditioned to assume a certain shape, *and* that identity is conditioned by certain unnamed inevitabilities. These ineluctable forces seem to have, because of their sheer predetermination, the status of natural forces. What intrigues me here is the summoning up of an unknown sphere of inevitability and instinct, which appears to counter the recurrently asserted constructedness of all conditioning forces and the reflexively self-contained quality of *Ulysses.*

The Schema: Encyclopedism and the Unknown

Ulysses produces within the terms of its own artistry an illusion of unmediated mind, of unstructured consciousness. At the same time, the narrative announces the dominion of culture over nature. In tandem with his ambivalent approach to the unknown unconscious, Joyce explored what in his notes for Ithaca he calls the "as yet unknown."[13] This negative space within and outside the text is suggested by the known, the disciplines that make up Western culture and on which Joyce drew for his many allusions. From that body of knowledge, *Ulysses* generates problems of heuristics, epistemology, ontology, and aesthetics; it also produces lacunae, ambiguities, and our sense of what I have alluded to as the "cultural unconscious" (a concept discussed below by way of conclusion). One efficient way to deal with this version of the enigmatic while developing an argument about Joyce's portrayal of consciousness, is to explore Joyce's own abstracts of *Ulysses,* the schemata that he prepared for his friends as aids to textual explication.[14] Certainly, the schemata cannot be considered authoritative guides to the fiction, for they are themselves only Joyce's fictions about *Ulysses.* Nonetheless, they continue to be reprinted, drawn on for clues, and distributed as hard classroom guides to the book. David Hayman's widely used study, Ulysses: *The Mechanics of Meaning,* includes a version of the charts. Similarly, Richard Ellmann's now classic *Ulysses on the Liffey* and Don Gifford and Robert J. Seidman's *Notes for Joyce* both liberally incorporate schemata information as readily as do many Joyce scholars when they want to emphasize this or that point of interpretation. Hence, although no one would grant the charts a sacrosanct status, very few readers, scholars, and teachers of Joyce have eschewed their use altogether.

The Linati-Gorman-Gilbert charts have long puzzled those readers who seek in them the keys to the work or a simplified model of its meanings. In fact, the lists of places, times, organs, arts and sciences, colors, symbols, stylistic techniques, and Homeric correspondences tend to muddy the waters. Attempting to take the charts seriously, we often pose more questions than answers. Some questions involve the seeming overexplicitness of the charts; for example, what relationship does the "technic" of "tumescence / detumescence" have to the meaning of Nausicaa beyond underscoring the already obvious sexual encounter of Bloom and Gerty MacDowell? Why, amidst the Homeric citations of the Correspondences, is it necessary to mention that the Stephen of Telemachus is like Hamlet? Other questions probe strategy. Why do episodes such as Lestrygonians, Eumaeus, and Ithaca lack designated colors? What accounts for the choice of listed organs? (Why, for instance, is there no episode for the gall bladder? Why are both muscle and flesh given space?) Still other questions involve relationships among parts of the schema or the interpretation of individual items. How much do Homeric details control, for instance, the problems of organicity mentioned above? Does the art of Calypso, in Stuart Gilbert's version designated as "economics," suggest or include, as has been argued, "home economics"? Any reader of the charts could supply a sizable list of queries.

Yet surely to pose such questions is to seek significance without first attending to the very process of categorization. Certainly, each column suggests a body of knowledge or a frame of reference in a way that highlights the conventionalities of Western culture. Like a university displaying in its catalogue its arbitrary division into what used to be regarded as self-evidently coherent "disciplines," Joyce's charts accept and even seem to authorize a divide-and-conquer mentality; they signify atomization as much as the encyclopedic wholeness that, following Joyce's lead, we often assume to be the point of the schematization.[15]

Hence, it is important that the bodily organs, the symbols, the colors—

all the columns—are made analogous or homologous to the arts and sciences, the disciplines through which our culture marshals and imposes the information it generates. Music, medicine, and mechanics, like theology and magic, are in *Ulysses* the categories by which a social status quo is maintained. Similarly, the many "scenes" that Joyce's schemata list and that his narrative describes are the typical points of political and socioeconomic domination. School, house, graveyard, newspaper office, library, streets, tavern, hospital, brothel, cabman's shelter, house, and bed—the cityscape is broken down into its institutional components, and these elements redefine as a cultural site the "natural" strand along which both Bloom and Stephen walk during their shared day. That Joyce was able to find in Ireland many a comic and many a serious parallel for the details of the society Homer portrays in *The Odyssey* reinforces our sense that Joyce's text reproduces the traditional organization of Western culture. The categories dividing and ruling the Dublin of 1904, including male and female, young and old, potent and impotent, rich and poor, country and city, science and theology, heart and loins, citizens and revolutionaries, are all implied by the terms of the schemata. They form a statement about what Joyce shows us in *Ulysses,* the swallowing up of the instinctual and unprogrammed by a form of highly organized urban culture that assimilates all experience. They represent the impossibility of conceiving of the self and of exploring nature, human and otherwise, except through this or a similar conceptual paradigm.

To summarize, both from within and from without *Ulysses* announces its approximation to a nature that is in fact absent from the work. The stream-of-consciousness technique, which seems to transcribe real thoughts and their typical patterns of association, may be more accurately described as documenting the emergence of what appear to be personal thoughts from an impersonal environment of conventions and texts. The schemata, which have long been used as external but reasonably reliable abstracts of *Ulysses,* must be recognized as signifying a wholeness or encyclopedism that they in fact undermine from within as they present more lacunae and differentiations than clues to coherence.

This external evidence from Joyce's charts provides suggestions that are borne out in the narrative. For instance, *Ulysses* is a book of divisions more insistent than those divisions of economic convenience, the Victorian novel's "parts," or even than those units of mnemonic and pedagogical convenience, novelistic chapters. Eschewing such conventions, the narrative refuses to divide itself using titles, numbers, or asterisks. On the other hand, the movement from one episode to another becomes increasingly clear in *Ulysses* owing to the changes in point of view and style. Like the analytic schemata, the narrative achieves through these unpredictable shiftings not only a quasi-encyclopedic scope but also a content that refuses at many points to compose a seamless whole.

In addition, just as the schemata do not make self-evident the logic behind the selection of arts and sciences they list, so Joyce's book fails to provide an *Ur*-rationale for all of the varied philosophical, philological, historical, mythical, literary, scientific, mathematical, and other information put to use in the narrative. Instead, the text seems to ground the information used in the story in the minds of its characters and to suggest that somehow Bloom, Stephen, and Molly directly or indirectly access their culture's most spiritually valuable knowledge. Certainly, one might argue that the controlling aim of Stephen's agonized self-examination is to engineer from the cultural material at his disposal an intuitive knowledge of some unifying code-system or other means of establishing connections among divine and human, person and person, philosophic theory and poetic lyric; this and more he appears to signify in the phrase "that word known to all men" (*U,* 3.435). Further, as already noted, Stephen's drunken entrance into Nighttown, during which he declares to Lynch his desire for a universal "language of gesture," recalls his morning's contemplation of the confluence of and perhaps potent parallels among natural process, linguistic variety, and primal matter. For all of his Aristotelianism, Stephen is also attracted to Giordano Bruno's Neoplatonic quest for grand design and substantial unity; he wants to connect the language of culture to the perhaps mystic vocabulary of nature and divinity. But the most that Stephen achieves is his morning's ironic restatement of Western humanity's chain of being: "God becomes man becomes fish becomes barnacle goose becomes featherbed mountain" (*U,* 3.477–79). Like Bloom, who repeatedly puzzles over the exact wording of various scientific principles as well as over their meaning ("Black conducts, reflects, [refracts is it?], the heat" [*U,* 4.79–80]; "what's parallax?" [*U,* 8.578]), Stephen has access to only a part—and arguably a marginal part—of human knowledge. Despite the frequently cited suggestion that Stephen represents Art and Bloom Science ("What two temperaments did they individually represent? The scientific. The artistic" [*U,* 17.559–60]), their interaction in Ithaca does not encourage the view that together they form a "whole" person with "complete" knowledge, or even that they together possess an epistemologically sound and comprehensive approach to human experience.

Hence, the extraordinarily diverse body of information alluded to in *Ulysses* defines an encyclopedism that is at best hollow; it serves to emphasize the distinctions which the schemata present in abstract—not wholeness but discrete sets that defy and thwart holism, terms for the deployment of institutional power. Given this framework, the more details

Joyce added to typescript, galley, and proofsheet, the more he signified in his practice the futility of the encyclopedic enterprise: he could never include all of even the culturally selected information at his disposal. Yet ironically, as Joyce embroidered into *Ulysses* the names of flowers, references to science, Homeric allusions, and the like, the text did take on a "life" of its own. That is, it engaged with the energy of Western culture in absorbing into its organizational and conceptual paradigms any raw material exposed to it. But this process, by which facts become ideology, is a hegemonic activity, whether in a society or in a work like *Ulysses* that reiterates its social environment. Hence, more than representing unity and completeness, Joyce's fictional encyclopedism reproduces and critiques the dominating divisions at the heart of the Irish life that he shows us.

Finally, like the schemata, the narrative prompts many questions and cannot help revealing many gaps, especially in the sphere of characterization. Like the schemata's list of "Organs," the text's references to organs, added together, would not form a whole individual, but only a textualized and scattered Osiris. Like the "Technics," which may appear to imply voices but actually include only such substitutes as "Narrative (mature)" and "Catechism (impersonal)," the narrative's voices are less personal than cultural. Above, I have tried to establish the sense in which *Ulysses* pretends to reveal identities but in fact undermines our traditional concept of mind by clearly deriving the content of consciousness from existing texts and conventions. As *Ulysses* has it, individuals conceive the truth of their selfhood to rest not in the enclosing culture but in an unspecifiable and largely inaccessible personal unconscious. Yet the derived discourses of *Ulysses* create a different sense of what it is to be a person in Joyce's world: one lives within a stream of consciousness that is finally not distinct from other discursive streams; one can never fully know the external imperatives that shape desire and condition action. In *Ulysses,* then, the signifiers of nature and individuality are indistinguishable from those of culture and conventionality.

A fiction often read as struggling to present the unified complexity of consciousness,[16] *Ulysses* thus produces characters largely reduced to compilations of received fictions enacting a life that at best recalls the natural by arguing the narrative's nostalgia for it. As a fragmented product, the narrative ultimately signifies something other than itself, a kind of "cultural unconscious" that can never be known except through the styles and strategies of the narrative, which transmit restricted ideological practices and stylized versions of lived experience. The enclosing culture does not know but substitutes for a nature that is never trapped in discourse, for what is missing from *Ulysses*—the living tissue of consciousness and a Gestalt that exceeds the mechanically charted—is missing as well from the society Joyce shows us; at the very least, the "cultural unconscious" that *Ulysses* evokes is perpetually chased, never grasped.

The result of Joyce's carefully engineered intersection of the social and the narrative is his exposing the insufficiency of our knowledge of self and society. For fifty years, readers have explained to one another what Stephen, Bloom, and Molly are really like, have unearthed the real reasons for Stephen's brooding inactivity, for Bloom's similar paralysis, for Molly's adultery. *Ulysses* has thrown the seeker after causes from Bruno to Vico to Aristotle to Jacob Boehme to Gaelic etymology to topographical study to Krafft-Ebing to Richmal Mangnall to the study of Joyce's school records. In these and in many other sources, valuable information has been discovered; we have enlarged our knowledge of what Joyce did know or could have known. We have understood more about the impact of life on art, even while the absorption of the first into the second demonstrated the artifice within both nature and culture. That is, Joyce's stream of consciousness is a gathering of discursive fragments from culture, and the schemata denote only an engineered unity that the novel partly produces and partly rejects—the unity of philosophic systems, the merely logical internal coherence of a cultural system or paradigm. The unconscious and the unknown are the same absent figures for both *Ulysses* and life, for nature and for a culture which cannot know themselves fully.

The Cultural Unconscious

Above, the term "cultural unconscious" referred to something unrepresented in *Ulysses,* whose reality is nonetheless affirmed, or at least desired, by the narrative. *Ulysses,* that is, may be read as nostalgically yearning to embody discursively the nature that it posits as desirable and necessary for truly gratifying human experience. To this end, *Ulysses* asserts its status as an encyclopedic book, as a work so comprehensive that it implies or can even capture glimpses of raw motivation, non-ideological concept, and uninstitutionalized experience. Bloom's thoughts, however continuously impinged upon and shaped by the city through which he moves, appear to offer the possibility of connection to uncensored impulse and unconditioned emotion. Especially when Bloom drifts off to sleep after his remote encounter on the beach with Gerty MacDowell, we seem to enter a gentle drift of uncontrolled idea, and this event seems to promise deep revelation when the reader gets to Circe. But the expectation is never fulfilled. In its place, the narrative provides a cycling through one cultural proposition after another. The minds that we see in *Ulysses* are very much the products of their environment, and tracking down the things alluded to in those minds has consistently driven scholars to the world external to the text. The book's cultural unconscious remains an inaccessible force which motivates the various searches by character, author, and reader for the chemical that will transform charted fragments into luminous certitudes about consubstantiality, the incorruptibility of the soul, and the meaning of experience.

In *The Political Unconscious* (1981), Fredric Jameson uses a term similar to "cultural unconscious," and clearly my own phrase alludes to his; in fact, the line of reasoning that Jameson follows in his exciting "Introduction" and problematic "Conclusion" must be partly rehearsed here if I am to round out my sense of the work enacted in *Ulysses.* Early in his study, Jameson states his belief that a chief task of the narrative analyst is to see every story as part of the "single great collective story" of, as Marx and Engels would have it, " 'oppressor and oppressed.' "[17] Jameson contends, "It is in detecting the traces of that uninterrupted narrative, in restoring to the surface of the text the repressed and buried reality of this fundamental history, that the doctrine of a political unconscious finds its function and its necessity."

Whereas Jameson sees the "political unconscious" as a "master-narrative" of historical struggle which is inscribed in various ways into every literary work, I find that in addition *Ulysses* has inscribed into it also a cultural master-narrative (no doubt specific to the social formation in and through which the work was written) of human connection with primal instinct and authentic wholeness. This vision, what Jacques Derrida and others might subsume into a myth of plenitude, might also be viewed as the logical outcome of bourgeois reality in a world of increasing social fragmentation, reification, alienation, and commodification. By this line of reasoning, nature is construed as transcendent or at least as a good to be sought outside of or in the usually unexamined folds of culture. The cultural unconscious is thus a narrative of nature which emerges from the pressure of modern society, though it has obvious affinities with the pastoral vision of earlier centuries and with various countercultural ("back-to-nature") movements of the postmodern decades. A Lacanian might argue additionally that this cultural unconscious, however much it may be a social construct, nonetheless functions as a motivating Other, a nature that speaks culture. Thus, nature is less a place or an ideal than it is a discourse whose themes are wholeness and psychological or even spiritual integrity. The measure of Bloom's and Stephen's inevitable defeat by a manipulative society is their steady inability to procure imaginative access to this extracultural language. The measure of the narrative's affirmation of this discourse's potency is the constant stream of coincidence that textures the fiction and tempts us always to discern within difference the presence of consubstantiality, connection, and communication. The nature in question here is quite other than the ideological construct that marks Molly as Gea-Tellus and as earthily polyphiloprogenitive; the latter marks only desire in submission to convention, while the former "exists" in the negative space outside the text.

One of Jameson's aims in *The Political Unconscious* is to broaden Marxist theory from its well-known concern with demystification to a recognition that "all literature must read as a symbolic meditation on the destiny of community."[18] To be sure, *Ulysses* itself accomplishes many kinds of demystification; the narrative's exploration of selfhood, gender distinctions, family relations, the social order, and Anglo-Irish interaction vigorously exposes the ideological practices shaping these concepts and dominating much of the life in Joyce's city.[19] However, *Ulysses* also addresses the issue of community, both by demonstrating the absence of the communal in the Dublin of 1904 and by emphasizing the events, actions, thoughts, and dreams linking meandering Stephen and wandering Bloom. In a city marked by clerical, patriarchal, economic, and political domination, Joyce signifies a consubstantiality of characters which, liberated from the theological doctrine that Stephen brings to the coding of coincidence, alludes to the many varieties of collectivity that the narrative aggressively lacks. Thus to contribute here my own coding of the characters' experience is neither sheer fabrication nor mere figure. Rather, to do so is to extrapolate the desire for community (as a version of nature) from the kinds of anomie experienced by Bloom, Stephen, and Molly; from the recurrent critical efforts to account for the novel's odd blend of depressing details and exuberant wit; and from Joyce's persistent interest in social forms and theories.[20]

One place in which theories abound is the penultimate episode of *Ulysses*, and it is from this site of rationalization that the cultural unconscious asserts its discourse of nature and community. In fact, it is the contradiction between culture and unconscious that accounts for the mixed readings of that chapter. Many critics have argued that despite the pseudo-scientific perspective, the narrative allows, via the good offices of Epps's Cocoa, a symbolic communion of father and son. Other readers maintain that even to suggest a meeting of minds is to indulge in the novelistic sentimentality that Joyce abhorred. But I detect in the Blephen-Stoom encounter the same voice of desire for nature that shapes the consensus perception of Molly as Earth Mother. It is not just by convention that readers have found Molly to be natural; such a reading also emerges from the dialectic between the culture and its unconscious. Strictly speaking, of course, we can never *know* the difference between these two terms; certainly, those of us who are caught within Western language and logic can conceive of the cultural unconscious only by analogy to our thoroughly conventional experience. What we can know, as

Vico proclaimed and Joyce undoubtedly noted, is the "world of civil society" (what Vico also calls the world of the "gentiles"), which "has certainly been made by men." Vico strictly distinguishes the human sphere from "the world of nature, which, since God made it, He alone knows."[21] Given the predilection for etymological study that Vico and Joyce shared, it is of interest that the word "nature" has affinities with the Indo-European root *gene-*, from which "gentile" derives; that is, "nature" contains Vico's world of culture. On the other hand, as anyone with an *American Heritage Dictionary* can determine, the word "culture" shares its Indo-European root *kwel-* with "entelechy," the Aristotelian term that Stephen seems in Circe to associate with the *quidditas* of an object. Perhaps because nature and culture writes themselves in each other, Joyce's fiction nostalgically projects wholeness despite the undeniable fragmentation in the work and its framing world.

Less positive assessments of Joyce's fiction have, of course, always been made. Early readers of *Ulysses* emphasized the "waste land" of Dublin life as portrayed by Joyce, and shades of that reaction color many different readings of the narrative, from Hugh Kenner's *Dublin's Joyce* (1956) to Franco Moretti's "The Long Goodbye." Moretti's argument about *Ulysses,* which appears in his very instructive *Signs Taken for Wonders* (1983), interests me because he argues unequivocally for Joyce's portrait of a Dublin caught in the "crisis of liberal capitalism," a "negative utopia" informed by the author's "consummate scepticism." Moretti grounds this view in the notion that the specific Irish context of the narrative is far less important than is the pressure of English economic history.[22] That is, the essay screens out the very details that *Ulysses* uses (the life it absorbs into art) to strike a balance between dystopia and community. Such a detail occurs in Aeolus, in which the stalled trams call to mind not only the celebrated paralysis of Dublin life as Joyce portrayed it in his short stories but also the 1913 Dublin Lock-Out.[23] That the Lock-Out was a brutally effective management strategy only highlights its equal success in generating some measure of class-consciousness. Such solidarity Jameson links to the Utopian desire for a communal society which he discerns in many literary works. Joyce's own text claims both less and more through its portrayal of the stalled trams, for swirling around those few paralyzed machines is the ongoing life of the city of words in which Irish laborers pursue their tasks, an Irish dilettante named Dedalus ponders consubstantiality, an Irish canvasser named Bloom seeks community, and the discourses of modern social life force us to recognize the significance of what is not said. It is at the margins of Joyce's discourse, where life and art entangle, that the dialectic of nature and culture enacts the work, in both senses, that we call *Ulysses.*

Notes

1. An excellent commentary on this phenomenon occurs in Fritz Senn's "Righting *Ulysses*," in *James Joyce: New Perspectives*, ed. Colin MacCabe (Sussex: Harvester Press and Bloomington: Indiana University Press, 1982), 3–28.

2. "The National Library of Ireland *versus* Walt Whitman," *Dublin University Review* 1 (May 1885): 97–98. It is likely that this or a similar story of censorship reached Joyce's ears. In *Finnegans Wake*, Jaun includes in his sermon some comments on censorship and mentions that "William Archer's a rompan good cathalogue and he'll give you a riser on the route to our nazional labronry" (*FW*, 440.3–5).

3. See John Henry Raleigh's *The Chronicle of Leopold and Molly Bloom:* Ulysses *as Narrative* (Berkeley and Los Angeles: University of California Press, 1977), 179–81. Raleigh finds 1903 to be the most likely date for the Blooms' move to Eccles Street.

4. For an account of Best's well-known defense of his extraliterary reality, see Richard Ellmann, JJII, 363–64. Ellmann speaks at some length of the peculiar relationship between Joyce's life and art, addressing an issue that recurs throughout the criticism as well as in Joyce's own theorizing about art.

5. Weldon Thornton, *Allusions in* Ulysses (New York: Simon and Schuster, 1973), 151–52.

6. Arthur Power, *Conversations with James Joyce*, ed. Clive Hart (London: Millington, 1974), 54.

7. Most thoroughly perhaps by Erwin R. Steinberg in his *The Stream of Consciousness and Beyond in* Ulysses (Pittsburgh: University of Pittsburgh Press, 1973). Also of interest in this discussion are Hugh Kenner's *Joyce's Voices* (Berkeley and Los Angeles: University of California Press, 1978) and Karen Lawrence's *The Odyssey of Style in* Ulysses (Princeton: Princeton University Press, 1981).

8. See Thornton, 41.

9. Joyce to Frank Budgen, 16 August 1921, *SL*, 285.

10. For a discussion of reflexivity in *Ulysses*, see Brook Thomas, *James Joyce's* Ulysses: *A Book of Many Happy Returns* (Baton Rouge: Louisiana University Press, 1982). Thomas argues that each episode destabilizes its own reality and the authority of all the others, an effect that the reader further complicates by interpretively acceding to the reflexive contours of the text.

11. A study of the conventional link between women and nature may be found in Carolyn Merchant's *The Death of Nature: Women, Ecology, and the Scientific Revolution* (San Francisco: Harper & Row, 1980).

12. *Women in Joyce*, ed. Suzette Henke and Elaine Unkeless (Urbana: University of Illinois Press, 1982), 165. Cf. Bonnie Kime Scott's *Joyce and Feminism* (Bloomington: Indiana University Press and Sussex: Harvester Press, 1984), 156–83.

13. Phillip F. Herring, ed., *Joyce's* Ulysses *Notesheets in the British Museum* (Charlottesville: University Press of Virginia, 1972), 455.

14. There was, of course, more than one version of the schema, Joyce having given somewhat different charts to Carlo Linati, Herbert Gorman, Stuart Gilbert, and others. My comments here on the schemata refer to the composite version printed in the appendix to Richard Ellmann's *Ulysses on the Liffey* (New York: Oxford University Press, 1972).

15. Joyce wrote of *Ulysses* to Carlo Linati on 21 September 1920: "È una specie di enciclopedia anche" (*SL*, 271).

16. For example, see James H. Maddox, Jr., *Joyce's* Ulysses *and the Assault upon Character* (New Brunswick, N.J.: Rutgers University Press, 1978).

17. Fredric Jameson, *The Political Unconscious: Narrative as a Socially Symbolic Act* (Ithaca: Cornell University Press, 1981), 19–20. Jameson cites Karl Marx and Friedrich Engels, "The Communist Manifesto," in Marx, *On Revolution*, ed. and trans. S. K. Padover (New York: McGraw-Hill, 1971), 81. Below, I quote from Jameson, 20.

18. Jameson, 70.

19. See Cheryl Herr, *Joyce's Anatomy of Culture* (Urbana and Chicago: University of Illinois Press, 1986).

20. For discussion of the last, we must turn to Dominic Manganiello's *Joyce and Politics* (London: Routledge and Kegan Paul, 1980); Manganiello comments (98–114) on the "vision" in *Ulysses* "of a classless, humanitarian, pacifist and co-operative society." Raymond Williams's *The Country and the City* (New York: Oxford University Press, 1973) also devotes attention to the question of community in *Ulysses.* Williams speaks of Bloom, Stephen, and Molly primarily as isolated figures whose internal experience—their unspoken streams of consciousness—not only is richer than their social interaction but also implies the reality of a "collective" mind: "In and through the intense subjectivities a metaphysical or psychological 'community' is assumed, and characteristically, if only in abstract structures, it is universal; the middle terms of actual societies are excluded as ephemeral, superficial, or at best contingent and secondary." It is the community of the collective consciousness—or, as Williams notes, of what Jung called the "collective unconscious"—that *Ulysses* calls forth. Finally and most importantly, Williams discerns in Joyce a "community of speech" (245–46). It is likely that Williams might see my notion of the "cultural unconscious" as identical to what he calls "rhetorical projections of connection or community or belief," but I find the multivalent nature sought in and through *Ulysses* to be less conventional than, strictly speaking, unsayable. Thus the largest effect of Joyce's use of the strategies of Menippean satire is to build by suggestion a sense of the extent and significance of what the text can never tell us, the nature of nature.

21. *The New Science of Giambattista Vico,* ed. and trans. Thomas Goddard Bergin and Max Harold Fisch (Ithaca: Cornell University Press, 1968), 96.

22. *Signs Taken for Wonders: Essays in the Sociology of Literary Forms,* trans. Susan Fischer, David Forgacs, David Miller (London-Verso-NLB, 1983), 201, 189–91. For Moretti's comments on stream of consciousness, which partly align with my own, see 194–98.

23. Cf. Colin MacCabe, *James Joyce and the Revolution of the Word* (New York: Barnes & Noble, 1979), 140.

The Politics of *Ulysses*

G. J. WATSON

I

Until comparatively recently a phrase such as "the politics of *Ulysses*" might have been regarded as a contradiction in terms. There was a general consensus that only the fall of Parnell caught Joyce's imagination in a political sense, and this precisely because it offered him a way out of Irish politics, which he could now dismiss as simply a morass of betrayals. Thus liberated, Joyce need show no interest in the kingdoms of this world as he assumed, in his masterpieces *Ulysses* and *Finnegans Wake,* sovereignty in the kingdom of art. Many writers on Joyce liked this portrait of the artist paring his fingernails above or beyond hot and messy politics; those who did not, such as Phillip Herring and Conor Cruise O'Brien, nevertheless assented to the notion that, for Joyce, aesthetics came first. For them, Joyce's politics are reactionary *because* he places aesthetics first. Herring's provocative essay puts it like this:

> Ireland's continual progress was a direct threat to him because it undercut the legitimacy of his prolonged exile. . . . and, further, threatened to obscure his gallery of paralytic portraits, to date them as the product of a particular era of Ireland's past.[1]

In other words, Joyce was nearly apolitical; or, insofar as he had political views, these were only that Ireland should not change too much and render *Ulysses* of somewhat antiquarian interest.

Such notions have been challenged in recent years. For instance, Dominic Manganiello's *Joyce's Politics* establishes convincingly the younger Joyce's genuine interest in socialism and anarchism during the years in Trieste, documenting Joyce's knowledge of Guglielmo Ferrero, Bakunin, and the American anarchist Benjamin Tucker (who wrote a book engagingly entitled *Instead of a Book by a Man too busy to Write One* in 1897). Manganiello, however, does not shed much light on the politics of *Ulysses,* and seems to undercut the whole thrust of his book when he writes: "Joyce's saving quality as an artist was that he distinguished, as

Pound did not, between the aesthetic and the political."[2] It is hard to see in Manganiello's account the relevance of socialism and anarchism to *Ulysses;* harder to see the connection between these (by this stage somewhat attenuated) political stances and the aesthetics, the writerly praxis, of Joyce in *Ulysses.*

The charge that Joyce's politics and aesthetics are left unconnected can certainly not be leveled against his poststructuralist critics. For them, *Ulysses* and *Finnegans Wake* are wholly political works—but in a highly specialized sense. That is to say, the politics turn out to be literary politics. Colin MacCabe's strategy, for example, is to offer us George Eliot as the paradigmatic example of the omniscient author, and then to proceed to show how, as he puts it, "Joyce refuses a hierarchy of discourses within the text."[3] In other words, what is by now a familiar and well-rehearsed quasi-political drama is enacted, in which the tyrant Omniscience is overthrown by the sans culottes of Shifting Narrative Stances, and the democratic Republic of Literature is born, the enfranchised reader actively and happily participating in the creation of the Text.

There is obviously much to be said for this sort of approach to a text such as *Ulysses.* It is, however, perhaps too broad an approach to the "politics" of modernist writing, and indeed too broad an approach for us, the finny tribe of "politicized" post-Fish readers. We may feel that such strategies do not tell us enough about the specifics of Joyce's writing, about what makes his "politics" in this sense, different from those of, say, Nabokov or John Barth or even—if we accept Hillis Miller's arguments—of Dickens in *Sketches by Boz.*[4] We need an analysis that will enable us, while profiting from the insights to be derived from the "new" criticism, to grapple more fully with literature seen as a social and historical product, and willing to go beyond the limited insights to be harvested from contemplating the Death of Omniscience and "unhierarchical discourses." Besides, is it actually true that Joyce's texts, especially *Ulysses,* offer a more democratic model of reader involvement, the reader participating creatively in the spaces left by the benignly absent author? Some years ago, David Hayman rightly drew our attention to the persistent and mischievous intrusions of "the Arranger" in *Ulysses;* and Christopher Butler more recently argues that in such a work we are reminded "not of the author's disappearance but of his varying status, and of the cunning ways in which his hand may be hidden."[5] The greater our sense of the author's "cunning," it might be argued, the greater our sense of his *power.*

II

The politics of *Ulysses,* which is indeed an intensely political book, are Irish (one might say, all too Irish). To see this clearly it is necessary to document in relative copiousness the political and cultural context out of which and against which it is written. I am not interested in providing inert "background"; I believe that only by contextualizing the novel are we able to see *Ulysses* as a complete and coherent political statement, to see the wood through the thickets of specialized articles and books. And, understanding the politics that underpin *Ulysses,* we can then see more clearly the significance of major aesthetic choices Joyce made as a writer.

First, however, we need to consider carefully *Ulysses* in relation to time. It is true that the work is set in 1904, but unfair to argue, *pace* Herring, that Joyce's own imagination and intellect are mysteriously frozen in the political outlook of that year, and that he lost interest in Irish events after 1904. *Ulysses* was written between 1914 and 1922. These years saw the formation of the Volunteers and yet another Home Rule crisis, Joyce being sufficiently interested to offer in 1914 the political articles he had written for the *Piccolo della Sera* to Formiggini for publication as a book, in "this year when the Irish problem has reached an acute phase."[6] There followed the Rising of 1916, the murder of Skeffington, with whom he had published "The Day of the Rabblement," the execution of Pearse (who had taught Joyce Irish), the triumph of Sinn Fein, the Black and Tan atrocities which included the murder of his friend Clancy (the Davin of *A Portrait*), the Treaty, and the origins of the Civil War. It is extremely unlikely, even *prima facie,* that the Joyce who could declare in 1918 "To me . . . an Irish safety pin is more important than an English epic"[7] was indifferent to these turbulent happenings in his own country, and that *Ulysses* is unmarked by them. The famous day in 1904 is seen by a consciousness saturated with this later knowledge. Further, of course, we must consider not only intention but effect. *Ulysses,* like all great books, perpetually renews itself in the circumstances of different times; and it is hard not to look again at the book with fresh interest—and respect—in the context of the last fifteen or so bloody years in Ireland, where "the irreconcilable temper" (as Joyce called it), molded and apotheosized in his lifetime, again stalks the streets and fields and pubs of the country.

The politics of Joyce's *Ulysses* may be seen as a characteristically massive attempt to deconstruct the mythology of Romantic Ireland. W. B. Yeats in 1913, famously, had proclaimed the death of Romantic Ireland, but in a poem of which the superbly defiant rhetoric testifies to the rude good health of the corpse. The chief features of this congeries of romantic attitudes may be summarized as: the cult of the peasant and a corresponding hatred of the commercial and urban; an exclusivist sense of the nature of "true" Irishness; a belief in the dynamic power of myth, that "great legends are the mother of great nations"; a deeply atavistic faith in blood sacrifice; and an attitude to history which is simultaneously aesthetic and theatrical, teleological and even apocalyptic. We may take as spokesmen for these attitudes two highly representative figures: Patrick Pearse, the militant "physical force" separatist, and W. B. Yeats, chief progenitor of the Literary Revival. At first sight unlikely bedfellows, what they share is more important than what divides them. They did not hold equally or to the same extent all the attitudes outlined above, but it is an agreed historical fact that the Literary Revival helped to develop the sacrificial and heroic elements in Irish life which prepared for 1916; Pearse, like many of his fellow insurgents, regarded Yeats's *Cathleen ni Houlihan* as a sacred text, and had, like Yeats, a romantic visionary view of early Ireland derived mainly from the pages of Standish O'Grady. Once again, as often in Irish history, nationalism and literature conjoined in a potent symbiosis. It is the systematic and comprehensive thoroughness with which *Ulysses* confronts and affronts the pieties of this romantic nationalism that enforces our sense of the work as vigorously political.

III

The sanctity of Irish peasant life was, of course, an article of faith for the literary revivalists. From Synge's Aran peasants through Lady Gregory's Kiltartan to Yeats's fisherman in gray Connemara cloth, the Irish peasant embodies the very soul of Ireland and his colorful speech is her authentic language. The problem with this partial if potent vision is that it necessarily leaves so much out. So much of Ireland—not only its urban centers, but what Yeats calls with distaste its "little gaunt towns"[8]—simply cannot be registered by the eye or ear concentrated on the noble Hibernian savage. If it is seen, it is seen to be dismissed—as Synge puts it, "in one place the people are starving but wonderfully attractive and charming, and in another place where things are going well, one has a rampant, double-chinned vulgarity I haven't seen the like of."[9] The world of the town, of commerce and business, is a world of fumblers in greasy tills, a filthy modern tide which must not be allowed to encroach on this "real" Ireland. The idealization of the peasant spawns a deeply reactionary politics. Patrick Pearse shares the Yeats-Synge view of the peasant, and their hostility to commerce; here we can see it with his characteristic sanguinary emphasis:

> When people say that Ireland will be happy when her mills throb and her harbours swarm with shipping, they are talking as foolishly as if one were to say of a lost saint or an unhappy lover: "That man will be happy again when he has a comfortable income." I know that Ireland will not be happy again until she recollects. . . . that laughing gesture of a young man that is going into battle or climbing to a gibbet . . . an eternal gesture in Irish history.[10]

The similarity of tone and viewpoint between this, written in June 1913, and Yeats's great "September 1913" needs no underlining.

Joyce resolutely opposes this simplification. One of the reasons for his attraction to the program of Arthur Griffith was its firm commercial bias—as he says in a letter of 1906 "at least it tries to inaugurate some commercial life for Ireland."[11] Well-known passages in *Stephen Hero* and *Portrait* illustrate his dissent from the Revival's view of Irish peasants, whom Joyce saw as a "hard, crafty and matter-of-fact lot."[12] In *Ulysses,* there are incidental parodies of Synge, not only in Buck Mulligan's amusing comparison of himself and Haines thirsting "like the drouthy clerics do be fainting for a pussful" (*U,* 9.565–66), or in Bloom's splendid appearance in Circe, *"in caubeen with clay pipe stuck in the band, dusty brogues, an emigrant's red handkerchief bundle in his hand, leading a black bogoak pig by a sugaun, with a smile in his eye"* (*U,* 15.1960–62); in larger ways the whole Hades episode is an oblique comment on Synge's superbly Wordsworthian account of a funeral on Aran amid the harsh grandeur of rocks and sea, and on the austere romanticism of *Riders to the Sea.*[13]

More importantly, the very subject-matter, the setting, the characters, their jobs (or lack of them)—all of this in *Ulysses* redeems into art the "unmannerly town" which was either ignored or excoriated by the writers of the Revival, and constitutes a major blow, the more effective because so unpolemical, against the cult of the peasant and the archaicizing politics implicit in that cult. Into the Yeatsian world peopled only by aristocrats, peasants and poets, into that "dream of the noble and the beggar man," steps the advertisement canvasser with *his* dream: "all creeds and classes *pro rata* having a comfortable tidysized income, in no niggard fashion either, something in the neighborhood of £300 per annum" (*U,* 16.1133–35). There are, in this context, political implications in what I have called Joyce's "unhistrionic and unostentatatious mode of treating the city":[14] the very largeness and obviousness of the point leaves it paradoxically in some danger of being overlooked.

The Revival's cult of the peasant was, for all its narrowness, at least genuinely idealistic and had its admirable aspects. Much less pleasant was the exclusivist notion of Irishness, a semi-mystical concept of what it is to be "truly" Irish, fostered particularly in the speeches and writings of Pearse, which issued in a deadening and virulent chauvinism. For Pearse, to be Irish meant to be a hater of England, a Gaelic speaker, a Catholic, and a believer in physical force.[15] Yeats was none of these things, yet he and Pearse shared a commitment to a dangerous kind of cultural nationalism. Elizabeth Bowen makes the point perceptively: "Ireland for the Irish had been the politician's promise, yet to be made good. *Irishness* for the Irish was the Gaelic League's promise, subtler and more essential."[16] Pearse and Yeats (obviously) had different views of who constituted "the indomitable Irishry"; each, however, in his different way, sought to establish a cultural identity as a criterion of "Irishness," and in doing so produced what may be felt to be more damaging "exclusivist" attitudes than arose in the course of the more straightforward quest for political freedom. The concept of nationality, for both, becomes sanctified: the Irish are the chosen people. Pearse writes:

> The people itself, will, perhaps, be its own Messiah, the people labouring, scourged, crowned with thorns, agonizing and dying, to rise again immortal and impassible. For peoples are divine and the only things that can properly be spoken of under figures drawn from the divine epos.[17]

Yeats strikes, slightly more circumspectly, the same note:

> It is hardly an exaggeration to say that the spiritual history of the world has been the history of conquered races. Those learned in the traditions of many lands, understand that it is almost always some defeated or perhaps dwindling tribe hidden among the hills or in the forests, that is most famous for the understanding of charms and the reading of dreams, and the seeing of visions. And has not our Christianity come to us from defeated and captive Judea?[18]

Election to the chosen people is not automatic: Pearse and Yeats apply different, but fairly rigid, criteria.

As the Aeolus episode of *Ulysses* demonstrates, Joyce was fully aware of the exclusivist, chosen-people strain in Irish cultural politics. It is, therefore, a fine touch to present to Irishmen obsessed with the Irish-Jewish parallel a Jewish hero, who then encounters rampant Irish anti-Semitism: "Ireland, they say, has the honour of being the only country which never persecuted the jews. Do you know that? No. And do you know why? . . . Because she never let them in" (*U*, 2.437–42). Mr Deasy, as almost always, is shown to be wrong, as evidenced by Bloom's travails in Barney Kiernan's pub in the ironically named Little Britain Street. It is an even finer touch that the Jewish hero should not even *be* Jewish, "properly speaking." As that wonderful reader of Joyce, Hugh Kenner, points out, Bloom "was never circumcised, was baptised a Protestant in consequence of his father's apostasy, and moved still farther from the tents of Judah when he underwent Catholic baptism in October 1888 prior to his marriage with Marion Tweedy. And whether Jewry would at any time have acknowledged him is doubtful: Jewish affiliation is traced through the mother, and Leopold's mother Ellen Higgins Bloom had herself an Irish mother, Fanny Hegarty."[19] No wonder that Bloom's attempt to define nationality in a pub full of racial experts is so humorously inadequate:

> A nation? says Bloom. A nation is the same people living in the same place. (*U,* 12.1422–23)

The inadequacy is deliberate, and we sympathize with Bloom, because *Ulysses* is a book that brilliantly mocks the whole notion of racial stereotypes and racial purity. The racists of Cyclops discredit themselves every time they open their (admittedly very funny) mouths about the English ("tongue-tied sons of bastards' ghosts"), the French ("set of dancing masters . . . never worth a roasted fart to Ireland") and the Germans ("sausageeating bastards"). Joyce had given up his study of Irish because his teacher, Patrick Pearse, found it necessary to exalt the Irish language by denigrating English; and despite some respect for Griffith's policies, Joyce wrote "what I object to most of all in his paper is that it is educating the people of Ireland on the old pap of racial hatred."[20] What *Ulysses* does so effectively is to bring the powerful weapon of humor to bear on all the manifestations of racial exclusiveness and racial "purity" encouraged in Ireland by cultural nationalists and militant separatists. Bloom is the chief means by which Joyce measures the inadequacies of the chosen Hibernian people. However, Joyce's challenge to the notion of a Gaelicized Ireland (insisted on by Pearse) is delivered as early as the opening episode of *Ulysses,* when he brings on his Cathleen ni Houlihan in the shape of the bemused old milk-woman who fails completely to understand when addressed in Irish—by (unkindest cut) an Englishman. Pearse, in particular, elevated nationalism to a religion and (Irish) nationality to sanctity: Joyce's great book queries the whole basis of nationalist stereotypes.

IV

Attitudes to myth and the use of the past also mark off the Joyce of *Ulysses* from Pearse and Yeats, and again these matters have their political implications. Irish nationalism was and is very largely shaped by a belief in the dynamic power of myth and legend—one looked to a heroic and epic past to make the future. In one of his earliest reviews, of the poetry of Ferguson, Yeats wrote:

> Of all the many things the past bequeaths to the future the greatest are great legends; they are the mothers of nations. I hold it the duty of every Irish reader to study those of his own country till they are as familiar as his own hands, for in them is the Celtic heart . . . I appeal . . . to those young men . . . whom the emotion of patriotism has lifted into that world of selfless passion in which heroic deeds are possible and heroic poetry credible.[21]

Practicing what he preached, Yeats's early plays and poems deal frequently with the matter of ancient Ireland, the Ireland of Cuchulain. The words quoted above show the considerable overlap between cultural nationalism of Yeats's kind and the more militant nationalism expressed by Pearse, for whom Cuchulain was the great prototype of the Irish patriot-martyr, and whom he regards euhemeristically, as a real historical character:

> The story of Cuchulain I take to be the finest epic stuff in the world . . . the story itself is as great as Milton's in *Paradise Lost:* Milton's theme is a fall, but the Irish theme is a redemption. For the story of Cuchulain symbolizes the redemption of man by a sinless God . . . it is like a retelling (or is it a foretelling?) of the story of Calvary.[22]

The boys of his school, St. Enda's, were to model themselves on Cuchulain, and to care not whether they lived for one day or one night so long as their fame lived after them. And it is quite clear that Pearse himself went into the streets of Dublin in 1916 to act out his destiny as a latter-day embodiment of Cuchulain and Christ, the figures whom he amazingly but characteristically links together constantly in his writings. Yeats's response to the Easter Rising was complex, but at one level he saw it as satisfying proof of his early theory: "great legends" can indeed breathe their powerful life into the casual comedy of the present. As he wrote in the late poem, "The Statues":

> When Pearse summoned Cuchulain to his side,
> What stalked through the Post Office?

One answer is: a romantic and atavistic view of Irish history, vigorously fostered by cultural nationalism.

A peculiarly dark aspect of this atavistic attitude to Irish history is the cult of the blood-sacrifice, which will redeem the nation. This has its roots in pagan times, but remained an active influence down through the centuries, mainly due to poets' knowledge of mythology and their unleashing of it in their work.[23] In the Ireland of Joyce's time, this belief issued in the conviction of the necessity for a periodic blood-sacrifice to keep alive the National Spirit (a suitably vague conception). The liturgy of the belief, as it were, ideally would involve the venerable tradition of the execution of the patriot-hero. We have already seen Pearse speaking of that "eternal gesture in Irish history," "that laughing gesture of a young man . . . climbing to a gibbet," which he illustrates by references to Robert Emmet and the Manchester Martyrs of 1867; Sean McDermott, also executed in 1916, addressed republican volunteers in Kerry in 1914 in these words:

> the Irish patriotic spirit will die forever unless a blood sacrifice is made in the next few years. The spark of nationality left is the result of the sacrifice of the Manchester Martyrs nearly half a century ago, and it will be necessary to offer ourselves as martyrs if nothing better can be done to preserve the Irish national spirit and hand it down unsullied to future generations.[24]

The canonical literary text embodying such beliefs is, of course, Yeats's play *Cathleen ni Houlihan* (1902). Pearse, in "The Spiritual Nation" (1916), remarks of it: "had Mr. Yeats's *Cathleen ni Houlihan* been then written [i.e., in Pearse's childhood], I should have taken it not as an allegory, but as a representation of a thing that might happen any day in any house."[25] One can see why Pearse and many of his fellow revolutionaries were so impressed. Yeats's play enforces most powerfully the binding nature of the call of total sacrifice of all merely personal ties and interests to the service of Ireland—as his Cathleen says, "If anyone would give me help, he must give me himself, he must give me all"; and it is quite clear that it is to be a blood-sacrifice—"They that have red cheeks will have pale cheeks for my sake, and for all that, they will think they are well paid." And later, in his poem "The Rose Tree," Yeats can effortlessly and with good reason absorb the actual historical event of the Rising into the mythos—

> Said Pearse to Connolly . . .
> "There's nothing but our own red blood
> Can make a right Rose Tree."

What made (and makes) the cult of the blood-sacrifice even more dangerously potent in Catholic Ireland was the way in which some of the men of 1916 managed to superimpose Christian imagery and emphases on what is essentially a pagan and barbaric code. Even James Connolly (committed socialist, and often critical of Pearse's more sanguinary views) could say in *The Irish Worker* of 5 February 1916, just two months before the Rising: "Without the slightest trace of irreverence but in all due humility and awe, we recognise that of us, as of mankind before Calvary, it may be truly said 'without the shedding of blood there is no redemption.' " As for Pearse, the messianic implications are even stronger. The clearly autobiographical protagonist of his play *The Singer* (written in late 1915) puts it like this in his last words, as he goes to face his enemies: "One man can free a people as one man redeemed the world. I will take no pike, I will go into battle with bare hands. I will stand up before the Gall [i.e., the foreigner] as Christ hung naked before men on the tree!"[26] He goes out to certain death, but his is, like Christ's, the redemptive triumph of failure, sealed in blood—another shining example of that "eternal gesture in Irish history."

Sentiments like these need to be documented in depth in order that one can appreciate more fully just how strongly Joyce opposed them, and how deeply scandalous *Ulysses* was and remains to a certain type of nationalist consciousness. Joyce was as opposed to the violence attendant upon "riotous and ruinous revolution" as to the romantic and sentimental simplifications—as he saw them—which gave rise to it.[27] In *Ulysses* the cult of the blood-sacrifice and its corollary, the image of the patriot-hero cheerfully climbing to his gibbet, are relentlessly exposed as sentimental cliché, or burlesqued in grotesque exaggeration, or reduced by comic juxtaposition, or by all of these means at once. For example, Tom Kernan in the Wandering Rocks episode is shown thinking about two historical patriot-martyrs, Robert Emmet and Lord Edward Fitzgerald, and the fictional Croppy Boy of the patriotic ballad. For him, however (and by implication the same is true of many an Irishman) such figures are merely sources for indulgent retrospection, merely provide, as it were, superficial local color: they are quickly banished from Mr. Kernan's mind by his much more lively disappointment at missing a closer view of the viceregal cavalcade of His Excellency, William Humble, Earl of Dudley. This does not indicate that Joyce favored a truly reverential view of the patriot-martyrs: indeed, in one of the book's cruder strokes of satire, at the close of the Sirens episode, Robert Emmet's famous words from the dock ("When my country takes her place among the nations of the earth, then and not till then let my epitaph be written. I have done") are counter-pointed by Bloom's burgundian eructation—"Pprrpffrrppff. *Done*." (Much more offensive to nationalist consciousness than Sean O'Casey's showing Irish flags in a pub in *The Plough and the Stars*, which was itself sufficiently offensive.) The execution of the patriot in the Cyclops episode, "the longest single set-piece in *Ulysses*" as Hugh Kenner calls it,[28] is an extraordinary—and extraordinarily funny—debunking of the mystique of the heroic death for Ireland. The whole thing is done in a clichéd journalese, which makes its own point about a good deal of nationalist effusions. At times, Joyce might almost seem to have in mind Pearse's cheerful gibbet-climber—"she would never forget her hero boy who went to his death with a song on his lips as if he were but going to a hurling match in Clonturk park" (*U*, 12.644–46). The Croppy Boy also meets his end, hanged by Rumbold, Demon Barber, in the Circe episode, in circumstances that recall some of the legends about Emmet's exeution (that ladies dipped their handkerchiefs in his blood), as well as Bloom's ill-timed explanation of a certain natural phenomenon (in Cyclops). It is, at any rate, not a pretty picture:

THE CROPPY BOY
Horhot ho hray hor hother's hest.

> *(He gives up the ghost. A violent erection of the hanged sends gouts of sperm spouting through his deathclothes on to the cobblestones. Mrs Bellingham, Mrs Yelverton Barry and the Honourable Mrs Mervyn Talboys rush forward with their handkerchiefs to sop it up.) (U,* 15.4546–52)

It would be hard to see here a terrible beauty being born. Indeed, it is even possible that Joyce, in including his monstrous regiment of Anglo-Irish women here, is glancing at the romantic attraction militant republicanism seemed to have for ladies such as Maud Gonne and Constance Markievicz.

At the more general level, Joyce's *Ulysses* is clearly as much at odds with the overall nationalist sense of the dynamic possibilities of myth and legend as it is with the particular case we have been examining, that of the blood-sacrifice. The point is just as crucial to our sense of the work's politics as is our registering of Joyce's spoofs of patriotic deaths and executions, though it can be made more briefly. First, we may note that Joyce pointedly prefers a Greek to an Irish story—we may remember in this context how Arthur Griffith's *United Irishman* rapped Synge over the knuckles just on suspicion that he had allowed the malign influence of the Widow of Ephesus near *The Shadow of the Glen*. Joyce's use of Homer, further, is very different from, say, Yeats's use of the Cuchulain saga. For Yeats, past and present exist in a vital and reciprocal relationship; they are in the same field of force, each exerting a magnetic pull on the other. (The same is true of T. S. Eliot, whose crowd of London commuters in *The Waste Land* is mediated to us through the powerful and somber cadences of Dante.) Joyce is not interested at all in the past in that kind of way—indeed it may even be said that he is not very interested in the past, and "never sets his imagination yearning after its echoing otherness."[29] Bloom in consequence is never allowed the slightest inkling that he is Ulysses—Pearse is all too conscious of himself as Cuchulain / Robert Emmet / Christ; and Yeats's art instructs Maud Gonne to see herself as Cathleen ni Houlihan or Helen of Troy or both. This does not mean that Bloom is ridiculed into insignificance by the shadow of his Homeric prototype. Rather, the parallel reflects Joyce's essentially democratic awareness of the wide applicability of a prototypical pattern; but we are always aware of the spirit of playful fun in which the details of the pattern are worked out, or confused, or stood on their heads.[30] This Dublin Odysseus is not condemned to slaughter, literally, Penelope's suitors. For Joyce, myth is not legislative: "great legends" are to be handled more cautiously, and in a more dispassionate way, than was congenial to Pearse, Yeats, and many of their countrymen.

V

It is obvious in the case of these two great contemporaries, Yeats and Joyce, that the crucial distinction in the politics of their very different arts stems from their very different attitudes to history. Yeats's way with history is masterful—he sees himself as a formulator, a maker, a shaper of history. Ireland for him in the aftermath of the fall of Parnell is "like soft wax for years to come"; and in an essay of 1904, where he is clearly thinking of himself, he writes: "We call certain minds creative because they are among the moulders of their nation and are not made upon its mould."[31] The creative mind, indeed, makes the world. Such is the claim of the poet Seanchan in the comparatively early *The King's Threshold* (1904): the poet hangs

> Images of the life that was in Eden
> About the childbed of the world, that it,
> Looking upon those images, might bear
> Triumphant children

Such is the claim of the late poem, "Long-Legged Fly." Inevitably, this view has the effect of aestheticizing history; and given the nature of Yeats's creative mind, the aestheticizing process will be romantic and heroic. Yeats approached history and politics with literary eyes and tried, as he says in a letter, to "turn all into a kind of theatre."[32] Certainly the poem "Easter 1916" sees the Rising as essentially an aesthetic gesture, in which the "motley" and the "casual comedy" of day-to-day mundanity is transformed at a miraculous stroke into the "terrible beauty" of heroic tragedy. This was not an unconsidered response. In a note to a late poem on the Rising which begins "Come gather round me, players all," Yeats writes:

> A nation should be like an audience in some great theatre—"in the theatre", says Victor Hugo, "the mob becomes a people"—watching the drama of its own history . . . that sacred drama must to all native eyes and ears becomes the greatest of all parables.[33]

(Of course, Yeats's theatrical sense found the republican version of Irish history so congenial precisely because it too articulates itself through myth and heroic images.)

In this aestheticized vision, gesture and image are all-important: the process of time is suspended and history is frozen, as it were, in a powerful gesture that renders, in Eliot's words, "ridiculous the waste sad time stretching before and after." Thus, in "The Municipal Gallery Revisited,"

Yeats in looking at the paintings is looking back at the recent history of Ireland, a history itself made by artists:

> "This is not," I say,
> "The dead Ireland of my youth, but an Ireland
> The poets have imagined, terrible and gay."

Thirty turbulent years are taken out of time, spatialized, and seen with a disarmingly total arrogance as merely part of the poet's self-generated mental furniture:

> Wherever I had looked I had looked upon
> My permanent or impermanent images.

We contemplate, with Yeats, the "images" (i.e., the portraits) of artists (John Synge, Augusta Gregory) who themselves create images: the poem's conclusion tells us that these manifestations of the creative spirit create history itself:

> come to this hallowed place
> Where my friends' portraits hang and look thereon;
> Ireland's history in their lineaments trace.

Yeats's vision is powerful and compelling, majestically expressed, but it is damagingly simplified and it leaves so much out. As Seamus Heaney says:

> Yeats, Lady Gregory and Synge strove to express a vision of Ireland that would alter for the better the destiny of Ireland, but it is also true that they seem to have assented to the Wildean paradox that nothing that actually occurs is of the slightest importance. They were intent on setting a faith in symbol against any sociological exploration, setting myth against history, ecstasy against irony, art against life.[34]

Heaney's words also apply, *mutatis mutandis,* to the mythology of the more extreme nationalist reading of Irish history. Irish history as a whole is a dismal record of oppression, abortive rebellions, betrayals, poverty, and cultural deprivations. It was therefore perhaps inevitable that the tides of nationalism which swept all of Europe in the nineteenth century should have led, in Ireland, to the construction of a set of compensatory myths which would appropriate, shape and glamorize the dismal story. This version of Irish history is powerfully teleological, even apocalyptic. The language of the Proclamation of the Republic, for instance, not only enshrines the cult of sacrifice, but conveys a sense of seven centuries of

Irish history leading to just this point, the perfect ending or closure for the predestinate nation:

> In this supreme hour the Irish nation must, by its valour and discipline and by the readiness of its children to sacrifice themselves for the common good, prove itself worthy of the august destiny to which it is called.

"Apocalyptic" may seem a strong word, but Pearse's speeches and writings from about 1912 onward are full of a frightening bloodlust and an itch to destroy the solid workaday bourgeois world almost regardless of cost. As he says in the ironically titled *Peace and the Gael,* "When war comes to Ireland, she must welcome it as she would welcome the Angel of God."[35] Yeats found the apocalyptic mode of thought alarmingly congenial—as he says in his introduction (1934) to the play *The Resurrection:*

> I took satisfaction in certain public disasters, felt a sort of ecstasy at the contemplation of ruin. . . . Had I begun *On Baile's Strand* or not when I began to imagine . . . a brazen winged beast (afterwards described in my poem "The Second Coming") that I associated with laughing, ecstatic destruction?[36]

Yeats also gave ennobling expression, in *Cathleen ni Houlihan,* to another aspect of this historical vision: its reliance on an enabling fiction of sudden metamorphosis, or transfiguration. To sacrifice oneself to Ireland (personified, as always in Irish literature since early times, as a woman) is to transfigure her—instantaneously:

> —Did you see an old woman going down the path?
> —I did not, but I saw a young girl, and she had the walk of a queen.

It is also to be transfigured oneself: the revolutionary steps from history into legend. His failure does not matter—indeed, failure gathers the revolutionary into the artifice of eternity. As the old woman (Ireland) says, in the play, of those who will die for her:

> They shall be remembered for ever,
> They shall be alive for ever,
> They shall be speaking for ever,
> The people shall hear them for ever.[37]

Joyce's *Ulysses* presents a powerful critique of this unholy alliance of romanticism, nationalism, and aestheticized history. First, it is so much more inclusive of many aspects of reality: it is a "chaffering allincluding most farraginous chronicle" (*U,* 14.1412). Karl Popper remarks relevantly:

> Kant was right that it is our intellect which imposes its laws—its ideas, its rules—upon the inarticulate mass of our "sensations" and thereby brings order to them. Where he was wrong is that he did not see that we rarely succeed with our impositions, that we try and err again and again, and that the result—our knowledge of the world—owes as much to the resisting reality as to our self-produced ideas.[38]

The massive documentation, in *Ulysses,* of that "resisting reality" is one means whereby Joyce queries the notion that the mind can simply or effortlessly impose itself on the world.

Joyce's attitude to history is profoundly different from that of Yeats and the teleologists of Irish nationalism. We may say that if Yeats is a formulator, a molder, Joyce is a recipient. In the Nestor episode of *Ulysses,* whose art according to Joyce's schema is history, Stephen rejects Mr Deasy's teleological vision ("All human history moves towards one great goal"); but he does not embrace instead the superiority of Blake's "Vision" ("a representation of what Eternally Exists, Really and Unchangeably") over history which—according to Blake—may only be "fabled by the daughters of memory."[39] As Stephen reflects:

> And yet it was in some ways if not as memory fabled it. A phrase, then, of impatience, thud of Blake's wings of excess. . . . Had Pyrrhus not fallen by a beldam's hand in Argos or Julius Caesar not been knifed to death. They are not to be thought away. (*U,* 2.7–49)

Neither Stephen nor Joyce wishes to "creepycrawl after Blake's buttocks into eternity of which this vegetable world is but a shadow." Rather, one must "Hold to the now, the here, through which all future plunges to the past" (*U,* 9.89). This involves the exercise of what Joyce called the classical temper, which "chooses rather to bend upon these present things,"[40] and to eschew romantic and aesthetic visions. In short, what one does with one's history is to put up with it.

Nor does Joyce in *Ulysses* throw Hegel out at the front door, as it were, only to allow the rough beast to slouch in at the back one. The apocalyptic strain in the thought of Pearse and Yeats is specifically mocked in the Circe episode, in one of the novel's great comic moments:

> *(A rocket rushes up the sky and bursts. A white star falls from it, proclaiming the consummation of all things and second coming of Elijah. Along an infinite invisible tightrope taut from zenith to nadir the End of the World, a twoheaded octupus in gillie's kilts, busby and tartan*

filibegs, whirls through the murk, head over heels, in the form of the Three Legs of Man.)

THE END OF THE WORLD

(with a Scotch accent) Wha'll dance the keel row, the keel row, the keel row? (*U,* 15.2174–82)

Circe, in fact, is rich in moments where Joyce can be seen confronting various tropes that go to make up the mythos of Romantic Ireland. We have already witnessed the grotesque end of the Croppy Boy; the notion of sudden and definitive transfiguration, which makes a miracle play of Yeats's *Cathleen ni Houlihan* and is rooted in extreme nationalist thought, is spoofed relentlessly in the bewildering variety of temporary metamorphoses which inform the episode throughout. It achieves particular definition at the moment Joyce's Cathleen, Old Gummy Granny, urges Stephen to attack the enraged Private Carr:

(thrusts a dagger towards Stephen's hand) Remove him, acushla. At 8:35 a.m. you will be in heaven and Ireland will be free. (*U,* 15.4737–38)

And earlier in the episode, the Utopianism that is a product of these romantic politics, when the chosen people enter their promised land, comes under Joyce's ironic scrutiny as the anointed Bloom welcomes his beloved subjects "into the golden city which is to be, the new Bloomusalem in the Nova Hibernia of the future" (*U,* 15.1544–45).

Joyce's hostility to the teleological narrative of romanticized Irish history may also in part be reflected in something more pervasive in the whole form and structure of *Ulysses,* in what may be called the aesthetic of incompleteness. Joyce's distaste for narrative closures seems deeply rooted in his sensibility. Many of the stories in *Dubliners,* for instance, are open-ended, none more so than "The Sisters," which ends (like "Counterparts" and "Grace") in midsentence, and includes the key word "gnomon," the incomplete geometrical figure which sums up in itself many of the themes and motifs of the collection. *Portrait* ends on a famous ambiguity; and in the very form of *Finnegans Wake,* with its haunting close which is not a close, there is a rejection of teleology.

In *Ulysses,* each episode is a new beginning, conspicuously separated from others, often involving a wholly new narrative method, requiring the reader's adjustment of his focus, confusing his sense of time and place, and deliberately frustrating his desire for forward narrative and chronological thrust. Further, as James Maddox has demonstrated in his lucid and subtle book, *Ulysses* operates through "many metaphors of incompleteness which fill the book (and through which the book describes itself): the disappointed bridge, the condition of almosting it, the Pisgah sight of Palestine, the life of Stephen's Shakespeare, 'untaught by the wisdom he has written or by the laws he has revealed.' "[41] Most famously, of course, on the narrative level, there is what Ellmann calls in a fine phrase the "resonant unfulfillment"[42] of the coming together of Stephen and Bloom: Joyce, connoisseur of anticlimax, shows Japhet in search of a father finding a place to pee. There is no need to rehearse here all the arguments about the much discussed question of whether the coming together of Stephen and Bloom really changes either of them.[43] That it remains a subject for critical discussion is the important point. The inappropriate reaction is Arnold Kettle's:

> The relationship between Stephen and Bloom, on which the pattern of the whole book depends, is a fraud, whose only significance is imposed from above by a vast apparatus of what can only be described as verbal trickery.[44]

Here we see a critical mind full of *a priori* notions of narrative, hungry for closure, for that apportioning out of destinies which Henry James so wittily mocks in the preface to *Roderick Hudson*. The whole tendency of Joyce's imagination is to celebrate moments of incipience, of potentiality, of possibility (and even the frustration of possibility), and to avoid not only "perverted commas" but the teleological full stop, or period.

Thus, the very forms of *Ulysses,* in their working to preserve indeterminacy and openness, and in pluralistic techniques that involve parallax, the stereoscopic vision, invite us to reflect, by contrast, on the monocular vision of the sacred march of Irish history endemic in the nationalist imagination. *Ulysses* implicitly as well as explicitly challenges that vision.

VI

What was Joyce *for?* What are his positives? The questions may be inappropriate—"the artist . . . remains within or behind or beyond or above his handiwork, invisible . . ." (*P,* 215). Besides, does a writer need to spell out his own political manifesto or credo? Chekhov thought not. He wrote to a friend in a famous letter: "You confuse two concepts: the solution of a problem and its correct presentation. Only the second is incumbent on the artist."[45] *Ulysses* "presents the problem" admirably, not least in the very obliquity of its treatment of politics. For it is still and mainly the chronicle of Leopold and Molly and Stephen, and steers firmly away from the abstractions of "pure" political theorizing, to which Yeats was so given. George Moore makes a point of some relevance to *Ulysses* when he writes in *A Drama in Muslin:* "The history of a nation as often lies in . . . domestic griefs as in the story of revolution . . . who could say which is of the most vital importance?"[46] Yet Joyce manages to avoid, through the sheer density of his book and its great comedy, the sentimental simplifications which lurk over Sean O'Casey's juxtapositions of domestic griefs with revolution.

The political outlook implicit in *Ulysses,* further, does not seem at all tame or irrelevant in the contemporary Irish context, where Cathleen ni Houlihan and Romantic Ireland are alive and well, and functioning on Armalites, Kalashnikovs, and car-bombs, and where once again there is an appeal to the past to give legitimation to violence. In that context Joyce's work seems not only political, but positive.

When Phillip Herring, with whom we began, writes of Joyce's hostility to "Ireland's continued progress," he begs the question. The vision of Ireland held by Pearse became canonical in the new Free State; and only comparatively recently has that canonical view been challenged by Irish historians.[47] Joyce with the artist's insight, intuition, and grasp of the forces that were working to make the new Ireland, asks us to consider whether it *is* "progress" to found a state on a politics construed as a theology and a history construed as a drama. *Ulysses,* in other words, demolishes the usual view of inevitable events leading to the present Irish State. Joyce the skeptic moves among the idealists of the time with his sane detachment, presenting us with another, corrective view of what has been so long taken for granted.

Yeats (rather ironically, it may be felt) wrote in 1915, in "Ego Dominus Tuus":

> The rhetorician would deceive his neighbours,
> The sentimentalist himself; while art
> Is but a vision of reality.

Joyce's great book confronts the rhetorician and the sentimentalist with a vision of reality honest, truthful, sane—and humorous.

Notes

1. Phillip Herring, "Joyce's Politics," in *New Light on Joyce from the Dublin Symposium,* ed. Fritz Senn (Bloomington: Indiana University Press, 1972), 6. See also Conor Cruise O'Brien, ed., *The Shaping of Modern Ireland* (London: Routledge and Kegan Paul, 1960), 14. Even Seamus Deane, in a subtle and agile essay, seems—for all his qualifications—to endorse the notion that Joyce seeks to transcend politics: "An act of writing which will replace all earlier acts; which will replace all politics; which will make the ignoble noble; which will make history into culture by making it the material of consciousness—this extraordinary ambition is at the heart of Joyce's enterprise" ("Joyce and Nationalism," in *Celtic Revivals: Essays in Modern Irish Literature 1880–1980* [London: Faber, 1985], 97).

2. Dominic Manganiello, *Joyce's Politics* (London: Routledge and Kegan Paul, 1980), 233.

3. Colin MacCabe, *James Joyce and the Revolution of the World* (London: Macmillan, 1978), 152.

4. Hillis Miller, "The Fiction of Realism: *Sketches by Boz, Oliver Twist,* and Cruikshank's Illustrations," in *Dickens Centennial Essays,* ed. Ada Nisbet and Blake Nevius (Berkeley and Los Angeles: University of California Press, 1971).

5. David Hayman, *Ulysses: The Mechanics of Meaning* (Englewood Cliffs, N.J.: Prentice-Hall, 1970), 70; Christopher Butler, "Joyce and the Displaced Author," in *James Joyce and Modern Literature,* ed. W. J. McCormack and Alistair Stead (London: Routledge and Kegan Paul, 1982), 71. Hugh Kenner says: "Joyce . . . is always present in *Ulysses,* and no talk of that dyad of technicians, the self-effacing narrator and the mischievous Arranger, should permit us wholly to forget that fact" (*Ulysses* [London: Allen and Unwin, 1980], 69).

6. Joyce's words. See Giorgio Melchiori, "The Language of Politics and the Politics of Language," *James Joyce Broadsheet* 4 (February 1981): 1.

7. Richard Ellmann, *JJII,* 423.

8. W. B. Yeats, *Autobiographies* (London: Macmillan, 1955), 225.

9. J. M. Synge, *Collected Works* (London: Oxford University Press, 1966), 2:283.

10. Pearse in *An Macaomh,* June 1913, cited in Ruth Dudley Edwards, *Patrick Pearse: The Triumph of Failure* (London: Gollancz, 1977), 177.

11. *JJII,* 237.

12. Arthur Power, *Conversations with James Joyce,* ed. Clive Hart (London: Millington, 1974), 33.

13. Given the concern with decent burial in Synge's play, and the vital importance of the coffin, Bloom's musings seem very profane: "Poor Dignam! His last lie on the earth in his box. When you think of them all it does seem a waste of wood. All gnawed through. They could invent a handsome bier with a kind of panel sliding, let it down that way. Ay but they might object to be buried out of another fellow's" (*U,* 6.815–18).

14. G. J. Watson, *Irish Identity and the Literary Revival* (London: Croom Helm, 1979), 242.

15. See Francis Shaw, "The Canon of Irish History—A Challenge," *Studies* 61 (1972): 116–53; and Dudley Edwards, *Patrick Pearse.*

16. Elizabeth Bowen, *Bowen's Court* (London: Longmans, 1942), 400.

17. Padraic Pearse, *The Collected Works of Padraic H. Pearse,* ed. Desmond Ryan (Dublin: Maunsel and Roberts, 1917–22), 2:91–2.

18. Yeats, *Uncollected Prose,* ed. John P. Frayne and Colton Johnson (London: Macmillan, 1975), 2:70.

19. Kenner, *Ulysses,* 43.

20. *JJII,* 237.

21. Yeats, *Uncollected Prose,* ed. John P. Frayne (London: Macmillan, 1970), 1:104.

22. Pearse, *Collected Works,* 3:156.

23. See G. F. Dalton, "The Tradition of Blood Sacrifice to the Goddess Eire," *Studies* 63 (1974): 343–54.

24. Cited in D. G. Boyce, *Nationalism in Ireland* (London: Croom Helm, 1982), 308.

25. Cited in Dalton, "Blood Sacrifice," 351.

26. *Collected Works,* 4:43–4.

27. Benjamin Tucker, whom Joyce had read with approval, had spoken of "Ireland's chief danger" as being "the liability of her people . . . to rush headlong and blindly into riotous and ruinous revolution" (cited Manganiello, 74). As Kenner shrewdly notes: "When the biscuit-tin [in the Cyclops episode], by heroic amplification, renders North Central Dublin a mass of ruins we are to remember what patriotic idealism could claim to have accomplished by Easter 1916. Thanks to a knot of hotheads with no prospect whatever of accomplishing what they proposed, Dublin had been the first European capital to undergo the bombardment of modern warfare, and James Joyce had little use for the oratory that fuelled hotheadedness" (*Ulysses,* 139).

28. Kenner, *Ulysses,* 93.

29. Kenner, "Circe," in *James Joyce's "Ulysses",* ed. Clive Hart and David Hayman

(Berkeley and Los Angeles: University of California Press, 1974), 345. See also Grover Smith, *The Waste Land* (London: Allen and Unwin, 1983), 55–60.

30. See Terry Eagleton, *Exiles and Émigrés: Studies in Modern Literature* (London: Chatto and Windus, 1970), 171–72; and Watson, *Irish Identity,* 240–41.

31. *Autobiographies,* 199; *Explorations* (London: Macmillan, 1962), 158.

32. Allan Wade, ed., *The Letters of W. B. Yeats* (London: Rupert Hart-Davies, 1954), 219.

33. Peter Allt and Russell K. Alspach, eds., *The Variorum Edition of the Poems of W. B. Yeats* (New York: Macmillan, 1966), 837.

34. "A Tale of Two Islands," *Irish Studies* 1 (1981): 11.

35. *Collected Works,* 2:217.

36. *Explorations,* 392–93. The apocalyptic strain in Yeats's work is fully documented in Fahmy Farag, *The Opposing Virtues* (Dublin: Dolmen Press, 1978), and Watson, *Irish Identity,* 128–50.

37. Compare *FW,* 13: "They will be tuggling foriver. They will be lichening for allof. They will be pretumbling forover. The harpsidischord shall be theirs for ollaves."

38. Karl Popper, *Objective Knowledge: An Evolutionary Approach* (London: Oxford University Press, 1972), 68 n.

39. Richard Ellmann, *The Consciousness of Joyce* (London: Faber, 1977), 3, argues that Joyce accepted Vico's idea that imagination is nothing but the working over of what is remembered.

40. *SH,* 83.

41. *Joyce's* Ulysses *and the Assault upon Character* (New Brunswick, N.J.: Rutgers University Press, 1978), 177.

42. *The Consciousness of Joyce,* 33.

43. See R. M. Kain, "The Significance of Stephen's Meeting Bloom: A Survey of Interpretations" in Ulysses: *Fifty Years,* ed. T. F. Staley (Bloomington: Indiana University Press, 1974), 147–60; and A. Walton Litz, "Ithaca," in *James Joyce's* Ulysses, ed. Hart and Hayman, 385–405.

44. Arnold Kettle, *An Introduction to the English Novel,* 2d ed. (London: Hutchinson University Library, 1967), 134–35.

45. M. H. Heim and S. Karlinsky, eds., *Letters of Anton Chekhov* (London: Bodley Head, 1973), 117.

46. George Moore, *A Drama in Muslin* (London: Vizetelly, 1886), 23.

47. Francis Shaw's "The Canon of Irish History—A Challenge" was written in 1966, but published only in 1972, well after the beginning of the present troubles. F. S. L. Lyons, in "The Burden of Our History" (The W. B. Rankin Memorial Lecture at Queen's University, Belfast, 1979), draws attention to the relatively recent demythologizing of Irish political history.

Ulysses and the Printed Page

PATRICK A. McCARTHY

A bone, a pebble, a ramskin; chip them, chap them, cut them up allways; leave them to terracook in the mutheringpot; and Gutenmorg with his cromagnom charter, tintingfast and great primer must once for omniboss step rubrickredd out of the wordpress else there is no virtue more in alcohoran.

(*FW,* 20.5–10)

In the course of Samuel Beckett's *Watt,* the narrator finds that it is necessary to invent the Lynch family, a clan that includes "Kate aged twenty-one years, a fine girl but a bleeder." Apparently recognizing that a female hemophiliac calls for some explanation, the narrator adds that "Haemophilia is, like enlargement of the prostate, an exclusively male disorder. But not in this work."[1] Such a statement necessarily reminds us that we are reading a book operating by rules different from those of what we call "real life," and the effect is increased by the fact that the narrator speaks not in an aside but in a footnote, the sort of device a writer uses only when he wants to remind us that he is writing, not merely narrating. Nor is this the only such device in *Watt,* for in addition to the footnotes (eight of them in all) there are various written documents—a song, a poem, a letter, a budget—printed on the page in their original forms (with some allowance for changes in typography), not to mention editorial comments on the condition of the manuscript that we are reading ("Hiatus in MS," 238; "MS illegible," 241) and the narrator-writer's complaints about the "hideous" semi-colon (158) and the necessity of underlining the "cursed preposition" *because of* (134). As the last instance indicates, however, we are not looking at the page that the narrator has written, but at something that has gone through the hands of a printer, for the preposition *because of* appears in the pages of *Watt* italicized, not underlined. We have, then, a process that demands a minimum of three people: a writer to put the words on paper in the first place, a typesetter or printer to transfer a handwritten or typewritten text into the medium of print, and a reader to look at the result.

A footnote is often a reader's aid, a gloss or guide to interpretation like the arguments to *Paradise Lost* and *The Rime of the Ancient Mariner;* but rather than leading to a clearer interpretation of the work, Beckett's footnote calls attention to itself and thereby deflects attention from the book's *meaning* to its physical existence as a book, an artifact of print technology. In this way, the footnote underlines the artificial and arbitrary nature of Beckett's fiction. Hugh Kenner traces this tradition to Swift's *A Tale of a Tub,* with its footnotes, marginalia, hiatuses, and the like.[2] It was also Swift who gave us an early lesson in the way an author is at the mercy of printers and publishers, for in the prefatory letter to the second edition of his *Travels* (1727) Captain Lemuel Gulliver complained that the word "Brobdingnag," which appeared in the first edition, was a corruption of "Brobdingrag,"[3] yet we would search in vain for a "correct" spelling of this name in the second, or any subsequent, edition of the book. Two centuries later, when James Joyce wrote *Ulysses,* the art of typesetting had not measurably improved, and the conditions surrounding the writing and production of the book—the author's poor eyesight, his almost equally poor handwriting in which he made numerous lengthy additions to typescript and proofs, and the use of French printers with little knowledge of English—conspired to produce a text in which, after much sets of proofs, there were still thousands of errors. Even the revised Random House edition of 1961, for a quarter century the text most readily available for general readers, has between four and five thousand textual errors.[4]

My purpose here, however, is not to lament the deplorable condition of the 1961 Random House text. Instead, I wish to examine the importance of the printed page, and its relationship to Joyce's social and aesthetic aims, in the novel. Few readers would disagree with Ian Watt's claim that "No book has gone beyond [*Ulysses*] in the literal transcription of all the states of consciousness, and no book in doing so has depended more completely on the medium of print."[5] Yet print was an important medium for Joyce not only because of its rich possibilities but also because of its limitations—for example, its tendency to perpetuate error along with fact and its power to force us in upon ourselves, to alienate us from the sense of community that an oral culture produces. Thus Joyce explores the rich possibilities of the print medium only to expose it as one more convention, one more artificial and inexact means of approximating reality.

Joyce's Dublin is a place caught between the aural and visual modes, between the spoken and the written word. This dichotomy is portrayed explicitly in the Cyclops chapter, which alternates between two forms of narration: a first-person account by an anonymous barfly who exemplifies the oral tradition of the Irish pub, and a sequence of pastiches of various kinds of written documents. It is interesting that the "I" narrator generally does what narrators are supposed to do in a novel: he tells us what he observes, in the order in which it happens, although he spices his account with assorted mean-spirited observations about the other characters, particularly Bloom. The effect of the pastiches, however, is to impede the development of the narrative and to lead us instead into a direct confrontation with the conventions and assumptions of a particular style of writing. Thus, a list of "Irish heroes and heroines of antiquity" begins predictably enough with genuinely Irish figures such as "Cuchulin, Conn of hundred battles, Niall of nine hostages" but proceeds to include such questionable entries as "the Last of the Mohicans," "Muhammad," and "Alessandro Volta" before concluding with the undeniably Irish "Jeremiah O'Donovan Rossa" and "Don Philip O'Sullivan Beare" (*U*, 12.176–99). A particularly interesting inclusion is "Murtagh Gutenberg," who appears in a sequence of four men with Irish or quasi-Irish first names and famous non-Irish surnames: "Patrick W. Shakespeare, Brian Confucius, Murtagh Gutenberg, Patricio Velasquez." It is, of course, the invention of another Gutenberg that has made possible this sort of absurd list that attempts to reduce human events to a uniform, homogeneous level; but the very absurdity of some of the inclusions betrays a human resistance to the leveling effects of print.

Throughout *Ulysses,* Leopold Bloom is Joyce's prime example of a modern reader, someone whose modes of thought often reveal the impact of printed texts. Bloom is in fact closely associated with print, for he makes his living by selling advertisements to newspapers; he is therefore aware of the way the arrangement of different items on the same printed page causes readers to associate one with another, as when an ad for Plumtree's Potted Meat is placed "Under the obituary notices" (*U*, 8.744). This emphasis on spatial form—on the appearance of print rather than on the sounds that printed words represent—is typically modern, as is the fact that Bloom reads silently, in contrast to other characters who generally read aloud: Ned Lambert, for instance, reads aloud a sentence from Dan Dawson's address (*U*, 7.243–47), the citizen reads a newspaper's list of recent births, deaths, and marriages (*U*, 12.225–36), and Joe Hynes reads to the other bar customers a letter from a hangman (*U*, 12.415–31). Marshall McLuhan has made the point that the advent of print led to silent reading and to the demise of a sense of community that exists in an oral culture; oral cultures tend to be tribal, literate cultures individualistic.[6] McLuhan's observation is certainly borne out by Cyclops, where the tribalism of the bar patrons is evident in the xenophobia of the drunken citizen and his friends, while Bloom stands alone as the exemplar of modern literate man. It is inevitable that in this chapter the clash of values between the closed-minded citizen and the open-minded, liberal Bloom would take the form of debate about the ethnicity of the characters, as the citizen challenges Bloom's right to call himself Irish:

—What is your nation if I may ask? says the citizen.
—Ireland, says Bloom. I was born here. Ireland.
The citizen said nothing only cleared the spit out of his gullet and, gob, he spat a Red bank oyster out of him right in the corner. (*U,* 12.1430–33)

Critics have rightly observed that it is Bloom's Jewishness that excludes him from this Irish company, but they have not noted that Bloom as Jew is inseparable from Bloom as literate man, and that he is excluded also because as a modern man, a purveyor and consumer of print, he is inevitably a stranger in this predominantly oral culture. The point becomes clear when we note that the occasions when Bloom most feels estranged, apparently on account of his religion, are those times when the claims of oral culture are in the ascendant: on the way to the funeral, for example, when Bloom's attempt to tell the story of Reuben J. Dodd's son results in the story being told by Martin Cunningham and being given a punch line by Simon Dedalus: "—One and eightpence too much, Mr Dedalus said drily" (*U,* 6.291). Bloom is aware of Simon's wittiness, and capable of appreciating it, as we see when he thinks, "One and eightpence too much. Hhhhm. It's the droll way he comes out with the things. Knows how to tell a story too" (*U,* 8.53–55). What Bloom does not seem to realize is that his own inability to tell good stories is reinforced by the immersion in print that is partly responsible for his acute sensibility—one of the marks of his superiority to most other characters in the novel.

Since Dublin is often described as a town of talkers, it is interesting that Joyce chose as his hero a man who is predominantly a reader rather than a speaker. Moreover, Joyce modeled *Ulysses* on the *Odyssey,* a work which we now know was the product of oral composition. Joyce wrote before the theories of Parry and Lord were developed and published, so he would have believed that the *Odyssey* was composed in writing; but even so, Joyce would have realized that Homer "wrote" for oral performance rather than private reading, and that even in translation the poem reveals many marks of its essentially oral nature. Oral cultures are distinguished by their emphasis on communal values, and oral narratives tend to focus on external action; literate cultures, on the other hand, come to focus on the individual, and their narratives lead necessarily to a concern with the shape of the individual consciousness. If Joyce's book lacks "action" in the classic sense, it is because the medium in which Joyce worked brought with it an emphasis on the interior worlds of its characters, so that in the end Bloom's sensitive mind will find a more appropriate (and modern) triumph than the slaying of Molly's suitor. Moreover, the discovery of various critics that the reader is the true hero in *Ulysses*[7] cannot legitimately be separated from the fact that Bloom is himself a reader, and that in watching Bloom we confront a mirror image of our own reading. If *Portrait* gives us one version of the Romantic theme that the writer is a hero, *Ulysses* shifts the emphasis to include the reader as well.

It will be illuminating to look at another brief episode that illustrates the clash between the written document and the spoken word. The incident occurs in the Ormond restaurant, where Bloom is having an early dinner with Richie Goulding, during the course of which Bloom decides to write a love letter to Martha Clifford, a woman with whom he has been corresponding under the assumed name Henry Flower. To prevent Goulding from knowing what he is doing, Bloom concocts the fiction of a business letter, and murmurs phrases supposedly from this second letter while he actually *writes* the letter to Martha:

> Hope he's not looking, cute as a rat. He held unfurled his *Freeman*. Can't see now. Remember write Greek ees. Bloom dipped, Bloo mur: dear sir. Dear Henry wrote: dear Mady. Got your lett and flow. Hell did I put? Some pock or oth. It is utterl imposs. Underline *imposs*. To write today.
>
> . . . .
>
> —Answering an ad? keen Richie's eyes asked Bloom.
>
> —Yes, Mr Bloom said. Town traveller. Nothing doing, I expect.
>
> Bloom mur: best references. But Henry wrote: it will excite me. You know how. In haste. Henry. Greek ee. Better add postscript. . . . P.S. . . How will you pun? You punish me? (*U*, 11.859–62; 11.886–91)[8]

Here we have a real (written) letter and a fictitious (oral) letter, the difference between the two being underscored by Bloom's determination to disguise his handwriting through the use of "Greek ees." This passage demonstrates a good deal about the subterfuges that Bloom uses to prevent his fantasy life from being discovered, but it also provides an intriguing illustration of McLuhan's argument that a literate culture dependent on a phonetic alphabet "lands men at once in varying degrees of dualistic schizophrenia" since it forces a separation of the visual and aural senses.[9] The passage raises serious questions about Bloom's identity, for in the letter Bloom is actually writing he assumes a false name and handwriting, thereby playing a role; in the letter he pretends to write, on the other hand, he uses his own name (and, we are almost tempted to add, his own handwriting), yet the entire document is a sham. Neither letter truly reflects his real identity, for the inevitable product of writing, real or feigned, is a fiction.

When we move from the written to the printed page we complicate matters further, for we introduce the generally unseen but necessary figure of the typesetter. Joyce knew about printers, having had trouble with them over the publication of his earlier work, and he would have recognized that the complexity of *Ulysses* would almost certainly insure that the new book would be plagued by printer's errors. Joyce was undoubtedly thinking of these matters when he had Bloom watch the typesetter at the newspaper office in the Aeolus chapter (*U,* 7.161ff.) and, much later, when he gave Bloom a glimpse at the results:

> So to change the subject [Bloom] read about Dignam R. I. P. which, he reflected, was anything but a gay sendoff. Or a change of address anyway.—*This morning* (Hynes put it in of course) *the remains of the late Mr Patrick Dignam were removed from his residence, no 9 Newbridge Avenue, Sandymount, for interment in Glasnevin. The deceased gentleman was a most popular and genial personality in city life and his demise after a brief illness came as a great shock to citizens of all classes by whom he is deeply regretted. The obsequies, at which many friends of the deceased were present, were carried out by* (certainly Hynes wrote it with a nudge from Corny) *Messrs H. J. O'Neill and Son, 164 North Strand Road. The mourners included: Patk. Dignam (son), Bernard Corrigan (brother-in-law), Jno. Henry Menton, solr, Martin Cunningham, John Power, .)eatondph 1/8 ador dorador douradora* (must be where he called Monks the dayfather about Keyes's ad) *Thomas Kernan, Simon Dedalus, Stephen Dedalus B. A., Edw. J. Lambert, Cornelius T. Kelleher, Joseph M'C Hynes, L. Boom, C P M'Coy, —M'Intosh and several others.* (*U,* 16.1246–61)

By this time we have survived several hundred pages of *Ulysses,* so there is nothing particularly mysterious about this passage: most of the passage is the newspaper account of the funeral, printed exactly as it is in the paper except for the substitution of italic for roman type, while the parenthetical insertions are Bloom's thoughts, his own version of the sort of scholarship in which we engage when we look at the circumstances surrounding the textual history of a novel or poem. Various features of this passage—the use of abbreviations for words that we would pronounce as complete words when we read them aloud ("solr" for "solicitor") and the "line of bitched type," as Bloom thinks of it (*U,* 16.1262–63)—serve as a forcible reminder that we are seeing a mirror image of ourselves, for we are watching someone read a text that is part of the text that we are reading. The difference is that the accuracy of Bloom's text can be gauged by reference to what actually happened at the funeral, so that Bloom is able to spot not only the annoying misspelling of his name but the inclusion of Stephen Dedalus and C. P. M'Coy, who were not at the funeral, and M'Intosh, a man inadvertently named on the authority of his raincoat;[10] our text, however, can only be judged by its internal consistency. The many cases in which Dubliners have complained that Joyce did not transcribe events the way they really happened are instances of people who are unable to maintain the delicate balance required by a book that takes place in a town called Dublin, involves many characters either bearing the names of, or being recognizably based on, real people, and contains massive evidence of its author's attention to realistic detail, yet often deviates from the very conventions of realistic fiction, not to mention the truth about turn-of-the-century Dublin.

The account of the funeral may not tally with what we witnessed, but then again this is Joe Hynes's version of reality, his own little fiction based on fact. If Bloom's activity in reading the obituary mirrors our reading of *Ulysses,* it is equally true that Joe Hynes is a portrait of the artist, and his production is a miniature of *Ulysses.* (This is hardly surprising, by the way, if we recall that Hynes has previously appeared in "Ivy Day in the Committee Room," where he reads a poem on Parnell's death, the subject of a lost poem by James Joyce.) Moreover, Hynes's piece has been damaged by an inept job of typesetting and proofreading, just as Joyce knew that his own book would certainly include printer's errors. The error in printing the obituary is only one of several printer's or writer's errors that are supposed to be part of Joyce's text; in each case, the error reminds us that we are experiencing something in the fallible realm of written communication. Note that this is a highly realistic presentation of the pitfalls in writing and printing, more realistic, in one sense, than the letters in *Pride and Prejudice,* which never seem to contain an illegible passage or an error in spelling or grammar; yet in another sense, Joyce's presentation of written and printed materials deliberately undercuts the book's realism, for the errors that we find in these materials are reminders that they, and *Ulysses* itself, are human productions, and therefore subject to fabrication (the presence of Stephen Dedalus and M'Coy), misunderstanding (M'Intosh), and careless error (the "bitched type").

I referred to "the errors that we find in these materials," but it would be more accurate to say "the errors that we *should* find," for one of the ironies of the printing of *Ulysses* is that at various stages printers and editors have "corrected" errors that rightfully belong in the book. Joyce wrote that, while in Paris, Stephen received "a blue French telegram, curiosity to show," reading "—Nother dying come home father" (U, 3.197–99); the printer changed "Nother" to "Mother"; Joyce changed it back when he read proofs; and, Gabler tells us, "An officious hand reintroduced 'Mother' in the final proofs after Joyce had last seen them."[11] The passage that we find in the 1961 Random House edition of *Ulysses* (42) therefore contains no typographical peculiarity, so the reader is left to suppose that the "curiosity to show" is merely that the telegram is blue and French. It does seem appropriate that a real French typesetter compensated for an error made by a fictional French telegraph operator,[12] but as it stands the passage differs little from what we might have encountered in a more conventional novel, where nobody ever makes an error of this sort unless the error is needed to move the plot in a particular direction. Instead, "—Nother dying come home father" has no lasting effect on Stephen's life that would not be accomplished by "—Mother dying come home father"; the difference is not in the *plot* of *Ulysses* so much as in the book's dependence on, and criticism of, written language.

Ulysses abounds in examples of marred texts, and while the telegram exists in Stephen's memory these texts are more often encountered by the man whose name will be reduced, in the newspaper obituary, to L. Boom (*U*, 16.1260) It is simple to trace this error to the Hades chapter, where Hynes is taking notes for the obituary:

> —I am just taking the names, Hynes said below his breath. What is your christian name? I'm not sure.
> —L, Mr Bloom said. Leopold. And you might put down M'Coy's name too. He asked me to. (*U*, 6.880–83)

Hynes is not malicious, but he is somewhat careless and insensitive: in asking Bloom for his "christian name" Hynes not only admits that he does not know the given name of a man from whom he has borrowed three shillings (*U*, 7.119) but shows, by his choice of words, his indifference to Bloom's Jewish heritage. Hynes's attitude towards Bloom's name represents one aspect of public opinion: Bloom is the outsider, always doomed to be treated in reductive terms, while Hynes and the others see themselves in the round. The difference between the two is signaled in a parodic newspaper article in Cyclops that allows Hynes his full name—Mr Joseph M'Carthy Hynes—while reducing Mr Leopold Paula Bloom to "L. Bloom" (*U*, 12.912). As we might expect from the difference in rank symbolized by the forms of the names used in the article, Hynes is described as the "wellknown and highly respected worker in the cause of our old [Gaelic] tongue," and his "eloquent appeal" for the revival of native Irish sports is described in detail; L. Bloom, however, meets "with a mixed reception of applause and hisses," and his position is shrugged off with the statement that he "espoused the negative." By the time we read the obituary in Eumaeus the name has been further reduced to "L. Boom," as if Bloom has been stripped of a first name and has had to cannibalize his last name to get even a first initial. That all of this indicates something about Bloom's importance is evident when we realize that Bloom is the last person actually at the funeral to be listed in the obituary, and the only member of the funeral party to be shorn of a first name or to have his last name misspelled.[13] Bloom is barely prominent enough to be invited to the funeral; he is not important enough to be made to feel that he is really one of the party, or to have his name spelled correctly.

Since Bloom will ultimately be victimized by having a letter dropped from his name, it is perhaps significant that the first text that we see Bloom reading is the legend on the band inside his "Plasto's high grade ha," and that he encounters this marred text while searching for a "White slip of paper" (*U,* 4.69–70) that, we later discover, identifies its bearer as "Henry Flower." This is the name Bloom uses when writing to the woman who calls herself Martha Clifford, and whose latest letter is another interestingly marred text that belongs in the same general category as Stephen's telegram, Bloom's hatband, and Paddy Dignam's obituary:

> Dear Henry
> I got your last letter to me and thank you very much for it. I am sorry you did not like my last letter. Why did you enclose the stamps? I am awfully angry with you. I do wish I could punish you for that. I called you naughty boy because I do not like that other world. Please tell me what is the real meaning of that word? Are you not happy in your home you poor little naughty boy? I do wish I could do something for you. Please tell me what you think of poor me. I often think of the beautiful name you have. Dear Henry, when will we meet? I think of you so often you have no idea. I have never felt myself so much drawn to a man as you. I feel so bad about. Please write me a long letter and tell me more. Remember if you do not I will punish you. So now you know what I will do to you, you naughty boy, if you do not wrote. O how I long to meet you. Henry dear, do not deny my request before my patience are exhausted. Then I will tell you all. Goodbye now, naughty darling, I have such a bad headache. today. and write *by return* to your longing
> Martha
>
> P.S. Do tell me what kind of perfume does your wife use. I want to know.
>
> X X X X (*U,* 5.241–59)

For several decades this was not precisely what we saw in most American copies of the book, however, for the Random House printers, spotting the error in "if you do not wrote," corrected not only that one but Bloom's wry comment further down the page, "Wonder did she wrote it herself."[14] The 1961 edition did restore another of Martha's errors, "that other world," which was "corrected" to "that other word" in the 1934 American edition.

In any event, "that other world" seems to me the more interesting of Martha's typographical errors, for it brings into play the dichotomy of word and world, art and reality, that underlies all of *Ulysses.* "Word" is fertilized into "world" by the addition of a phallic "l," just as in a later chapter the removal of another "l" will reduce Bloom to Boom, rendering him symbolically impotent. It is a chance error on a typewriter that opens up these possibilities, just as later in the same chapter Bloom's chance comment that he is going to throw away a newspaper inadvertently results in a valid tip on a twenty-to-one outsider in the Ascot Gold Cup race. Other elements in the letter seem familiar, including the question about "the real meaning of that word," which seems to echo Molly Bloom's earlier request for the definition of "metempsychosis" (*U*, 4.337–40), and the letter's sado-masochistic emphasis on punishment. In fact, while its short sentences, sterling phrasing, and limited vocabulary seem to place the letter at the opposite end of the literary spectrum from *Ulysses* as a whole, there are several signs that the letter, like other written or printed documents, is a microcosm of the book: the unimaginative repetition of phrases (Dear Henry, Henry dear; naughty boy, naughty darling) and the tendency to circle back to the same idea (punishment, the demand that he write, their future meeting) parody Joyce's use of repeated themes and images to unify and lend meaning to his novel. The text, moreover, contains its own mysteries just as *Ulysses* does: we may guess that the other word for which Martha substitutes "naughty boy" is voyeur, masochist, or exhibitionist, just as we are all entitled to hazard guesses as to the "real" identity of M'Intosh, but Martha's text, like Joyce's, remains mysterious and resistant to reductive analysis.

It is typical of *Ulysses* that we see a printed version of Martha's letter, then wait 644 pages (in the 1961 text) before discovering that the original of this printed letter was typewritten (*U*, 17.1841).[15] While the printed page can reproduce many features of written documents, it cannot reproduce all of them, so that we imagine that the italicized phrase *"by return"* was underlined in the actual letter. The same principle means that Stephen's "blue French telegram" will be represented by black letters on a white page or, in Stephen's phrase, "Signs on a white field" (*U*, 3.415). Likewise, when we read the postscript to Milly Bloom's letter—"Excuse bad writing am in hurry. Byby" (*U*, 4.413)—we do not actually see Milly's sloppy penmanship but we can be reasonably certain that "bad writing" refers to Milly's assessment of her handwriting rather than her prose style. Our own act of interpretation here is paralleled by Bloom's subsequent thoughts about the same postscript: "Excuse bad writing. Hurry. Piano downstairs." Bloom is putting together two parts of the letter to conclude that the reason for Milly's hurry was the presence downstairs, as she was writing, of some people playing the piano while waiting to go on a picnic. The fact that Bloom is looking at a relatively simple text, while we are engaged with a very complex one, should not obscure the clear parallel between the way we and Bloom both draw inferences on the basis of available textual evidence.

At times, however, we have at hand less evidence than the characters do, and we experience a written text not exactly as it really looks, nor even as it appears when translated into print, but as it impresses itself on the mind of a character. Take, for instance, the postcard received by Denis Breen:

> [Josie Breen] took a folded postcard from her handbag.
> —Read that, she said. he got it this morning.
> —What is it? Mr Bloom asked, taking the card. U.P.?
> —U.p: up, she said. Someone taking a rise out of him. It's a great shame for them whoever he is. (*U,* 8.255–59)

Various critics have taken a stab at interpreting this passage—and, indeed, the book itself contains one character's interpretation, J. J. O'Molloy's opinion that the postcard is libelous because it "implies that [Breen] is not *compos mentis*" (*U,* 12.1043–44). To interpret the passage, however, we first need to know what the card actually says. Robert M. Adams writes that the postcard "contains simply the message, 'U. P. up,' "[16] a version of the text that Mrs Breen seems to be reading, albeit without the colon. David Hayman, however, contends that the entire text of the postcard consists of "the letters 'U.P.' "[17] Hayman's unstated assumption is that Bloom reads the entire card ("What is it? Mr Bloom asked, taking the card. U.P.?"), while Mrs Breen provides us with not only a literal reading but a sort of interpretation: "U.p: up, she said" (*U,* 8.258). Subsequent occurrences of Mrs Breen's version, or a corrupted form thereof (*U,* 8.274, 8.320, 11.903, 12.258, 12.1044, 13.1239, 15.485, 15.1609, 18.229), would then simply perpetuate her reading, passing it off as part of the text, so that many years later an ingenious critic like Adams would engage in speculation about the possibility that the card refers to upward urination or a whole range of other meanings, all of which assume that the message is "U.P. up."

The colon in Mrs Breen's statement of the message (missing when Adams reproduces the message) is perhaps our best evidence that the message is indeed "U.P."; the colon would seem to indicate that what follows is a restatement or clarification of what precedes it, whereas if the entire message appeared as such in the postcard it would be hard to see what the function of that colon might be. For what it is worth, the evidence of the text seems to me to support Hayman's position over that of Adams, but one piece of extra-textual evidence might throw the matter back into doubt: in a letter to Valery Larbaud dated 17 October 1928, Joyce wrote about his eye problems and commented that "Apparently I have completely overworked myself and if I don't get back sight to read it is all U-P up."[18] Surely the evidence in the case is inconclusive, and Shari Benstock rightly observes that the mysterious postcard has no definitive form in the novel.[19]

The problems raised by the Breen postcard are much the same as those of the mysterious letter in *Finnegans Wake,* whose authorship, tone, style, meaning, and the like are subjected to endless analysis without getting us closer to any ultimate truth. Commenting on the impossibility of selecting *one* meaning from a *Wake* passage that is deliberately ambiguous, Kenner has noted that "one thing *Finnegans Wake* is about is the seemingly insuperable difficulty of reading anything at all."[20] The printed or written documents that appear in *Ulysses* often reflect this same ambiguity of language, as well as its liability to error and the ease with which one message can be transmuted into another. Thus Bloom, walking along wearing a hat whose headband once said "Plasto's high grade hat" but now says "Plasto's high grade ha," recalls (or imagines) having seen a "POST NO BILLS" sign that someone had altered to read "POST 110 PILLS" (*U,* 8.101). Paul van Caspel has observed that this prankish alteration of the sign "depends largely on the use of capitals,"[21] so that the joke calls attention to the typeface in which it is set. We are also often directed to concern ourselves with the way the book is printed in such chapters as Aeolus, with its capitalized headlines, Circe, with its dramatic form and stage directions in place of more conventional narrative, and Ithaca, with its alternation of question and answer. Occasionally, in *Ulysses,* we find the sort of typographical oddity that reminds us of *Tristram Shandy:* the giant capital letters on pp. 2, 54, and 612 of the pre-1986 Random House editions were Bennett Cerf's idea rather than Joyce's, but they are perfectly appropriate in a book that presents us with a speech in blank verse, a form in which we can be certain the characters have no intention of speaking (*U,* 9.684–706), or that includes, in two separate places, both the lyrics and the music for a song (*U,* 9.500, 17.808, 17.828).

It was inevitable that the fractured surface of *Ulysses,* which tends to expose and discard the conventions of printing just as it does the conventions of fiction, would offend a serious man like Holbrook Jackson, the William Morris scholar who later wrote *The Printing of Books* (1939). In a 1922 review, Jackson complained that *Ulysses* is "an ungainly, loose-limbed book which falls to pieces as you read it. . . . The very format of the book is an affront." Even worse is "the arrangement of the book," for "All the conventions of organised prose which have grown with our race . . have been cast aside as so much dross." Jackson complains about the punctuation, or absence thereof; about sentences which "begin and forget to end"; and about the Penelope chapter, in which "the enormous stretches of type are condescendingly broken into occasional paragraphs." As a result, "the reader is continually losing his way and having to retrace his steps."[22]

What can be said in response to Jackson's charges? First, it must be admitted that he is partly right: Joyce does abandon many of the conventions of English prose, and the reader inevitably loses his way and retraces his steps. This, however, is a deliberate exploitation (and subversion) of the print medium, for like Laurence Sterne, Joyce uses the printed page to make readers aware that his work "is digressive, and it is progressive too,——and at the same time."[23] Already in the eighteenth century, Sterne had begun to recognize the extent to which print forced readers into a passive, consumer role, and he explored ways of bringing them into a more active involvement with the text. Likewise, we may begin *Ulysses* with the assumption that we will be spoon-fed information in an orderly fashion, but very soon we either abandon this assumption or abandon the book. It is partly through the exposure of the pitfalls of print that *Ulysses* becomes, in Kenner's felicitous phrase, "a new kind of book altogether, a Berlitz classroom between covers: a book from which we are systematically taught the skills we require to read it."[24] Or, as Joseph Frank put it four decades ago, "the reader is forced to read *Ulysses* in exactly the same manner as he reads modern poetry—continually fitting fragments together and keeping allusions in mind until, by reflexive reference, he can link them to their complements."[25]

All of this might help us to give an answer—by no means the only one—to the oldest question in *Ulysses* criticism: whether this big, sprawling book is a novel at all. The novel, it is often said, developed in the eighteenth century because there was a group of consumers (readers) who wanted extended prose accounts of middle-class life. The printing press made all this possible, just as it had made inevitably the translation of the Bible into the vernacular; in any event the mass production of books is inseparable from the development of the novel as a significant art form. But that art form was based upon a sense of reality that we associate with Euclidean geometry and Newtonian physics: other geometries may be just as coherent as Euclid's, and Einsteinian physics may answer many questions that Newton failed even to ask, but these relatively recent developments do not correspond so easily to what we observe and experience in everyday life. Likewise, *Ulysses* commences in the tradition of the realistic novel but soon veers off in other directions, introducing stylistic parodies, expressionistic devices, and other forms of non-realistic writing in order to force the reader into a more complex relationship to the world of the book.

That it is print that accomplishes all this is appropriate, for McLuhan connects the development of the phonetic alphabet—the necessary forerunner of print—with the assumptions about the continuity and homogeneity of time and space that underlie Euclidean geometry, and notes that these assumptions are reinforced by the homogeneous and reproductible medium of print.[26] Similarly, he shows that the maintenance of a fixed or consistent point of view—a phenomenon that is crucial to the development of the early novel—becomes possible (or at least desirable) only when works are printed.[27] Yet Joyce uses print precisely to undermine these very assumptions, as when the headlines in Aeolus introduce a variety of new viewpoints into the chapter to challenge the authority of the "primary" narration, or when Joyce builds upon the model of non-Euclidean geometry for the narration of Ithaca.[28] Ezra Pound objected strenuously to the use of "a new style per chapter,"[29] but the shifting styles and viewpoints of *Ulysses* are an essential aspect of Joyce's determination to offer alternatives to the Euclidean and Newtonian viewpoint fostered by the printed text. We may begin *Ulysses* with assumptions borrowed from Flaubert, or even Defoe, but we conclude it in the spirit of Beckett, recognizing, for example, when Bloom becomes a mother, that childbirth is an exclusively female activity, but not in this work.[30]

Notes

1. Samuel Beckett, *Watt* (New York: Grove Press, 1959), 102; other page references are given parenthetically.

2. Hugh Kenner, *Flaubert, Joyce and Beckett: The Stoic Comedians* (Boston: Beacon Press, 1963), 37. I am indebted to this book, and to Kenner's work generally, for the direction that I have taken in this paper. See also Bernard Benstock's "Bedeviling the Typographer's Ass: *Ulysses* and *Finnegans Wake*," *Journal of Modern Literature* 12 (March 1985): 3–33, which appeared after I wrote this paper.

3. Jonathan Swift, *Gulliver's Travels*, ed. Robert A. Greenberg (New York: Norton Critical Edition, 1970), vi–vii.

4. See Jack P. Dalton, "The Text of *Ulysses*," in *New Light on Joyce from the Dublin Symposium*, ed. Fritz Senn (Bloomington: Indiana University Press, 1972), 102, and Hans Walter Gabler, Forward to *Ulysses: A Critical and Synoptic Edition*, ed. Gabler (New York: Garland Publishing, 1984), vii. Quotations from *Ulysses* conform to the Garland text except in places where I am calling attention to the corruption of the Random House edition.

5. Ian Watt, *The Rise of the Novel: Studies in Defoe, Richardson and Fielding* (Berkeley and Los Angeles: University of California Press, 1962), 206.

6. Marshall McLuhan, *The Gutenberg Galaxy: The Making of Typographic Man* (Toronto: University of Toronto Press, 1962), passim.

7. Marilyn French, *The Book as World: James Joyce's* Ulysses (Cambridge: Harvard University Press, 1976), 3–4.

8. The English translation of Edouard Dujardin's *Les Lauriers sont coupés*, the book Joyce credited with the invention of *le monologue intérieur*, contains an odd reference to *Ulysses:* when Daniel Prince composes a note to Leah, he makes a mistake, tears it twice, then tries to tear it again but fails: "Again; no, imposs." (*We'll to the Woods No More*, trans. Stuart Gilbert [New York: New Directions, 1957], 27.) This passage has no basis in the French text of *Les Lauriers sont coupés* (Paris: Editions Messein, 1925), 43, which reads, ". . . encore en deux; là, encore; plus moyen." Another Joycean echo is "love's old sweet song" (48), which appears in the French text (57) as "la romance de l'éternal amour."

9. McLuhan, 22.

10. M'Intosh gets his name at *U*, 6.894–96. The most thorough and intriguing investigation of the M'Intosh phenomenon has been undertaken by Brook Thomas in *James Joyce's* Ulysses: *A Book of Many Happy Returns* (Baton Rouge: Louisiana State University Press, 1982), passim. I take issue, however, with Thomas's statement that "we can be relatively certain . . . that 'M'Intosh' does not have the real name of M'Intosh" (116); if this enigmatic character did in fact have a real name, it would seem most appropriate that Bloom would accidentally hit upon it.

11. Hans Walter Gabler, "Stephen in Paris," *James Joyce Quarterly* 17 (Spring 1980): 311.
12. This insight developed out of a conversation with Hugh Kenner.
13. Dublin is a town in which an imprudent borrower like "Stephen Dedalus B. A." gets his full name and university degree included in the account of a funeral that he did not attend, while a lender like Bloom gets slighted.
14. Kenner, *Dublin's Joyce* (Bloomington: Indiana University Press, 1956), 203 n. The original edition of *Ulysses* (Paris: Shakespeare and Company, 1922) has the passage right.
15. The typed letter might, however, have been deduced from the "typed envelope" specified in Lotus Eaters (*U*, 5.61).
16. Robert Martin Adams, *Surface and Symbol: The Consistency of James Joyce's* Ulysses (New York: Oxford University Press, 1962), 192.
17. David Hayman, Ulysses: *The Mechanics of Meaning,* rev. ed. (Madison: University of Wisconsin Press, 1982) 54.
18. *Letters,* III, 182. Adams, who does not even recognize the existence of any doubt over the form of the message, cites the French translation, "Fou Tu," in support of particular textual interpretations (Adams, 193). The problem here is that a translation of a phrase like this is itself an interpretation that tends to focus on one meaning while eliminating others; Joyce, however, usually wanted to include rather than exclude meanings.
19. Shari Benstock, "The Printed Letters in *Ulysses,*" *James Joyce Quarterly* 19 (Summer 1982): 424–25.
20. Kenner, *A Colder Eye: The Modern Irish Writers* (New York: Alfred A. Knopf, 1983), 219.
21. Paul P. J. van Caspel, *Bloomers on the Liffey: Eisegetical Readings of James Joyce's* Ulysses *Part II* (Groningen, 1980), 147.
22. Holbrook Jackson, "Ulysses à la Joyce," in *James Joyce: The Critical Heritage,* ed. Robert H. Deming (New York: Barnes & Noble, 1970), 198–200.
23. Laurence Sterne, *The Life and Opinions of Tristram Shandy, Gentleman,* ed. James A. Work (New York: Odyssey Press, 1940), 73. Sterne frequently undermines the conventions of printed fiction, as for example when his characters read earlier volumes of the novel in which they appear (218) or when Tristram says that a turn of events has saved him from writing a "chapter on chances" to go with the other chapters that he has promised his readers (280).
24. Kenner, *A Colder Eye,* 155.
25. Joseph Frank, "Spatial Form of Modern Literature," *Sewanee Review* 53 (1945): 234.
26. McLuhan, 177–80.
27. Ibid., 126–27, 135–36.
28. See Patrick A. McCarthy, "Joyce's Unreliable Catechist: Mathematics and the Narration of 'Ithaca,'" *ELH* 51 (Fall 1984): 605–18.
29. Richard Ellmann, *JJII,* 459.
30. *"Bloom . . . bears eight male yellow and white children. . . . All are handsome, with valuable metallic faces, wellmade, respectably dressed and well conducted, speaking five modern languages fluently and interested in various arts and sciences"* (*U,* 15.1821–26).

Fifty Years of Joyce: 1934–1984

RICHARD M. KAIN

The anniversary of the first authorized American edition of *Ulysses* in January 1934, and the appearance of the Synoptic Edition on Bloomsday 1984, afford an opportunity for a veteran Joycean to comment on the position of Joyce then and now, to describe a few items of little-known Joyceana, and to indulge in some recollections.

In 1934 Random House printed 10,300 copies (plus 100 for copyright) of *Ulysses*, at the price of $3.50 and issued a complimentary flyer, undoubtedly now more of a rarity than a first edition. This throwaway, one of my treasures, is entitled "HOW TO ENJOY / James Joyce's / ULYSSES / presented with the compliments of / RANDOM HOUSE AND YOUR BOOKSELLER." A sheet, twenty-two inches wide and sixteen inches high, is folded into a five- by eight-inch format. The center spread contains a photograph of Joyce, looking left, right hand behind his ear and left eye covered by a patch; a plan of Dublin, with five views; a list of major characters, a summary of episodes, and some critical opinions.

The text begins:

> FOR THOSE who are already engrossed in *Ulysses* as well as for those who hesitate to begin it because they fear that it is obscure, the publishers offer this simple clue to what the critical fuss is all about.

The account is helpful, if not penetrating. Stuart Gilbert is quoted:

> "It is like a great net let down from heaven including in the infinite variety of its take the magnificent and the petty, the holy and the obscene. In this story of a Dublin day we read the epic of mankind."

An unsigned commentary isolates three elements of structure: "the symbolic narrative of the Odyssey, the spiritual planes of the Divine Comedy and the psychological problem of Hamlet." As to theme: "The theme of the Odyssey has been called 'the dominance of circumstance over mind.' " Three "planes of reality" are also indicated: the naturalistic, the classical, and the symbolic. Then, in a disarming statement, "these things need not concern the general reader whose enjoyment of Ulysses depends on its humor, its wisdom, and its essential humanity." Apart from two of the small photographs on the Dublin map—one which certainly is not Joyce's Martello Tower, and a view of the Bray promenade instead of Sandymount Strand—the presentation is acceptable.

Several years ago I found at the Gotham Book Mart Bennett Cerf's account, "Publishing Ulysses," in the James Joyce Issue of *Contempo*, 15 February 1934. The publisher tells of being summoned to the brokerage office of Robert Kastor, Giorgio Joyce's brother-in-law, in December 1931, almost exactly two years before Judge Woolsey's famous decision regarding *Ulysses*. Cerf's recollection was that Kastor had suggested fighting the ban, and that on the same day Morris Ernst drew up a contract which was taken to Joyce in Paris by Kastor the next February. As for possible sales, Cerf was optimistic: "My own guess would be about 50,000 in the first year, and a steady sale of a few thousand each year thereafter." The Slocum-Cahoon Joyce bibliography records a Random House run of 187,625 copies printed by June 1950, and Sylvia Beach issues of 28,000.

Bennett Cerf realized that Joyce held a special position in the world of letters. Joyce was never destined to become a widely popular writer. Nor, indeed, did he intend to be. Frank Budgen records that Joyce said of those who produced two books a year, "I feel quite capable of doing that if I wanted to do it. But what's the use: It isn't worth doing."[1]

As for the Paris first edition, a prospectus, given to me by Sylvia Beach, announced that "ULYSSES by JAMES JOYCE will be published in the Autumn of 1921." The actual date was to be 2 February 1922, Joyce's fortieth birthday. Prices, at an eight-cent franc, ranged from $28 for one of the hundred copies signed by the author to $20 for the next 150 copies and $12 for the remaining 750 copies. Few investments were to enjoy such meteoric appreciation. But even years later I was only a superficial reader, and by no means a collector. I had bought a bootlegged copy of a later Beach edition at the University of Chicago Bookstore in 1930, which I had perused with interest, and only partial comprehension.

Miss Beach also gave me two leaflets, "EXTRACTS from PRESS NOTICES OF ULYSSES BY JAMES JOYCE." They deserve brief description, as I do not recall having seen any published account of them. Each is a folded sheet, four pages, one on white paper, the second, apparently later, with many more quotations, on pale rose paper. Both contain favorable comments by Valery Larbaud ("formidable . . . vivante . . . humaine"), Exra Pound ("l'art flaubertian"), Arnold Bennett ("astonishing phenomenon"), Edmund Wilson ("Extraordinary poetic facility") and others, each about a dozen lines. Then, more briefly, remarks such as "fearful travesty," "impossible to read and undesirable to quote," "clotted nonsense," and "enough to make a Hottentot sick." Both leaflets conclude with an anticlimatic one-liner from the *Irish Independent: "Ulysses* has come in for some severe criticisms."

Harriet Weaver was responsible for publishing these items, and she told me that Joyce had helped select the quotations, even those unfavorable, as is shown in several letters to her in the autumn of 1922. Considering current widespread interest in everything Joycean, these press notices should probably be published, as well as similar sheets on *Chamber Music, Dubliners,* and *A Portrait of the Artist as a Young Man.*

Ulysses had become an international phenomenon even before publication. The "usylessly unreadable Blue Book of Eccles" (*FW*, 179) had a pre-publication debut in the "SÉANCE CONSACRÉE A / L'ÉCRIVAIN IRLANDAIS / JAMES JOYCE / CONFERENCE PAR M. VALERY LARBAUD" on 7 December 1921, to quote an invitation given to me by Sylvia Beach. The first biographical booklet was Francini Bruni's *Joyce Intimo Spogliato in Piazza* (Trieste, 1922), a rare item, fortunately now available in English.[2] Although Joyce is said to have resented it, the sketch has the mocking tone that the author of *Ulysses* should have relished, had it been at someone else's expense. My copy was given to me by Joseph Prescott, whose 1944 Harvard thesis was the first American Ph.D. dissertation on Joyce.

In the twenties current literature was virtually unknown in college curricula. Although metropolitan newspapers and major journals were constantly noting theatrical productions by Eugene O'Neill and others, as well as a steady stream of poetry and fiction, English literature ended in 1900 or 1914 as far as English departments were concerned, and American literature was almost totally unrecognized. I do recall seeing a copy of *Ulysses* in the college dormitory, and in an unguarded moment one instructor mentioned the name of Virginia Woolf.

By 1934 *Ulysses* was already recognized as a masterpiece, though in the popular mind it was notorious for its frankness or at best considered impenetrably obscure. Yet after fifty years of analysis it still yields rich rewards to the investigator. The matter is put succinctly by Thomas F. Staley in his survey of Joyce studies for the volume *Anglo-Irish Literature: A Review of Research*: "No novel written in English in this century has been studied more widely or more deeply over so impressive a range of topics as *Ulysses*—studied not only because of its own intrinsic complexity, depth, and worth but also because of its impact on the whole of modern literature."[3]

Fritz Senn has described *Ulysses* as a "Book of Many Turns," using the literal translation of the Greek *polytropos*, applied by Homer to the hero Odysseus in the first line of the *Odyssey*.[4] Joyce himself had indicated some of these many turns in a letter to Carlo Linati on 21 September 1920: "It is an epic of two races (Israelite-Irish) and at the same time the cycle of the human body as well as a *storiella* of a day (life)." "It is also a sort of encyclopaedia," he continued. "My intention is to transpose the myth *sub specie temporis nostri*," and "Each adventure (that is, every hour, every organ, every art being interconnected and interrelated in the structural scheme of the whole) should not only condition but even create its technique."

My serious interest in Joyce came about indirectly, through reading Mann and Proust, who, like Joyce, extended the novel beyond the limits of conventional fiction. Joseph Warren Beach's *The Twentieth Century Novel* (1932) was for me a major influence. Beach's allegiance to the well-made novel, particularly as written by Henry James, led him to do less than justice to the Modernists. Nonetheless, his type of analysis, an early anticipation of structuralism, showed that the post-Jamesian novel had its own aesthetic principles of composition, point of view, style, and tone. In lighter moments during my course in the modern European novel I used to observe that to pick up an experimental fiction was somewhat like sorting out a bridge hand, since both are filled with unpredictable possibilities.

Although it was some fifty years ago, I still retain vivid memories of my first readings of *Ulysses* as an uninstructed novice. I recall my delight and bewilderment at the opening chapters with their compelling sense of immediacy, and the surprise I felt at the appearance of "Agenbite of Inwit," which I thought had been safely buried in that dreaded graduate-school course in Middle English.

I had read *Dubliners* and *Portrait*, but to me at that time Joyce was no more than *primus inter pares*. After all, Joseph Warren Beach had devoted more space to Conrad and almost as many pages to D. H. Lawrence as he did to Joyce. As I look back on those pages in Beach I find him somewhat apologetic regarding *Ulysses*. If it were not for its influence, he argues, "we might leave it out of our account, as being a freak of nature, a thing *sui generis*." Motifs and correspondences he considers "a pure luxury—the unbridled play of the poetic or musical faculty." Yet he does make some interesting comparisons: with "the close-up and the slow-up, or *ralenti*, in the moving picture" and with Browning, Carlyle, and post-impressionist painting, which creates "an abstract composition for rendering some truth" of the artist's thought.

I was pleased to find the Hades chapter included in the college-level anthology, *This Generation* (1939), edited by George K. Anderson and Eda Lou Walton, a text I used in a contemporary literature course at that time. The introductory essay is of historical interest. The style of *Dubliners* is considered "distinctly orthodox," but *Portrait*, despite "passages of great powers" contains "many examples of execrable taste that defy analysis." *Finnegans Wake* is summarily dismissed as "the reductio ad absurdum of the subjective" but somewhat excused as "the natural result of the excessive growth of . . . self-portrayal through one's own imagination and emotions." The evaluation of *Ulysses* is equivocal. One head-note asserts that "however great the enthusiasm for the pyrotechnics of this work and the homage due the unquestioned influence of its brilliant writer, no praise can truly counterbalance the censure of Joyce's work" expressed in the introduction, an essay which, paradoxically enough, concludes: "No longer is it intelligent to throw up one's hands in horror. . . . Joyce has, for better or for worse, achieved that which will leave its mark upon English letters for a long time to come."

The editors provide notes on characters, places, allusions, and Homeric parallels. These annotations are competent, though with the usual quota of error; Artane and Todd's, for instance, are not "prominent private schools," but an Institute for Destitute Children, and the silk mercer's shop of Todd, Burns, and Co.

At the Modern Language Association meeting in New Orleans in 1939 I heard a paper by William Powell Jones on the recently published *Finnegans Wake*, possibly the first appearance of Joyce on such a program. At that time Edmund Wilson's excellent review of the *Wake* had given a satisfactory introduction, as had his earlier essays, dating from 1922, and his account of Joyce in *Axel's Castle* (1931). In 1939 Herbert Gorman's biography, inadequate though it was, presented something of a portrait, but it was Harry Levin's brief but comprehensive *James Joyce: A Critical Introduction* (1941) that consolidated Joyce's position in the mainstream of modern literature. Levin's book, far-reaching in its insight and interpretation, remains one of the best general guides to Joyce.

Having conducted research seminars in modern fiction at the University of Louisville for several years, I asked my department head, Ernest C. Hassold, whether I could concentrate on Joyce in the fall of 1944. Hassold, a profound thinker and an innovative educator, gave his consent. So far as I know, this was the first such course to be offered. (By 1982 *A Guide to Irish Studies in the United States* listed 116 courses on Joyce.)

The course announcement created something of a sensation on campus. Senior college enrollment was small at the time, and had been further curtailed by the draft, but the seminar attracted some of the keenest young minds I have encountered in years of teaching, here and abroad. Two of the thirteen students were to earn doctorates, and a term paper was later printed in *PMLA* (Joseph E. Duncan, "The Modality of the Audible in James Joyce's *Ulysses*" [March 1957]).

Even in 1944, *Ulysses* was by no means unexplored territory. Stuart Gilbert had, with Joyce's help, elucidated the Homeric correspondences, and Frank Budgen had conveyed a rich personal impression of Joyce as friend and artist. My approach, influenced by Edmund Wilson and Harry Levin, was to read *Ulysses* for its human values, and as a social document.

To me at that time *Ulysses* was, on one level, a historical novel, for Joyce had been recreating the Dublin of his youth from a distance of hundreds of miles and some fifteen or more years in time. In a memorable passage Budgen had recalled a conversation with Joyce in Zurich:

> "I want," said Joyce, as we were walking down the Universitatstrasse, "to give a picture of Dublin so complete that if the city one day suddenly disappeared from the earth it could be reconstructed out of my book."
>
> We had come to the university terrace where we could look down on the town.
>
> "And what a city Dublin is!" he continued. "I wonder if there is another like it. Everybody has time to hail a friend and start a conversation about a third party. . . . I suppose you don't get that gossipy, leisurely life in London?"[5]

Ulysses also seemed to me a metaphysical novel. I had not yet encountered another statement by Joyce, but I sensed the tenor of his concept. To Arthur Power he said, "if I can get to the heart of Dublin I can get to the heart of all the cities of the world," for "In the particular is contained the universal."[6]

My first *Ulysses* course was offered just ten years after the Random House edition, and, by a Joycean coincidence, the first copy of my *Fabulous Voyager* arrived exactly twenty-five years after *Ulysses* had been placed in Joyce's hands on 2 February 1922. In writing *Fabulous Voyager* I attempted to evoke from *Ulysses* the Dublin of Bloomsday—the streets, the happenings, the characters, the "friend" and "third party" of Joyce's comment. In the war years travel was out of the question, and I had to reconstruct from maps, from the pages of Thom's *Directory*, and from *Ulysses*, a Dublin I had never seen. One problem perplexed me, one that could have been solved in Dublin within minutes. Only after laborious cross-checking did I learn that buildings are numbered, not by the American system, but consecutively to the end of one side of the street, then returning on the other side. Thus Bloom left his door at 7 Eccles Street, and "crossed to the bright side, avoiding the loose cellarflap of number seventyfive" (*U*, 4.77–78).

A microfilm of the *Evening Telegraph*, a copy of which Bloom glances at in the cabman's shelter, provided evidence of Joyce's documentary bent, since the wording in *Ulysses* regarding general news, shipping, theatre attractions, and sports follows that in the newspaper. Tracing these topics through *Ulysses* proved fascinating—the disastrous fire on the excursion steamer "General Slocum," the Ascot Gold Cup race, the hoof and mouth disease problem, the cycle race at Trinity College, even the presence there of the band of the Second Seaforth Highlanders.

Stuart Gilbert had observed that "Through the greater Odyssey of

Bloomsday there runs a 'Little Odyssey', a *Saponeia*, the wanderings of the soap." Countless other themes are to be found, many of which I followed through the text. They range from the trivial—the evangelistic throwaway "Elijah is Coming" or the pornographic book *Sweets of Sin*—to the philosophical concepts of metempsychosis or parallax.

Of greater interest to me was a hint from Harry Levin's *James Joyce* that in Ithaca "Joyce contemplates his characters *sub specie aeternitas*, from the scope of planetary distances." I followed Levin in citing Pascal and in addition mentioned comparable attitudes in Montaigne and Sir Thomas Browne, together with passages in *Ulysses* suggestive of relativity and the cosmic perspective such as divergent calendars or Bloom's meditations on water and on the starry sky. The medieval formula, "Ubi Sunt," is suggested as one turns the pages of Thom's *Directory*; "Where, now," I wrote, "Thomas Johnson and his neighbor, the retired registrar?" I suggested that *Ulysses* "anticipates the thought of *Finnegans Wake* that 'we are circumveiloped by obscuritads.' "

One chapter on Bloom's humanitarian proclivities, with its epigraph "*Love, says Bloom. I mean the opposite of hatred*," seems vindicated by the recent discovery of five lines omitted from all previous versions of *Ulysses*, first printed in the Synoptic Edition (1984). The restored lines, from the library scene, include "Love, yes. Word known to all men" (*U*, 9.429–30). These words, according to Richard Ellmann, "will have a considerable effect upon the interpretation of the whole book."

In fact, one contribution made by my study was to assert the importance of Leopold Bloom. My first appendix was entitled "THE TEMPERAMENT, PERSONALITY, AND OPINIONS OF LEOPOLD BLOOM," in which I compared our intimate knowledge of Bloom with what we know in the same vein about Montaigne, Pepys, Johnson, Rousseau, and Proust. One reviewer suggested adding Sherlock Holmes to this list.

Each of the subjects of the four appendices has since given rise to a book itself. *The Chronicle of Leopold and Molly Bloom* (1977), by John Henry Raleigh, and Peter Costello's *Leopold Bloom: A Biography* (1981) construct Bloom's life from his frequent memories, the Costello book even projecting a "life" that continues to his "death" in 1937, when "By some oversight no notice of his death was put in the papers." The second appendix, "A BIOGRAPHICAL DICTIONARY OF *ULYSSES*," has been followed more thoroughly (and with the inclusion of Joyce's earlier works) by Shari and Bernard Benstock, *Who's He When He's at Home* (1980). My DIRECTORY OF SHOPS, OFFICES, PUBLIC BUILDINGS, PROFESSIONAL AND CIVIC PERSONAGES," derived from Thom's *Directory*, was enlarged and provided with excellent maps by Clive Hart and Leo Knuth in *A Topographical Guide to James Joyce's* Ulysses (1975). The "INDEX OF VERBAL MOTIFS" has been exhaustively listed by William M. Schutte, *Index of Recurrent Elements in James Joyce's Ulysses* (1982).

My study was itself dependent upon the Miles L. Hanley *Word Index to James Joyce's* Ulysses (1937), done by hand before the age of computers. An interesting note: "The cost of materials used between June and September, 1936, amounting to $148, was paid by a grant from the Special Research Fund of the University of Wisconsin." That expenditure deserves an exclamation point!

The publication of *Fabulous Voyager* brought me in contact with the collector John Slocum, whose superb library, now at Yale, formed the basis of the Slocum-Cahoon *Bibliography of James Joyce* (1953). In 1948 I went with Slocum on a "Joyce tour" of Dublin, London, Oxford, Paris, and Zurich. This trip afforded me the privilege of seeing Dublin before it was invaded by modern commercial development, sometimes called progress. The city was still eighteenth-century in appearance and spirit. The disintegration of Georgian facades had not begun; trams and horse-drawn drays, outside cars, and cabs constituted the major traffic, thanks to gasoline shortages. The original Abbey Theatre had not been destroyed, and the magnificent public buildings had been restored after their destruction during the "Troubles."

Best of all, many of Joyce's contemporaries were there, ready to talk about the old days. Constantine Curran's vivid recollections of his years with Joyce at University College made me aware that Dublin in the time of Joyce had been a scene of lively literary activity and political enthusiasm. For Curran, Joyce's college mates—Kettle and Clery and Skeffington and the rest—were as interesting as Joyce himself.[7] As an expert on Dublin before the Union (Curran hated the term "Georgian"), he introduced me to Dublin's city planning, architecture, plasterwork, and the early views by James Malton. It is noteworthy that Joyce ignored the elaborate plasterwork, the fine staircases, and the Palladian windows that grace the buildings of Belvedere College and University College, many full-page plates of which are included in Curran's handsomely illustrated study, *Dublin Decorative Plasterwork of the Seventeenth and Eighteenth Centuries* (1967). Father John Conmee, in fact the one-time rector of Clongowes Wood College and later rector of Belvedere, does reflect, briefly, en route to Artane, on a "drawingroom, ceiled with full fruit clusters" (*U*, 10.176–77). So much for the beauties of Ascendancy Dublin—or so little. Curran remarked to me that it was like Joyce to describe Sandymount Strand at low tide, with flotsam on the sand.

The collectors P. S. O'Hegarty and Seumas O'Sullivan generously showed us their fine libraries. Booksellers and librarians freely dispensed information. I heard that the National Library had only recently destroyed call slips going back many years, but in Marsh's Library, where Stephen Dedalus presumably had spent much time in study, I saw two entries of one James Joyce. "Only two," the librarian observed.

Gogarty, despite his obsessive bitterness toward Joyce, was a source of witty invective and a fund of brilliant historical and literary comment, ranging from Danish and Irish place names to Grace O'Malley. These men recreated for me the Dublin of Bloomsday, as the later generation of Niall Sheridan, Michael Scott, and Donagh MacDonagh brought to life the aftermath of the revival, the Dublin of the late twenties and the thirties.

The generosity of Dubliners must be recorded. Not only generous of their time—I recall an evening when Michael MacLiammoir read some of the Cyclops episode in the dialect of the Dublin slums—but also as givers of such irreplaceable ephemera as a catalogue of the Municipal Gallery opening in 1908 or an issue of a Castle newssheet dating from the Anglo-Irish War.

A recent talk by John Slocum, printed in the *Gazette of the Grolier Club* (new series, 33/34 [1981–1982]) brings to mind other recollections, as when I directed a taxi driver to follow the funeral route from Sandymount to Glasnevin, via Great Brunswick and Sackville Streets. The jarvey looked at me in amazement, remarking, "Those names were changed after the Treaty. Sure you're not old enough to remember that!" Slocum also recalls Niall Sheridan's account of Joyce's sister at her home on Mountjoy Square, with the same "washed-out forget-me-not blue eyes and that pen-wiper nose" as her brother.

When I asked for an old copy of Thom's *Directory* at a Dublin bookstore the clerk said that they didn't have any, but as an afterthought asked me what year I might want. When I said that it would be 1904 or 1905 he reconsidered. After all, in 1948 that wouldn't be *old*. After a few moments in the basement he emerged with a 1904 edition, which I bought for a few shillings. On the shelf behind his desk I saw Sir Robert Ball's *The Story of the Heavens*, a copy of which was in Bloom's library. So on one visit I acquired two unusual items of Joyceana.

One other bit of ephemera deserves special mention. Mr. O'Hegarty mailed me a photostat of his copy of a 1904 pamphlet, "The Language of the Outlaw," an account of John F. Taylor's speech defending the Irish language movement. Quoted in *Ulysses* (*U*, 7.828–69), it was selected by Joyce for his reading on a phonograph recording in 1923. In a clever comment Brook Thomas traces the circuit of these words as "An impromptu speech, recorded in print by memory, reconstructed as a fictional text, where it masquerades as an impromptu recreation" by Professor MacHugh, after which it is "finally recorded by gramophone."[8] The text of this pamphlet has been published in *The Workshop of Daedalus* (1965).[9]

As an early Joycean I enjoyed some experiences never again to be duplicated: conversations with Sylvia Beach, Lucie Leon, Maria and Eugene Jolas, and Stuart Gilbert in Paris, Nora and Giorgio Joyce in Zurich, Harriet Weaver in Oxford, and Frank Budgen in London.

A few other recollections from my visit to Dublin with John Slocum may be of interest. A librarian at Trinity College asked me confidentially, "Tell me frankly, if it's not too personal, do you admire James Joyce." Remarks heard in a pub: "If you're following the footsteps of Joyce, you'd better get water-proof boots," and "To censor that book you'd have to mark all the objectionable passages, and no one here is likely to spend the time doing that." Seumas O'Sullivan, poet and editor, told me he was not in *Ulysses* "because Joyce had no use for me at all, and I never did him any harm" (O'Sullivan was mistaken, for as Starkey, his real name, he is mentioned among the younger poets in the library chapter). Regarding Joyce's obscurity, I remember Jack Yeats, gazing at the turf smoldering in his fireplace, musing that "The idea of understanding everything you read is a curious modern superstition." At her apartment in Zurich Nora Joyce reflected, "I'm a simple woman but I had a great man for a husband and that's enough."

In Sylvia Beach's Paris apartment I appreciated her enthusiasm as much as the Joyce treasures she showed us. She was unbelievably generous, giving me, in addition to the press notices of *Ulysses*, one from a pile of covers for *Pomes Penyeach*, rejected by Joyce as an incorrect shade of green. At her table I transcribed the 1904 manuscript, "A Portrait of the Artist," the germ of the famous novel, written in his sister Mabel's copybook, one of "VERE FOSTER'S RULED EXERCISE BOOKS." We recall that Bloom treasured as a souvenir "A Vere Foster's handwriting copybook, property of Milly (Millicent) Bloom," with its childish drawing of her father (*U*, 17.1775–76).

At that time the essay as virtually unknown, though Sylvia Beach had listed it in an unpriced catalogue that included seventeen Joyce items, among them the second numbered copy of *Ulysses*, the *Stephen Hero* manuscript, the broadsides, the typescript pages of *Ulysses*, which "may be acquired separately by those who might like to enrich their copy of 'Ulysses' with a little manuscript." Ms. Beach gave me a copy of the catalogue, but, alas, none of her many pages of proof and manuscript which we handled with awe. Robert Scholes and I edited the "Portrait" essay, first in *The Yale Review* in 1960, and in *The Workshop of Daedalus* (1965).

There was also my discovery of two Joyce book reviews in the Dublin *Daily Express*.[10] Thanks to a hint from Padraic Colum, that gracious and genial spirit, at the National Library I found in the 11 December 1902, issue, "An Irish Poet," unsigned, but with the telltale phrase later used in *Ulysses*, "those big words which make us so unhappy" (*U*, 2.264), an example of Joyce's memory and verbal economy. The book was *Poems and Ballads*, by William Rooney, patriotic versifier and contributor to *The United Irishman*. Griffith must have resented this insult to his recently deceased protégé, but he made ironical use of the review for advertising, as he was later to evade censorship by printing press cuttings in his Sinn Fein journal *Scissors and Paste*.

The second review is mentioned in *Ulysses*, when Mulligan refers to Stephen's attack on Lady Gregory's *Poets and Dreamers*: "She gets you a job on the paper and then you go and slate her drivel to Jaysus" (*U*, 9.1159–60). Joyce's many reviews are included in *The Critical Writings* (1959), edited by Ellsworth Mason and Richard Ellmann.

I remember too my visit to the La Hune Bookshop on the Left Bank, where Maria Jolas showed me the cases of materials once in Joyce's apartment and saved despite the Nazi occupation of Paris. Here were remnants of his library, some manuscripts, family portraits, and other mementoes, about to be mounted in the exhibit catalogued by Bernard Gheerbrandt, *James Joyce: Sa Vie, Son Oeuvre, Son Rayonnement* (1949). This important collection, now in the Lockwood Memorial Library of the State University of New York at Buffalo, is catalogued in Peter Spielberg's *James Joyce's Manuscripts and Letters at the University of Buffalo* (1962). Through the generosity of the curators and the James Joyce estate I was able to edit an interesting example of Joycean homework, his chronology of Shakespeare's life, biographical data for the library chapter of *Ulysses*.[11]

Joyce continues to inspire musical settings, recordings, radio and television programs, stage and film versions, exhibitions, symposia, journals, and annual publications of books and articles. The centennial of Joyce's birth was celebrated in many countries, and the Synoptic Edition of *Ulysses* in 1984 became a front-page story.

The "Joyce Industry" has been viewed with alarm—and ridicule—since the term first appeared in the sixties, but as early as 1951 the Joyce issue of the Dublin journal, *Envoy*, printed Patrick Kavanagh's satiric verses, "Who Killed James Joyce?" The poem begins:

> Who killed James Joyce?
> I, said the commentator,
> I killed James Joyce
> For my graduation.

A book review by the Irish writer Bernard Share was entitled "Any Old Irony?," echoing a call from an itinerant monger and mocking critical extravagances. Some Joyceans, too, reveal a sense of humor, notably Adaline Glasheen, whose addenda to her useful list of characters in *Wake* was entitled "Out of My Census." In the *Wake Newslitter* she once announced, "I am going to tell all I know about these paragraphs, no matter how boring I get."

Throughout my own forty-year involvement with Joyce studies—as teacher, scholar, editor, and reviewer—I have had a special interest in the growth of Joyce's reputation. Few writers have had such an extraordinary following, Yeats perhaps excepted. In March 1948 I spoke on the topic at a meeting of the newly formed James Joyce Society of New York. The Society's early programs featured reminiscences by Joyce's daughter-in-law Helen and her brother Robert Kastor, as well as by Joyce's friends Lucie Leon, Maria Jolas, and Padraic and Mary Colum.

In 1954, while in London looking up periodical materials on Joyce in the British Museum, I heard the BBC celebration of the fiftieth anniversary of Bloomsday with a reading of two episodes, Hades and Sirens, the latter with a background of Irish song. Unfortunately, because of a labor dispute the program was not preserved.

My accumulation of approximately 2,500 notes about books and articles on Joyce became part of *Joyce: The Man, The Work, The Reputation* (1956), co-authored with Marvin Magalaner. My opening chapter was on "The Enigma of Joyce," and in the final chapter I classified major critical opinions of the author as humorist, indifferent observer, nihilist, divided soul, Catholic, Dubliner, and symbolist. Reviews of this book in Europe as well as India and Australia, and an English edition, testify to widespread interest in Joyce at that time. A much enlarged study is now needed.

The extent of the Joyce Industry can be suggested by the 5,885 items in Roberty H. Deming's revised *Bibliography of James Joyce Studies* (1977), which covers the years through 1973, and about 200 entries in the annual editions of the Modern Language Association's *International Bibliography*. Supplements are periodically compiled by Alan M. Cohn for the *James Joyce Quarterly*. The editor of this excellent journal, Thomas F. Staley, has contributed useful surveys of Joyce scholarship to the volume, *Anglo-Irish Literature: A Review of Research*, edited by Richard J. Finneran (1976) and to the supplement published in 1983. *The James Joyce Quarterly* recently announced that it had 800 subscribers in 39 countries, with foreign subscriptions of 430 (West Germany, 80; Japan, 70; Canada, 67; England, 53; Italy, 24; Netherlands, 23; and Ireland, 22, being the leaders).

One can only smile at Joyce's speculating to Harriet Weaver three months after the first publication of *Ulysses*: "I wonder if any criticism of the book will be published—apart from these articles."[12]

Joyce is such a seminal writer that every aspect of his work is of interest, no matter how trivial it might seem. *Ulysses* is, as Joyce observed, "a kind of encyclopaedia." its range can be compared to that of Proust or Mann, touching upon the larger issues of the modern world and the human psyche. An incomparable stylist, he continues to evoke ever more subtle analyses. No account of his genius can exhaust the subject.

The most amazing fact of his career is that with his weak eyesight, impaired health, and domestic problems, he was able to absorb so much from others and to shape it in his own imagination. Literally thousands of casual facts and allusions have been found in *Ulysses, vide* the Gifford and Seidman and the Weldon Thornton volumes, and others continue to be discovered. Joyce endows each reference with the magic of his style so that uncovering a source can be an illuminating experience.

A few of my findings come to mind. Serendipity led me to learn that the titles of the Puritan tracts Anne Hathaway was supposed to have read, according to Stephen, were not entirely fictitious, ridiculous as they are.[13] One of my favorites was tracking down Stephen's reference to Shakespeare's appearance on stage as the ghost in *Hamlet*, clad "in the castoff mail of a court buck" (*U*, 9.164–65). Joyce is here alluding to the elaborateness of Elizabethan actors' costumes as well as suggesting Buck Mulligan and Stephen's wearing Buck's boots: "My two feet in his boots" (*U*, 3.16–17). Some years ago, as I was browsing through F. E. Halliday's *A Shakespeare Companion* (1964), I found a relevant quotation from a Swiss doctor, Thomas Platter, who recorded in his diary of 1599 that "The actors are very expensively and handsomely dressed," for "when distinguished gentlemen or knights die, almost their best clothes are given to their servants, but as it is not fitting that they should wear them they sell them cheaply to the actors." There it was, but how did Joyce come across it? E. K. Chambers cited Platter in *The Elizabethan Stage* (1923, II, 364) as having been published in the German text in *Anglia* (1899), but the earliest English mention I could find was in the 1916 translation of Wilhelm Creizenach's *The English Drama in the Age of Shakespeare*. Joyce might have seen the German edition of 1909, or this English version, or he could possibly have heard of the 1899 publication from Father Darlington, whose lecture on Shakespeare had recently been published.[14] In *Ulysses* Eglinton mentions Darlington's theory that Shakespeare was "a holy Roman" (*U*, 9.764). Joyce was in college at the time, and his lifelong friend Constantine Curran recalled that the dean's interpretation of *Hamlet* "had for me a particular flavour."[15] Several years later I found the text of Darlington's article, "The Catholicity of Shakespeare," in *The New Ireland Review*, (8 [1897–98]: 241–49, 304–10). Of such details is the text of *Ulysses* woven.

As for the text itself, we now have the three-volume facsimile of the Rosenbach manuscript of *Ulysses* (1975), sixty-three volumes of the *James Joyce Archive* (1978), reproducing most of the extant rough drafts and notes of the various works, and the three-volume Synoptic Edition of *Ulysses* (1984), with its full record of revisions, misprints, and omissions.

The edition is a tremendous achievement, and demands extensive study, which reveals still more illustrations of Joyce's genius. One happy addition to the definitive text may be mentioned. We read in Ithaca of the "socalled fixed stars, in reality evermoving from immeasurably remote eons to infinitely remote futures" (Random House 1961 ed., p. 698). A passage of sheer poetry, as it appears in all ten previous printed versions. But one word, "wanderers" has always been omitted. The correct reading, "Evermoving wanderers" (*U*, 17.1053), suggests not only the infinite spaces, the cosmic view that was my first venture in Joycean interpretation, but also alludes to the theme of the Wandering Jew, and, Joyce being so aware of etymology, the Greek *planes*, "wanderer," the source of the word "planet." Thus the fixed stars are only "socalled," in reality being wanderers or 'planets.'

The prospect of confronting almost seventy volumes of source material may well daunt all but the most dedicated scholar. Though the task be long, results should be rewarding. I speak from limited personal experience, my Modern Language Association papers, read at the 1947 and 1952 annual conferences, being in this area: a comparison of *The Little Review* text of *Ulysses* with the first edition, a task now completed by the editors of the Rosenbach volumes, and a discussion of the importance of the newly discovered notes for *Exiles*. These modest efforts, and perusal of the Synoptic Edition, lead me to predict a welcome emergence of new insights into Joyce's art and into the creative process itself. For the annotated text of the three-volume Synoptic Edition, once its complex symbols are decoded, reveals *Ulysses* as a work in progress. Unfortunately some of Joyce's material is irrecoverable, but enough remains to challenge an investigator. One can only imagine how we would welcome a comparable Shakespeare archive.

Regarding the immense volume of interpretation, perhaps a synoptic or variorum edition of commentary might be considered. I have found that of the many books, articles, reviews, notes, and manuscripts that I have read over the years, there is usually some insight, no matter how minor, in almost every bit of Joyceana. To compile such an archive might be a seven-year task, like that represented by the Synoptic Edition.

Some have expressed fears that the huge volume of Joyce material may condemn his work to the confines of academe. It does impose considerable burdens on the scholar-teacher, but in itself it need not restrict appreciation of the work. I have always urged readers to plunge into Joyce's texts unaided, so that they may enjoy the same thrill of recognition, and imperfect understanding, which was mine fifty years ago. Of course the timid will inevitably be tempted to fall back on some guide or handbook, but they will miss a unique experience. My most recent venture has been rewarding. In leading a discussion group of middle-aged persons, I was encouraged by their responses to continue to view Joyce, not as an easy or a popular author, but as one who can be approached and appreciated intelligently by a well-educated general reader.

After the initial shock, students will welcome the aid of a qualified teacher, who should present Joyce not as a problem but as a vital and exciting author, and, above all, as a humorist. Many reviewers of *Fabulous Voyager* quoted my remark, "*Ulysses* is fun to read," which showed that they had got as far as the third page! For me, after innumerable readings, Joyce is still fun—and much more.

But I must stop. I just got another Joyce book to review, my fiftieth I believe. And what was Tom Kernan thinking about as he walked along James Street at 3:30 on 16 June 1904?

Notes

1. Frank Budgen, *James Joyce and the Making of* Ulysses, with an Introduction by Hugh Kenner (Bloomington: Indiana University Press, 1960), 22.
2. Willard Potts, ed., *Portraits of the Artist in Exile* (Seattle: University of Washington Press, 1979), 7–39.
3. Thomas F. Staley, "James Joyce," *Anglo-Irish Literature: A Review of Research,* ed. Richard J. Finneran (New York: Modern Language Association, 1976), 412.
4. Fritz Senn, *Joyce's Dislocutions,* ed. John Paul Riquelme (Baltimore and London: Johns Hopkins University Press, 1984), 128 and *passim.*
5. Budgen, *James Joyce,* 67–68.
6. Richard Ellmann, *JJ II,* 505.
7. Reminiscences by Joyce's contemporaries are reprinted in Robert Scholes and Richard M. Kain, eds., *The Workshop of Daedalus: James Joyce and the Raw Materials for* A Portrait of the Artist as a Young Man (Evanston, Ill.: Northwestern University Press, 1965), 138–237. See also *A Page of Irish History. . . . Compiled by Fathers of the Society of Jesus* (Dublin and Cork: Talbot Press, 1930); *Struggle with Fortune: A Centenary Miscellany,* ed. Dr. Michael Tierney (Dublin: Browne and Nolan, 1954); and *Centenary History of the Literary and Historical Society, 1855–1955,* ed. James Meenan (Tralee: The Kerryman Ltd., 1955).
8. Brook Thomas, *James Joyce's* Ulysses: *A Book of Many Happy Returns* (Baton Rouge: Louisiana State University Press, 1982), 180.
9. Scholes and Kain, 155–57.
10. Richard M. Kain, "Two Book Reviews by James Joyce," *PMLA* 67 (1952): 291–94.
11. Richard M. Kain, "James Joyce's Shakespeare Chronology," *The Massachusetts Review* 5 (1964): 342–55. Also in Robin Skelton and David R. Clark, eds., *Irish Renaissance* (Dublin: Dolmen, 1965), 106–19.
12. *Letters,* I, 184.
13. Richard M. Kain, "Anne Hathaway's Puritan Tracts, *Ulysses,* 204; 206," *JJQ* 4 (1967): 160.
14. Richard M. Kain, "Shakespeare in *Ulysses:* Additional Annotations," *JJQ* 8 (1971): 176–77.
15. Constantine Curran, *Under the Receding Wave* (Dublin: Gill and Macmillan, 1970), 80.

Paternity, the Legal Fiction

KAREN LAWRENCE

"Paternity may be a legal fiction," prodigal son and would-be creator Stephen Dedalus tells a skeptical audience in *Ulysses*. Legal *fiction*—fatherhood is made up, fictionalized, a product of language and imagination rather than a fact of nature. *Legal* fiction—an authoritative fiction, not only sanctioned by law but, perhaps, the basis of law, for as Stephen puts it, fatherhood is the *founding* fiction of the Church of Rome and even the world itself.

Stephen's idea of fatherhood serves as a focus for discussion of important issues in *Ulysses,* a focus and not a "key," since keys, like fathers, are legal fictions which posit an ultimate source of meaning, a unifying trope to explain the whole. From Stephen's speeches on paternity—brilliant, yet defensive and ambivalent—we can extrapolate Joyce's more comprehensive treatment of fatherhood in *Ulysses*. In the novel, Joyce demonstrates both the incertitude and potency of fatherhood; on the level of theme, language, and character, *Ulysses* enacts the estrangement betweeen father and son while acknowledging the power of the fiction of paternal origin.

Stephen's pronouncement on paternity comes in the midst of his oration on Shakespeare. Observing that Shakespeare wrote *Hamlet* in the months following his father's death, Stephen argues that with his death John Shakespeare passes on to his son the "mystical estate" of fatherhood. He goes on to say:

> Fatherhood, in the sense of conscious begetting, is unknown to man. It is a mystical estate, an apostolic succession, from only begetter to only begotten. On that mystery and not on the madonna which the cunning Italian intellect flung to the mob of Europe the church is founded . . . like the world, macro and microcosm, upon the void. Upon incertitude, upon unlikelihood. *Amor matris,* subjective and objective genitive, may be the only true thing in life. Paternity may be a legal fiction. Who is the father of any son that any son should love him or he any son? (*U, 9.837–45)*

Stephen's stress on both the fictionality and power of fatherhood derives, at least in part, from his own personal situation—in particular, his ambivalance toward his father. His idea of paternity frees him from biology in a number of ways: he is free to invent his own spiritual father rather than reconcile himself with Simon Dedalus, "the man with [his] voice and [his] eyes" (*U,* 3.46). Once dispossessing his real father, Stephen can trade filiality for fatherhood and biological paternity for literary paternity; being no more a son, he can imagine himself a father creator like Shakespeare, whom he calls "the father of all his race" (*U,* 9.868–69). Finally, the mystical estate of fatherhood preempts the role of the mother and leaves the male artist self-sufficient, free to create his world. Thus, although couched in "theolologicophilolological" jargon, Stephen's theory also reflects his desire and defensiveness.

In arguing that a child never really knows the identity of his father, in contrast to his mother, Stephen echoes Telemachus who says, "My mother says I am his [Odysseus's] son; I know not/surely. Who has known his own engendering?"[1] Legacy and inheritance are matters of naming, of designating a son a son and a father a father. For the hazy origins of biological paternity, Stephen wishes to substitute the authority of a spiritual begetter. "Old Father, old artificer, stand me now and ever in good stead," Stephen says at the end of *A Portrait of the Artist as a Young Man,* hoping to inherit the artist's mystical estate. The very incertitude of paternity becomes a virtue; a dubious connection gives way to a spiritual one and assumes a privileged position.[2]

By analogy with God the father's creation of the world, paternity is the founding fiction of literary creation as well. Summarizing Stephen's discussion of Shakespeare, Edmund Epstein says, "a son does not become a father until he becomes capable of projecting his image in the real world in the form of a child and in the realm of art, by producing a true work of art."[3] It is the latter act of fathering (that is, literary paternity), that makes a more compelling claim on Stephen, who describes intercourse as an "instant of blind rut" (*U,* 9.859). Although Stephen says that mother love may be the "only true thing in life," he is much more comfortable with the thought of literary creation *ex nihilo* rather than human creation with the help of a woman (as Buck Mulligan acknowledges in his parody "Everyman His own Wife"). "In woman's womb word is made flesh," Stephen says, "but in the spirit of the maker all flesh that passes becomes the word that shall not pass away" (*U,* 14.292–94). Although he does reflect on the "womb" of the imagination in *Portrait,* both in *Ulysses* and *Portrait,* Stephen's dominant metaphor for artistic creation is paternal. In fact, the image of the powerful, authoritative and self-sufficient male Creator is provided by Western culture itself.[4]

In his essay "Plato's Pharmacy," Jacques Derrida analyzes the authority and the incertitude that attend the concept of paternity in Western culture. He shares Stephen's two basic ideas: that an ultimate and identifiable origin is a fiction, and that the fiction is so powerful precisely because it underlies Western culture and metaphysics, whether reflected in the paternity of God the father or the analogy between paternity and the act of authoring. The Western tradition, he says, "assigns the origin and power of speech, precisely of *logos,* to the paternal position."[5]

> But the father is not the generator or procreator in any "real" sense prior to our outside all relation to language. In what way, indeed, is the father/son relation distinguishable from a mere cause/effect or generator/engendered relation, if not by the instance of logos. . . . In other words, it is precisely *logos* that enables us to perceive and investigate something like paternity.[6]

One cannot understand fatherhood in any natural, biological sense, outside of culture and language; precisely what distinguishes the concept of fatherhood from engenderment is its inscription in the world of reasoned speech. Thus, an ultimate and identifiable source or origin behind language is a fiction, but the potency of this fiction dervies from our whole system of language and culture.

Interestingly, Derrida discusses the relationship between text and author as an estranged filial relationship. "Writing, he says [is] a structure, cut off from all absolute responsibility, from *consciousness* as the ultimate authority, orphaned and separated at birth from the assistance of its father."[7] According to Derrida, writing has been regarded with such suspicion throughout history, precisely because it is obviously cut off from the authority of the author/father, making him, in a sense, unnecessary. Writing advertises the estrangement between father and son, author and text, for it seems to substitute "the breathless sign for the living voice."[8] In a complex discussion of the myth of the origin of writing in Plato's *Phaedrus,* Derrida calls Thoth, the god of writing, the "signifier-god," who stands for or replaces his father, Ra, the Sun-King, just as writing is said to replace or supplant the living voice. Thoth, Derrida says, doubles for the King, his father: "the god of writing is thus at once his father, his son, and himself. He cannot be assigned a fixed spot in the play of differences . . . he is . . . a sort of *joker,* a floating signifier, a wild card."[9]

Like Derrida's analysis of Thoth, Stephen's analysis of Shakespeare involves the absence of the father and the son's replacement of him. The death of the father enables the paternity of the son; as Stephen observes, Shakespeare is able to write *Hamlet* only after the death of John Shakespeare. Fathers are most useful in their absence; the death of the father initiates the action of the son, who both memorializes and replaces his father, rendering him unnecessary. "Remember me," the ghostly father enjoins Hamlet in act 1 of the play, but must renew the injunction once again in act 3. Analogously, the text, like Thoth, remembers and replaces the father/creator. Shakespeare's plays embody the hidden father as they dispossess him. According to Stephen, the name of Shakespeare is scattered throughout his creation: "He has hidden his own name, a fair name, William, in the plays, a super here, a clown there, as a painter of old Italy set his face in a dark corner of his canvas" (*U,* 9.921–23).[10] The tradition that Shakespeare himself acted the part of the ghost further conveys an image of the writer simultaneously haunting and dispossessed by his own text.

Stephen calls paternal authority into question in other ways besides in the image of the father's dispossession. In his analysis of Shakespeare Stephen acknowledges the anonymity and collectivity of authorship that can also undermine the image of the single, original creator. He says, "When Rutlandbaconsouthamptonshakespeare or another poet of the same name in the comedy of errors wrote *Hamlet* he was not the father of his own son merely, but, being no more a son, he was and felt himself the father of all his race" (*U,* 9.865–69). The name of the all-powerful father-creator here gives way to a Saturnalian confusion of proper names, a comedy of errors and letters that turns ghost into ghostwriter and trades single authorship for collectivity and anonymity. The ghostwriter writes someone else's lines (a reason, perhaps, for Shakespeare to speak in "ventriloquy" in Circe). Although Stephen designates Shakespeare the father of his race, at the same time he casts doubt upon the authority of the father.

Joyce extends Stephen's sense of the fictionality of fatherhood in numerous ways in the novel. Pater texts, as well as authors, as sources of authority are called into question throughout *Ulysses,* with its grab bag of quotations, allusions, parodies, and rewritings. Even the title reflects the incertitude as well as the power of paternity; it tells us that *The Odyssey* is the pater text of *Ulysses,* its "legal fiction," so to speak, but exactly what fatherhood means in this context, too, is in doubt. First, there are very few references to Homer's story. Second, the one-word title suggests a more complicated inheritance than it might at first appear, for the book is called *Ulysses* and not *The Odyssey* partly because the former evokes an entire tradition of revisions and rewritings. Hidden in the title are Dante and Tennyson who ensured that posterity would know Odysseus as Ulysses.

It is in the language and style of *Ulysses,* however, that Joyce most radically questions the singleness and authority of authorship and the corollary idea of the originality of the author as source of his own language. With its multiple styles, and tissue of preexisting texts, *Ulysses* decenters the idea of language as attributable to a fathering source. In its use of language either borrowed from specific but multiple sources (i.e., unacknowledged and acknowledged quotations) or from the storehouse of received ideas and generic forms (i.e., clichés, journalese), *Ulysses* flaunts the citationality of its language. (The primary meaning of the word "citational" is a "mention" of some previous text, style, or type of language. It also refers to the bracketing of language as language, as when quotation marks are placed around a word we wish to discuss as a word.) It is a book which advertises its own derivativeness, an aspect of modern literature that Geoffrey Hartman has called "self-exposing plagiarism"[11] and that Joyce has called "stolentelling" in the *Wake*. This citationality suggests that writing is always rewriting, that we can never truly be the author of our language. Perhaps the most striking gesture of citation in the text occurs in Aeolus. The boldface headings import into the text the catchy, formulaic, alliterative language of journalistic titles: **"SHORT BUT TO THE POINT," "ERIN, GREEN GEM OF THE SILVER SEA."** This is "borrowed" language that appears suddenly and glaringly; it is anonymous, collective, homeless discourse.

This collective discourse fills up the narrative of Cyclops and Eumaeus. The interpolated passages in Cyclops present a kind of travesty of Irish consciousness; they represent the anonymous cultural voice that codifies Ireland's received ideas or myths from past (epic and romance) to present (journalism). The anonymity of the parodied discourses of society, exaggerated by their canned, propagandistic quality, presents an attack on the whole notion of an identifiable point of linguistic origin. This generic, anonymous, promiscuous language is apotheosized in Eumaeus. Like Flaubert's *Bouvard et Pécuchet,* Eumaeus presents the received locutions of society. It is the epitome in *Ulysses* of the citationality of all language, a rejection of the notion of both originality and identifiable origin.[12].

But it is Oxen of the Sun that treats paternity, origin, and language most interestingly, for the chapter comes closest of any in *Ulysses* to suggesting that Western literature is a series of great books written by a succession of great literary forefathers. As criticism reflects, Oxen of the Sun is most conducive to source hunting for fathers whose signatures are hidden in the style. Anthony Burgess once labeled Oxen an "author's chapter,"[13] a description à propos not only of Joyce's attempt to surpass his literary forefathers by incorporating them, but also of the notion that Literature is the domain of the proper name, of paternity. For a chapter that takes place in a maternity hospital and, according to its author, imitates the development of a fetus, it is remarkable the extent to which the paternity of authorship displaces the maternal, on the level of plot (the baby's birth) and the level of language (the development of the fetus). In tracing the development of language, Oxen powerfully raises the question of origin within a literary tradition and the apostolic succession of literary fathers. And, as Geoffrey Hartman writes, although quotations are always "homeless" and "cannot be fully assimilated to any context," they still imply a "hope" of being "attributed, as well as integrated, and so an ultimate recognition scene."[14] They borrowed styles and quotations in *Ulysses* are indeed "homeless," cut off from their contexts and not quite at home in their new surroundings, but it is Oxen more than any other chapter that suggests the possibility of the exiled offspring's return. The theme of the prodigal son is repeated on the level of language: it would seem, in the chapter, that words and phrases can be "returned to" (i.e., attributed to) a particular father/author.

Yet even in this chapter, Joyce tends to subvert the notion of origin. Stylistic pastiche, indirect quotation and allusion, and the characters' quotations of literary sources call into question the authority and singularity of the father and the order of apostolic succession. Joyce's errant and echoing language produces a process of literary transmission that is both comical and chaotic. He complicates pastiche with multiple allusion and anachronism, deliberately subverting the integrity of the texts he expropriates. Pater texts are thereby ransacked, vandalized. The prodigal word finally cannot be pinned down—there is no ultimate recognition scene between father and son, despite attempts of critics to attribute the homeless quotations. Thus, in Oxen of the Sun, the power of literary paternity and apostolic succession is both asserted, *and* ultimately called into question. Finally, even in this "author's chapter," the unbridgeable gap between father and son, author and word, finds expression.

Both the desire for a reconciliation between father and son and its impossibility are dramatized in the characters' relationships as well as the language of the text. Bloom seeks a replacement for his dead son Rudy; an unknown clown is "in search of paternity"; Stephen tries to convince himself that he has inherited the mystical estate of the Greek artisan Daedalus. The scene that most often has been interpreted as dramatizing the reconciliation between spiritual father and son, Leopold Bloom and Stephen Dedalus, is Bloom's vision of Rudy as he gazes at Stephen in Circe. Has the child, snatched from his father so prematurely, been restored to that father in some way? My own feeling about the vision is that it manages to convey the desire for reconciliation *and* an unbridgeable gap between generations. The vision of Rudy does not speak to Bloom—the sense of loss is expressed in the incompleteness of the dialogue. Bloom does not recover his son Rudy in Stephen; rather, he acts like a father to him.

Similarly, Bloom's desire for Rudy's replacement is expressed and then frustrated in Oxen. The hope is held out that the young men with Bloom in the hospital might be his sons—"Who can say?" the narrative asks, as Bloom thinks of a fling with Bridie Kelly that might have produced one of these strapping young men. We teeter on the brink of the kind of ingenious revelation found in Victorian novels—will the dissolute, rowdy youth turn out to be the true heir of the lonely hero? "Nay, fair reader. . . . No,

Leopold. Name and memory solace thee not. . . . No son of thy loins is by thee. There is none now to be for Leopold, what Leopold was for Rudolph" (*U,* 14.1071–77).

In Eumaeus, the episode of recognition and reconciliation between generations in *The Odyssey,* the coming together of Stephen and Bloom is also provisional, expressed in broken syntax and redundancy, yet expressed nonetheless: "The queer suddenly things he popped out with attracted the elder man who was several years the other's senior or like his father" (*U,* 16.1567–69). "A certain analogy there somehow was," the narrative goes on to say—simile, likeness, analogy—"as if" rather than "is," incertitude rather than certain paternity.

It remains for me to consider briefly the maternal, the "only true thing in life" (according to Stephen), preempted by the metaphor of paternity until the book's final chapter, biology seemingly displaced by a "legal fiction." We have seen how Joyce presents the incertitude of paternity even as he demonstrates its power. Now I want to suggest that offstage (as in Oxen), in the interstices (as in Stephen's thoughts on mother love in Nestor), the maternal silently undermines patriarchal power and the cultural and linguistic structures it underwrites. In an essay on paternity in *Portrait,* Maud Ellmann suggestively discusses the episode in which Stephen, searching for his father's initials in a school desk, is startled to find the word "Foetus" inscribed instead. She reads this as an image of the mother's anonymity flaunting the name of the father. She says, "the mother's namelessness engraves itself upon the flesh [i.e., the navel] before the father ever carved his signature."[15] "The name of the father . . . necessarily entails a fresh unstained creation. . . . The scarletter on the belly tells another story, that has neither a beginning nor an end."[16] She rightly sees anonymity rather than the authority of the proper name in the maternal image. Maternity, then, is a different kind of "fiction" than paternity, a fiction of a source *before* law and identity, the "alaphbed" of Anna Livia.

I'd like to close with an image in the text that juxtaposes paternal signature and maternal stain, the name of the father with the anonymity of the mother. In Nestor, scrawny, pathetic Cyril Sargent copies out his sums, as Stephen, reminded of his own youth, gazes at an ink stain on his student's face:

> On his cheek . . . a soft stain of ink lay, dateshaped, recent and damp as a snail's bed.
>
> He held out his copybook. . . . at the foot a crooked signature with blind loops and a blot. Cyril Sargent: his name and seal. . . .
>
> Ugly and futile: lean neck and thick hair and a stain of ink, a snail's bed. Yet someone had loved him. . . . But for her the race of the world would have trampled him underfoot, a squashed boneless snail. . . .

> Was that then real? The only true thing in life? . . .
> . . . *Amor matris:* subjective and objective genitive. With her weak blood and wheysour milk she had fed him and hid from sight of others his swaddlingbands. (*U,* 2.126–67)

The ink stain, the blemish on the face: a birthmark. The ink itself comes before the signature; the blemish on the face is the sign of female anonymity rather than the signature of the father, of maternal stain rather than the fresh unstained creation.[17] The smudge on the face vs. the name and seal (and perhaps the name "Sargent" suggests not only the boy's Englishness, but also the patriarchal worlds of finance [argent] and the military [sergeant], each linked with Mr. Deasy, Joyce's counterpart to patriarchal Nestor). The stain reminds Stephen of the vulnerability of the flesh. Motherlove is like the shell of the snail, protecting the child from the world's cruelty, just as Moses, the Patriarch in swaddling bands, is protected by a woman. "Whatever else is unsure in this stinking dunghill of a world a mother's love is not," Cranly says in *Portrait*. Stinking dunghill, mother, ink stain—curiously anticipate that stained letter scratched out of the dungheap by Belinda the hen in *The Wake*. The letter

> has acquired accretions of terricious matter whilst loitering in the past. The teatimestained terminal . . . is a cosy little brown study all to oneself and, whether it be thumbprint, mademark or just a poor trait of the artless, its importance in establishing the identities in the writer complexus . . . will be best appreciated by never forgetting that both before and after the battle of the Boyne it was a habit not to sign letters always. (*FW,* 114–15)

Both legal fictions and illegal stains subvert the authority of fathers and the integrity of their signatures.

Notes

1. *The Odyssey,* trans. Robert Fitzgerald (New York: Doubleday Anchor, 1963), 8.
2. In *The Mermaid and the Minotaur,* Dorothy Dinnerstein suggests that the privileging of the patriarchal position in Western culture is compensatory; the male, she says, stresses the importance of legitimacy and inheritance via the patronym, precisely because he is insecure about his "loose mammalian connection with children" (New York: Harper & Row, 1963), 81.
3. Edmund Epstein, *The Ordeal of Stephen Dedalus: The Conflict of the Generations in James Joyce's* A Portrait of the Artist as a Young Man (Carbondale: Southern Illinois University Press, 1971), 7.
4. For an excellent discussion of male creation and female silence in *Paradise Lost* see Christine Froula, "When Eve Reads Milton: Undoing the Canonical Economy," *Critical Inquiry* 10 (December 1983): 321–47.

5. Jacques Derrida, "Plato's Pharmacy," *Dissemination,* trans. Barbara Johnson (Chicago: University of Chicago Press, 1981), 76.
6. Ibid., 80.
7. Derrida, "Signature Event Context," trans. Samuel Weber and Jeffrey Mehlman, *Glyph* 1 (Baltimore: Johns Hopkins University Press, 1977), 181
8. "Plato's Pharmacy," 92.
9. Ibid., 93. One finds interesting connections between Joyce and Derrida by way of Thoth. In a footnote to his discussion of Thoth in "Plato's Pharmacy," Derrida cites the relevance of the *Wake;* and his epigraph to a section of the essay is the following quotation from *Portrait:* "A sense of fear of the unknown moved in the heart of his weariness, a fear of symbols and portents, of the hawk-like man whose name he bore . . . of Thoth, the God of writers, writing with a reed upon a tablet and bearing on his narrow ibis head the cusped moon" (quoted in "Plato's Pharmacy," 84). In Joyce's mind, as in Derrida's, Thoth is linked to questions of origin, paternity, and creation—witness the line in the *Wake,* "Where did thots come from?" (*FW,* 597.25). A number of fine critics have discussed the implications of this line. See Jennifer Schiffer Levine, "Originality and Repetition in *Finnegans Wake* and *Ulysses,*" *PMLA* 94 (1979): 109; Maud Ellmann, "Polytropic Man: Paternity, Identity and Naming in *The Odyssey* and *A Portrait of the Artist as a Young Man*" in *James Joyce: New Perspectives,* ed. Colin MacCabe (Bloomington: Indiana University Press, 1982), 76; and Stephen Heath, "Joyce in Language," in *James Joyce: New Perspectives,* 141.
10. Stephen Heath observes that Joyce's name is scattered throughout the *Wake:* " 'Joyce' as name never appears: only a succession of transformations, so many drifts—'joycity' (*FW* 414), for example—that are never brought to any final stasis, to the 'proper name.' " (See "Joyce in Language," 129.)
11. Letter from Geoffrey Hartman, *PMLA,* 92 (March 1977), 307–8.
12. For more on citationality in Aeolus, Cyclops, and Eumaeus see Karen Lawrence, *The Odyssey of Style in Ulysses* (Princeton: Princeton University Press, 1981), chaps. 3, 5, and 8.
13. Anthony Burgess, *ReJoyce* (New York: W. W. Norton, 1965), 156.
14. Geoffrey Hartman, "Monsieur Texte II: Epiphony in Echoland," *The Georgia Review* (Spring 1976), 193.
15. M. Ellmann, "Polytropic Man," 96.
16. Ibid., 101.
17. One is reminded of "The Birthmark," a wonderful short story by Hawthorne, in which a scientist tries desperately to remove a "crimson stain" from the cheek of his beautiful wife, because it symbolizes "his wife's liability to sin, sorrow, decay and death." The mark, resembling a "bloody hand," represents a challenge to the husband's male authority and knowledge, symbolizing, as it does, female sexuality and creation.

Ulysses: Trinitarian and Catholic

JOHN HENRY RALEIGH

The excuse for parts of *Ulysses* is the WHOLE of *Ulysses.*
—Ezra Pound to James Joyce (1920)[1]

Joyce had a mind both Irish-Catholic-Jesuitical and catholic that was simultaneously highly schematic ("I have learnt [from his Jesuit education] to arrange things in such a way that they become easy to survey and judge" [*JJ* II, 27]), was enamored of detail ("I have a grocer's assistant's mind" [*JJ* II, 28]), was a connoisseur of chaos ("Complications to right of me, complications to left of me, complex on the page before me, perplex in the pen beside me, stuplex on the face that reads me. And from time to time I lie back and listen to my hair growing white . . ." [*Letters* I, 222]); was addicted to mysteries and puzzles ("I've put in so many enigmas and puzzles that it will keep the professors busy for centuries, arguing over what I meant, . . ." [*JJ* II, 521]); was inveterately and deeply archaic and superstitious ("It seems as if this year [1921] (1+9+2+1=13.) is to be one incessant trouble to me" [*Letters* I, 161]); and was both haunted and fascinated by madness and the thin line that exists between reason and unreason ("Nonetheless, that book [*Ulysses*] was a terrible risk. A transparent leaf separates it from madness.")[2]

What will be discussed here principally will be the schematic tendencies and the passion for detail, although some of the other aspects will be touched on. No other major novelist in Western culture has arranged his central characters in such a diagrammatic fashion as has Joyce with his central triad in *Ulysses*. Since in the work as a whole there was to be so much local detail, he seems to have wanted to suggest in the larger outlines of the novel a sense of universality and timelessness and give an allegorical cast to his principals. The choice of a triad alone is significant, as three is one of the most potent as well as one of the most archaic of the primary magic numbers, laden with multiple meanings per se for either the superstitious or the non-superstitious mind: to take only two that would be expressly relevant for Joyce—the Godhead of the Father, Mother, Son, which is also reflected in the human family, and Aristotle's gloss, "The Triad is the number of the whole, inasmuch as it contains a beginning, a middle, and an end." This is not to mention all the other basic properties of human existence that are comprehended in triads: the world as heaven, earth, and waters; man as body, soul and spirit; life as birth, life, death; time as past, present, future, and so on. Moreover, the sacred properties ascribed to the number three are among the most ancient and widespread of such ascriptions in religion, magic, and philosophy: not only the divine family but many lesser divinities come in triads, such as the Three Fates, the Three Graces, the Three Furies, the three-headed Gods in Ireland and India, and so on. In biblical numerological symbolism three is a superlative, i.e., a thing is entirely what it is said to be, as God is thrice holy.[3]

In the creation of his Three Graces Joyce seems to have conceived of them in their larger outlines and in their schematic deployment in almost allegorical terms, the young genius-to-be, the common man (who turns out to be remarkably uncommon), and the sexual-giantess-earth-mother, all suggesting the timeless and the universal although matters become considerably more complicated with the fleshing out of the abstract types. With the filling out of the three members of his Trinity several other purposes are discovered. Most obviously, he wished for each of his central characters to stand for and embody discretely distinct physical and mental properties and, as it turns out, to represent differing periods of history or historical outlooks. Second, and more important, there is manifested at the very heart of *Ulysses,* a powerful urge on Joyce's part to contradict the assumptions of both the English and the Irish Catholic Church about the basic elements of the celebrated, maligned, infamous, stereotyped "Irish character." In his lecture, "Ireland, Island of Saints and Sages" (1907) Joyce remarked on "the curious character of the modern Irishman," and went on to explain what a diverse and complex racial/cultural heritage lay behind these people.

> Our civilization is a vast fabric, in which the most diverse elements are mingled, in which nordic aggressiveness and Roman law, the new bourgeois conventions and the remnant of a Syriac religion are reconciled. In such a fabric, it is useless to look for a thread that may have remained pure and virgin without having undergone the influence of a neighboring thread. What race, or what language (if we except the few whom a playful will seems to have preserved in ice, like the people of Iceland) can boast of being pure today? And no race has less right to utter such a boast than the race now living in Ireland. (*CW,* 165–66)

What Joyce was saying in *Ulysses* in the creation of his central characters is that they have verisimilitude, that is, they could have been real people living in the real Dublin, but that they are precisely not what the English say that the Irish are and what the Irish Catholic Church, in its vulgar day-to-day parishioners' outlook, not at its higher intellectual level, says they are. At the same time he was distancing himself from the quite different set of assumptions about "Irishness," and about the relationship between the present and the past of Ireland, propounded by the Gaelic movement. His chief chosen opponents in order of importance were, first and foremost, the Church, second, the English, and third the proponents of the Gaelic Revival, the "Cultic Twallete," as he called it in *Finnegans Wake*. Seldom, if ever, did a writer conceive and execute so ambitious a literary rebellion/revolution whose aim was to diminish or demolish the three central cultural forces by which he thought his own people were enslaved or misled or bamboozled. The "Irishman," according to Joyce, could not be epitomized by any label, certainly not by the clown of the English imagination nor by the pious believer of the Church's ever-hopeful imagination, nor by the Cuchulain-cum-peasant of the Gaelic League's imagination. Each of these imaginary "Irishman," that of the English, the Church, and the Gaelic League, were in actuality more complex than my condensed summary above, but as a shorthand designation it is fairly accurate.

But, as a final irony, the three characters turn out to be in the long perspective three of the basic types of humanity that have either been assumed by or engendered by the Roman Catholic church. So *Ulysses,* considered as a map of possible human configurations of character, is both anti-Catholic and quintessentially representative of the kind of psychology, that is, in its basic assumptions about human nature, that the Catholic Church, whether as conscious doctrine or instinctive wisdom, had always assumed and acted upon.

Joyce's schematic triad in *Ulysses* is composed of two diametrically different polar types, which comprise the beginning (Stephen Dedalus) and the end (Molly Bloom), with between them an enormous middle term, Leopold Bloom, who is at one end and at the same time distinctly different from the polar opposites by which he is enclosed, is a mean between the two extremes, shares affinities and likenesses with each, and has an actual personal relationship, however imperfect (Joyce's precise point) with both the other terms. As such, he constitutes a true middle term, looking back to the beginning and forward to the end, connecting the dissimilar two, making "extremes meet" and parallel lines cross.

If one stands back from the dazzling complexities and richness of detail of the novel and looks at it from the abstract trinitarian perspective adopted here, it looks as if Joyce had conceived an immense spectrum of a single androgyous human being, at each end of which there was an almost complete 180° difference or opposition. More precisely, the spectrum could be diagrammed as the bottom half of a globe:

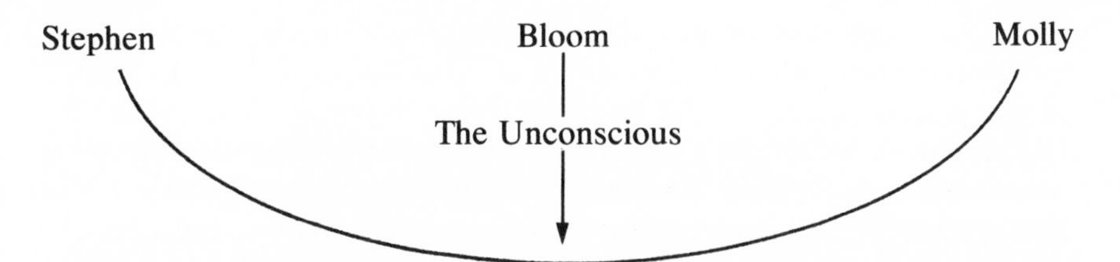

Thus Bloom takes up not only most of the horizontal dimension but most of the vertical dimension as well, since Stephen's unconscious is only briefly revealed, almost solely filled by his mother, Molly's not at all, and only Bloom's fully and in excruciating detail. It is as if Joyce had slowly swung a pendulum through his human spectrum beginning at the Stephen-pole and ending at the Molly-pole. Like a pendulum, the arc would not only spend most of its duration in the Bloom orbit, it would also achieve its perigee in that same territory.

The primary polar opposition in the book, then, is not between Stephen Dedalus and Leopold Bloom but between Dedalus and Madame Bloom. Their "beginningness" and "endness" is even indicated by such matters as pagination, always an important consideration in Joyce's work, with the first fifty-one pages given almost solely to Dedalus and the last forty-five given quite solely to Molly. Both, of course, are large presences throughout the middle section of the novel, Stephen intermittently in person, Molly as an unseen but very powerful force by way of Bloom's memories of their mutual past and his ever-active consciousness in the present of 16 June 1904, in which she is often on the surface of his mind and never far below that surface, and through collective Dublin gossip about her. Seldom in literature has a person been so thoroughly introduced, described, characterized in advance as has Molly Bloom. Joyce could not have done otherwise than to end the book as he did, to banish his entire cast of characters, even Dublin itself, and leave the last words to her, of which occasion she so felicitously takes advantage.

The polar contrast between Stephen and Molly extends from the sexual and the physical to the emotional, moral, intellectual, and almost any other aspect that comes to mind. The fundamental polarity, and the root source, in both the literal and figurative senses, of the human condition in Joyce's world is that of the male and the female. In *Ulysses,* as in the Genesis story, his male(s) come first and his woman last although all three characters are, each in his or her own way, outside of Eden at the start of Joyce's novel.

Dedalus, the male, is tall, slim ("lithe"), clad in black, dirty (he has not bathed since 10 October 1903), with decaying teeth, a snotgreen-colored handkerchief, is probably suffering from a hangover, and will soon start to prepare himself for another one for the morning of 17 June. What he actually is supposed to look like is one of the many mysteries of this mysterious book, wherein after the initial, detailed, complete description of the countenance and the body of Buck Mulligan, each succeeding character is either faceless or is lightly sketched impressionistically or is described by way of his impression upon other characters. We are told later on that Stephen looks in certain respects like his father and sister and in others like his mother although we don't know what they looked like either. But that he is a comely youth there can be no doubt, as other characters remark.

His polar opposite is a short, stout woman approaching middle age and possessed, by reason of her raven hair, her olive skin, her countenance (unknown in any precise way once more) and her voluptuous figure, of considerable sexual appeal. Bloom keeps stressing her "Moorish," oriental exotic appearance, but she says that she has the "map" of Ireland on her face; so I take it that Joyce meant her to look like her heritage, half Spanish-Jewish and half Irish, with features looking, as has been suggested by others and by myself, somewhat like those of Kitty O'Shea (Joyce possessed Mrs. Parnell's memoirs, with its photographs of the author). The exact degree of her voluptuousness is lost in the usual Joycean maze; all we know is that when she married Bloom she weighed 154 pounds, put on, perhaps, another nine pounds after weaning Milly Bloom and has added considerable weight since then. So what is it: 180? 190? We do know for a certainty that she is a full-blown Victorian "broth" of a woman and needs no padding to fill out either her front or rear. In any event, tall, slim, male set off against short, Junoesque female, the curves of whose body are of epic dimensions, just as he is as lean as a lathe.

In every other respect, way of life, emotions, ways of thought, they are polar opposites in a radically schematic manner: solitary and single vs. conjoined, both licitly and illicitly; homeless rover vs. stationary huswife (or husey); at large vs. at rest; drunk vs. sober; abstract vs. concrete; rationalistic vs. intuitive; subjective vs. objective; intellectualistic vs. materialistic; solipsistic vs. pantheistic; guilt-obsessed vs. self-forgiven; skeptical vs. credulous; idealistic vs. naturalistic; infidel/heretic/agnostic/atheist (it is impossible to tell whether he disbelieves or disagrees or half-believes or totally rejects) vs. believer; frustrated vs. fulfilled (momentarily); sex-less vs. sex-full. It has always seemed to me that for a man, especially for a man his age, Dedalus thinks remarkably little about sex; while she for a woman, although I have no authority to speak for women in this important matter, thinks obsessively about that same function—perhaps, of course, the result of her rather full afternoon and evening. Although I am sure that women think about men as much as men think about women, I believe men by far exceed women in the frequency of sexual fantasies. Bloom of course certifies to this aspect, but in the contrast being sketched here the woman has all the sexual memories and fantasies, the man virtually none of either. One could go on with this list of antitheses but I think the general point is made.

But both sides of the schema should be placed in their novelistic contexts to reveal the full meaning of each. Both are concerned with the sea and often think of that immensity in characteristic, and characteristically divergent, ways. Through their agencies Joyce both opened and closed his great Irish, or Dublin, epic with visions of the sea, eminently appropriate for historical, cultural, meteorological, and psychological reasons. The sea has always been the primordial fact of Irish history, constituting simultaneously a mechanism for isolation and entrapment, for invasion by superior powers, and for, finally, a kind of quasi-protection. If Ireland had directly abutted England geographically, as had Scotland and Wales—and there had once been a land bridge between Scotland and Ireland—it would no doubt have been absorbed and incorporated (or absolutely devastated) into the English polity and culture, as have Scotland and Wales. Instead it has been semi-incorporated and ambiguously incorporated with its northern portion still under direct English rule and its southern part, while actually "free," still with an immense impress upon it, in social habits and attitudes, in education and learning, in a more and more secularized outlook—the Irish Catholic Church notwithstanding—of English, or Western, culture. But the final fact of the English occupation of Ireland was that the conquest was never complete, and the results therefore have always been, and still are, ambiguous.

Historically, islands have generally been paradoxical in their relationship to the world: on the one hand, isolated, backward, provincial, narrow-minded; on the other hand, since they lie open to the sea on all sides for any incoming enterprise, military, commercial, cultural; they are also great crossroads as well, where the most cosmopolitan and the most provincial outlooks and attitudes exist side by side. In Irish history a native culture existed side by side with two universalisms: the Catholic Church, which it embraced with a fervor known in no other land, and the British Empire, with its powerful accompanying idea of "Englishness," which it tried to reject with a hatred seldom engendered, or sustained as long, in few other lands. It was Ireland's misfortune to have been subjected to two of the most potent and most penetrating imperialisms in Western history. History aside, the sea is an omnipresent fact of Irish life at any time—nowhere in the island is one ever far from it and one is always aware of it. All the meteorological phenomena that Joyce wove into *Ulysses,* such as constant changeability and windiness, are attributable to it. "So," as Joyce might have had a character say in the Eumaeus episode, "—the sea."—nothing furthermore needful to be said.

And the all-encompassing sea was not only an avenue for escape and a highway for invaders, it also bred the psychological sense of being enisled, so pervasive a sense in Joyce's world. Indeed this feeling may well have gone back to his boyhood days, and in an unforgettable way. From 1887–92, Joyce aged five to ten, the Joyce family lived by the sea at Martello Terrace, Bray, in the first of eight arcaded houses that face south toward Bray Head. The sea wall was so close to the Joyce residence that on windy days sea spray blew on the porch of the home. In stormy weather it was not uncommon for the Joyce residence to be surrounded by water on three sides.[4] Thus the young Joyce was living at times in a virtual island which, of course, was part of a real island, which, in its turn, was one of two islands lying off the northwest coast of Europe. Not only was Stephen Dedalus the "bullock-befriending bard," but also the "thrice-enisled bard." This sense of being doubly or triply enisled or encircled had great metamorphical appeal to both Yeats and Joyce, and it was a historical fact that in all the Celtic countries eremites shared a predilection for islands, at first in lakes and then in the sea. These senses of concentric encirclements are dramatized quite beautifully by the St. Kevin episode of *Finnegans Wake,* the saint who lived in a beehive cell on an isle in the lake of Glendalough: "an enysled lakelet yslanding a lacustrine yslet" (*FW,* 605.20), accompanied by such words as (*FW,* 605–6) "midmost," "amiddle," "amidships," "centripetally," "epicentric," "centre," "concentric," and so on. An island existence breeds the twin contradictory senses of being both on the edge of things and at the center of things, of centrifugality and centripetality, two of the basic senses that pervade *Ulysses* and Joyce's other work.

The initial section of *Ulysses,* the Telemachiad, was not only introducing the parallel to Homer, among many other matters, but was also concerned with asserting the primacy of the role of the sea in Irish history and with asserting the primacy of the Irish imagination and intellect over that of the English, a gesture of patriotism on Joyce's part that is often overlooked, most notably by the Irish themselves. *Ulysses* opens with two seascapes (Telemachus and Proteus) encompassing some speculations on the mysteries, ambiguities, and necessitarian character of human history (Nestor)—plus a picture of human frustration and guilt (Dedalus)—this arrangement alone points to what is really being said. Dedalus has two different relations to and reactions to the sea (each is to contrast with that of Molly Bloom, and Leopold Bloom as well). In the Telemachus episode Dedalus looks down at it from a height, contemplating its endless extent and all-encompassing nature, but it is associated with the bowl of green bile vomited up by his dying mother; it also comes into his mind that a man has recently drowned there; thus it is associated for him with guilt and death. However, in the Proteus episode, in which he walks along the seashore, it is the immediacy and the ever-changing characteristics of the sea seen close-up that are represented and are used by Joyce as a physical analogue for the protean nature not only of Dedalus's brilliant, ironical, mocking, well-stocked mind but for the protean nature of human speech and thought itself. And, of course, the sea-line, shore-line, was a particularly felicitous choice for the staging of Joyce's intellectual display and verbal pyrotechnics. As Frank Budgen described it in what is still one of the best books on *Ulysses:*

> Through his [Stephen's] senses the seashore comes to life. The natural abode of change is that area between low water and high water mark. It is easier to believe that life began here than that it began in a garden. Tides ebb and flow, cheating the clock every day, lagging behind. The volume of water changes, spring to neap and neap to spring again. Cold water flows over hot sand. Sea breeze and land-wind alternate. The colour of sea and sky changes like shot-silk. The sea makes and unmakes the land. Steel-hard rocks are broken up, firm contours of land are dissolved and remade. A sea-town drifts inland and the houses of an inland town topple into the sea. Yellow sand, lying neatly round rocks, is taken away by an overnight storm and a floor of black boulders appears. Then with the smooth lapping of the next calm the yellow carpet is laid again. There is a whole population of plants and animals here and of living things that are neither plant nor animal. Carcasses of man, beast, bird, fish, washed ashore, decompose. Sea and sand bury them. Wreckage rots and rusts and is pounded to pieces and every tide brings new flotsam and jetsam, lays it on other ribbed sand, other stones. The seashore is never twelve hours the same.[5]

As has often been said, the universe seems to have arranged itself for Joyce's purposes. Joyce himself said of this aspect of his work: "Chance furnishes me what I need. I am like a man who stumbles along; my foot strikes something, I bend over, and it is exactly what I want."[6]

For the Irish patriotic assertion by Joyce in the Telemachiad the chief elements are the presentation of the Englishman Haines in Telemachus and Dedalus's intellectual acrobatics in Proteus. Up to this point in Joyce's work, *Dubliners, Portrait,* and *Exiles,* although English power and culture were overwhelmingly present, there were virtually no representations, curiously enough, of individual English. The sole exception is the Dean of Studies, an English convert, in Book V of *Portrait,* described as "a poor Englishman in Ireland . . . —a late comer, a tardy spirit." Stephen speculates that he may be a refugee from the Protestant sectarianism of England, but that he had entered into the Jesuit order too late, as history had by now passed it by. But when Joyce came to broaden his picture of Irish life and culture so immensely in *Ulysses* one of the first things he did was to introduce a "representative" visiting Englishman who would embody the Irish stereotype, at least as old as John Mitchel's formulations and fulminations on the breed, of the English. Both the Irish and the English had, to the full, derogatory stereotypes, with much foundation in fact, of one another. The Irishman's Englishman was dull, ponderous, inarticulate, materialistic, humorless, inhibited, lacking in wit, overconcerned with his digestion, devoid of charm, sexless, avaricious, power-obsessed, snobbish, and so on. The Englishman's Irishman was pig-headed, indolent, irresponsible, improvident, undisciplined, verbose, incapable of either sustained labor or thought, priest-ridden, bigoted, idolatrous, credulous, drunken, factious, and violent: in a word, mad, or as bad or worse, so futile and ineffectual as to be in the large sense harmless except for sporadic outbursts of violence. Last but by no means least, especially since cleanliness was next to godliness in the Anglo-Protestant scale of values, the Irishman was smelly and unwashed. In addition, the Englishman had behind him that vast stretch of high English culture, Shakespeare and Company, from which eminence he could look down disdainfully on the Irish Yahoo.

Haines, Joyce's Englishman, is presented pretty much according to the Irish stereotype, dull, ponderous, slow-witted (John Mitchel himself would have approved although he would have thought Joyce's picture much too brief), but Joyce borrowed from the Englishman's Irishman one of the most devastating ascriptions, madness or lunacy or insanity, and attached it to his Englishman who is described by Mulligan as "a woeful lunatic." Joyce was also clever enough to endow his young Irishman, Dedalus, with quite a few of the English negative stereotypical qualities: he is indolent, irresponsible, improvident, ineffectual, lacking a home and having just quit his occupation, which he only pursued half-heartedly anyway (in English parlance he is a lay-about with no fixed abode), not a little mad, and drunken. And, of course, he is supremely unwashed. But mentally or intellectually he is superb. So what Joyce was doing in Proteus, besides further characterizing his enigmatic and difficult young man and displaying and deploying his own preciously stored up shards of arcane learning, is to say: here is a detailed and precise picture of the mind of a young literary genius-to-be, roaming around in its own consciousness in multiple, overlapping and contradictory ways, playing with philosophical and religious conundrums, ranging back and forth between the present and the past, both the historical and the personal, many of these memories being of living in Paris, the City of Light and the home of the permanent avant-garde (no mere provincial is this young man). There is, so Joyce is silently saying, no picture like it, or even remotely like it, in the whole sweep of English literature, as in truth there is not. Furthermore, Buck Mulligan fits virtually none of the qualities of the stereotypical Englishman's Irishman—Oxford-educated, knowledgeable in Greek, in the process of becoming a doctor, and a man of immense vitality and considerable wit, although Joyce is careful to give some of the best witticisms and aphorisms in Telemachus to Dedalus. Thus in the Telemachiad what Joyce has done with "the Irish question" is to place a dull Saxon, batty to boot, between two brilliant Celts. As a final irony, it is only the Englishman who is a student of Gaelic and a supporter of the Gaelic League.

As the book opens with the sea, it closes with it as well in Molly Bloom's elemental romantic rhapsody about sea, sky, flowers and sex: thus as Dedalus's sea is associated with guilt and death and with intellectual brilliance, hers is emblematic of young sexual love and an emotional intuitionism and pantheism. Her two greatest memories, her first sexual experience with Mulvey at the age of 15 on Gibraltar in May 1886, and her acceptance of Bloom's plighted troth on Mt. Howth in Ireland in May 1888, both took place on great heights overlooking the sea. Moreover, she has always lived enisled first on Gibraltar and then in Ireland.

This similarity between these two disparates constitutes a reminder that Joyce hardly ever let an absolute contrast stand, for he was always, in great ways and small, knitting together his huge imaginary world which like the universe itself seems often to be in the process of flying apart. For example, both Stephen and Molly are singers; both are bereaved, Stephen for his mother, Molly for her son; both are loners and lonely; both are frightened by that fearful thunderclap that resounds over Dublin—not a familiar phenomenon, it should be said—at 10 P.M. on 16 June. Thus even virtual opposites do cross lines in certain ways. But none of these resemblances alters the schematic opposition between them.

Molly Bloom also constitutes a large scale reversal—explosion is the better word—of the stereotypical Irishwoman, who though supposedly inordinately prolific, especially in producing sons, was also supposed to be a vessel of sexual purity, unlike the contaminated male. Molly Bloom has produced only one living child, and a daughter at that, and is the only one of the central characters who enjoys a full-scale, uninhibited sexuality, complete with prolonged orgasm. Far from being meek and submissive, she is massively self-assertive and independent and possesses a rude mother wit. Once more, no previous Irish writer, not to mention all the writers of other lands, has ever conjured up anything like her.

Bloom considered physically is a mean between the two extremes: shorter than Dedalus, he is taller than his wife; heavier than Dedalus, he is not so heavy as his wife; more exotic looking, for an Irishman, than Dedalus, he is not so "Moorish"-looking as his wife, the quality in her that he precisely prizes. Like them both, he is virtually faceless, since we are never told precisely what he looks like although the perception of him by other people is often noted; but since these vary enormously—to Gerty McDowell he appears distinguished-looking, to the narrator of Cyclops he is repulsively Semitic—then all this tells us is that human perceptions of things outside them vary enormously. But that he is an attractive man there can be no doubt; and thus each of Joyce's central characters is pleasing to the observer's eye. They are then complete reversals of that ape-like "Paddy," the Caliban-Yahoo, prognathous and melanous, that had come into being in English cartoons in the 1870s and 1880s. But, it should be added, they also owe nothing to the counter-image that the Irish generated: Erin, a stately, sad, wise woman with dark hair and Pat, a handsome, honest, sturdy man, and a farmer.[7] The great differences in their looks, of Dedalus and the Blooms, are a reminder of the great diversity of racial-cultural heritages that Joyce had ascribed to his race. Christine Longford in her book on Dublin remarked:

> The stranger searches for a racial type. Dubliners seem Irish to him because they have fresh complexions and an animation expected of the Irish, and speak with Irish accents. But they are dark or fair, tall or short. . . . Among the crowds there is a sprinkling of the easily-recognized stage-Irish type, with dark curly hair and blue or grey eyes; but there are plenty of blondes and nondescript, brown-haired western Europeans.[8]

While Bloom's consciousness is markedly different from those of Dedalus and Molly Bloom, yet, as all readers of *Ulysses* know, Bloom has many specific affinities to each and shares some of their few similarities as well, being both a manly man and a womanly man. Molly appears especially to have prized the "woman" in her man. It would be tedious to recite all of the interconnections between the three, which have been traced in great detail many times. Suffice it to say that Bloom is never as extreme and consistent as they are in their habitual outlooks. He can become at certain moments solipsistic and at others pantheistic, both rationalistic and intuitive, both subjective and objective, both skeptical and credulous, and so on. He exceeds them only in the immensity of his lucubrations on the sea (*U,* 17.183–228), and his attitude toward it is as characteristic of him as theirs is of them: he attaches no specific meaning to it but carefully catalogues its vast number of physical properties and the ways by which the sea in its totality manifests itself. In keeping with the schematic tendencies of *Ulysses* and remembering that both Stephen and Molly conclude their respective solo appearances with visions of the sea, it is near the end of Bloom's day that the sea begins to "surface" in his consciousness: first, in a general way, in Nausicaa when he is actually on a strand; second, more specifically, in Eumaeus (*U,* 16.624–29) and set off by the presence of a sailor, one Murphy; and culminating and concluding with the amplitudinous summation of Ithaca in what is Bloom's final appearance in the book.

Bloom's consciousness is of a totally different order, and seems in fact to come out of a different world (as in fact it does), from either of the disparate consciousnesses that exist on either side of him. As Dedalus is an inversion of the Englishman's Irishman in the matter of native intelligence, Bloom is a complete inversion of the entire stereotype. But just as Dedalus is endowed with many of the enduring traits of the Englishman's Irishman, so Bloom is surrounded by ambulatory personifications of practically all the elements of the Englishman's Irishman: lunatics, drunks, bar-flies, layabouts, pig-heads, nonstop talkers, losers, drifters. For many of them to utter a witticism is the height of human felicity and the world would be well lost—it is their Cleopatra, as Dr. Johnson observed of Shakespeare's love of the "quibble"—to utter it in the proper company, where it would be appreciated, and, better, repeated and thus finally take its place in Dublin folklore.

It should be added that Joyce was well acquainted with the world of middle-class Irish Catholics, of which he was one himself, such as the Sheehy family and Kettle and Skeffington and others whom he knew at Clongowes, Belvedere, and University College, who were anything but stereotypical "Irishmen," but he chose not to represent them in *Ulysses*. We get just a glimpse of Mrs Sheehy, wife of M.P. David Sheehy, conversing briefly with Father Conmee at the beginning of the Wandering Rocks. This is the barest of insights into a quite different Dublin world than the world Joyce chose to present. According to Conor Cruise O'Brien, who is the grandson of Mrs Sheehy, this was a meeting of two forces, composed of the Catholic elite, confidently expecting Home Rule and the subsequent control of the new state by them and theirs: "The Jesuits were helping to train such an elite. So was my grandmother."[9] The uprising of 1916 was to destroy these expectations.

But Joyce wanted expressly to people his fictional world with the losing and the lost, mostly lower-middle-class people, some of whom had once been members of the middle class proper, and for several reasons. Their constant presence would set off in even more noble relief his temperate and magnanimous protagonist. Probably too he thought his gallery of layabouts was more representative of Ireland as a whole and of Irish history than would be examples drawn from what was a rather small middle class. The Irish Catholic middle class was tiny in the eighteenth century and never very large in the nineteenth century, and it had seldom been of any great importance in the torturous process of Irish history. Moreover, Dubliners below the level of "respectability" were often, as the novel demonstrates, colorful, high-spirited, uninhibited and witty, as was his own father, his favorite Irish "character." They were much more apposite for the great Irish comedy he was writing than would have been the more staid, sober and conventional members of the middle class proper. Finally, since England was preeminently the "bourgeois" nation, the last thing Joyce wished to do was to present an Irish equivalent, and it was the Irish Catholic middle class that of all the Irish Catholics most resembled their English counterparts in education, social outlook, even habits of mind.

So where does Bloom, and the concept of Bloom, come from? Joyce was always complaining that he lacked "imagination," by which he seems to have meant that he could not have composed Yeats's verse or *Wuthering Heights*, as he could not have, and that he could only assemble his characters by stitching together remembered traits of the many people that he or his father knew. But it is difficult to see how he could have found among his father's friends, who make up most of his secondary cast, a human consciousness quite like that of Bloom, although one cannot, of course, rule this out. But as all Joyce scholars know, no precise archetype, or archetypes, for Bloom have ever been identified either in Dublin or on the Continent, although Ellmann has suggested several possible partial models. Bloom then, unlike Dedalus, Molly Bloom, Simon Dedalus, Ben Dollard et al., seems to have been a more or less pure invention of Joyce's imagination; further, there is nothing or nobody in all of his earlier work that remotely resembles, and thus prepares for, Leopold Bloom. Thus, so I think, one of the strangest and most mysterious things about this most strange and mysterious book—it is the only one I know of that the more closely and repeatedly it is studied and pondered, the more enigmatic it becomes—is the character of the protagonist. The only possible general analogue for Bloom in Anglo-Irish literature is the Gulliver of Book I and the King of the Brobdingnagians of Book II of *Gulliver's Travels.* When one remembers that Bloom is taller than most of his Dublin associates, the analogy is apt, and when he coolly and silently dissects Bantam Lyons, Nosey Flynn, Richie Goulding, and others, one is reminded of the King of the Brobdingnagians looking down, humorously-contemptuously, on little Grildrig.

One of the great creative acts of the book consists in the fact that while Joyce on one side of his complicated and intricate mind was so "Irish of the Irish" (in Thomas Flanagan's words, "His [Joyce's] was the deep and envenomed hate which a man may feel toward that to which he is bound by love and by spirit"[10]—superstitious, medieval, Jesuitical, Judas-obsessed, a sometime participant in that triad of "learning, drink, and lunacy" that Benedict Kiely says characterized the wonderful, wild, grotesque teachers of the peasants in Carleton's early days,[11] he also should have put at the center of his Irish epic an immense replica of nineteenth- and twentieth-century liberal humanism: secular, tolerant, steady, humane, perceptive, sober, composed, self-possessed, inclined toward the objectivity of science but valuing letters, literature, and music, given to utopian notions of the future for humanity but without illusions about individual human beings, ever curious about the world around him, rather thin in his culture, possessed of no profound historical sense. It is, or was, a type engendered in greatest profusion by the middle classes of America and Europe, although not Ireland, in the nineteenth century and the first part of the twentieth. Although his heyday may have passed, it should not be forgotten what an admirable type it was, and still is. Peter Gay in his large-scale survey of the culture of the middle classes of Europe and America concludes that the single greatest achievement of middle-class culture in the nineteenth century was the engendering of liberalism. He describes this accomplishment in terms particularly relevant to Bloom and his situation in Dublin:

> Real situations are rarely clear-cut, real feelings often nests of ambivalence. This is something the adult learns to recognize and to tolerate, if he is fortunate; it is a strenuous insight from which he will regress at the first opportunity. That is why the liberal temper, which taught men to live with uncertainties and ambiguities, the most triumphant achievement of nineteenth-century culture, was so vulnerable to assaults of cruder views of the world, to bigotry, chauvinism, and other coarse and simplistic classifications.
>
> . . . .
>
> The mixture of generosity and rationality that characterizes the liberal spirit was a hard-won acquisition for the few and under persistent pressure.[12]

But Joyce immensely enriched and complicated his picture of his humane and liberal man by dramatizing a descent into his Hell, i.e., his unconscious, in the Circe episode, wherein is exhibited his homosexuality, fetishism, masochism, coprophilia, self-abasement, passivity, and impotence, which constitutes a kind of psychological equivalent to the nadir of human existence as his conscious mind can conceive an objective end for himself: "the aged impotent disfranchised ratesupported moribund lunatic pauper" (*U,* 17.1946–47). Having punished himself enough and temporarily relieved his guilts, Bloom returns to the surface once more to become the savior of Dedalus and the affable man of good will; as Freud said, masochists are the most decent of human beings.

Bloom then is a kind of unattached free-floating consciousness, expressive of no particular institution or institutional training, as is Dedalus, or of a sex, as Molly is supposed to be so monumentally Woman, or of a culture, as Simon Dedalus and others are so quintessentially Irish, or Dubliners. So at the center of his Irish epic Joyce put a consciousness that could hardly be in any way accounted for by the fact that it was born and come to maturity in Ireland. Rather he is modern, secular man, an international phenomenon produced in the Western world at large in fairly sizable numbers by the secular currents of the eighteenth, nineteenth, and twentieth centuries, a type often both homeless in any specific locale and at home in any of the diverse middle-class worlds in the Europe and America of those centuries. But—Joyce's real point—he was born, grew up, matured, learned all he knew in Dublin.

One of the most significant ways by which the three are distinguished from one another is by their widely differing senses of time, an eminently appropriate touch for a novel so quintessentially concerned with the temporal and the myriad of ways in which time manifests itself in human consciousness.

Dedalus's time-sense is a peculiar combination of disparates. On the one hand, he embodies that familiar Dublin time-sense, shared by virtually all the secondary characters in the book, wherein ordinary clock-time does not exist and one lives in an ambience in which each day is "the afternoon of the day before yesterday"; on the other hand, this time-sense, or lack of time-sense, in Dedalus is coupled to, and occasionally broken into by, the twin Blakean senses of seeing eternity in a grain of Sand (God is "a shout in the street" [*U*, 2.386]), and of intimations of an impending apocalypse (*Time's livid final flame leaps and, in the following darkness, ruin of all space, shattered glass and toppling masonry* [*U*, 15.4244–45]). In other words in Dedalus is combined the ordinary Dublin sense of time of a street-roamer and a pub perambulator crossed by eruptive forces within him which look back to Romantic propheticism and to the eschatological visions of the religious belief from which he has defected; that is to say, ordinary Dublin time periodically broken into by microcosmic and macrocosmic senses of eternity. This, I take it, was Joyce's way of saying that here is a young man living the life of his kind who yet has within him the seeds of genius.

Molly's time-sense is of quite a different order and is the most primordial of the three chief characters. Bloom had given her a watch but it never works properly and thus, as she says, "I never know the time" (*U*, 18.344–45). Her deepest and truest sense of time is archaic: cyclic and rhythmic, suggestive, as Joyce himself remarked, of the turning of the globe upon its axis, of the everlasting and repetitive sound and pattern of the sea, of the menstrual cycles of the daughters of the moon, of the procession of the seasons, of diurnal and nocturnal turns. Insofar as she tells clock time at all it is by the ringing of nearby St. George's Church's bells, one of the oldest ways of telling time. Historians argue endlessly over the origins of the time-sense of Western man which were to lead finally to the invention of precise clocks and watches, but there is general agreement that two of the fundamental impulses were the religious and the secular. The Catholic monastic system—the Rule of St. Benedict first spelled out the Church "hours" with some precision ca. A.D. 530—had a need to divide the twenty-four hours into fairly accurate segments for reasons of prayer; and early urban existence had to have a way to remind its citizens, now divorced from their natural habitat in the country with its manifold natural senses of time, what approximate hour of the day or night it was for secular, very often business, reasons.[13] Either way, monastery or town, it was usually done by bells, and thus an urban church bell system, such as St. George's, combines both senses, the religious and the secular. Joyce was careful to insert into Molly's monologue near its end a reminder of the religious origin for the telling of time: "well soon [she thinks at 2 A.M. on the morning of 17 June] have the nuns ringing the angelus . . . an odd priest or two for his night office" (*U,* 18.1541–43). This observation is immediately juxtaposed with a reference to a most modern device for the telling of time, an item that the Blooms do not possess and which she detests, an alarm clock: "the alarm clock next door at cockshout clattering the brains out of itself" (*U,* 18.1543–44). So with Molly what we have is a fundamentally natural sense of time regularly visited by clock time through the agency of the sound of the most archaic of time-tellers, church bells, and once each morning invaded by the unpleasant clatter of the device by which time-bound modern mankind reminds itself of the imminence of DUTY.

Bloom is modern urban man, living by precisely measured clock time, the only such person in the book. Through him principally the reader of *Ulysses* is constantly reminded of the incessant ticking of the clock that dominates modern existence; as he thinks to himself in Sirens: "Time ever passing. Clockhands turning. On" (*U,* 11.188). It could be argued that on 16 June 1904, Bloom is particularly aware of the passing of time because of the impending assignation between his wife and Blazes Boylan. This is true, but we are also told that Bloom has always been a habitual and inveterate watch-watcher, to the incomprehension and amusement of his cohorts who live in that "afternoon of the day before yesterday." So when Bloom enters Davy Byrne's "moral pub," and before he orders his luncheon repast, he takes out his watch to tell the time. Later in this scene, with Bloom off-stage, Nosey Flynn says:

> —God Almighty couldn't make him drunk. . . . Slips off when the fun gets too hot. Didn't you see him look at his watch? . . . If you ask him to have a drink first thing he does he outs with the watch to see what he ought to imbibe. Declare to God he does.(*U,* 8.978–81).

It is true that on 16 June Bloom's watch stops at 4:30 P.M., just about the time that at 7 Eccles St. Boylan is mounting his wife, but one can be assured that he will get it repaired; he even thinks he could repair it himself (*U,* 13.847–48).

Bloom also, as befits a "scientific" man, is interested in the most complex and bizarre mysteries of astronomical time, as when he reads Sir

Robert Ball in order to confront parallax (*U,* 8.110) and contemplates a visit to Professor Joly, Astronomer Royal of Ireland and Director of the Dunsink Observatory (*U,* 8.572–78), and also in the most concrete workings of time-pieces, as when he uses the clock of Connemara marble (stopped at 4:46 A.M., 21 March 1896), given to the Blooms as a wedding present, to explain to his daughter with some precision how the mechanism of a clock actually works (*U,* 17.913–19).

These remarkably different time-senses of the central triad constitute, of course, only a portion of the many ways in which Joyce dramatizes the protean nature of time in the book as a whole, but that is another story.

So what are we being shown by this triad? First, three Dubliners who are completely unlike what the Irishman-woman was supposed to be according to what the Catholic church, the English and the Anglo-Irish establishment, and the Gaelic League said such creatures were supposed to be, and unlike anything that had ever appeared before in Irish literature. Second, they are gigantic portraits, and like the close-ups in movies when these first appeared, were a complete novelty at the time of the publication of *Ulysses*. Nowhere in previous fiction had the reader seen such massive outlines so close up, filled with such an immensity of detail, both revelatory and obfuscating, such trenchant touches mingled with so much trivia, contradictions, ambiguities, mysteries, puzzles. So Joyce had a concern with Irish giants, but they were not mythic: they were contemporary Dubliners. Each was meant to be, and is, absorbing in its own right. Of them Joyce said to Budgen that they "remind me of the persons of the Trinity. Get firm hold of one of them and you lose grip on the other."[14] But, of course, it is their triadic relationship that both shapes the outline of the entire book and provides its central meanings as well, as the reader is plunged in succession into three distinctively different body-soul configurations. Once again human physiology never had played such a role in a novel. Thus we pass from a mind to a mind-body to, at the last, being virtually lodged inside a body; or from a state of celibacy, through a large-scale picture of sexual frustration, to a monumental representation of animal sexual fulfillment (however imperfect in any complete and human sense that it was). In a wider sense we pass from an intense inverted Catholic consciousness, through a secular, modern, liberal consciousness, to find final rest in an ahistorical materialist consciousness; philosophically, from realism (the beginning) to nominalism (the end) by way of a middle term that shares propensities in both directions, but is basically pragmatic and empirical, thinking human perceptions made up of both abstractions and things; or from the subjective and solipsistic, through the average, normal, common-sensical, to the pantheistic and the organic.

Historically, the large swing of the arc of the pendulum travels from past history through present history to non-history in a book that reverberates with the patterns of Irish history itself. Even the journey through Bloom's unconscious in Circe has a historical dimension. Bloom's first self-abasement, culminating in his desire to be beaten by the infuriated Mesdames Talboys, Bellingham, and Barry, is followed by his brief wild flight into the imaginary empyrean of ultimate success, the successor to Parnell and the Savior of the human race, which is quickly annulled and followed by more prolonged and worse abasements. This sequence reduplicates in miniature the basic pattern of Irish history: extended periods of oppression periodically interrupted by uprisings, usually wholly unrealistic and without the least chance of success but accompanied by the wildest and most unfounded optimism—up like a rocket and down like a stick—as the forces and powers of oppression close in quickly and more powerfully than ever. This same pattern is endemic in the book as a whole which consists of a series of anti-climaxes.

If *Ulysses* should be considered as prophecy, it would seem to say that after the present has consumed the past, and the present has consumed itself,[15] we shall be left, perhaps, with a human body, preferably a female body, and a natural landscape. Joyce's overpowering urge, like that of his nation, was to escape the toils of history; hence the end of *Ulysses* points, in a multitude of ways, to *Finnegans Wake* where synchronicity has annulled time. Beginning in the time-bound, historically-entrapped world of the *Dubliners,* and moving through the loosening of these grips that the last part of *Portrait* encapsulates, especially in the image of the winged form in the sky, Joyce, through the agency of *Ulysses,* successively discards first the past and then the present, finally steps outside of time, and later, into the "coincidental universe" of the world of *Finnegans Wake* where all history certifies that there is no history. Thus in his career as a whole he was not only using up and discarding literary styles, forms and genres, he was also using up and discarding human history, at least in its familiar periodicalized forms, and was finally to discard history itself when he moved into his timeless world where everybody was anybody else, time out of mind. He had one more thing to discard and that was humanity, at least as it had manifested itself customarily in fiction. Some kind of such urge was also present in his greatest contemporary novelist in the English language (the two thoroughly detested one another's work), D. H. Lawrence, who, apropos of *The Rainbow,* wrote a letter to Edward Garnett describing where he was going as a writer of fiction:

> but somehow—that which is physic-non-human, in humanity, is more interesting to me than the old-fashioned human element—which causes one to conceive a character in a certain moral scheme and make him consistent. . . . You mustn't look in my novel for the old stable *ego* of the character. There is another ego according to whose action the individual is unrecognizable and passes through, as it were, allotropic

> states which it needs a deeper sense than any we've been used to exercise, to discover are states of the same single radically unchanged element.[16]

This is not an inaccurate capsule description of certain aspects of *Finnegans Wake,* but Joyce's trajectory as a writer was almost vertical, much more radically so than Lawrence's, and when one contemplates the distance between *Dubliners* and *Finnegans Wake,* one does wonder what could possibly come next. Once when asked what he planned to do after *Finnegans Wake* Joyce replied that he contemplated an epic on the sea, which does seem just and fitting, whatever were his real feelings on this subject, which I am sure he kept to himself. But given the trajectory that has just been pointed out one feels, or at least I do, that on the Day of Judgment Joyce's world would consist only of the sea, the island, the mount, and the river. No human beings need apply or, more appropriately, in the formulation of advertisements for jobs in nineteenth-century New England, "Irish Need Not Apply." One unmistakable drift—there are others—in Joyce's complicated creative dispositions was toward eschatology: FINIS for history and humanity. However, on other occasions when asked about future intentions, he indicated that his sleeper would awake and that Joyce would return to humankind the English language, de-*Wake*-ified. And the impulsion toward the eschatological climax that I have posed here may have been only a Viconian turn, the end of one era and the beginning of another. Thus his next words, had he lived to write them, might have been:

> Once upon a time and a very good time it was
> there was a moocow coming down along the road. . . .

Looked at from quite another perspective, remembering always Joyce's claim for having constructed a novel whose perspective was always changing throughout its entire course, the central triad come out as three of the major archetypes of Catholicism, a fact that should come as no surprise, as should not the eschatology I have surmised. Deciding whether the three archetypes were partially formed by centuries of Catholic discipline or whether the Church in its centuries of accumulated practical wisdom discovered that the three were three of the essential types of humanity and accordingly founded its rock upon them is analogous to trying to settle the chicken-and-egg riddle. In any event, St. Augustine had said that three vices comprehend all sins: carnal pleasure (Molly), pride (Stephen), and curiosity (Leopold).

From this angle the central cast of characters of *Ulysses* is made up of two important, but relatively infrequent, polar opposite types and one very major and numerous type. Dedalus, the most infrequent type, is the potential saint and/or Church Father turned inside out or upside down and become the arch heretic or infidel, one who in an earlier age might have been "terribly burned," as was Bruno, one of Joyce's intellectual patron saints. Just as in Dostoyevski's world where there is only the slightest difference, a hairline, between the great sinner and the great saint, so in the world of historical Catholicism there was only the slightest differentiation between the genius-as-saint and genius-as-heretic. It is not difficult, for example, to imagine St. Augustine and Joyce changing places. Commentators on the *Confessions,* such as Rebecca West or Peter Brown, who in his classic biography *Augustine of Hippo* quotes a passage describing the inner life of Stephen Dedalus in *Portrait* to parallel a similar moral stage of St. Augustine's, remark on Augustine's potentialities as a novelist (Rebecca West compares him especially to Tolstoy but also to Lawrence, Proust, and Joyce, among others). Thus there could have been, exchanging a few centuries, the *Confessions* of St. James of Dublin, in many senses a book that we have, and Augustine's *A Portrait of the Artist as a Young Man,* similarly a book that in many respects does exist. And in Augustine's massive and complex disquisitions on memory and time we have two of the most important subjects of serious modern literature. Toward secular life Augustine appeared to have had a Joycean or *Ulyssean* attitude and once said, "this life is nothing but the comedy of the human race."[17]

What is usually emphasized in discussions of Dedalus-Joyce and Catholicism is the rebellion, the *non-serviam;* what I shall stress here is the attraction for him of this formidable institution and how conceivably, except for the celibacy which would always have constituted an insuperable barrier for him, he could have been at home in certain fundamental ways within its intellectual precincts at their highest levels, as he himself explains in some complex detail in chapter 25 of *Stephen Hero.* Louis Gillet, a French Catholic, drew parallels between Joyce's thinking and that of the Church Fathers and theologians and concluded that the generic outlines were quite similar: experienced in dialectics; psychologists without illusions; minds, poetic in cast, disenchanted with all vanities and concerned solely with eternal problems. It has been said by many observers that the word "eternal" was always on the lips of the Jesuits, and the note of eternality that Joyce was always striving for in his later work had one of its primary bases in that fact of his schooling. When Joyce was planning to move from Paris in the winter of 1938–39, he drastically reduced his personal library, and of the 468 items that remained the most heavily underlined single work in his library was *Casus de matrimonio fere quingenti quibus applicat et per quos explicat sua asserta moralia circa eadem materiam* (1892) by M. M. Matheram, 497 cases of marital matters and problems, from betrothal to incest. For each crux Father Matheram gives the official decision of the Church, citing authorities, and Joyce underlined the judgments.[18] For not only was he interested, first and foremost, in marriage and its problems, he also prized the manner in which over the ages Catholic theologians have systematically laid out in orderly file *all* possible human sins and peccadillos and then with uncompromising, though often tortuous, logic, assessed each and every one and passed a judgment on each. It requires no great imaginative leap to see Joyce, with "the robes upon him," compiling such a list and making such assessments, or compiling a penitential, as in effect he finally did in *Finnegans Wake*.[19]

Molly represents the two elements, which were often the same, the feminine and the pagan, that had been officially condemned by the early Church and supposedly banished to the pagan past but were in actuality in the first centuries of the Catholic Church incorporated into Church doctrine and ritual on a massive scale. The female element of the Trinity, which was finally to become the Mariolatry whose extravagances are satirized in the Nausicaa section of *Ulysses*, goes straight back to the fertility goddesses of the Middle East in the ancient past, as does virtually everything else in Christian belief. Max Weber in his *Sociology of Religion* said that only Judaism and Islam are strictly monotheistic in principle, as Christian trinitarianism as well as the Catholic cult of the saints make Christianity come very close to the polytheism of the Greco-Roman practices of the Near East. In the nineteenth and twentieth centuries the claims made by Protestant theologians and scholars of the subject for the capture of Christianity by paganism have become ever more sweeping. Of this considerable literature I shall quote only two such assertions. First, an American scholar, John Strong Newberry: "The Christianity we profess today is sublimated paganism";[20] second, an English Protestant theologian, Arthur Weigall: " . . . a great deal of ecclesiastical Christianity being, indeed, so definitely paganism re-dressed that one might almost speak of it as the last stronghold of the old heathen gods."[21] In other words, the pagans have the last word, just as one does in *Ulysses*. I have already said that Molly represents a kind of ahistoricity; considered from the present perspective she represents a return to the depths of time, remembering that modern biblical scholarship asserts that in certain segments of pre-biblical Middle Eastern society and mythology a matriarchy prevailed, which was finally overturned by a patriarchy.[22] The same thesis has been argued for Greek culture, and thus Greek-Jew/Jew-Greek were once under the authority, so it has been speculated, of the Great Mother.[23]

It has often been remarked that Molly's birthdate, 8 September, is the same as that of the Virgin Mary, and asserted that this is some kind of irony on Joyce's part. This may well be so, but it also underlines Molly's descent from the pagan goddesses from whose iconography and symbolism, which were elaborated in the earlier centuries of the Christian era, the modern picture of the Virgin descends. The *Catholic Encyclopedia* says that it is unclear why 8 September should have been chosen for the nativity of Mary, the apocryphal only child of the apocryphal Anne and Joachim, but says these legends first surfaced in an important way out of the East in the sixth century and were not adopted by Rome until the seventh century, the Latin Church being rather slow to accept what was, as it knew, an "oriental festival."[24] There are a couple of other touches in Penelope that underline Molly's pagan heritage. That side of the by now complex picture of the Virgin signified by the Mater Dolorosa, the mother sorrowing for her dead child, with which we associate the Virgin, also had it archetypes in the pagan goddesses: Cybele mourning for her dead son Attis and Demeter for her daughter Persephone; just so, if briefly, Molly becomes the Mater Dolorosa (*U,* 18.1445–51). Again Molly is a diviner, an augurer both by dreams and by playing cards. An anathema for the early Christian missionaries to the pagans were pagan superstitions: it was forbidden to believe in the Fates. Although the early Church accepted or allowed divinations by dreams, it severely rebuked, and imposed heavy penances for, augury by any other means. In a larger perspective, although it appears that Molly is a professing Catholic and a participant in the confessional—it also appears that her "last confession" was some years behind 16 June 1904—she is not a participant in that sense of sinfulness and resultant guilt complexes, so intense in Dedalus, so extensive in Bloom, that Pauline and Augustinian Christianity had imposed on Western humankind and of which, so far as we know, the world of paganism was largely free, although it had its own form of subjective negativities. As Dedalus represents Catholicism in its pitch of greatest intensity, Molly embodies that large residue of an older world that refused to die and had to be incorporated into Catholic belief—"myth outlasts the ages."[25]

Bloom obviously represents the flock, the mass of humankind, *l'homme moyen sensuel,* given not to sins of the spirit, like Dedalus, but not free of guilt, like Molly. His sins, such as they are, are the sins of the flesh, and for such as him the confessional exists, or used to exist. It was thus appropriate on Joyce's part to have his hero at the beginning of his day in Lotus Eaters attend a mass, observe communicants partaking of communion, and speculate with shrewd common sense on the psychology of the confessional. He understands quite clearly how it works and why most human beings need it, or something like it. Its equivalent is provided for him by the psychological mechanisms of the Circe episode.

In the larger psychological perspective Joyce's anti-Catholic, Catholic novel is a comedy about human feelings of guilt. Joyce happened to have been born into a religious environment, Catholic-Ireland, that engendered such feelings on a massive scale. He escaped to the Continent, only to encounter a massive new secular and "scientific" elaboration on the same theme, man as the "guilty animal," in the work of Freud, with which, and in despite of his own denials and deprecations, it now appears that Joyce was quite conversant. What Joyce found then was that feelings of guilt about sins and transgressions, real or imaginary, were not only mass-produced in Catholic Ireland but mass-produced by the human race, although he once said he would much prefer the ministrations of the confessional to those of psychoanalysis. *Ulysses* itself constitutes a kind of symbolic absolution of this universal human condition. As Joyce moved through his central triad, the guilts successively lessen at each stage. The overriding fact of Dedalus's inner life on 16 June 1904 is guilt about his mother, and there is no indication, despite his passionate rejection of her ghost in Circe, that his guilt about her has been expiated in any deep sense. Bloom's guilts are both lesser in intensity and multiple in their manifestations, ranging from those concerned with his father and mother, his wife, his own position in life, and so on, and these are, temporarily, relieved by the early morning of 17 June. Through the agency of Molly, Joyce made his final comment on Irish Catholic morality, which had put at its center sexual purity, of which his heroine makes in her masive way a massive rejection. So at the very end of her monologue, and the end of the book, we are in a kind of sexual paradise, reminiscent of the heaven of Islam, with human feelings of guilt utterly banished, as is Dublin and human history itself. Only the sky, the sea, the mount, flowers, and sexual love, highly romantic in nature and quite unlike her encounter with Boylan, survive. This is the meaning of that final "Yes."

But to conclude with this assertion would be tantamount to saying that the end of the book is the meaning of the book, which it is not: the meaning is the *whole,* as Pound wrote to Joyce in 1920. This meaning is both extensive, residing in the entire verbal sequence in all its enormity, from "Stately, plump" to "Yes"; multiple, that is, literal, moral, allegorical, and anagogical; and finally unformulable in any kind of single or simple proposition. From the perspective adopted in the present essay, it can be argued that the most important meaning-constituents in the mighty labyrinth are the central characters themselves, some of their many significances having been suggested in the foregoing remarks. In the history of Western literature they constitute the most complete examples of what Hegel called the "concrete universal." In no other work of literature is there such a wealth of physiological details, allied to, even expressive of, such a multiplicity of moral, emotional, and intellectual qualities, richly diverse in each principal. And each of the principals, each in its own way, is expressive of large historical resonances, some of them emanating from the depths of time; others suggesting modes of thought and feeling from the Middle Ages to the twentieth century; still others prophetic, and—like most serious nineteenth- and twentieth-century literature—rather ominously so, of the unknowable future.

Finally, through the agency of *Ulysses* Irish culture for the first time, and so far the only time, contributed a large fictional presence to that great pantheon of European-American fictional presences, whose avatars, Don Quixote and Sancho Panza, were engendered in sixteenth-century Spain and whose numbers were so copiously multiplied by the major novels of England, France, Russia, America, and Germany in the eighteenth, nineteenth and twentieth centuries—namely one Leopold Bloom.

Notes

1. Forrest Read, *Pound/Joyce* (New York: New Directions, 1967), 185.
2. Jacques Mercanton, "The Hours of James Joyce, Part I,"*Kenyon Review* 24 (Autumn 1962), 725. Mercanton's memoir is reprinted in *Portraits of the Artist in Exile*, ed. Willard Potts (Seattle: University of Washington Press, 1979), 205–52.
3. *New Catholic Encyclopedia* (New York: McGraw-Hill, 1967), "Numbers and Number Symbolism," vol. 10, 567–70. Joyce once said to Adolph Hoffmeister: "Number is an enigma that God deciphers. Along with Beckett . . . I have discovered the importance of numbers in life and history. Dante was obsessed by the number three." Potts, *Portraits*, 129.
4. Bruce Bidwell and Linda Heffer, *The Joycean Way* (Baltimore: Johns Hopkins University Press, 1982), 11.
5. Frank Budgen, *James Joyce and the Making of* Ulysses, (1934; Bloomington: Indiana University Press, 1960), 49.
6. Potts, *Portraits*, 213.
7. L. Perry Curtis, *Apes and Angels* (Washington, D.C.: Smithsonian Institution Press, 1971), 21–22, 75.
8. Christine Longford, *A Biography of Dublin* (London: Methuen, 1936), 4.
9. Conor Cruise O'Brien, *States of Ireland* (New York: Pantheon Books, 1972), 64.
10. Thomas Flanagan, *The Irish Novelists* (New York: Columbia University Press, 1959), 339.
11. Benedict Kiely, *Poor Scholar* (London: Sheed & Ward, 1947), 27.
12. Peter Gay, *The Bourgeois Experience*, vol. 1, *Education of the Senses* (New York: Oxford University Press, 1984), 31, 59.
13. For the most up-to-date, and the best, discussion of these matters see David G. Landes, *Revolution in Time* (Cambridge, Mass.: The Belknap Press, 1983), 58–72.
14. Frank Budgen, "Further Recollections of James Joyce," *Partisan Review* 23 (Fall 1956), 531.
15. As Joyce put it in *Portrait* in a Diary entry near the end: "The past is consumed in the present and the present is living only because it brings forth the future"(*P*, 251).
16. *The Letters of D. H. Lawrence*, ed. Aldous Huxley (New York: Viking Press, 1932), 197–98.
17. E. R. Dodds, *Pagan and Christian in an Age of Anxiety* (Cambridge: Cambridge University Press, 1966), 11.
18. Thomas Connally, *The Personal Library of James Joyce* (University of Buffalo: University Bookstore, 1957), 25–28.
19. In an interesting and neglected essay Edward Duncan argues that Joyce's ideal church was the early monastic Irish Church which had presumably existed before Adrian IV's Bull *Laudabiliter* and the Norman invasion:

> My purpose [says Duncan] in this essay is to show, if possible, that Joyce was influenced by the dream of Joachim of Floris of an age of the Holy Spirit, when the church would be

completely monastic, no longer clerical and sacramental. Joyce felt that the primitive Irish Church corresponded somewhat to Joachim's dream. Thanks to Adrian's Bull the semi-independence of this Church was destroyed and now the present day Irish Church is strongly clerical and is, furthermore, an ally of the State, an alliance which, like Blake, Joyce thoroughly detested. Now in his own time, he finds this alliance operating (strange bedfellows though they be) between the English government and the Roman Catholic Church.

Duncan's evidence for his thesis is drawn from all of Joyce's work but most substantially from *Finnegans Wake*. "James Joyce and the Primitive Celtic Church," *Alphabet,* no. 7 (December 1963), 17–38.

20. John Strong Newberry, *The Rainbow Bridge* (Boston and New York: Houghton Mifflin, 1934), 2.

21. Arthur Weigall, *The Paganism in Our Christianity* (New York: Putnam's, 1928), 9. In Weigall's analysis the Trinity, the Virgin Mary and her Virgin Birth, much of the life of Jesus and all his miracles, the Crucifixion, the Resurrection, the Ascension, the Atonement, the Saints, Christmas, Easter, Sunday observance, the Eucharist, the Epiphany, and so on, all disappear into the maw of paganism. What is left is part of the story of the historical Jesus in the Gospels. He was a fine fellow, says Weigall, and all we need for a Founding Father.

22. Walter Beltz, *God and the Gods: Myths of the Bible*, trans. Peter Heinegg (New York: Penguin Books, 1983), 21–22.

23. When *The Father*, which is an adaptation of Aeschylus's *Agamemnon*, was gestating in Strindberg's imagination, he read a Marxist interpretation of the *Oresteia*, an article by Paul Laforgue called "Le Matriarcat" (1886), arguing that Aeschylus's trilogy reflected the development of ancient society from an organization in which the mother was central, because parentage could be indubitably determined by her, to a social organization in which the father was central. Strindberg thought there was a possibility that history was completing a cycle in the late nineteenth century and that European society, beset by feminist demands, was entering a second matriarchal era and that women's cunning and immorality would probably defeat the male. Evert Sprinchorn, *Strindberg as Dramatist* (New Haven and London: Yale University Press, 1982), 47.

The notion that a matriarchy had once prevailed in most ancient societies had first been advanced in a scholarly way by Bachhofen's *Das Mutterrecht* (1861) and later by Lewis Morgan's *Ancient Society* (1887). Engels had borrowed extensively from Morgan for his *The Origin of the Family* (1884). Vico, with his idea of a sexually promiscuous stage in the evolution of primitive society, is usually thought to be the ultimate precursor of the matriarchal thesis.

24. *The Catholic Encyclopedia* (New York: Appleton, 1911), "Nativity," vol. 10, 712–13.

25. Beltz, 21.

Redrawing the Artist as a Young Man

MICHAEL PATRICK GILLESPIE

In the opening paragraph of "A Portrait of the Artist," a narrative essay written in January of 1904, Joyce first articulated a concept for depicting the nature of an individual that he would develop with increasing sophistication in each of his succeeding works. In this essay he questioned the preeminence given in most descriptions to incidental, physical features distinguishing a person at any particular time, implying that a more accurate, a more artistic rendering includes a reflection of the influence of the past.

> The features of infancy are not commonly reproduced in the adolescent portrait for, so capricious are we, that we cannot or will not conceive the past in any other than its iron, memorial aspect. Yet the past assuredly implies a fluid succession of presents, the development of an entity of which our actual present is a phase only. Our world, again, recognizes its acquaintance chiefly by the characters of beard and inches and is, for the most part, estranged from those of its members who seek through some art, by some process of the mind as yet untabulated, to liberate from the personalised lumps of matter that which is their individuating rhythm, the first or formal relation of their parts. But for such as these a portrait is not an identificative paper but rather the curve of an emotion. (Reprinted in *P*, 257–58)

This idea of the individual evolving out of an aggregate of shaping experiences found little sympathy with William Magee, the editor of the Irish magazine *Dana,* who refused "to publish what was to my self incomprehensible."[1] The rejection, however, did nothing to blunt Joyce's determination to develop his approach to fictional characterizations along lines suggested by ideas contained in the passage above, and I believe that with the advantage of critical hindsight unavailable to Magee one can draw upon the elements of this youthful essay to comprehend Joyce's mature vision of the artist, personified in Stephen Dedalus in *Ulysses,* and to delineate his refined abilities to create such a figure.

In each of his succeeding works Joyce sharpens his depiction of the "individuating rhythm" that shapes his characters. His earliest fictive efforts call attention to the mutability of a human personality, yet they also reflect the technical difficulty of tracing "the curve of an emotion" from recollections truncated by the selective suppression of elements that individuals prefer not to confront. Specific stories in *Dubliners* imply the power of personal experience to affect the lives of characters like Eveline, Maria, Mr Duffy, and Gabriel Conroy, but as a whole the collection places greater emphasis on the suffocating influence of a general, cultural past, a feature of the society separate from any single character and yet imposing limits on everyone. *Exiles* develops more explicitly the influence of private and public pasts on the individual's present. It examines the efforts of Richard Rowan to resist the formal constraints of his heritage: moral traditions enforced by institutions like Church, State, and family; yet it lacks the scope necessary to establish a context for these events or to elaborate upon the evolution of the consciousness of the artist. *Portrait* attempts a more ambitious examination, moving toward a depiction of the cumulative influence of a collection of discrete experiences on the artist's perception of his present condition. It records "a fluid succession of presents" in the early life of Stephen Dedalus unfolding in tension with the larger events that have shaped the society he enters. As the work progresses, tension gives way to antagonism, and antagonism fosters alienation. With little capacity for self-reflection, Stephen implicitly rejects the prospect that experiences, like the trip to Cork with his father, can exert any positive influence on the development of his artistic consciousness. (At the same time, while touring the anatomy theatre with his father, Stephen's evocation of the scene of the student carving the word *Foetus* in a desk provides an early example of the impact of the Irish ambience on his artistic powers [*P*, 89–90].) This rejection of the past leaves Stephen with a flawed self-portrait: one that only imperfectly recognizes the elements constituting his nature.

The crucial difference between Stephen's character in *Portrait* and in *Ulysses* rests on his emerging ability to acknowledge the incremental effect of experience. In *Portrait* Stephen endures immersion in experience, while naively assuming that personal genius alone will carry him to the status of artist. *Ulysses,* a novel that begins after a brief self-exile in Paris has loosened the restrictions of youthful assumptions, shows Stephen's initial efforts to examine his personal and public pasts reflectively. He is in the process of discovering that becoming an artist is not a purely natural process. It must be brought on through an apprehension of the self as it is derived from the culture, and Stephen, having left Ireland and returned, can now re-view his Irish ambience with the empathy of one coming to regard it as the foundation of his art.

This development of Stephen's sensibilities also marks the mature convergence of Joyce's artistic vision and his technical powers. *Ulysses* finally unifies general and particular associations of the past through formal and contextual manipulations. It overlays the description of a single day with allusions underscoring the shaping force of custom on personal identity. Traditional temporal and spatial barriers disappear as the narrative reforms in Stephen (and less overtly in Bloom) conceptions of the boundaries of an individual's consciousness. As a consequence, *Ulysses* presents a view of the artist radically opposed to those articulated in *Exiles* and in *Portrait,* and it would be a mistake to see the Stephen Dedalus of *Ulysses* as nothing more than an extension of the protagonist of *Portrait*. Despite his continuing feeling of isolation, he emerges as a figure unavoidably conditioned by his personal past and unconsciously moving toward reconciliation with his cultural heritage. Yet even after one acknowledges the clear differences between the two characterizations, the problem remains of reconciling impressions of Stephen derived from *Portrait* with aspects of his nature emanating from *Ulysses.*

Critics have generally sidestepped the problem by using *Portrait* as a standard against which one measures formal and contextual changes in *Ulysses,* but the analogue has produced no consensus on the evolution of Stephen. Robert Scholes and Robert Kellogg, examining the impact of variations in forms of characterization on narrative development, contrast the "attenuated" depiction of Stephen in *Portrait* with the "ramified" one in *Ulysses* to illustrate distinctly different textual strategies.

> One of the major reasons for the apparent differences in the character of Stephen Dedalus in *A Portrait* and in *Ulysses* stems from Joyce's having emphasized a different kind of characterization in the two works. In *A Portrait* Stephen's character is attenuated so as to show his development along esthetic lines as an artist who combines the religious functions of priest-teacher and sinner-scapegoat. But in *Ulysses* he is seen in a temporal rather than a developmental manner, as frozen for a day in time, rather than progressing swiftly through it toward an evolutionary goal, and his character is presented in a much broader and less attenuated manner.[2]

While their distinctions capture perfectly the contrasting atmosphere of the two works, their approach necessarily places little emphasis on Joyce's conscious efforts to form a conjunction between the novels. This, in turn, causes them to ignore the evolutionary progress in Stephen's nature that Joyce traces.

Individuals, places, events, even phrases from *Portrait* appear throughout *Ulysses* and extend its temporal limits well beyond a single June day in 1904. Repeated allusions affirm the shaping impact of the past on Stephen's present. Playing upon the reader's presumed knowledge of the preceding novel, *Ulysses* presents Stephen as a figure influenced by events that need little elaboration or recapitulation. Other critics, beginning with Joyce's friend Stuart Gilbert writing on *Ulysses* in 1930, have recognized these links to Stephen's past, but they see no significant growth in his character.[3] Such a synchronic view of Joyce's artistic abilities unrealistically assumes that the sophisticated advances in thematic articulation, evident throughout the novel, have had little impact on the constitution of characterization. I believe that one forms a clearer sense of Joyce's conception of an individual's development by acknowledging the complex relationship between depictions of Stephen in the two works. Joyce's retrospective arrangements in *Ulysses* manipulate awareness of Stephen's past in a manner that both enhances and contradicts previous impressions, reforming Stephen's nature for the reader by depicting Stephen's changing perspective of himself.

Initially at least, convergences between the depiction of Stephen in *Ulysses* and in *Portrait* appear more often than do contrasts. Just as chapters 2 through 5 of *Portrait* open with anti-epiphanies that undercut the lyrical moment of the episodes immediately preceding them, on the opening page of *Ulysses* Stephen, like a fallen Icarus, broods over Dublin Bay. Recollections of his immediate past bridge the unrecorded period between the two novels and imply that his present condition merely continues unresolved conflicts.

The action of the opening scene contributes to the sense that Stephen's present is no more than a variation of his past. Figures from the previous work undergo a form of metempsychosis as Buck Mulligan reproduces the patterns of behavior that inflicted so much pain on Stephen in *Portrait*. Like Nasty Roche, Stephen's early tormentor at Clongowes Wood (*P,* 8–9), Mulligan opens the novel with an assault on Stephen's identify by questioning his name (*U,* 1.34). Previously, using tactics similar to those of the bully Wells (*P,* 14), Mulligan had offended Stephen with a flippant reference to his mother (*U,* 1.189–229). In his role as "gay betrayer," he resembles on several levels Vincent Heron, a rival in Stephen's Belvedere days, who, like Mulligan, had pale hair and favored superficial, iconoclastic poses. Both demonstrate avine affinities: Heron in his surname and his "flushed and mobile face, beaked like a bird's" (*P,* 76); Mulligan with his "winglike hands" and "birdlike cries" and his declaration in the Ballad of Joking Jesus—"My father's a bird" (*U,* 1.585). Despite their inflammatory rhetoric, both Mulligan and Heron are reactionary by nature. They prefer a static society where their positions seem secure, and each is quick to use violence to suppress any idea or person who questions his assumptions. The beating that Heron and two stooges administer to Stephen as punishment for his "heresy" (*P,* 79–82) parallels the "ragging" that Mulligan threatens to administer to Haines (*U,* 1.160–64).

Although he has no illusions about Buck's friendship, Stephen makes no connection between Mulligan, Nasty Roche, Wells, and Heron. The links to earlier adversaries, however, are clear to the reader, and they seem initially to announce a replication of the conditions that impelled Stephen to declare his intention to fly by the nets of nationality, language, and religion (*P*, 203). What distinguishes past from present is Stephen's response. While the tactics of his opponents remain the same, Stephen demonstrates an ability, refined beyond a mock recitation of the Confiteor (*P*, 82), to use his heritage as a defense against forces that threaten him.

In a detailed assessment of his current adversary, Stephen makes what readers of *Portrait* might see as an unusual comparison, for Stephen's imagery suggests a shift in his own values: a lessening of aversion for institutions that, as a younger man, he had rejected. Recollecting controversies in Church history involving the evolution of doctrine, Stephen thinks of "[a] horde of heresies fleeing with mitres awry: Photius and the brood of mockers of whom Mulligan was one" (*U*, 1.656–57).[4] Placing Mulligan (in the middle of a birdlike brood) in the role of heretic that Heron had once assigned to him, Stephen now seems to feel less antipathy for the structure of orthodoxy, modifying the position of *non serviam* articulated in *Portrait*.[5] Stephen has not ceased to rebel (cf. his *non serviam* in Circe [*U*, 15.4228]), but he has refined his sense of what he must defy. His allusion to heresies introduces an attitude absent in Stephen's temperament since the early sections of *Portrait:* an implicit perception of efficacy and of legitimacy within traditional structures of his society.

Other elements in the opening chapter mark a shift in the attitudes that Stephen articulated so forcefully at the close of *Portrait*. His interior monologue, recording a range of vignettes created on the spur of the moment, emphasizes his increasing tendency to draw on evocative material from his Irish background to articulate affinities as well as animosities. Lyrical images—like his sketch of the old milkwoman (*U*, 1.396–407)—combine sympathy for his environment with resentment at being ignored. "She bows her old head to a voice that speaks to her loudly, her bonesetter, her medicineman: me she slights" (*U*, 1.418–19). His thoughts suggest a unified wish for accommodation markedly different from the mixture of apprehension, defiance, and confusion integrated into the scenes of Irish life that he constructs in the diary section of *Portrait*. There he sums up his response to a story about a peasant in the west of Ireland by saying:

> I fear him. I fear his redrimmed horny eyes. It is with him I must struggle all through this night till day come, till he or I lie dead, gripping him by the sinewy throat till . . . Till what? Till he yield to me? No. I mean him no harm. (*P*, 252)

The unfolding action of *Ulysses* extends the central concerns of *Portrait* by elaborating upon the influence exerted by Irish culture and Irish life on the consciousness of Stephen. Incidents reflecting a growing within Stephen of the importance of Ireland to his work chart a concentric rather than a linear development in character. Stephen seems to be acquiring a more precise sense of the artist's need to reflect the mores of society, a sense he elaborates in his Shakespeare lecture in the National Library. He begins to make efforts to gain from his fellow Dubliners esteem for his position as an artist. Although in *Ulysses* Stephen moves away from solipsistic fascination toward an awareness of the necessary interplay between the artist and his society, experiences from *Portrait* exert a pronounced residual effect upon him and upon the reader's apprehension of the evolution of his consciousness. In Stephen's mind perception stimulates memory, and experience reforms response. Not only does the maturing Stephen behave differently in the present than he had in analogous situations in the past, his recollections often display a sympathy and understanding that were absent when the event occurred.

This new consciousness in Stephen is introduced slowly, through a series of analogous situations presented over the first three chapters. Building on naturalistic links to *Portrait* planted in Telemachus, the narrative joins the action of Nestor more overtly to Stephen's past, and it continues to highlight aspects of Stephen's nature that previously had been given little or no consideration. Knowledge of events in *Portrait* add a touch of irony to his current situation; no longer the rebellious student, he is now a gentleman usher at Garret Deasy's school for boys in Dalkey. The position gives him no sense of security; it only aggravates his sense of isolation built up throughout *Portrait* and continued in Telemachus. His inclination to maintain this alienation, however, has diminished significantly. While he sees himself separated from the comfortable, middle-class world of his Protestant pupils (*U,* 2.22–38), he can now feel sympathy for one of them, the ineffectual Cyril Sargent.

Although not a mirror image of Stephen, Sargent does serve to call attention to Stephen's changing attitude toward his past. He identifies in Sargent a vulnerability akin to what he felt on first coming to Clongowes: "Like him was I" (*U,* 2.168). Stephen's associations resemble Bloom's remembrance of a seedcake kiss that took place sixteen years earlier on Howth, "Me. And me now" (*U,* 8.917), but they go beyond mere recollections of personal experiences. Stephen is acknowledging a psychological bond, a convergence of his past and another's present. In so doing he reveals a conjunction, in his artistic consciousness at least, of his own experiences with those of others. This movement away from isolation and toward amalgamation makes possible observations that a younger Stephen would very likely have scorned. Like his remarks on Mulligan and heretics, Stephen's musings on maternal love—"The only true thing in life" (*U,* 2.143)—and his allusion-laden parsing of "*Amor matris:* subjective and objective genitive" (*U,* 2.165–66) signal a new facet of his nature. He paraphrases opinions expressed by Cranly when he berated Stephen for refusing to perform his Easter duty: "Whatever else is unsure in this stinking dunghill of a world a mother's love is not" (*P,* 241–42). At the time Stephen seemed to respond to the remark with studied indifference. Now his sympathetic recollection suggests a softening of his attitude toward familial bonds, and with this shift in feeling he can create a sharply defined, lyrical picture of Sargent's mother, unsentimental yet not devoid of sympathy. "With her weak blood and wheysour milk she had fed him and hid from sight of others his swaddlingbands" (*U,* 2.166–67).

Echoes of Stephen's schooldays persist throughout Nestor, recalling not just the ambience of his youth but also the attitudes he held as a boy. These analogues, in contrast to the tone established in the closing pages of *Portrait,* do not emphasize Stephen's separation from his heritage; rather they suggest a movement toward reconciliation. The athletic field scene provides a spatial and temporal transition, transferring Stephen from the role of putative master to that of a student, again confronting a figure of authority. Raucous descriptions of Deasy's boys playing field hockey, the game Sargent has assiduously tried to avoid, call to mind little Stephen on another athletic field keeping "on the fringe of his line, out of sight of his prefect, out of the reach of the rude feet, feigning to run now and then" (*P,* 8). The disorder of the classroom, his association with Sargent, and Deasy's peremptory request to "wait in my study for a moment" (*U,* 2.191) overturn our image of Stephen as teacher and make him appear a vulnerable, sensitive child. Approaching the meeting with Deasy, Stephen shows a little of the eagerness that one would expect in an impoverished young man about to receive his wages. His salary represents a form of spiritual death. He thinks of previous paydays as "[t]hree nooses round me" (*U,* 2.234), suggesting an association with the nets he wished to fly in *Portrait,* but now Anglo-Irish rather than Irish institutions threaten Stephen.

Elements in the scene recall earlier encounters between Stephen and Father Conmee, the Director of Belvedere, and later with the dean of studies at UCD. Superficially, Deasy seems to conform to models of authority established by Jesuits depicted in *Portrait,* but the narrative discourse reveals, through the dynamics of the exchange, a shift in Stephen's attitude and a realignment of the forces that he faces. The connections between Deasy and figures from Stephen's boyhood establish standards for comprehending evolutions in Stephen's nature and the consequent change in his perception of the Dublin ambience.[6] In *Portrait,* even when Stephen rebelled, the figures in power maintained a concern for his welfare. In *Ulysses* new, less solicitous antagonists have arisen, and in response to their hostility Stephen finds greater affinities with his environment.

The Anglo-Irish ruling class and its supporters, both overt ones like Deasy and covert ones like Mulligan, have displaced in Stephen's mind the native Irish as his principal opponents. Joyce has hinted at this change earlier through a conversation between Stephen and Mulligan's friend, Haines. Responding to obtuse and insensitive probing Stephen describes himself aphoristically:

> —You behold in me, Stephen said with grim displeasure, a horrible example of free thought. (*U,* 1.625–26)
>
> . . . .
>
> —I am the servant of two masters, Stephen said, an English and an Italian. (*U,* 1.638)

A puzzled Haines questions the Italian reference, but Stephen ignores him to expand, within his thoughts, on the English allusion: "A crazy queen, old and jealous, kneel down before me" (*U,* 1.640). The discussion ends with Haines's tepid remark: "It seems history is to blame" (*U,* 1.649).

The exchange with Deasy in the Nestor chapter clarifies the nightmare that Stephen now wishes to escape as the version of history created by English imperialism. His embarrassment over his connection with Deasy's letter and his disdain for Deasy's anti-Semitism reflect a reluctance to be drawn into a particularly English perspective, adumbrated by his coolness toward Haines's opinions on Ireland and on the Jews in England in the preceding chapter. Although Stephen still rejects the oppressive authority of the Church and the constrictive insularity of his countrymen, contact with the Protestant Ascendancy has made him aware of the support provided to him by his cultural identity.

After the examination in the first two chapters of the social and the personal selves of Stephen, Proteus offers insights on his artistic nature: a record of aesthetic impressions emphasizing his facility for enlarging casual sensations into lyrical descriptions. In the Telemachus and the Nestor episodes Stephen's mind suggests its capabilities through scattered imaginative creations generated more or less on the spur of the moment and derived from ideas suggested by people around him: Mulligan's remarks about Clive Kempthorpe's ragging leads to a picture of Oxford students bullying a classmate; Deasy's racial slurs produce an image of Jews at the Bourse. In this chapter similar but more personal sketches come in rapid succession as Stephen reforms his own random thoughts into arresting descriptive passages. Like the creative flashes hinted at in the diary material from the closing pages of *Portrait,* these interludes derive their significance from their Irish background, but in *Ulysses* Stephen's perceptions of that background have changed. Now there is an easy acceptance, a lessening if not a total absence of the scorn and the apprehension that characterized Stephen's imagined picture of Cranly's father or his meditations on the old man whom John Alphonsus Mulrennan encountered (*P,* 251–52).

Although Stephen does not seem to regard them as serious artistic efforts, these unfocused musings lend credibility to his creative abilities and to the impression that Joyce is creating of Stephen's evolving artistic consciousness. The description of an imagined visit to the home of Aunt Sally and Uncle Richie in Strasbourg Terrace moves with a fluid grace, capturing nuances of the speech patterns of his father, uncle, and cousin while summarizing the desperate financial conditions of the Goulding family. Its mimetic force underscores Stephen's emerging skill as an artist, and on first encounter all but the most careful readers tend to forget its fictive beginning and to assume the visit is actually taking place.

Stephen draws the basic material for the creative daydreaming of Proteus from the Ireland that he knows. Images of the Paris he visited touch on a variety of details, but they develop most completely in his recollections of the expatriate Kevin Egan. Powerful in its own right, the scene also serves as a reminder to readers that, unlike Egan, Stephen has returned to practice his art in his homeland. A view of medieval Dubliners carving up a beached whale springs from a sense of his heritage strong enough to imply absorption into its daily routine.

> [M]y people . . . Their blood is in me, their lusts my waves. I moved among them on the frozen Liffey, that I, a changeling, among the spluttering resin fires. I spoke to no-one: none to me. (*U,* 3. 305–9)

A description of the bloated body of the man drowned nine days earlier in Dublin Bay is inspired by the chance remarks of two Dubliners (*U,* 1.669–77). These evocative moments, produced with careless ease, underscore the creative force of personal experience, social conditions, and cultural bonds upon his art.

The chapter also contains a paradoxical example of Stephen's self-conscious efforts at artistic creation, and, through a perspective that both evokes and mimics Stephen's earlier moment of artistic awakening in chapter 4 of *Portrait,* the narrative underscores its equivocal significance. While the setting on Sandymount Strand replicates the epiphanic location of Dollymount, the proximate stimulus for Stephen's poem—the gypsy woman who "trudges, schlepps, trains, drags, trascines her load" (*U,* 3.392–93)—lacks the physical charm of the birdgirl. Significantly, however, this does not deter Stephen. He transforms her from a nondescript itinerant into "the handmaid of the moon," and in this pose she elicits a much more concrete response from him—a poem—than did the earlier vision. I believe that the difference serves to mark a significant development in Stephen's nature: In the first incident he behaves intuitively and solipsistically as a visionary exulting in what he feels without translating it into an experience that can be shared; in the second he acts like a working artist, a creative writer who recognizes the possibility for deriving profoundly moving emotions from banal occurrences, and he attempts to convey those feelings through his art. This change in attitude points up a maturing consciousness: able to draw inspiration from the mundane, intent upon articulating personal reflection in a form accessible to others, and yet reluctant to give himself over, without any reservation, to the allure of art.[7]

In the studied awkwardness of the poem itself, the narrative invites us to acknowledge the qualitative difference emphasized by its juxtaposition with the vivid daydreams that have preceded it. The poem, unfolding in clumsy disjointed phrases, lacks the coherence and assurance of Stephen's musings. Its stilted tone, borrowed as Robert Adams has discovered from a portion of a work in Douglas Hyde's *Love Songs of Connacht,* gives an example of the sort of art that Stephen thinks he should produce.[8] In contrast, the more evocative, less contrived prose narratives of his random thoughts draw their force directly from the Irish ambience, and, in its studied alignment of the two genres, the narration focuses the reader's attention on a crucial juncture in Stephen's artistic development. His self-conscious verse necessarily calls to mind the awkwardness of the villanelle of chapter 5 of *Portrait,* written several years earlier. The second poem—derivative and inchoate—maintains the level of mediocrity established by the first, and it emphasizes Stephen's stagnation as a poet. The forceful images that enliven his diegetic daydreaming suggest, in contrast, an artistic ability wanting only disciplined application. The reader can see clearly the emergence of this creative facility as Stephen, although he makes no conscious decision to abandon his efforts to write poetry, instinctively spends most of the day honing his narrative talents.

From the moment Stephen arrives at the offices of *The Freeman's Journal,* the reader experiences with growing awareness evidence of the marked personality changes produced by artistic ambitions. For the first three chapters of the book, despite moments of empathy already mentioned, Stephen has remained self-absorbed with his art, disdaining to perform for either the English Haines or for the Anglo-Irish Deasy. Now among his fellow Dubliners Stephen moves from one public building to another—newspaper office, library, hospital—in search of a forum for his art, seeking stimulus and recognition.

Each attempt draws upon experience from Dublin life for its content and upon the techniques of accomplished Dublin performers for its form. And each meets with progressively diminishing approval (corresponding inversely to the level of Stephen's intoxication), but the themes and structures of his perfomances suggest new dimensions of his artistic development. Stepping out of the newspaper office and into Abbey Street, Stephen pauses before beginning his "Parable of the Plums" to offer an unvoiced tribute to his native city. "Dublin. I have much, much to learn" (*U*, 7.915). He then endeavors to convert urban experiences into art by constructing his tale from his impressions of the two old women whom he saw on Sandymount Strand (*U*, 3.29–40).[9]

As he speaks, Stephen must contend with clamorous distractions and blunt interruptions, but he forges ahead. His determination (a bit more reserved but equally as persistent as Lenehan's attempt to recount his Rose of Castille joke) makes apparent his desire to secure the approval of his audience, and his deft inclusion of local color and sardonic social commentary gains both attention and commendation. "—Onehandled adulterer! the professor cried. I like that!" (*U*, 7.1019). Stephen stumbles only in his conclusion with the two women "spitting the plumstones slowly out between the railings" (*U*, 7.1026–27). Although the ending produces little more than bewilderment among the listeners, it suggests to me an effort within the narrative discourse to underscore the spontaneity of Stephen's composition. It is possible that Stephen may have entertained vague ideas for the story for a much longer period. However, the abrupt and unsatisfying conclusion combined with contemporaneous details from his walk on the beach and Mosaic allusions from the account in the newspaper office of John F. Taylor's speech indicates that Stephen patched together his most recent impressions in an ultimately unsuccessful attempt to emulate the style of an extremely effective storyteller. Along broad thematic lines, the story serves as an ironic comment on the impulse of the Irish Literary Revival to sentimentalize the peasantry, but, for the reader's conception of Stephen, the parable, despite its flaws, stands as evidence of an emerging willingness to draw art from his environment.

Stephen's impulse to perform on the spur of the moment may come out of a sense of competitiveness. He has been listening to accounts of accomplished orators and tale-tellers, and he has been goaded by Crawford to demonstrate his ability. "I want you to write something for me, he said. Something with a bite in it. You can do it" (*U*, 7.616–17). Stephen's tale seems at least a provisional answer to Crawford. Stephen, unlike Ignatius Gallaher, does not "paralyse Europe" with his story, but the Dublin tramway system does grind to a halt shortly after he finishes speaking (*U*, 7.1043–49). "The Parable of the Plums" disappoints MacHugh and Crawford, who understand the genre better than Stephen does, for it lacks the punch line that they have been led to expect. At the same time it presents readers with an intimation of the type of fiction that Stephen, in time, could shape into something significant.

In the National Library Stephen attempts a different type of performance, and again he seems to make a conscious effort to draw the pattern for his discourse from personal experiences. Before beginning his disquisition, Stephen must endure the first onslaughts of hostile jibes from another brood of mockers, John Eglinton and A.E. In response to their skepticism, he collects his thoughts and silently invokes his Jesuit training. "Composition of place. Ignatius Loyola, make haste to help me" (*U*, 9.163). Although he addresses his prayer to St. Ignatius, he identifies a rhetorical strategy associated with one of the founders' spiritual descendants: Father Arnall, the retreat master (*P*, 127). In *Portrait* Father Arnall uses a description of hell to give a local habitation to the abstract concept of divine punishment, a concrete depiction of the central concern of his sermon. Like Father Arnall, Stephen intends to use composition of place to lend color to his argument, but he also uses it to make a highly personal statement about his own qualifications for assuming the role of artist in his society.

Stephen says little to point to the true topic of his disquisition, but his internal monologue underscores the reflective quality of his mind while pointing up the central concern of his talk: the influence of the past on his own emerging consciousness. When A.E. criticizes him for "prying into the family life of a great man," Stephen silently responds by examining events in his own life in a way that never had occurred to him in *Portrait*. Following the same logic articulated by Joyce in the passage quoted at the opening of this essay, Stephen creates a vignette centering on the pound that A.E. has previously lent to him. His thoughts wander from how he squandered the money in a whorehouse, to his own unwillingness to discharge a legally incurred debt in contrast to Deasy's fiscal probity, to a sophistic attempt to evade his obligation, to a final acknowledgment of a debt not simply to A.E. but to his Irish heritage. Stephen's musings illustrate his own recognition of how memory holds events from the past to condition one's present. It concludes with the implication that to deny the past is to deny the self.

> How now, sirrah, that pound he lent you when you were hungry?
> Marry, I wanted it.
> Take thou this noble.
> Go to! You spent most of it in Georgina Johnson's bed, clergyman's daughter. Agenbite of inwit.
> Do you intend to pay it back?
> O, yes.
> When? Now?

Well . . . No.
When, then?
I paid my way. I paid my way.
Steady on. He's from beyant Boyne water. The northeast corner. You owe it.
Wait. Five months. Molecules all change. I am other I now. Other I got pound.
Buzz. Buzz.
But I, entelechy, form of forms, am I by memory because under everchanging forms.
I that sinned and prayed and fasted
A child Conmee saved from pandies.
I, I and I. I.
A.E.I.O.U.

(*U,* 9.192–213)

Stephen's unvoiced commentary on the discussion in the library provides for readers a link between his discourse and his personal concerns.[10] In describing Shakespeare's relations with his wife as a powerful influence on the creative process, Stephen examines the same strong drives he feels acting on his own consciousness: normal sexual energy and remorse of conscience produced by his mother's death. The narrative makes the connection clear to readers when, in his thoughts, Stephen conflates his "Agenbite of inwit" over his mother with sexual guilt of his longing for Georgina Johnson's bed. The older-woman/younger-man relationship of Anne Hathaway and Shakespeare provides him with a vehicle for publicly articulating his feelings of self-reproach while protecting his privacy. In assessing the futility of an artist attempting to distance himself from his past, Stephen represents the solution he chose at the end of *Portrait*—escape—in the action of his surrogate, Shakespeare. "He carried a memory in his wallet as he trudged to Romeville whistling *The Girl I left behind me*" (*U,* 9.246–47).

As the sardonic musical allusion suggests, escape could not erase the trauma of Shakespeare's sexual initiation, and it has had no more salubrious effect on Stephen's feelings. However, by metaphorically linking biological and artistic creativity, Stephen asserts the artist's ability to transmute without denying experience. Exploring the impact of paternity on Shakespeare, he repeats lines from Nestor that announce but do not reveal his own feelings of guilt. "*Amor matris,* subjective and objective genitive, may be the only true thing in life" (*U,* 9.842–43). With the reappearance of Cranly's views, the narrative again turns our attention to Stephen's capacity to reassess ideas and feelings apparently rejected in *Portrait*. Thus, Stephen can speak as much of himself as of Shakespeare in saying "[a] man of genius makes no mistakes. His errors are volitional and are the portals of discovery" (*U,* 9.228–29). Having struggled in *Portrait* to break free of the influence of his past, Stephen's evolving consciousness now views the past as a source for artistic inspiration and reciprocally revalues previous experience in terms of this new perspective.

The discussion in the National Library also brings out Stephen's heightened concern for his position of social isolation. Stephen's sensibilities are assaulted by impressions of intellectual rejection, beginning with recollections of separation from Cranly (*U,* 9.36–40) and exacerbated by the knowledge of being excluded from George Moore's literary party (*U,* 9.273–74). His sense of isolation and his impulse to retreat into a personal past increase as his listeners mix ad hominem attacks with resistance to his theory. Eglinton, like Mulligan and Nasty Roche before him, reminds Stephen of the strangeness of his name, and this thinly veiled insult turns Stephen back to thoughts of artistic escape building on the mythical and literal consequences of the conclusion of *Portrait*. "Fabulous artificer. The hawklike man. You flew. Whereto? Newhaven-Dieppe, steerage passenger. Paris and back. Lapwing. Icarus. *Pater, ait*. Seabedabbled, fallen, weltering. Lapwing you are. Lapwing be" (*U,* 9.952–54). This acknowledgment of vacillation and remorse of conscience,[11] more than anything else in the chapter, signals to the reader Stephen's recognition of his failure to gain the position he seeks. As in Aeolus, the lack of success comes in part from the material—a theory that Stephen himself ultimately rejects (*U,* 9.1065–67)—and in part from Stephen's untenable position, one that pushes him toward acceptance while preventing him from embracing the company he scorns. As Mulligan reminds him, Stephen has not yet learned to "do the Yeats touch" (*U,* 9.1160–61) to curry the favor of those whom he wishes to impress.

At the Holles Street Hospital, Stephen, in his last conscious attempt of the day to achieve public acclaim, joins a group of medical students for a symposium on maternity, in a sense complementing the topic of paternity discussed in Scylla and Charybdis. Stephen with the "mien of a frere . . . at head of the board" (*U,* 14.192) may initially have hoped to preside and to present a performance similar to the one he gave earlier in the afternoon, but the drunken and disorderly conduct of the others and imperfect control of his own intellect, muddled by alcohol, preclude any such attempt. No single voice dominates as each man, with the exception of Bloom, strives to display wit and erudition.

Conversation careens around discussions of sexuality, creativity, and the essence of self—topics that Stephen has toyed with all day—but he remains unsure of himself and of his subject. He vacillates between physical and metaphysical approaches and settles on neither. Since the chaos of the room and his own ambivalence prevent Stephen from holding forth as he did at the National Library, he tries to make his presence felt by emulating another model from his Dublin ambience: Simon Dedalus, taproom wit. Stephen, however, lacks the practiced polish of the man he dismissed in *Portrait* as

> —A medical student, an oarsman, a tenor, an amateur actor, a shouting politician, a small landlord, a small investor, a drinker, a good fellow, a storyteller, somebody's secretary, something in a distillery, a taxgatherer, a bankrupt and at present a praiser of his own past. (*P.* 241)

Despite his desire for public attention, he still retains an aloofness strong enough to inhibit the conviviality necessary to capture and to hold the others' interest. Further, a day of drinking has blunted his glibness, leaving him open to the harsh criticism of spongers like Vincent Lynch when he attempts just the sort of self-aggrandizement that he had disparaged in his father:

> I, Bous Stephanoumenos, bullockbefriending bard, am lord and giver of their life. He encircled his gadding hair with a coronal of vineleaves, smiling at Vincent. That answer and those leaves, Vincent said to him, will adorn you more fitly when something more, and greatly more, than a capful of light odes can call your genius father. All who wish you well hope this for you. All desire to see you bring forth the work you meditate, to acclaim you Stephaneforos. I heartily wish you may not fail them. (*U,* 14.1115–22)

As the episode progresses, Stephen falls further short of his aspirations as an entertainer, growing increasingly alienated from both language and audience. His contributions become desultory, regaining animation only to suggest more drinks: "Burke's!" (*U,* 14.1391). At the pub the indirect discourse that had rendered remarks articulate for most of the chapter disappears, and the dialogue that follows shows speech degenerated into polyglot. Just as Proteus summarizes themes of the opening chapters, pointing out Stephen's failure to recognize his creative strengths, Oxen of the Sun, capping a series of progressively unsuccessful performances, shows Stephen still searching for a form for articulating his art.

In the nighttown episode Stephen's impulse to gain recognition continues to surface sporadically, but at this point in the day alcohol, hunger, and fatigue have considerably blunted his powers of expression. Still, at various instances when he wishes to capitalize on the brief attention of an audience, he turns to experiences from his past to provide sources for impromptu performances. In the opening pages of the chapter, Stephen attempts a reprise of the disquisition on aesthetics with which he entertained Lynch in *Portrait:* "So that gesture, not music not odour, would be a universal language, the gift of tongues rendering visible not the lay sense but the first entelechy, the structural rhythm (*U,* 15.105–7)." His discussion of art, however, takes a form even denser than the diction which framed his theories in *Portrait,* and his own senses are too dull to vary the presentation enough to keep Lynch's mind from more concrete pleasures: "Damn your yellow stick. Where are we going?" (*U,* 15.120).

Later, when the whores ask Stephen to describe life on the Continent, he offers them a disjointed sketch of a Parisian debauch. His description, however, conveys none of the sensitivity of his earlier recollections in Proteus: "In Rodot's Yvonne and Madeleine newmake their tumbled beauties, shattering with gold teeth *chaussons* of pastry, their mouths yellowed with the *pus* of *flan breton*" (*U,* 3.212–14). Finally, in his confrontation with Private Compton, Stephen achieves what he has sought all day, an audience devoting full and complete attention to his words. Unfortunately, he can say nothing without it being misconstrued and further enciting the already enraged soldiers. "I seem to annoy them. Green rag to a bull" (*U,* 15.4497). The chapter ends with the prostrate Stephen *hors de combat* and done performing for the day. The final two chapters in which he appears, Eumaeus and Ithaca, show a torpid Stephen suffering from human contact rather than relishing the opportunity for any further exchange.

Ulysses ends with Stephen's artistic nature still in a state of flux, but the skill with which Joyce describes that character attests to the maturity of his own talents. Whether conscious of it or not, following guidelines articulated in his essay, "A Portrait of the Artist," Joyce forms our conception of Stephen through allusions to experiences from *Portrait* enhancing rather than echoing the characterization of the preceding novel. Consequently, events in *Ulysses* do not make up a coda to *Portrait* but a reevaluation of the development of an artist conditioned by Joyce's own changing attitudes. Emotional concerns have intensified, and Stephen no longer enjoys the protection of childhood, as tenuous as it might have seemed in *Portrait*. His artistic powers have increased, but he has not yet come to grips with his creative strengths and weaknesses. Stephen's condition encourages speculation as to what he may become, but it seems to me that our real pleasure in his character is derived from tracing the progression from his past to his present.

Notes

1. Quoted in *The Workshop of Daedalus: James Joyce and the Materials for* A Portrait of the Artist as a Young Man, ed. Robert Scholes and Richard M. Kain (Evanston, Ill.: Northwestern University Press, 1965), 56.

2. Robert Scholes and Robert Kellogg, *The Nature of Narrative* (London, Oxford, and New York: Oxford University Press, 1966), 170.

3. Gilbert's study probably did as much as any to establish this reading of Stephen's

character as static rather than as evolving. "Despite the encounters [Stephen] has had with the reality of experience, he remains the young man we knew in the Portrait of the Artist" (*James Joyce's* Ulysses: *A Study* [1930; rpt., New York: Vintage Books, 1955], 102).

4. Weldon Thornton clarifies the allusion, underscoring its Trinitarian implications. "It was Photius (*ca.* 815–97) who . . . became leader of what developed into the Greek schism that finally separated the Greek Church from the Roman in 1054. Probably Photius is called a mocker because of his refusal to accept the *Filioque* clause of the Nicene Creed, which says that the Holy Spirit proceeds from the Father and Son" (*Allusions in* Ulysses: *An Annotated List* [New York: Simon and Schuster, 1973], 24).

5. Hugh Kenner aptly points out the careful limits that Stephen in *Portrait* has placed on his rebellion against the Church: "his *Non serviam* is not a *non credo*" (*Dublin's Joyce* [Bloomington: Indiana University Press, 1956], 127). In *Ulysses,* as I read the text, Stephen may still be unwilling to serve, but he has greatly increased his capacity for tolerance.

6. Like the Jesuit teachers whom Stephen has known, Deasy does not confine lecturing to the classroom. His own pedagogical philosophy appears to center on persuasion over learning. Badgering Stephen about economics, Irish history and the influence of women, and the ethnic mix of the British Isles, he gets his facts wrong as often as not. Like Father Conmee, Deasy redresses grievances (*U,* 2.187ff.), but his motivation stems from a regard for order rather than from a concern for the individuals involved. Like the director of Belvedere, Deasy does not perceive his profession idealistically, but his crass materialism (*U,* 2.236–39) goes beyond the Director's urbanity. Unlike the Director, Deasy does not attempt to encourage Stephen to follow his profession; instead he concludes their meeting with a veiled threat of dismissal (*U,* 2.401–2). Deasy most resembles the dean of studies, another practical man and, again like Deasy, someone perceived by Stephen as a foreigner, "a poor Englishman in Ireland" (*P,* 189). Neither the dean, as he fusses with his fire, nor Deasy, as he settles accounts and dashes off a letter, gives much more than patronizing attention to Stephen. But both, as representatives of institutions that Stephen perceives as diametrically opposed to his ideas, crystallize his position. In *Portrait* he struggles to define his aesthetics. In *Ulysses* he is coming to recognize the inspiration that his art takes from the environment of Ireland.

7. J. Mitchell Morse in "Proteus," *James Joyce's* Ulysses: *Critical Essays,* ed. Clive Hart and David Hayman (Berkeley, Los Angeles, and London: University of California Press, 1974), 30–33, traces parallels between Stephen's interview with the Director of Belvedere and his subsequent walk on Dollymount Strand. Morse views Stephen's consciousness as developing along a more linear, solipsistic pattern than I do. For yet another view see James Maddox's *Joyce's* Ulysses *and the Assault upon Character* (New Brunswick, N.J.: Rutgers University Press, 1978), 34–35.

8. Robert Adams, *Surface and Symbol* (New York: Oxford University Press, 1962), 123–24. On the significance of Joyce's use of Hyde as a model for the passage see further remarks in Michael Patrick Gillespie, *Inverted Volumes Improperly Arranged* (Ann Arbor, Mich.: UMI Research Press, 1983), 65–66.

9. Strictly speaking, Stephen has performed publicly while teaching at Deasy's school, but his story in Aeolus marks his first endeavor before an other than captive audience. Joyce introduces an ironic parallel to his own artistic career into these efforts. Stephen, or perhaps the narrator, prefaces "the Parable of the Plums" with a single word: "Dubliners." The story itself has a framework similar to the patterns of Joyce's own collection, blending local color with political and religious references and moving toward an ambiguous, epiphanic conclusion. The parallel to Joyce's work continues in Stephen's library lecture which is based on his image of Shakespeare as a young man and is seasoned with allusions from *Portrait.* Shari Benstock pursues points similar to these in an analysis of Stephen's storytelling in Proteus, Aeolus,and Scylla and Charybdis in her "The Dynamics of Narrative Performance: Stephen Dedalus as Storyteller," *ELH* 49 (Fall 1982): 707–38.

10. Stephen's thoughts also bring out a conflict in his own temperament already suggested in exchanges with Mulligan and with Deasy, absent from or at least heavily muted in *Portrait.* In his discussions with the dean of studies, for example, Stephen maintains an internal aloofness, slipping only in his thoughts on the tundish, corresponding to the aplomb he presents externally. In Scylla and Charybdis he rebuts the remarks of his listeners in

unvoiced criticisms, but he generally maintains an appearance of accommodation. He has developed a need for acceptance that the Stephen of *Portrait* would have disdained.

11. The entry for lapwing in W. W. Skeat's *An Etymological Dictionary of the English Language* (Oxford: At the Clarendon Press, 1879–82), 329, enhances our sense of the significance that Joyce intended this passage to impart, highlighting connections with "ambivalence" and "Ayenbite of inwyt."

Mockery in *Ulysses*

JAMES MADDOX

When Little Chandler goes to meet Ignatius Gallaher at Corless's in "A Little Cloud," their conversation at once becomes a struggle for dominance, and Little Chandler never has a chance. "And is [Paris] really so beautiful as they say?" he asks; and, a little later, "is it true that Paris is so . . . immoral as they say?" In his answer to the first question, Gallaher shows that "beautiful" is an inoperative word in the vocabulary of a bon vivant such as himself, and in his answer to the second he magisterially transforms "immoral" into "spicy" (*D*, 76, 77). Chandler, who is dependent upon hearsay in the first place (". . . as they say"), is quelled by this man who dictates with such authority the meanings and efficacy of words.

Gallaher's discourse has mastered Chandler's—not a particularly grand feat, since Chandler habitually thinks of himself in the terms described by the discourses of others. (He can imagine his future success as a poet only by imagining the words the English critics might evolve to describe his Celtic-twilight poetry.) But Gallaher too has a discourse that the story presents as being easily mastered. Here, for example, mediated through Joyce's free indirect style, is Gallaher's description of life abroad:

> Ignatius Gallaher puffed thoughtfully at his cigar and then, in a calm historian's tone, he proceeded to sketch for his friend some pictures of the corruption which was rife abroad. He summarised the vices of many capitals and seemed inclined to award the palm to Berlin. Some things he could not vouch for (his friends had told him), but of others he had had personal experience. He spared neither rank nor caste. He revealed many of the secrets of religious houses on the Continent and described some of the practices which were fashionable in high society and ended by telling, with details, a story about an English duchess—a story which he knew to be true. Little Chandler was astonished. (*D*, 78)

The thoughtful puff at the cigar (compare the dramatic striking of the match in Aeolus, which takes place in the newspaper office that is Gallaher's old stamping grounds); the denomination of the "corruption" as "rife"; the cosmopolitan pause before the journalistic "awarding the palm" to Berlin; the soft-porn stories of nuns and duchessess—every cliché reinforces the sense of Gallaher's vulgar parade of noblesse oblige. The passage is humorous because it mocks by imitation, and mockery is so aggressive and effective a form of humor because it seems to reduce another's discourse to a relatively simple and knowable code.

Free indirect style in *Dubliners* reveals the limitations of a character's discourse while showing at the same time the character's blithe comfort within that discourse. The technique works in many of these stories to create a war between discourses, in which one character seeks to dominate another by demonstrating a superior description—hence knowledge—of the world. "An Encounter" is about the relationship between the two discourses we can hear in the following sentence: "Mahony said it would be right skit to run away to sea on one of those big ships and even I, looking at the high masts, saw, or imagined, the geography which had been scantily dosed to me at school gradually taking substance under my eyes" (*D,* 23). Both Farrington and Alleyne in "Counterparts" sneeringly mimic the speech and accent of the other; they know that to mimic is to reduce and to control. Most complexly of all, Gabriel Conroy labors all evening to demonstrate his superiority to and facility with various forms of discourse, none of which he quite succeeds in mastering: noblesse oblige (every Dubliner's dream) with Lily, banter with Molly Ivors, assumed dongiovannism with his wife. None of these ploys quite works, and it turns out that Gabriel has no confident voice of his own. His dilemma is to be taken up by other characters later in *Ulysses.*

Stephen Dedalus in the *Portrait* experiences, exactly, the obverse of this discovery of one's voicelessness. The chapter-by-chapter progression of this novel shows Stephen mastering more and more complex forms of speech; every new realm of experience presents itself as a new language to be acquired; even a prostitute's lips pressed upon his own seem to him "the vehicle of a vague speech" (*P,* 101). Moreover, the book is celebratory of Stephen's ability not only to master but then to escape limiting discourses. In one passage, which has always seemed to me the least distanced paragraph in *Portrait,* the passage in which one feels authorial "authority" backing Stephen more than anywhere else in the book, Joyce gives us a Stephen who has successfully resisted "the constant voices of his father and of his masters, urging him to be a gentleman above all things and urging him to be a good catholic above all things" as well as other voices, one of which bids him "be true to his country and help to raise up her fallen language and tradition" (*P,* 83–84). We later see in a more fully dramatized form this escape from the discourse of others when Stephen stands aside from competition with the discourses of MacCann and Davin in the final chapter. At the end, Stephen finds his own voice in the journal that constitutes the closing pages of the novel. He feels himself controlled only by that large discourse of the English language (*home, Christ, ale, master*), in whose shadow his soul frets. This is all before Paris and before Buck Mulligan.

Ulysses brings together the hero of *Portrait* and the dramatis personae of *Dubliners,* and it plunges Stephen Dedalus into an acute form of the battle of discourses to be found in the short stories. Paris has had its effect upon Stephen, in part simply by encouraging that predilection for the polyglot which was already becoming clear in him near the end of *Portrait.* Paris has created the Frenchified Stephen of *Ulysses,* with his Latin quarter hat, but it also seems to have released all his polylingual powers as well as an anxiety at what Bakhtin has called polyglossia, the polyglot's awareness of the inadequacy and relativity of any single language-system.[1] Post-Paris Stephen, with his *naturlich,* his *oinopa ponton,* his *maestro di color che sanno,* his *frate porcospino,* as well as his *Lui, c'est moi,* is lost in a welter of discourses and wishing he had land under his feet. And now Stephen finds himself living with a man who seems to need no land under his feet, who in fact is a powerful swimmer, and who is a tirelessly inventive and protean talker. We need only read Mulligan's conversation over breakfast with Stephen and Haines to understand why Stephen feels such panic and hatred in his presence. Mulligan is Stephen's Gallaher, not because he is in control of one dominant discourse, but because he seems capable of mastering *so many* discourses (he absolutely preempts the aesthetic Swinburne-Nietzsche line), and the intimidating insouciance of Mulligan's manner effectively silences Stephen. Mulligan has confidence, presence, and, to Stephen's knuckle-gnawing grief, authority. He can parody and trivialize Stephen's Shakespeare-theory and have Haines believe him: he has this kind of authority. And, much more importantly, Mulligan has immense authority within Stephen's own mind, where his strong, taunting voice echoes all day.

Mulligan wields such almost magical power because he is the catalyst that has brought to completion the destabilizing process begun in Stephen by his experience of Paris and the death of his mother. It took Mulligan to complete the process because Mulligan himself is a destabilized play of voices, offering, with a cynical Cheshire-cat smile, the principle that no voice or discourse is really important. For Mulligan, all that is real is the mocking smile itself, left suspended derisively in the air. And the truth is that Stephen must come to agree that Mulligan is in some way right, even as he rejects Mulligan's solution of mockery. That is why, in one of the most important Homeric details of the book, Mulligan is the equivalent of Scylla, the danger Stephen-Ulysses has to steer toward and then escape.

In the following few lines from Proteus, Stephen remembers three phrases of Mulligan's from earlier in the day, and they initiate a monologue—a dialogue, rather, or even a mini-drama—in which Stephen talks back and forth to himself and effectively finds it impossible to grant faith to any stance, any single voice that exists in his head:

> My Latin quarter hat. God, we simply must dress the character. I want puce gloves. You were a student, weren't you? Of what in the other devil's name? Paysayenn, P. C. N., you know: *physiques, chimiques et naturelles.* Aha. Eating your groatsworth of *mou en civet,* fleshpots of Egypt, elbowed by belching cabmen. Just say in the most natural tone: when I was in Paris, *boul' Mich',* I used to. (*U,* 3.174–79)

A quality that recent critics have found in the text of *Ulysses* is here grounded in the mind of Stephen Dedalus. Stephen can find no "metalanguage" within his own consciousness. He is aware of the fragility of every statement he makes and the tenuousness of every stance he assumes because of the reflection that his own internalized Mulligan shows him in a mocking mirror.[2]

"The mockery of it," says Mulligan on the first full page of *Ulysses:* he opens the book with a mock mass, and he performs a fair mock-Synge and mock-Yeats in the library scene. And that particularly aggressive form of mockery, the mockery of the jeer and jibe, extends far beyond Mulligan in *Ulysses* and is indeed something of a Dublin tic: think of Martin Cunningham and (the report of) Paddy Leonard taking off Tom Kernan or Simon Dedalus doing the Goulding family or (in Bloom's memory) doing Larry O'Rourke. Think of the newsboys taking off Bloom's walk and the boots in the Ormond responding to Miss Douce: "Imperthnthn thnthnthn" (*U,* 11.100). Mockery in all these cases is an act of aggression, an effort to make ridicule manifest. Compulsive mockery—and foremost among the book's compulsive mockers is Mulligan—is the signature of the frustrated and impotent and seems, in Joyce's work, the terrible Scylla for all the Irish. The compulsive mocker is still chained to the object of his scorn: there is something servile in this mockery. (Recall the linkage between these qualities in the description of Lenehan in "Two Gallants": "A shade of mockery relieved the servility of his manner" [*D,*52].) This insight of Joyce's accounts in part for the peculiar treatment of politics in *Ulysses.* The major form of political feeling exposed in the book is, precisely, the Citizen's luxuriating in his impotent mockery which is a form of bondage to the object of his hatred. And Joyce's perception also explains why Mulligan looms so large as Stephen's bogeyman. Not only does Mulligan mock Haines even as he envies his Oxford manner; vis-a-vis Stephen, Mulligan is envious of artistic power and therefore composes ditties and pastiches to trivialize art and bring it low. Ah, the mockery of it.[3]

It is worth remembering that Yeats was meditating upon the Irish penchant for mockery during the time that Joyce was bringing *Ulysses* to a close. Thoughts upon the uses of mockery (and, secondarily, upon his own fear of mockery)—thoughts never very far from Yeats's poems—are absolutely central to the magnificent "Nineteen Hundred and Nineteen," which presents a Yeatsian version of Stephen's dilemma. The bitter ironies following upon failed idealism; the desire for some cold-eyed knowledge beyond irony, some transcendent desolate heaven; the collapse of that superhuman effort into the malice of all-too-human mockery; the perception of mockery itself as an inauthentic superiority, a superiority of bad faith—the poem offers up a cold-heaven, bleak version of the polyphony of voices and attitudes in Stephen's head. And both Stephen and Joyce, though in different ways, devise an idea of voice or discourse that is a radical extension of the polyphonic form of the poems that Yeats was writing and would gather together in *The Tower:* for Yeats, for Stephen and for Joyce, the work of art comes to be conceived of as a panoply of discourses arrayed beneath a hypothetical ultimate discourse—"hypothetical" because it is unattainable. For Yeats, that ultimate discourse, which could master all other discourses, had a metaphysical reality undiscoverable in life because it was the knowledge of Byzantium, the knowledge of the afterlife, disdaining all mere complexities. To understand Joyce's rejection of an ultimate discourse (except perhaps as a hypothetical construct), we must first look at the still-evolving thought of Stephen Dedalus, who has not yet reached that point.

In *Ulysses,* Stephen thinks several times of the notion of the Great Memory, the great universal storehouse where all that has been thought and said is recorded and remembered. Recalling the pathos of his mother's souvenirs of her youth, her tasseled dancecards and her memories of old Royce in *Turko the Terrible,* he muses that all those tokens of her past are now "Folded away in the memory of nature" (*U,* 1.265). Later, amid the rhetorics of Aeolus, he thinks of O'Connell's speeches for repeal of the union in the 1840s and of the mystical place where O'Connell's wind-scattered words still exist: "Akasic records of all that ever anywhere wherever was" (*U,* 7.882–83). Stephen recalls the Great Memory, not because he has a Yeatsian belief in the *Spiritus Mundi* but because the Great Memory is an image of his remembering soul, the form of forms, the form that contains the forms of all that he has perceived and experienced. And the soul (in Stephen's Aristotelian terminology) is capable not only of receiving the forms of the things it experiences but, in its ultimate act, of comprehending those forms in one act of understanding which is an act of self-understanding. That is the endpoint of Stephen's striving: "Thought is the thought of thought. Tranquil brightness. The soul is in a manner all that is: the soul is the form of forms. Tranquility sudden, vast, candescent: form of forms" (*U,* 2.74–76).

And here, we realize, we are in the presence of Stephen's idea of an ultimate discourse. Stephen posits a future Stephen who will one day know the Truth, who will have arrived at some attitude of equanimity toward himself of which he is still, today, incapable. (It is the dream of the young. We may recall Lily Briscoe's dismay in *To the Lighthouse* that at age forty the muddle still has not disappeared. But we really need not go outside *Ulysses,* of course: the example of Bloom is an ample reminder that young kinesis never gives way completely to mature stasis.) His anticipation of such a future all-knowing self is especially evident in Scylla and Charybdis, where he virtually predicts the composition of the book we are reading: "So in the future, the sister of the past, I may see myself as I sit here now but by reflection from that which then I shall be" (*U,* 9.383–85). Elsewhere in the same chapter, as he listens to discussion of a volume of young poets' verse that will not include the poems of Stephen Dedalus, he dictates to himself: "See this. Remember" (*U,* 9.294). Another scene has been stored away in the Great Memory, to be selected out and used years later. Thus, perhaps with some vagueness, Stephen characterizes his own future knowledge as understanding and transcending his present experience of anxiety. That future, superior understanding will itself be the ultimate discourse, a magical set of terms we might call maturity, that will clarify and redeem his life.

It is tempting to conjecture that Joyce himself began *Ulysses* with an idea about discourses rather like Stephen's. In the opening chapters of *Ulysses,* the interior monologues of Stephen and Bloom and the dozens of other competing discourses are set against the supple, meticulous "initial style," which in the opening chapters seems to function as the book's ultimate discourse. This third-person attendant to the characters' interior monologues and dialogue is extraordinarily, famously adept at conveying narrative information in free indirect discourse. In Calypso it can do this:

> His hand accepted the moist tender gland and slid it into a sidepocket. Then it fetched up three coins from his trousers' pocket and laid them on the rubber prickles. They lay, were read quickly and quickly slid, disc by disc, into the till. (*U,* 4.181–84)

And, as late as Wandering Rocks, it can do this:

> A tiny yawn opened the mouth of the wife of the gentleman with the glasses. She raised her small gloved fist, yawned ever so gently, tiptapping her small gloved fist on her opening mouth and smiled tinily, sweetly. (*U,* 10.125–27)

The great authority of this style derives from its slightly obtrusive elegance, the precision of its notation of gesture, and, as is especially clear in the second passage, its effortless absorption of the tonalities of the characters within its immediate vicinity.[4] It is even more tempting to see this entirely confident because entirely adequate initial style as the very voice that Stephen desires for himself; for Stephen represents the will toward Olympian authorial power, and the initial style impresses with how much it *knows,* how much it has observed: again and again, it records gestures we have never before seen set down on paper. The Stephen who posits the nail-paring God-like author of the *Portrait* is, after all, still alive in *Ulysses,* seeking some place to stand and imaginatively rule over experience. But just when we have begun to formulate the theory that this style is something like the telos toward which Stephen is headed, Joyce alters the rules of the game: just when Stephen finishes his Shakespeare-theory, the book undergoes a profound change.

In his examination of Joyce's composition of *Ulysses,* Michael Groden helps us see how crucial to Joyce was the completion of Scylla and Charybdis. Joyce at one time hoped to finish *Ulysses* in 1918, but by the end of that year he had finished only half the book's chapters and far less than half the completed book's pages. Nevertheless, he had completed *something.* As Groden tells us, "On the last page of 'Scylla and Charybdis' he wrote 'End of First Part of "Ulysses" ' and the date, 'New Year's Eve 1918' . . . , as if to indicate that one phase of *Ulysses* was ending and something new was about to begin."[5] What was finished in 1918 was the great effort of the initial style, the style that seems to imply an author something like a mature Stephen-Shakespeare. Then, all changes, and, after the entr'acte of "Wandering Rocks," the radical chapter-by-chapter metamorphoses of style usurp the narration of the novel.[6]

That usurpation is the most notable formal characteristic of *Ulysses,* and it constitutes the most momentous change that ever took place in Joyce's conception of his art: after these new styles take over, the composition of *Finnegans Wake* seems to become virtually an inevitability. There is no doubt that the change in conception took place as a result of a long meditation of Joyce's upon the nature of language and narrative authority—a meditation that seems implicit in Joyce's work from "The Sisters" through *Finnegans Wake.* I wish now to propose that Joyce reached the critical point in this meditation and changed the stylistic nature of *Ulysses,* not simply because that meditation, of its own forward momentum, reached a great crisis in 1918 or 1919, but because the very subject-matter and dramatis personae of *Ulysses* brought him to that point. I wish to propose, in short, that the two things *Ulysses* is "about"—its novelistic concern with character and plot on one hand and its metanovelistic concern with narrative authority on the other—have more to do with one another than we have lately thought. If the initial style is the projected ultimate discourse of Stephen Dedalus, the multiple styles of the second half of the book are extrapolations from Joyce's discovery of the character of Leopold Bloom.[7]

Stephen desperately wants an assured voice of his own because he is so acutely aware of the voices of others crowding out everything else in his consciousness. He fears the mockery and intimidation of those other voices, he is uneasy that his gestures are only imitations of the gestures of others, and he seems to dread that his very life is a sort of plagiarism of other lives already lived. "Whom were you trying to walk like?" he asks himself on the beach, and a few minutes later he admonishes himself, "That is Kevin Egan's movement I made . . ." (*U,* 3.184, 438–39). He can hear (and other characters hear this too) that he speaks with his father's voice, and he doesn't like that. It is not surprising that when this young man writes a poem he plagiarizes from Douglas Hyde, or that when he expounds his Shakespeare-theory, his "voice" is a tissue of quotations. Stephen's desire to make a voice, to hammer out an authoritative, persuasive personal discourse, is intense.

Such a desire is very weak in Bloom, who, as Fritz Senn has been the most skillful at showing, is unlike most Joycean male Dubliners in having no strong, characteristic spoken idiom.[8] His interior monologues have the indelible Bloomian imprint, but when he comes to speech he is something of a muff. Bloom is not really a member of the male tribe that creates the brilliant Dublin argot, nor does he have the necessary brassiness for speaking it. Probably the best of many examples of his relative incapacity is his funny, lame attempt to tell the story of Reuben J. and the son in Hades, when Martin Cunningham rudely—but, for the sake of the story, mercifully—intrudes to give the narration a much-needed oiling. Martin steals most of the story from Bloom, and when Bloom tries to reinsert himself into the narration at the end, Simon steals the whole show by proffering the punchline:

> —Isn't it awfully good, Mr. Bloom said eagerly.
> —One and eightpence too much, Mr. Dedalus said drily. (*U,* 6.290–91)

Imagine Stephen's reaction to having his story stolen by one listener and capped by another: "Hast thou found me, O mine enemy?" would not even begin to express his exasperation. Imagine that, and then notice how Bloom responds a couple of hours later, when he remembers Simon's capping remark: "One and eightpence too much. Hhhhm. It's the droll way he comes out with the things. Knows how to tell a story too" (*U,* 8.53–55). Without even trying to describe the powers that so often enable Bloom to escape rancor and resentment ("a good man," Joyce called him) let us simply note for the moment Bloom's unruffled ability to admire a turn of phrase and a narrative method.

Bloom's attitude—curious, diffident, appreciative—toward the discourse of others is especially clear in his many acts of reading during the day, acts in which he is strikingly aware of the textuality of what he is reading. (He is far more aware of the textuality of written language than Stephen on this particular day. The comparison of course is skewed by the fact that Stephen reads so little on 16 June: his glasses, remember, are broken. When he does read, at the bookcart in "Wandering Rocks," he characteristically reflects that even reading itself is somehow a repetition, a plagiarism: "Thumbed pages: read and read. Who has passed here before me?" [*U,* 10.845–46].) When Bloom reads, he moves constantly into and out of the text, regarding it alternately as a transparent window opening onto a world of content and as an opaque object, a textual medium interesting to consider in itself. This tendency is no doubt heightened by his being a newspaper man and an ad man, but it seems deeply embedded in his temperament anyway. In Dlugacz's, reading the planting company prospectus, he is aware of the transparent language, the accompanying picture, the paper itself: "He held the page from him: interesting: read it nearer, the title, the blurred cropping cattle, the page rustling" (*U,* 4.157–58). Later, in the funeral-carriage, he will be alternately aware of a list of names on the obituary page and of "Inked characters fast fading on the frayed breaking paper" (*U,* 6.160). His attention to textuality is reinforced by a very strong habit he has when a printed or written page is before him: he is a great re-reader. He usually scans first and then reads more closely (as with the planting company prospectus or Martha's letter); in the early chapters his eyes move over *Matcham's Masterstroke* three times, and he reads Milly's letter four times. Bloom re-reads, not simply in order to be certain that he has absorbed information but just as often to adjust himself to the reading and to appraise it as a text. (He is drawn to texts in something like the same way he is drawn to the clothed bodies of women: he alternates between the naive surrender to desire and an equally pleasurable musing over the media that solicit and engage his attention—words, or details of clothing. Reading newspapers or women, Bloom enjoys the pleasures of fetishism.) Here is Bloom the critic in the jakes:

> It did not move or touch him but it was something quick and neat. . . . Smart. He glanced back through what he had read and, while feeling his water flow quietly, he envied kindly Mr. Beaufoy who had written it and received payment of three pounds, thirteen and six. (*U,* 4.511–17)

Kind envy: not bad as a description of Bloom's response to other Dubliners who draw profit (laughter; three pounds, thirteen and six) from their more capable and more public ways with words. Bloom does not hanker after an ultimate discourse; he has instead a wry, curious, observant play of mind that is attentive to discourse and is usually unthreatened when the discourse is superior to his own.

What happens, though, when those other forms of discourse become more openly antagonistic toward Bloom? How do his mental habits enable him to cope with mockery? There are mocking discourses aplenty in Cyclops: aggressive, snarling, competitive discourses are at once the subject-matter and the procedure of the whole chapter. There is something of Dublin in excelsis here as Joyce presents a confrontation between city and hero; it is rather as if Gabriel Conroy's after-dinner speech were to be answered by hoots and catcalls all up and down the table. To the non-Irish reader—to *this* non-Irish reader at any rate—Cyclops is the most Irish chapter in the book or, rather, virtually a parody of what Joyce usually presents as "Irish," in its competition of voices, each voice brilliantly and violently imposing a point of view—very often through mockery—and each voice also fretting under the consciousness of being itself the target of other mockers. The virulent power of the Citizen's rhetoric is the sign of a subjection that the rhetoric itself seeks to deny but only intensifies, for the whole chapter is about the complicitous nature of mocking hatred, which only rivets more securely the hater to the hated object. And, over the heads of the characters, the "gigantic" narrator, a sort of impassive parody-producing machine, constantly destabilizes the scene by offering mocking echoes of the characters' "sincere" statements. Everyone in the scene is in *the* paradigmatic Joycean dilemma: each character stands, with his own discourse, in the presence of another, mocking discourse.

How does Bloom respond? He is of course the target of multiple mockeries; he is being Ignatius Gallaher'd from all sides—outside his awareness by the two narrators, in his presence by the Citizen and company, and within his own consciousness by Boylan (" . . . hated and persecuted. Also now. This very moment. This very instant"). He for awhile keeps his distance from the Citizen's conversation with his cronies by treating the conversation as a discourse to be mused over and tested by reason. Rower's heart, the natural phenomenon of a hanged man's erection, the universality of military discipline—those are some of Herr Professor Luitpold Blumenduft's well-observed but of course howlingly inappropriate footnotes added to the conversation in the bar. There, although on edge, is your usual Bloom, skeptical, curious, two-eyed. But, finally, only so many of the Citizen's increasingly barbed innuendos can be endured.

There is nothing more well-observed in Joyce's sharp-eyed fiction than his treatment of a character's being drawn into the competition of argument: think of Simon and Mr. Casey feigning to ignore Dante's remarks at the Christmas dinner-table or think yet one more time of Chandler for awhile refraining from responding to Gallaher's patronizing remarks. Then the pose of indifference becomes insupportable, and the character turns upon his heckler and becomes locked in dialectical combat. Something rather different from this happens to Bloom in Cyclops.

> —Those are nice things, says the citizen, coming over here to Ireland filling the country with bugs.
> So Bloom lets on he heard nothing. . . . (*U,* 12.1141–43)

Thus is a taunt launched forth into the obscure murk of Barney Kiernan's. Bloom at first seems to refuse a response, but he can't fully resist. More than two pages after the original taunt, he replies, with the same pretense as the Citizen's, that he is addressing absolutely no one in particular:

> —Some people, says Bloom, can see the mote in others' eyes but they can't see the beam in their own.
> —*Raimeis,* says the citizen. There's no-one as blind as the fellow that won't see, if you know what that means. (*U,* 12.1237–40)

Does Bloom know he is quoting Christ? Very probably, for he has had some time to consider an answer, and it is likely that, for once, he has come up with a felicitous phrase to speak. In Aeolus he fumbled for some time over what he should have said to Menton at the cemetery (*U,* 7.171–73). In this moment of Cyclops, he seems to wait until the happy phrase comes. (Could even Bloom, with this much time to think, mistake the source of the phrase with that striking, unique "mote/beam" locution?) Bloom does not respond directly to the Citizen; he tries instead to fracture the basic vocabulary of the Citizen's discourse by responding to the Christian anti-Semite in the words of Christ. And that remains his strategy for the rest of the scene, as he first speaks, gamely if lamely, in defense of love and then in parting tries to unsettle the Citizen's anti-Semitic discourse completely with reminders of Christ's origins in Judaism.(By now, verbal felicity is quite out the window, as Bloom tries to bring in Christ's uncle.)

Bloom engages in argument with the Citizen by refusing to engage, by refusing to accept the Citizen's terms of discourse—by, in short, refusing to grant him authority. Bloom is not of Hungarian descent for nothing: this refusal to acknowledge unjust authority *is* exactly the "Hungarian system" Martin Cunningham speaks of in Cyclops.[9] The Citizen is so painfully stung, not because Bloom has argued with him (the Citizen deeply, almost erotically *desires* an argument and Bloom will not oblige him), but because Bloom's blurted-out "Christ was a jew like me" destroys the opposition upon which the Citizen's whole discourse is based. Moreover, later in the day, when Bloom in a retrospective arrangement looks back upon this scene, he dissolves the Citizen's dialectic of hatred even further: "Look at it other way round. Not so bad then. Perhaps not to hurt he meant. Three cheers for Israel. Three cheers for the sister-in-law he hawked about, three fangs in her mouth" (*U,* 13.1219–22). Bloom's dislike of the Citizen is clearly there in that final phrase of *Schadenfreude,* but it is counterbalanced by curiosity about the Citizen, even by a faint attempt to apologize for him. Here we are close to a central component of Bloom that could be fully clarified only if we were approaching him from a more purely psychological perspective: his readiness to identify with his enemies and his mockers.[10] For my purposes, I want to stress only the peculiarly liberating effects of that identification, as it operates to break down the circuit of antagonism. The play of mind that allows Bloom a curious and detached critical attention to discourse makes him skeptical of any authority—even his own—and so releases him from the deadly, closed dialectic of mockery.

Just a few pages before Bloom's bemused reconsideration of the Citizen in Nausicaa (where his post-orgasmic languor no doubt encourages this relatively anxiety-free identification with the Other), he has a similar moment as he reflects upon a stroller on the beach: "Walk after him now make him awkward like those newsboys me today. Still you learn something. See ourselves as others see us" (*U,* 13.1056–58). This last phrase, from Burns, is evidently something of a favorite of Bloom's, since he has quoted it earlier (*U,* 8.662). It is the motto of a consciousness that frees itself from mockery precisely by giving partial assent to the mocker's point of view. The occupational hazard of this form of consciousness is a certain want of confidence and self-esteem, a want of faith in its own authority because it constantly experiences the relativity of personal authority by projecting itself into the attitudes of others. One of the strengths of this consciousness is that it alone of the consciousnesses registered in *Ulysses* seems capable of thinking, as everyone stands silent around the grave into which Paddy Dignam's coffin has just been lowered: "If we were all suddenly somebody else" (*U,* 6.836).

Bloom's mind contains an attitude toward discourse that, extrapolated, gives rise to the second half of *Ulysses,* and I would even guess that the extraordinary experience of creating Bloom (think of making Bloom up!) led Joyce to the discovery of how his book would continue. Stephen, as I have proposed, imagines something for himself very like the book's initial style. He wants a future knowledge that will set today's events in the lucid, all-revealing light of pure understanding. In such an effort as his "Parable of the Plums" he seems intent upon finding some language to be the stylistic equivalent of that knowledge (and he is at least in part successful).

Even his conversation often strives for a marmoreal, aphoristic quality: "You behold in me, Stephen said with grim displeasure, a horrible example of free thought" (*U,* 1.625–26); "I fear those big words, Stephen said, which make us so unhappy" (*U* 2.264). These are sentences every word of which has been rung on a mental counter; these words are pre-tested to be mockery-proof. (Do we not imagine them to have been stored up, as Stephen stores up his "disappointed bridge" for Haines?) Ah, how sensitive this young man is to mockery, and how he longs to transcend it.

It is possible that Joyce originally set out to show his own style transcending all mockery, as if free indirect style could mimic and yet through its very purity escape the antagonism that consistently hovers around mimicry. If all the novel had been written in that style, *Ulysses* would be the greatest Flaubertian novel ever written, its style claiming for itself an Olympian calm, but its implied aesthetic rationale would reveal that the novel itself was still caught up in a battle of mockeries. When Joyce gave his first novel a title that called attention to its autobiographical nature, the very last words—"Dublin 1904/Trieste 1914"—had the implication that those ten years account for the gap between the still-callow young hero and the mature, understanding artist: by living through those ten years, the author now comprehends and controls the past. *Ulysses* up through Scylla and Charybdis (and especially *in* Scylla and Charybdis) seems to be following the same plan. But all is changed by Joyce's deeper, more searching portrayal of mockery in *Ulysses.* The *Portrait* at one point asks us to accept that Stephen "bore no malice now to those who had tormented him. . . . Even that night as he stumbled homewards along Jones's Road he had felt that some power was divesting him of that suddenwoven anger as easily as a fruit is divested of its soft ripe peel" (*P,* 82). This is more a description of what an angry person wants his enemies to feel than it is a convincing presentation of an overcoming of rancor.[11] *Ulysses* makes Stephen morbidly sensitive to mockery and denies him the ease of that earlier immunity to anger and resentment as it places him at once in the presence of Buck Mulligan. The admirably honest opening of *Ulysses* at once makes Mulligan's mockery a central problem—in a way altogether different from the too-easily transcended taunts of the *Portrait.* Were *Ulysses* to continue with its initial style to the end, its own strategy of mockery and revenge would lie revealed: the young man in the novel who anticipates the novel we are reading may have been reviled and scorned in 1904 ("Ten years, he said, chewing and laughing. He is going to write something in ten years" [*U,* 10.1089–90]), but see how he has turned the light of understanding back upon those persecutors in 1922! This much could be inferred from the text itself, quite without our ever knowing of Gogarty, say, or of Messrs. Rumbold, Bennett, Compton, and Carr. The novel would then be what indeed, to a lesser degree, it still is: an attempt to play the final card in the game of mockery, as the book achieves its superiority by mastering all the subsidiary discourses of Dublin.

The full discovery of Bloom at least helped to alleviate Joyce's dilemma. Bloom saves Joyce from Stephen not only because of the evident attractiveness and variety of Bloom, but also because Bloom is content not to win, content not to have the one last word. The second half of *Ulysses* thus shows Joyce letting go of one sort of power: the book gives up its initial style and fiddles with new ways of writing, as if it were setting out to explore that Bloomian musing at the cemetery, "If we were all suddenly somebody else." The book deprives us of the lucidity it at first seemed to proffer as it places us in a competition of discourses, with no hope of our ever regaining even the semblance of an ultimate discourse. Bloom ousts Mulligan, not only by taking Stephen's arm in Eumaeus as Mulligan took it in Telemachus, but also by suggesting through his example a replacement of Stephen's fear of mockery with some actual acceptance of mockery and a curious-minded attraction to the discourses of others.

That is my main contention, but I must admit that it needs a final qualifier. This cannot be the total view of *Ulysses;* this view is a little too sweet. Joyce creates Bloom and in creating him discovers a new attitude toward discourse, but Bloom is finally put back into the service of Stephen Dedalus. (This is one thing that the meeting of Stephen and Bloom *means.*) When, late in Oxen of the Sun, the Carlylean voice addresses Theodore Purefoy, it calls him "the remarkablest progenitor barring none in this chaffering allincluding most farraginous chronicle" (*U,* 14.1411–12). This voice makes the claim that the book containing it is "allincluding," as if *Ulysses* actually *were* equivalent to the akasic records holding *all* the discourses of Dublin. The artistic will to power of Stephen Dedalus and the wry humility of Bloom constitute the inescapable dialectic of Joyce's art in *Ulysses.* In his great novel Joyce sought some way out of competition and the battle for mastery; nevertheless, he could not resist showing that he was the master of more discourses than all the other Dubliners put together.

Notes

1. The great relevance of Bakhtin's "dialogism" to Joyce's narratives, especially *Ulysses* and *Finnegans Wake,* has not yet received the major attention it deserves. Let it suffice here to mention how Bakhtin's description of the mentality that produced a "novelistic" consciousness among Roman writers aware of literary Greek is remarkably like Joyce's depiction of an Irishman's attitude toward literary English. "Only polyglossia fully frees consciousness from the tyranny of its own language and its own myth of language. Parodic-travestying forms flourish under these conditions, and only in this milieu are they capable of being elevated to completely new ideological heights." And again, in a passage that seems to me very accurate as a description of certain dilemmas of the Anglo-Irish writer: "It was extremely charac-

teristic for the literary Roman to perceive all of language, from top to bottom, as style—a conception of language that is somewhat cold and 'exteriorizing.' Speaking as well as writing, the Roman *stylized,* and not without a certain cold sense of alienation from his own language" (Mikhail M. Bakhtin, "From the Prehistory of Novelistic Discourse," in *The Dialogic Imagination,* ed. Michael Holquist, trans. Caryl Emerson and Michael Holquist [Austin and London: University of Texas Press, 1981], 61, 62–63).

Other formulations of Bakhtin's—for example, that the novel appears when the epic can no longer be looked upon without humor—make him a critic potentially invaluable for an analysis of Joyce's work. Interestingly, however, Bakhtin seems to have had little use for that work itself; in *Problems of Dostoevsky's Poetics* (ed. and trans. Caryl Emerson [Minneapolis: University of Minnesota Press, 1984]), his Marxism is uncharacteristically reductive and predictable as he approvingly quotes another critic's description of "the degenerate decadent psychologism of Proust or Joyce" (37).

2. See in particular Colin MacCabe, *James Joyce and the Revolution of the Word* (New York: Barnes & Noble, 1979), chap. 2.

3. It is interesting to find this ambivalence between mockery and artistic aspiration in the work of Gogarty himself. A fascinating instance is "Leda and the Swan," a poem Gogarty first published in *Selected Poems* (1933). The poem is a jeu d'esprit (what else would Gogarty make of copulation between a lady and a bird? we already know what Mulligan can do with *that* subject), but Gogarty doesn't seem quite willing to leave it at that. No poem entitled "Leda and the Swan" could possibly be published by an Irishman in 1933 without courting comparison with Yeats (even though Gogarty apparently claimed that his poem was written before Yeats's), and there is something like an echoing of Yeats in Gogarty's closing stanza, which ends—as Yeats's sonnet ends—with a musing rhetorical question:

When the hyacinthine
    Eggs were in the basket,—
Blue as at the whiteness
    Where a cloud begins:
Who would dream there lay there
    All that Trojan brightness;
Agamemnon murdered;
    And the mighty twins?

The poem careens between facetiousness and "seriousness."

4. The initial style has been the subject of intense scrutiny in recent years. See in particular Hugh Kenner's *Joyce's Voices* (Berkeley and Los Angeles: University of California Press, 1978), in the second chapter of which he proposes his famous Uncle Charles Principle (which is in reality free indirect style); his *Ulysses* (London: Allen and Unwin, 1980), in which he impressively extends the argument of the previous book; chap. 2 of Colin MacCabe's work already cited; Shari Benstock's "Who Killed Cock Robin? The Sources of Free Indirect Style in *Ulysses,*" *Style* 14 (1980): 259–73; chap. 1 and 2 of Karen Lawrence's *The Odyssey of Style in* Ulysses (Princeton: Princeton University Press, 1981); and the long section on *Ulysses* in John Paul Riquelme's *Teller and Tale in Joyce's Fiction: Oscillating Perspectives* (Baltimore: Johns Hopkins University Press, 1983). MacCabe, Benstock, and Riquelme are especially interested in demonstrating that the diffusion of authorial presence, so obvious late in the book, has already taken place within the initial free indirect style itself.

5. Michael Groden, Ulysses *in Progress* (Princeton: Princeton University Press, 1977), 17.

6. Obviously, the shift from the initial style to the various styles in the latter half of the book is immensely more involved than I express it as being here. Both Groden and Lawrence have written entire books tracing that shift.

7. See the related argument of William B. Warner, "The Play of Fictions and Succession of Styles in *Ulysses,*" *James Joyce Quarterly* 15, 1 (1977): 18–35. Warner writes: "Bloom's play with fictions and use of language in the first half of *Ulysses* prepare for the more exotic gyrations of language in the last nine episodes" (20). See also Robert Storey's "The Argument of *Ulysses,* Reconsidered," *Modern Language Quarterly* 40 (1979): 175–95. Storey writes: "*Ulysses* is the vehicle that effected this imaginative transference of psychic sympathies

[from Stephen to Bloom] for Joyce; I want to argue, in fact, that to a large extent that transference is what *Ulysses* is 'about' " (182).

8. Fritz Senn, "Bloom among the Orators: The Why and the Wherefore and All the Codology," *Irish Renaissance Annual* 1 (1980): 168–90.

9. The question of whether Bloom could have been the source of Arthur Griffith's knowledge of "the Hungarian system" has its own rather acrimonious critical history. See Dominic Manganiello's résumé of the dispute in *Joyce's Politics* (London: Routledge and Kegan Paul, 1980), 121. The important point is not the undecidable question of whether Bloom did indeed speak to Griffith (Manganiello is right that such a happening is not really all that improbable, if we are going to discuss the probabilities of fictional characters meeting historical personages in the first place) but rather the Bloom-Hungary analogy the whole issue raises. Bloom follows a Hungarian policy in refusing to acknowledge the Citizen's authority, and he follows it again when he stays away from home all evening (as the Hungarian representatives stayed away from Vienna) and thereby piques Molly's curiosity. It is of interest to remember that the founding of the Dail Eireann in Dublin in 1919 could be described as an act according to the Hungarian system.

10. Bloom's feelings toward Boylan obviously constitute the clearest example of this identification with the enemy. His most overt identification with Boylan takes place in the unanxious post-orgasmic pages of Nausicaa (not long after his reconsideration of the Citizen that I have quoted), following his thoughts of the sexual allure of women's clothing: "Us too: the tie he wore, his lovely socks and turnedup trousers" (*U*, 13.800–801).

11. I am not necessarily assigning an inadequate psychological sense to Joyce here. It can very well be argued that these words do not show Stephen's actual superiority to anger, but are signs of that chilly affectlessness that begins to grow upon him as he enters adolescence. (To the adolescent Stephen's inability to hate—or to love—compare Gabriel's disarmingly honest thought on the closing page of "The Dead": "He had never felt like that himself towards any woman but he knew that such a feeling must be love.") In *Ulysses* the death of May Dedalus has released in Stephen powerful feelings, formerly repressed, of love and hate that the *Portrait* did not record for the simple reason that they were unavailable to Stephen's consciousness. This sort of back-reading is an instance of a principle very perceptively formulated by Mark Shechner: "What *Ulysses* does is make manifest the subtle thread of irony that is latent in so much of Joyce's previous work, liberating it and giving it a voice of its own" (*Joyce in Nighttown: A Psychoanalytic Inquiry into* Ulysses [Berkeley and Los Angeles: University of California Press, 1974], 186).

Ulysses as a Comic Novel

ZACK BOWEN

Few devotees of Joyce would deny that his last two major works, *Ulysses* and *Finnegans Wake,* were very funny books. In particular, the *Wake,* through linguistic incongruities, parody, and general tone and demeanor, is first of all a hilarious celebration of life. *Ulysses* is a more problematic book in this regard, since many of its readers and commentators over the years have described its dilemmas, its ambiguities, its lack of definitive answers as ultimately posing some of the darkest existential problems facing modern man. Freudians, Marxists, and deconstructionists have painted particularly negative pictures of the basic philosophy or lack of one underlying the book. In a sense, they have confused the novel's lack of a moral purpose of the sort inherent in tragedy with their even grimmer view that any lack of moral direction implies the absence of the generally pleasant sentience that life affords.

It has always bothered me that such a funny and rewarding book as *Ulysses,* a work that ends with the resounding affirmation "Yes," should be seen as an embodiment of hopelessness by so many, when to others like myself it represented such an affirmation of the spirit of life. I do not mean to imply by this that funny things, such as the black humor of post–World War II books, are not essentially as grim and occasionally tragic as the plays referred to in the *Poetics.* However, I do think that *Ulysses* is in the mainstream of comedy, which provides the vital life force of the novel.

This essay will be greatly indebted to the work of Suzanne K. Langer, whose brilliant essay on "The Comic Rhythm" reflects her extraordinary depth and understanding of the relationship of art and human sensibility.[1] Langer's basic proposition is that "the pure sense of life is the underlying feeling of comedy, developed in countless different ways."[2] Comedy reflects a basic biological pattern of life, or life rhythm, which when disrupted tries to restore itself and the natural balance of existence. Langer's examples of a tree growing taller in the shade and a fish assuming new functions with its other fins when part of its tail is bitten off are representative of biological life confronted by obstacles and attempting to restore a balance, the process reflecting the vitality of life itself. Langer associates comedy with the same attempts at renewal and its attendant religious rites that celebrate the bringing of life into balance and emphasize the rhythm of sheer vitality which makes comedy its happy secret. In the same way the comic novel depicts conflicts or dilemmas, resulting from accidents of fate or man's perversions and the attempt at restoring a social, biological, or psychological balance. The revivification, so closely associated with spring, plays no small part in *Ulysses.* Beginning with the choice of date, associated with a new beginning with Nora, Joyce has constructed a novel which has as one of its central propositions the conflict between men and women. This subject, according to Langer, is the greatest and perhaps sole subject of comedy because it is the most universal, humanized, civilized, most primitive and joyful challenge to our existence—self-preservation and self-assertion, whose progress is the comic rhythm. Women are, of course, also at the center of great tragedy: such characters as Jocasta, Gertrude, and perhaps even May Dedalus are to their male counterparts the origins of ambivalent messages representing love, sin, and truth. Contests between the sexes, however, have an attitude of joyful, regenerative sexuality, which is part of the vitality of life. Stephen, as the would-be tragic figure of *Ulysses,* sees women initially as disruptive, as in their role in *Oedipus* and *Hamlet.* Representing sources of sin and guilt, even though passive, they are linked somehow with the temptress of his villanelle. Bloom, the comic center of the novel, is, in fact, engaged in a classic comic contest with Molly, the ultimate affirmation of the vital continuity which Langer refers to as the comic spirit. Molly is both antagonist and affirmer of Bloom's efforts and life. It is Molly's soliloquy in Penelope which finally confirms the fact that the obstacles facing Bloom are all trivial, and she becomes spokesperson for the ultimate common sense which is the hallmark of comedy.

Unlike tragedy, comedy has no agon, no great moral struggle. What aspects of that tragic impulse there are in the book are relegated to the still undeveloped Stephen; his is the moral struggle with the past, with the guilt over his mother, with the great choices of whether to assume the sins of his countrymen and lead them messianically out of bondage. But the tragic spirit is inimicable to the comic hero because comic characters have a morality which is complete, in the sense that their principles are generally clear and coherent enough so that they do not face soul-rending moral decisions. Thus the action in comedies, Langer suggests, derives from the changes of fortune that the comic heroes encounter. Leopold Bloom, from his first discourses with the cat in Calypso through his final reflections in Ithaca, is the ultimate comic hero. His challenges derive from such obstacles on the path of his marital bliss as Blazes Boylan, from such changes in fortune and financial setbacks as his inability to bring about communal kitchens and endowments for infants, and from his seeming inability to appear as a heroic figure to his wife. While Stephen is still engaged in a great search for a moral blueprint for his place in the universe, Bloom proceeds with moral certitude into the void. He will meet his misfortunes with reason, the highest virtue of the human soul, and in a sense emerge victoriously, still combative in a struggle that will never be resolved and for which no ultimate victory is possible.

Thus, even Stephen's position as would-be tragic hero in a bildungsroman search for his personal truth, which initially sets the tone and direction of the novel as a potentially tragic and serious work, must give way to the mundane certitudes and rationality of the central comic figure, Leopold Bloom. In the past Stephen has sought an intellectual answer to his moral dilemmas in an attempt to reconcile the artist and his work to the psychological and physical changes in his environment. His past, bound up in allusions to church, state, and family, a Catholic sense of guilt over sins in relationships with country, father, and mother, has led Stephen to seek an amoral philosophy in an art whose beauty is detached from its maker, an art representing a truth outside the moral or political spheres. This non-didactic truth, which Stephen calls "dramatic," is the kind that can be found only in comedy. Thus, by the time Stephen reaches the state of mind that embraces his new Shakespearean aesthetic theory in *Ulysses,* the relationship of artist to art (of Shakespeare's writing *Hamlet* to free himself of his own personal feelings regarding his cuckolding wife) has become in a sense trivialized by reason.The flippant tone of the narration which mirrors Stephen's mindset in Scylla and Stephen's admission that he doesn't believe his own theory indicate that he realizes that the conjunction of his own plight to Shakespeare's has become more comic than tragic. His forced parallels and altered facts in his presentation to the librarian's company in Scylla begin, for the first time in *Ulysses,* to take on more comic than tragic overtones. It is the Shawn-like spirit of the invading trickster figure, Mulligan, who, in Scylla as in Telemachus, makes all of Stephen's would-be attempts at justifying his own high place in the tragedy of his life appear ludicrous. Mulligan, the debunker, paves the way for Bloom's quiet certitude. The latter's comic, often zany, upside-down way of looking at both life and Molly's rump, his enjoyment of life's vital processes of ingestion and elimination, his ever-present, oft-thwarted sexual drives, his sexual surrogates of ladies' ankles, knickers, and other fetishistic garments and activities, and his pleasant, calm acceptance of masturbation as a substitute for coition, are all like Langer's fish who navigates as nearly as possible with the remaining pectorals and dorsals at his disposal in an attempt to restore nature's balance. If Bloom can't take satisfaction in either traditional societal approbation or financial remuneration for his talent, and if he is no longer the sole or even infrequent proprietor of Molly's body, he nevertheless achieves a measure of satisfaction from his own, more basic bodily functions such as taste, flatulence, and elimination. He derives sensual pleasure not only from self-manipulation but from a host of female fetishistic surrogates. In doing so Bloom has in a curiously comic way become more independent, more able to survive in the often inhospitable environs of dear dirty Dublin.

While Stephen's all-encompassing theories about life and art and *Hamlet* are trivialized in the library scene, Bloom's trivial philosophy and rationality gain importance as natural functions of survival and vitality for the common man. Stephen's vision is trivialized because it has the vitality missing, whereas while Bloom's unique if zany solutions to both his and society's problems seem ridiculous, they nevertheless possess the vital energy that transcends traditional morality and that informs the comic vision, a vision which takes the greatest epic in Western civilization and reduces it to a set of domestic circumstances. The absurdity of the whole idea, with its comic logic, provides the sense that the epic, the past recapitulated in contemporary life, is not tragic, or dark, but if, like our mundane hero, Bloom, we are not carried away, its very paradoxicalness is its salvation. The conjunction of Ithaca and Eccles St. is the source of the comedy that enables us to carry on, to see things in the mundane terms, which, in fact, are more characteristic of our lives than the tragic ones we project on to them. The fear of apocalypses as yet unsuffered, the aggrandizing of our condition into cosmic and tragic terms, which we somehow see as bearing artistic truth is, when reduced by the comic rationality and sense of where we are, rendered laughable by the welter of the mundane things which comprise the vitality of life. *Ulysses* reaffirms that comic sense of vitality.

The novel abounds in testimonials to the comic view of life, in both theme and language. Trivializing the grand and aggrandizing the trivial linguistically as well as thematically is a part of the comic tradition. Joyce, the consummate self-reflexive artist, reproduces himself caricatured in Stephen Dedalus, and he invites comparison to the modern ineffectual epic hero, Leopold Bloom. In doing so, Joyce abandons the tragic mode, because his artistic protagonist ceases to loom larger than life and becomes another stock comic character, another actor living through the trivia of contemporary detail. In a sense, the paradoxical impression the reader is left with is that the everyman in each of us is vital and unique, that the trivial aspects are in fact more rationally and meaningfully heroic than the rantings of tragic heroes caught in self-inflicted moral dilemmas. The audience, lulled into a sense of comic detachment by the possibility that neither Bloom nor Stephen is more noble than themselves, fails initially to identify with either character. It is one of the great ironies of the comic situation. For comedy, with its attention to the trivial in everyday life, really inspires an even closer ultimate identification than the audience feels with its tragic heroes, an identification that we consciously shun, but unconsciously accept.

Thus, when we laugh at the hero's plight and his fumblings, we are assured, without realizing that pity and fear exist, that our own problems are universal, and that we are at least as able to cope with them as the hero is, and finally, that a satisfactory struggle has in itself a measure of sufficiency no matter how badly we bumble our attempts at solutions. If Bloom can be a hero, inviting comparison with Ulysses, then so can we all. If Bloom's life is not so horrible, if his sense of equanimity, his inability to realize that he has lost, somehow makes his ignorance a triumph, it assures us that we, as good as he, might experience something of the same. At the end of the novel Stephen's plight is not resolved anymore than is Bloom's. Comedies do not bring ultimate solutions to life; they depict the vitality in the ongoing struggle.

None of this is meant to imply that Bloom is wholly a buffoon; he is a rational, sensitive, compassionate, humane man. There is so much good about Bloom that an identification with him assures us that we ourselves are better. If he learns nothing, no moral answers from the day's dilemmas, we are assured that because the answers have not come to us we are no more lost than he. If he, like Stephen, wants to feel an identification with the past and the future, then so do we. Like Aeneas leaving burning Troy with his father on one side, his son on the other, we want to be assured of a continuity. That continuity, a source of the comic vitality Langer speaks of, is represented in a number of ways in *Ulysses,* but it is no more apparent than in the father-son theme.

Stephen, like Telemachus, sets out in search of a father figure. While a great deal of philosophical speculation among *Ulysses* critics turns on whether Bloom fulfills the role of Stephen's spiritual father, Bloom, unlike his putative offspring, is searching for a flesh-and-blood son to replace the dead Rudy. Stephen, on the other hand, has already got a real father, Simon Dedalus, a character we see several times during the day, much to our delight, for Simon is a funny man. His aphorisms, his clichés, his exaggerated and comic sense of his own tragic dilemmas, his bombastic railing at his in-laws, and his generally lackadaisical attitude regarding the financial and spiritual support of his family are but a few of the delights making Simon a classic comic character. Stephen's perhaps subconscious and certainly grudging respect for his father's comic presence is manifested in Proteus, when Stephen recites nearly word-for-word an entire litany of Simon's traditional raillery regarding his in-laws. We learn later of the accuracy of Stephen's mimicry when we hear nearly the same words from Simon's own lips. While his comedy is often at others' expense, his own figure is the object of satire. Whether Stephen approves or not,

Simon's excuses, his bombast, his Macawber-like character, provides his son a sense of the comic, the ironic, and the incongruous in life. For Stephen, Simon is certainly no tragic hero wrestling with great moral dilemmas, and consequently Stephen's understanding of his father's shortcomings brings him a great deal closer to accepting the mundane comedy of a father like Bloom than Stephen consciously knows.

The other paternal motifs that augment the central triangle of Simon, Stephen, and Bloom are the *Hamlet* and Holy Trinity motifs on one side and such mundane domestic pairings as Paddy Dignam and Son, Reuben J. Dodd and Son, and W. B. Murphy and Son on the other. The latter all have comic associations. Reuben J. Dodd and Son are the subjects of a joke started by Leopold Bloom and finished by the Shakespeare-father-surrogate, Martin Cunningham, while they are on the way to Dignam's funeral, accompanied by Simon Dedalus, whose genuinely funny line, "One and eightpence too much" (*U,* 6.291) completes the Dodd story. In another comic variation on the paternal motif, the entire company is seated upon sperm-stained seats, the result of love-making in the funeral carriage. The comic incongruity underscores Langer's basic comic thesis. Like most of the essentially comic events in the Hades chapter, the atmosphere, as Bloom speculates, represents life or vitality in the midst of death.

In a way Bloom plays a comic Panza to Stephen's Quixote. While both are funny characters, Panza's simplicity, grubby earthiness, and will to survive provide the realistic vital background for the Don's demented projections. Panza is the mundane father-protector of the idealistic Quixote. One comic key to *Ulysses* lies in the similarly ludicrous father-son conjunction of Stephen and Bloom. Whether or not Stephen is actually looking for inspiration from a surrogate father such as Bloom, Bloom does provide a comic inspiration for the novel as a whole. On the other hand, Bloom will not ask for much from his son-surrogate Stephen, perhaps a chance to make a little money from the joint concert tours of his newfound progeny and his wife. It does not cross Bloom's mind that he could be either subject or object of any potential literary artistry, though Molly certainly sees her role as sexual inspiration figure during her Penelope musings.

W. B. Murphy, one of the great comic characters of modern literature, is another Ulysses-Sinbad traveler with a runaway son, Danny, who left a draper's shop in Cork for a life at sea. Murphy's comic and highly dubious accounts of his own adventures parallel the Odyssean motif and regale both would-be father and son. His comic vitality and the artistry of his fabrications rival those of Odysseus, and underscore the link between the paternal theme and artistic creation, especially when Murphy claims to know Simon personally and then tells a completely phony story about Simon's marksmanship in the Hengler circus in Stockholm.

Bloom's father's suicide, certainly not a comic theme, is overshadowed by Bloom's attachment to the past through his grandfather, Lipoti Virag, whose id in Circe projects a vigorous sensuality in the form of a funny libidinous impulse toward women and sex. He is the patriarchal counterpart to Stephen's paternal predecessor, Simon Dedalus. Fathers and grandfathers, it seems, provide a basis for coping with reality rather than with spiritual dilemmas. They are the mundane Panza figures whose low roads to life supply the comic vitality necessary to survive.

Stephen's initial vision furnishes the framework of the novel, much like his Odyssean counterpart, Telemachus, provides the *medias res* entrance to the *Odyssey* and shapes our expectations of what his father may eventually do. Stephen becomes the architect of *Ulysses,* shaping our expectations of what his father-surrogate might be like, and how Stephen, like Telemachus, will meet his father and the relationship between them will be reestablished. In the comic world of *Ulysses* however, nothing is resolved. The action of the novel is incomplete and ongoing, an experience of the vital continuity of life rather than the completed action of the *Odyssey.* For Bloom is not a father in control, the action is not finished, and the continuity between father and son is subsumed into the greater continuity of mundane events in an everyday work of *Ulysses.*

The comic is a world in which the senseless turns of events are transformed by artistry into a sort of drollery, a world where the plights of the characters invite instant everyday identification and where the crude and the sublime exist side by side. In *Ulysses,* Bloom-Panza provides the comic counterpart to most of Stephen-Quixote's serious, high-artistic vision. In counterpoint to Stephen's deification of art, Bloom's own artistic ventures are of a much lower order. The conjunction of the art work "Matcham's Masterstroke" and Bloom's own artistic production of a turd "just right . . . quick and neat" (*U,* 4.510–12), is confirmed by Bloom's use of the prize titbit as toilet paper, a conjunction, lest we missed it, underscored again in Circe with Beaufoy's exhibiting "a specimen of my maturer work disfigured by the hallmark of the beast" (*U,* 15.844–45). Bloom's own aspirations as an artist writing his experiences in a cabman's shelter are the comic projections of Stephen's own ambitions and perhaps Joyce's own writing of Eumaeus.

Two great comic characters in the book, Leopold Bloom and Buck Mulligan, both serve to debunk or reduce the artistic visions of Stephen Dedalus; Mulligan through irony, satire, and wit in his parodies of Stephen as priest in the beginning, of Dedalus-Christ as artist in "The Ballad of Joking Jesus," and of Stephen as self-reflexive artist in Mulligan's masturbatory version of *Hamlet.* Bloom's commentary, never intended to be a didactic satire on another's work, is a more constructive reduction of the artistic impulse to the lower common denominator of comedy. The final conjunction between the would-be father and would-be artist son is manifested in the crossing of the trajectories of their urinations, a final ironic and genuinely funny comment on their aspirations.

Bloom also fits the traditional comic picture of the spiritual misfit. From Dogberry to lucky Jim comedy has long embraced the concept of the person who simply does not fit into a traditional spiritual-theological system. While his own misfit role is a source of anguish for Stephen, Bloom comfortably looks at the church's power, money, and ludicrousness from a healthy sense of commonplace agnosticism. Bloom is a quasi-Protestant, Catholic, and Jew, fitting no creed and untutored in all, except bits and pieces of Hebraic lore. There is just enough earthy Jewishness in Bloom to cast him as a schlemiel figure, the traditional comic Jewish masochist, an intelligent, yet chronically mistake-making creature who revels in his misery. *Ulysses* is tinged with this bit of ethnic humor, but it is only a part of Bloom's multifaceted makeup. As spiritual misfit, Bloom embodies the traditional comic salvation of the powerless against the powerful, the individual against the social order. In the comic spirit, he operates outside the traditional conventions of religion by seeking as much meaning as possible between the natural poles of birth and death. The vitality of this philosophy embodies his natural religion, so closely akin to the comic spirit. While religion, like tragedy, depends upon the fatalistic, comedy, exemplified by Bloom's approach to religion and the rest of his life, depends upon fortune. He reacts to events as they occur in the day. His life, therefore, is essentially contingent, episodic, and ethnic, the very hallmarks of comedy as outlined by Langer. His schemes for tram lines to the cemetery and social reform are part of both his Jewish and Irish heritage, and his search for a son to replace Rudy is inextricably linked to his Semitic background. His chance meetings with Stephen, coincidental with the birth of Mina Purefoy and the *Hamlet* aesthetic highjinks in the library, are used by Bloom to develop a relationship which spans but a few hours of his life, in a day largely dependent upon such transitory factors as place, time, social conventions, and Bloom's ethnicity both as Irishman and Jew.

Social convention and constraints play a far larger part in comedy than they do in tragedy. Because the characters in a comedy are part of a vital continuity, they are a part of life as it exists rather than acting as reshapers or changers, as tragic heroes do. Comic characters, like the fish and the tree, adapt to existing circumstances and do not affect large changes in the social order. The comic hero's enemy is an uncongenial world in which he shapes or adapts his own fortune. Thus, if *Ulysses* were indeed a comedy, one would not expect the cosmos of Dublin and environs to be radically changed or reshaped. The lack of purposeful action oft cited by early critics would be a flaw in a tragic novel, but it is the norm in a comic one.

As readers of a tragic *Ulysses,* we hope to impart dramatic impact into such trivia as who will get whose breakfast the next morning. But the very ludicrousness of the breakfast question as an answer to tragic problems is funny in itself. Of course nothing much is changed. The question is how Bloom and Stephen cope with existing circumstances and how they change or adapt themselves to meet those circumstances.

Once we have established *Ulysses* as a comic novel, the other features of comedy embodied in it become apparent. As Langer again points out, the laughter in comedy comes about as a result of the totality of the action. Having established itself in a comic milieu, each individual scene produces laughter not merely because it is indigenously funny in itself, but because it is a part of the entire comic action of the work, so that, for instance, Molly's memory of Bloom's suggestion about milking her breasts into his tea in the morning, a mild joke in itself, produces a disproportionate laughter because it is a general part of Bloom's entire comic personality. When we laugh at acts like W. B. Murphy's emptying his bilge beside the cabman's shelter, we are laughing at the whole novel and not merely the immediate action. Comedy sustains itself through its individual elements, and as the audience's awareness of the comic sensibility heightens, each individual comic incident becomes funnier, rather than merely tragically ironic. Thus the final *Yes,* translated by unimaginative or pessimistic critics into *No,* becomes anomalous if it is not an affirmation of life's comic vitality.

Of course it is not merely a string of situations that maintains the comic atmosphere of the novel, but Joyce's whole plethora of comic, particularly linguistic, devices. On the first page Joyce commences with ribald parody, burlesque, and blasphemy to destroy the seriousness and potential tragedy of Stephen's outlook, and continues with increasingly comic linguistic acrobatics from the headlines in the Aeolus chapter, through the Gregorian notation of Scylla, to the musical-comedy world of Dublin in song in Sirens. As the narration itself shifts gears, the comedy increases in Cyclops with its mundane barfly and hyperbolizing narrators jointly trivializing or magnifying to the point of ridiculousness. The meanness of the barfly's and citizen's points of view, counterpointed by the aggrandizements of the omniscient narrator, are, however, all to be seen in contrast to Bloom's doctrine of love and his humanitarian efforts on behalf of the Dignams. The ineffectuality of both Bloom and the citizen's last exchange completes the comic scene. Joyce leads us a merry chase through the parodies of the mundane literature of a Dublin adolescent girl, to the grotesque twistings and turnings of a series of opinionated period narrators in Oxen of the Sun; through the farce of Circe, in which the libido itself is objectified in all its drollery; through the cliché-ridden half-truths and vitality of Eumaeus; to our final non-answers in catechism and science in Ithaca, before the whole novel is culminated with the comic Gea-Tellus omniscience of the earthy Molly. The linguistic situations enhance the aggrandizements of the mundane. The Irish hyperbole of describing Bloom as Elijah ascending "at an angle of fortyfive degrees over Donohoe's in Little Green street like a shot off a shovel" (*U,* 12. 1917–18) is typical. The great comic technique of *Ulysses* is that the actions which seem to appear so important, and hence tragic, are made trivial by aggrandizement. Joyce's long discourse on the trifling contents of a drawer in Bloom's house, the elaborate elucidation of Bloom's fantasies in Circe, Gerty McDowell's fashioning Bloom's masturbation into a classic romantic moment, all are indicative of the length comedy goes to render normal activities trivial through aggrandizing them. At the same time, the reader is left with a sense of the genuine vitality of the mundane, with a sense that life's continuity and vitality have been reestablished. The unrealistic epic proportions to which Joyce takes the action through his linguistic parodies restores proportion by emphasizing the importance of the trivial which remains at the core. The whole idea of the Odyssean epic of Eccles Street itself assumes greater comic tone with each new outlandish linguistic feat, each new mundane circumstance made artificially important, increasing our laughter at the totality of the comic experience.

Langer admonishes that comedy must guard against backsliding into anxious intent and selfish solicitude. The comic art in essence represents a generalization about life's mundane complications without arousing the terror of tragedy. We are to be reminded that we are witnessing a funny artifice, although its ultimate truth is universal. Joyce accomplishes this by his use of such devices as varying his narrative methods and by the absurdity of the coincidences and crisscrossing of motifs and meanings. If we ever tend to forget that *Ulysses* is a funny book, we need only refer to the comic innovations and devices of Joyce's style, his scores of variations on established motifs and themes, until at last its protagonist becomes the symbol of the vital continuity of life, never destroyed, if momentarily defeated, as nature and life go on. Whatever Molly's "Yes" signifies, it is, as Langer points out, the final aspect of the comic spirit, because vital continuity begets affirmation of process rather than ultimate answers. Langer sums up her comedy chapter with the following statement:

> Not the derivation of personages and situations, but of the rhythm of "felt life" that the poet puts upon them, seems to me to be of artistic importance; the essential comic feeling, which is the sentient aspect of organic unity, growth, and self-preservation. (350)

The reader leaves *Ulysses* with the idea that Bloom and Molly's life will continue with the same vitality and urgency. If there were answers to their problems the vitality would be less than realistic, but we are left with the more fundamental comic assertion that life goes on.

Notes

1. Susanne K. Langer, *Feeling and Form* (New York: Charles Scribner's Sons, 1953), 326–50.
2. Ibid. 327.

Transformatio Coniunctionis: Alchemy in *Ulysses*

ROBERT D. NEWMAN

Without Contraries is no progression.
—Blake, *The Marriage of Heaven and Hell*

To accept unquestionably James Joyce's mockery of occult practices and of those associated with them in *Ulysses* is to be caught in yet another of the traps that this consummate trickster sets for his readers. Despite a seminal article written thirty years ago by William York Tindall, critical investigation of the Hermetic tradition in *Ulysses* has been largely limited to explications of allusions.[1] In contrast, critics have been more receptive to the placement of *Finnegans Wake* within the realm of hocus-pocus, some viewing its aberrant convolutions as fodder to keep the eccentrics occupied while the real issues might be debated in reference to the works written before Joyce's revolutionary impulses seemingly went awry. This attitude has certainly softened with the recognition of the structural and conceptual integrity of *Finnegans Wake;* however, the intellectual parochialism that it manifests points to a dominant tendency in the Western empirical tradition that I believe Joyce is attempting to confute through the Hermetic infrastructure that informs his work.

Despite the Aristotelian bias of his Jesuit training, there was something about Hermeticism that appealed to Joyce and that persists as an undercurrent in his work, particularly in *Ulysses* and *Finnegans Wake*. The appeal is rooted primarily in Joyce's vision of himself as the artist who could heal the breach between the naturalistic and symbolic perceptions of life and art that was inherited by the twentieth century. In this sense, we might compare him to Paracelsus, who sought to combine the mystical and the practical by liberating alchemy from its obsession with goldmaking and placing it in the service of medicine as a tool for healing the cosmos. Joyce considered *Ulysses* to be a prophetic book and his belief that in it he could reconcile inner and outer reality while infusing wholeness, harmony, and radiance is close to the vision of a Hermetic magus. Like the world of the magus, the world of *Ulysses* is ultimately one of correspondences, from the thought fragments that Stephen and Bloom mysteriously share to the elaborate schemas that Joyce constructed linking time, color, and anatomy to episodes of the novel, thereby presenting the book as world. For Joyce, the word becomes world, as Martha Clifford's epistolary slip demonstrates. In comparing *Ulysses* to Phineas Fletcher's *Purple Island,* Joyce acknowledged his preference for the analogical, a manner of thinking that is the cornerstone of Hermetic thought, but which succumbed to the analytic bias that dominates the modern world view.[2]

Despite his public scoffing, Joyce was interested in and influenced by the various occult movements that pervaded the intellectual milieu of late nineteenth-century Ireland. While his youthful defensiveness led him to condemn Yeats's beliefs as involving a "treacherous instance of adaptability," Joyce also praised Yeats's occult short story, "The Adoration of the Magi" (*CW,* 71), and has Stephen in *Stephen Hero* commit another of his occult short stories, "The Tables of the Law," to memory (*SH,* 176–78).[3] Yeats's essay, "Magic," in which he states "that the borders of our mind are ever shifting and that many minds can flow into one another"[4] (an idea that adumbrates *A Vision,* the most important Hermetic book since Bruno's last works on the art of memory), might be taken as describing the *modus operandi* of Circe. Yeats's introduction to W. T. Horton's *A Book of Images,* which Joyce owned, maintains that the essence of symbolism is defined by one phrase from the Emerald Table of Hermes Trismegistus, a series of thirteen precepts that offer the fundamental statement of alchemical doctrine. The phrase, "what is below is like that which is above," maintained a place in Joyce's own great memory for use in *Finnegans Wake:* "the tasks above are as the flasks below, saith the emerald canticle of Hermes" (*FW,* 263.21–22). The early manuscripts of *Portrait* also show Joyce likening the artist to the alchemist, "bringing together the mysterious elements, separating the subtle from the gross."[5]

Joyce encouraged Stuart Gilbert to read Madame Blavatsky's *Isis Unveiled* and his library contained other works by theosophists. In addition to reflecting mystical poets like Blake and Dante, *Ulysses* demonstrates Joyce's knowledge of the Egyptian *Book of the Dead,* the Kabbalah, Cornelius Agrippa, Dionysus the Areopagite, Emanuel Swedenborg, *The Golden Bough,* astrology, Rosicrucianism, and Freemasonry. Gilbert reports that he and Joyce discussed Eliphas Levi's theories of magic,[6] and Tindall's article points out that it was Levi's *Dogme de la Haute Magic,* published in 1855, that introduced much of Hermetic philosophy to the French Symbolist poets whom Joyce studied.[7] This work pays little attention to demons and spirits. Rather, it concentrates almost entirely on magical symbolism, taking an approach that is almost Jungian. Joyce also read Jung's early work, and the affinities of the 1916 English translation of

Psychology of the Unconscious with the psychological method of *Ulysses* deserve further attention, particularly regarding the emphasis that Jung gives in this version to the son's battle for deliverance from the mother and the debt owed to it in the climactic hallucinatory appearance of Stephen's mother in Circe.[8]

It is also difficult to neglect Joyce's reading of Giordano Bruno and to accept Joyce's intellectual deification of him as based solely on Bruno's heroic defense of his beliefs rather than on the beliefs themselves. In a letter to Harriet Shaw Weaver that discusses Lewis McIntyre's book on Bruno, Joyce writes, "I would not pay overmuch attention to these theories, beyond using them for all they are worth, but they have gradually forced themselves on me through circumstances of my own life" (*Letters*, I, 241). Allusions to the thought of this Renaissance magician, particularly the idea of the coincidence of contraries, recur throughout Circe and underscore the psychological transformations implicit in this episode.[9]

Joyce's parodies of the occult, then, should not be interpreted as a dismissal of this mode of thought. Part of the appeal, and indeed the consequent difficulty of *Ulysses*, is the inclusive rather than exclusive consciousness expressed within the novel. The implied values of the novel include an attack on intellectual reductionism. The parodic impulse in *Ulysses*, therefore, might more properly be construed as a rejection of simplifications, whether practiced by the Citizen or by A.E. Joyce's irony is seldom sardonic, but rather is intended to tease us out of circumscribed simplifications of life, whether they be Stephen's obsessions or Bloom's escapism. Joyce's concern seems to be with seeing life as a whole and with seeing a dynamic relationship among the parts that constitute the whole—both of which are concepts that define the core of the Hermetic tradition.

Given the influence of the Hermetic tradition in *Ulysses*, I would like to focus on the metaphoric significance of one aspect of that tradition, alchemy, as a means for reflecting the unified psychological design of the novel. The contention is that the underlying psychological mechanisms of the novel can better be understood by analogy with certain basic alchemical processes, and that several situations and images of the novel seem to allude to these processes. But first I would like to establish some of the primary alchemical beliefs and to redeem the intellectual respectability of that neglected and maligned tradition.

As Frances Yates has demonstrated in her books on the occult philosophy in the Renaissance, the Hermetic philosophers were not a splinter group of quacks and satanists as the witch-hunts fomented by Church dogmatism claimed, but a serious and influential group of thinkers who were striving not only for spiritual illumination but also for the advancement of scientific and intellectual knowledge.[10] And they were considered seriously by many of the intellectual giants of the day. The humanist

Patrizi proposed to Pope Gregory XIV that Hermetic philosophy take the place of Aristotle in ecclesiastical doctrine. The magical precepts of John Dee, Philip Sidney's teacher, underscore the design of the *Fairie Queene*. Shakespeare's *The Tempest* was written, in part, as a corrective to Ben Johnson's attack on alchemy in *The Alchemist*. John Donne frequently alludes to Paracelsus and demonstrates a sophisticated knowledge of alchemy. Even Newton, one of the architects of the mechanical view of the universe, was passionately interested in his alchemical notebooks.

Alchemy derives from a mixture of Greek natural philosophy and Egyptian technology. The Greeks, who first applied rational thought to the problems of nature, made very few experiments while the Egyptians, who developed sophisticated magical-chemical techniques, simply passed on formulas without theoretical amplification. When the two civilizations came together in the Alexandrian period, alchemy was born. As it developed in the highly Christianized Western world, alchemy was never hostile to prevailing religious ideas, but rather formed a kind of complementary undercurrent. Just as the soul was imprisoned in the body and was striving to reach its end in union with God, the alchemists believed that metals were trying to reach their end in the purity of gold. The soul of gold was caught in the body of earthly materials and could be released through alchemical practice. Those concerned with mercenary ends were derided as "puffers" by the true adepts, an allusion to their erroneous belief that their failures to produce gold were the result of the lack of heat of their fires, and their use of a bellows to puff up the fire.[11]

The belief in the unity of matter and spirit and the correspondence between the physical and spiritual planes is the basis of alchemical thought. Redemption of base metals into gold is akin to the redemption of the soul. Thus, the alchemists did not view transmutation as anything unnatural. For them, converting lead and mercury into gold and silver was no more unusual than nature transforming grass and rain water into flowers, or wheat and hay into the bones and muscles of animals.[12]

Despite great variation regarding minor points in alchemy, there was general agreement on the basic steps of the process. The starting material was some extremely common substance, often earth or water, sometimes mud or excrement (which may remind us of Shem the Penman writing with his own excrement in *Finnegans Wake).* The term *alchemy* itself derives from the Egyptian *"al-khem"* meaning "black earth,"[13] and an alchemical proverb reads "the corruption of one thing is the generation of another." This *prima materia* presumably contains two elements that are contradictory yet complementary and is purified by being pulverized, mixed with fire, and placed in the sealed Hermetic vessel to be heated. The two elements are dissolved and united, then blacken and putrefy, the process known as *"nigredo."* The black substance then slowly turns white, the process known as *"albedo."* The product of this phase, the white stone, is a moon symbol, sometimes represented as a white tree with silver apples. The white stone is the basis of the next stage, and is gradually purified through the addition of mercury until it turns red, symbolized by the sun. This new compound is the Philosopher's Stone, which can turn base metals into gold and give immortality.

Thus, alchemy has a theological analogue and, as Carl Jung has shown, a psychological one as well. In his interpretation of these phases, Jung sees the *prima materia* as psychic energy that contains the conscious and the subconscious, which must be united by the fire of experience, a painful confrontation of the conscious ego with the shadow nature within the subconscious. Jung explains the shadow as the repressed and guilt-laden facets of the personality that manifest themselves in terms of projections onto other people or things.[14] The strain of this confrontation, a dark night of the soul, produces exhaustion that, if the process of individuation is successful, is slowly succeeded by a resurrection.

Jung was struck by the numerous alchemical references encoded in the dreams of his patients, and eventually decided that the unconscious undergoes processes that express themselves in alchemical symbolism. In a letter to Erich Neumann, he states, "analytical psychology . . . has its roots deep in Europe, in the Christian Middle Ages, and ultimately in Greek philosophy. The connecting link I was missing for so long has now been found, and it is alchemy."[15] Just as the goal of alchemy is the philosopher's stone, possession of which permitted transmutation into gold, the individuation process sought by the unconscious leads man toward the attainment of the self. For Jung, alchemy, with all its symbolisms and operations, is a projection onto matter of archetypes and processes of the collective unconscious.[16]

Just as the alchemical process has transformation as its raison d'etre, so does the transformation process underscore *Ulysses,* as is implied by the discussion of metempsychosis in the first sustained conversation between Bloom and Molly. Transformation and unity are also knit into the basic fabric of the novel, which reconciles its naturalistic and symbolic threads. In tracing the events of one day, the novel moves from the light of morning to the darkness of night, ending in the shadows of Molly Bloom's consciousness approaching light before dawn. The symbolic associations of this natural progression are woven throughout the texture of *Ulysses* to offer patterns that ultimately reveal its basic values, which extend from the tangibly psychological to the mythical and cosmic, akin to the levels of correspondences in alchemy. Stephen's inversion of the phrase from John 1:5 that recurs throughout the novel, "darkness shining in brightness which the brightness comprehended not," offers the basic scheme of these patterns. Stephen and Bloom may either follow the artificial and seductive path traveled by cynics and escapists like Buck Mulligan, Deasy, and Father Conmee who are associated with the superficial qualities of light through dress, physical setting, and behavior; or they may follow the path of self-illumination achieved through a descent into the darker aspects of the psyche that imprison the self, an effort that may in turn liberate it. In Yeats's words, they "must lie down where all ladders start / In the foul rag-and-bone shop of the heart."[17] *Ulysses* follows Stephen and Bloom in the course of this descent and in the initial stages of their emergence from it. Joyce also plays magus by manipulating his readers, plunging us with his two main characters into darkness in search of light and forcing us to grope through the transitional yet indefinite nature of shadows in our search. We experience the complementary qualities that aid them on this psychic journey and identify with their emergent potentialities as the text concludes.

In an essay on the concept of the archetype, Jung discusses the *Corpus Hermeticum* and its description of God as the "archetypal light . . . pre-existent and supraordinate to the phenomenon 'light.' "[18] While we might think of Stephen's comment concerning "the playwright who wrote the folio of this world and wrote it badly (He gave us light first and the sun two days later)" (*U,* 9.1046–48), we can use the Hermetic distinction between archetypal light and the phenomenon of light to clarify the two uses of light in *Ulysses* and the implicit attack on the overreliance on rationalism contained therein. Scientific empiricism often operates by reductionism, ignoring the *a priori* existence of light while focusing exclusively on the derived phenomena. Using its Occam's razor of simplicity, it tends to neglect the more labyrinthine but fertile possibilities of concepts such as the unconscious, while erecting categories of explanation that apply stasis rather than dynamism to life. One logical outgrowth of this tradition is behavioristic psychology, an academically influential form of reductionism. The point here is that the exclusive nature of the tradition of Western rationalism, founded on Aristotelian reasoning, attempts to categorize what is and what is not experience, and has achieved domination over the general receptivity of the Platonic tradition. It has also historically sought to suppress the offshoots of that tradition, including alchemy and the entire Hermetic line of thought, whether through political advantage, sarcasm, or witchhunts.[19] We see Stephen bemoaning this loss in the passage that includes his inversion of John 1:5: "Gone too from the world, Averroes and Moses Maimonides, dark men in mien and movement, flashing in their mocking mirrors the obscure soul of the world, a darkness shining in brightness which brightness could not comprehend" (*U,* 2.157–60). Through his references to the healing correspondences of the Hermetic tradition, Joyce creates a mocking mirror in *Ulysses* wherein he flashes "the obscure soul of the world." Like alchemical theory, where the corruption of one thing is the generation of another—which draws on biblical teaching where death is a necessary preliminary to regeneration—*Ulysses* proceeds by the *via negativa* in accomplishing transformation to a higher realm.

In applying alchemy as a metaphor for psychological transformation in *Ulysses,* I want first to offer a rapid overview of the psychological relationships of the major characters, followed by a more detailed analysis. The culminating episodes of the Telemachiad and the Bloomiad, for example, most poignantly reflect a low state of their respective character's self-regard and sense of the world. The Blooms' empty marriage, Stephen's unfulfilled poetic promise, Paddy Dignam's body, the Dedalus household, and the moral spirit of Dublin are all examples of decay associated with the primary characters of *Ulysses.* Fleeting encounters with the shadow self become more sustained although still temporary confrontations in episodes like Scylla and Charybdis, Sirens, and Cyclops, foreshadowing the full-scale descent into the dark night of the unconscious in Circe. During this episode, the contradictory yet complementary characters of Stephen and Bloom are united. Bloom also fulfills the prophecies signaled in earlier episodes by functioning as Mercurius, the alchemical agent of transformation. In doing so, he replaces Mulligan as Stephen's spiritual messenger, thereby affecting a triumph for compassionate involvement and Hermetic reconciliation over objective detachment and rational division. The exhaustion from the strain of their descent is reflected in Eumaeus as they move arm in arm toward 7 Eccles Street where the product of alchemical albedo is reflected in Molly as unifying moon symbol. The white tree with silver apples becomes "the heaventree of stars," and Ithaca ends with a symbolic portent of harmony between conscious and unconscious. Penelope concludes *Ulysses* with references to the sun, the symbol of the Philosopher's Stone, and with the healing union of man and woman and past and present amplified in an affirmation that completes the circle of the episode and of the book as a symbol of eternity.

Although Stephen confidently proclaims to himself "signatures of all things I am here to read" (*U,* 3.2), quoting the mystic Jacob Boehme, Proteus might be seen as an epitome of his incertitude. Vacillating from solipsism to objective reality, Stephen is obsessed with mutability and eschatology. He seeks a firm sense of identity within a world of flux, brilliantly articulating philosophical and theological antitheses in a fervent search for some sense of synthesis. His dialectics are based on emotional conflicts that block his access to his creative process. Rather than producing art, he spins sparkling but futile webs of sticky meditations that attach themselves to nothing outside of himself. Mired in intellect, with no integrity or soul to reinforce them, these intellectual sallies cast an ephemeral glimmer before collapsing back on him to make him a prisoner of his own empty gestures.

Alchemical nigredo finds a correlate both in Stephen's emotional confusion and in his intellectual preoccupation with the dissolution of matter, with corruption rather than creation. Indeed, having witnessed the rotting carcass of a dog, Stephen goes on to imagine a drowned human corpse and, after a meditation on his urination and a contemplation of his decaying teeth, he picks his nose and carefully places his dried snot on a rock. Throughout the episode, Stephen links sex with death, thereby conjoining procreation (both biological and artistic) with cessation. He thinks of his conception as taking place "wombed in sin darkness" (*U,* 3.45), between his mother, now a "ghostwoman" (*U,* 3.46), and his father, now a failure. He applies Aquinas's term, "morose delectation" (*U,* 3.385), to sex, and thinks of women as "pickmeups" (*U,* 3.430) who are physically and morally blemished: "when night hides her body's flaws calling under her brown shawl from an archway where dogs have mired" (*U,* 3.375–76). He watches two women who he presumes are carrying a misbirth. Turning his back to the midday sun, he scribbles a poem in which the lover is a vampire. Stephen's own sexual experiences, from *Portrait* to present, have consisted solely of rendezvous with whores. Hence, the procreative urge has become tinged with guilt and disease for him. Though he desperately needs to create in order to approach an individuated sense of self, the process of creation has become repugnant.

In its positioning within the text, the preoccupations of its protagonist, and its overall tone, Hades parallels Proteus. As an example of Bloom's nigredo, it presents the familiar equation of the grave to the alchemist's distilling vessel, which refines and purifies just as the grave transmutes all earthly into heavenly flesh. As is fitting for a funeral, the mood of the episode is oppressive, and Joyce indicates in the Linati and Gorman-Gilbert schemas that the "sense" is "descent into nothing." "Brown," "grey," and "dull" are prominant objectives. The sun is "veiled" (*U,* 6.136). Bloom meditates on his dead son, his dead father, and his dead dog as well as on death in general. He listens as Simon Dedalus breaks down at the thought of his dead wife and stands by as his fellow mourners lament Ireland's dead heroes. He endures the anti-Semitic remarks of his companions while considering their troubled family situations and, by extension, his own. The images of bodily decay generated by his interior monologue are grossly physical, serving as a complement to the metaphysical conceptions of dissolution that Stephen's meditations conjure in Proteus. The sight of a grey rat in the cemetery, for example, sends him into the following grim soliloquy:

> One of those chaps would make short work of a fellow. Pick the bones clean no matter who it was. Ordinary meat for them . . . Regular square feed for them. Flies come before he's well dead. Got wind of Dignam. They wouldn't care about the smell of it. Saltwhite crumbling mush of corpse: smell, taste like raw white turnips. (*U,* 6.980–94)

Jung's notion of the initial stages of alchemy as psychological descent is expressed within the dark, musty confines of the library in which Stephen offers his Shakespeare theory and of the pubs into which Bloom descends. These episodes are largely transitional in that we observe Stephen and Bloom move from confusion and utter subjugation to their problems to tentative attempts to confront these problems.

Stephen's own isolation is cloaked in his analysis of Shakespeare. Not only does he identify Shakespeare with the ghost of Hamlet's father as a means of working out Shakespeare's personal frustrations, but Stephen unconsciously makes that same identification for himself. By presenting his theory, Stephen is indirectly addressing his paralyzing guilt over his refusal to pray at his mother's deathbed as well as his own artistic frustrations.[20] While linking Anne Hathaway with Gertrude, the guilty queen, he goes on to associate her with his mother through the image of death. While Anne Hathaway is seen as an agent of potential psychological destruction for Shakespeare, the fact that Stephen continually recalls May Dedalus in imagery of death and decay places her in an equivalent role for him. In one discussion Stephen states that Socrates learned "from his mother how to bring thoughts into the world" (*U*, 9.235–36), a lesson that Stephen has not learned.

Whereas Shakespeare is able to avenge his wife's adultery through writing his play, Stephen is still bound to his mother's ghost. Whereas Shakespeare, upon accepting the incertitude of fatherhood as a "mystical estate, an apostolic succession from only begetter to only begotten" (*U*, 9.838–39), is able to write *Hamlet* and become father and son consubstantial; Stephen is unable to accept incertitude, unable to "battle against hopelessness" (*U*, 9.828), and unable to create. In the development of his theory, Stephen presents to himself the sources of his own problems. However, his shadow self lurks on the fringes of his consciousness to deflate his energy and to restore his mental bondage.

When Mulligan enters the library, interrupting Stephen's speech, Stephen thinks to himself, "Hast thou found me, O mine enemy?" (*U*, 9.483). Mulligan serves as a messenger of his shadow self, a self that Stephen has temporarily escaped. Mulligan also represents a materialistic and deterministic view of the world to which Stephen is in danger of succumbing. Upon seeing Mulligan, Stephen's self-doubts and negative projections are once again activated, and he ultimately denies his own theory and goes drinking with Mulligan. Resigned, he tells himself, "Cease to strive" (*U*, 9.1221).

Both Sirens and Cyclops are barroom episodes imbued with the vices of an alcohol-drenched environment, including sentimentality and pugilistic nationalism. The characters who frequent the Ormond Hotel and Barney Kiernan's are generally idlers who pose a marked contrast to Bloom's persistent activity. Lydia Douce and Mina Kennedy indulge in gossip and flirtation, their language full of nonsense expressions. Simon Dedalus lounges around the bar in sentimental laments while his children barely maintain a subsistence level of existence. The Citizen apparently spends his days bar-hopping with his dog, Garryowen, trading on his past athletic glory and the Irish penchant for nostalgia, to procure free drinks. The nameless narrator of Cyclops also begins his narrative by stating that he "was just passing the time of day" (*U,* 12.1). In contrast, we observe Bloom entering the Ormond Hotel in a temporary burst of bravado as he decides to follow Blazes Boylan at this third sighting of him. Later, he comes to Barney Kiernan's for the purpose of meeting Martin Cunningham and Jack Power to discuss providing for Paddy Dignam's family. Bloom's distinction from the bar-dwellers is demonstrated not only by the fact that he is ostracized by them, but also by his ability to emerge from the emotional cave in which they have imprisoned themselves.

Looking out the window of the Ormond Hotel, Bloom reads "Aaron Figatner," a jeweler's name, and thinks of the name as "Figather" (*U,* 11.149–50). By linking agricultural and mining metaphors, Joyce suggests a connection between Cyclops and Sirens regarding the alternative that Bloom presents to psychological escapism. Like the Cyclops of Book IX of the *Odyssey,* who reside in a fertile land but are ignorant of agriculture, the inhabitants of the two bars fail to probe the depths of their lives. Instead they wallow in their losses and failures or find scapegoats for their frustrations. Bloom alone seems capable of learning from his personal lapses, of unconsciously tunneling into the problem-laden, but fertile passageways of his emotions and of mining the embedded jewels that give him the capacity for psychological richness. This metaphor is introduced in the prelude of Sirens: "Low in dark middle earth. Embedded ore" (*U,* 11.42), and is repeated in association with Bloom's decision to leave the Ormond Hotel, a decision that reflects his growing recognition of the dangers of the behavior practiced there. This phrase recalls scene 3 of Wagner's *Das Rheingold* where Wotan, the threatened king of the gods, descends into Nibelheim, the cavern residence of the dwarf Nibelungs and strips the dwarf Alberich of the ring and his power.[21] Bloom functions as Wotan, threatened by the dwarfed vision of the bar-dwellers. He descends into their cavern residence and, through Joyce's juxtaposition of his character to that of the Citizen, deflates the power with which the two narrators have attempted to imbue the Citizen while enhancing his own psychological resources through self-knowledge. Wotan (Woden) is also linked to Mercury (Hermes) through his association with Wednesday and as a messenger figure. Bloom's function as a messenger figure, a bringer of "light to the gentiles," also possesses an alchemical context.

As a messenger and spiritual guide for Stephen, Bloom functions as

Mercurius, the agent of transformation in alchemy. In *Alchemical Studies,* Jung interprets Mercurius as the archetype of the unconscious, a dark, hidden god and an adumbration of the primordial lightbringer, Christ, who is the archetype of the conscious.[22] Mercurius is associated with Lucifer, not in a diabolical aspect, but as the morning star preceding the emergence of light from darkness. In Proteus when Stephen thinks "allbright he falls, proud lightning of the intellect" (*U,* 3.486), he indicates not only Joyce's famous fear of thunderstorms, but also the diabolical nature of Lucifer and his own overreliance on intellect which imprisons his creativity.

Stephen has committed himself to the bondage of Mulligan as "usurper" of his home and messenger of his shadow self. Throughout Telemachus, Stephen is lugubrious and Mulligan lambent. While Mulligan carries on an incessant stream of brilliant jokes, word-play, and literary allusions, Stephen the poet broods and follows him "wearily" (*U,* 1.36). It is Mulligan who has saved a man from drowning, while Stephen admits "I'm not a hero" (*U,* 1.62). "Stately, plump" Buck Mulligan's robust health is in stark contrast to Stephen's rotting teeth and general physical decrepitude. Mulligan immerses himself laughingly in the sea for his morning bath, while Stephen sulks, a hydrophobe. In contrast to Mulligan's insouciance, Stephen stoops under the weight of his barbed comments. Stephen refers to him as "Mercurial Malachi," "Malachai" being Hebrew for "my messenger." As Mulligan leaps for his morning ablution, he is described in mercurial terms as "fluttering his winglike hands, leaping nimbly, Mercury's hat quivering in the fresh wind that bore back to them his brief birdsweet cries" (*U,* 1.600–2), a reference to Mercury's association with the Egyptian ibis-headed Thoth, the god of scribes, whom Stephen invokes while auguring his poetic destiny in *Portrait*. Mulligan is a perversion of this mythological ancestry, detached from the compassionate interaction with life that art requires.

Mulligan uses Stephen, as he probably uses everyone with whom he is associated, for amusement. Although in training to be a physician, he expresses little human concern. In contrast to Stephen's metaphysical brooding, Mulligan posits a reductionistic view of life. "I remember only ideas and sensations" (*U,* 1.192–93), he tells Stephen. His response to Stephen's turmoil over the death of his mother reveals his personal philosophy to be based solely on the empirically physical:

> And what is death, he asked, your mother's or yours or my own? You saw only your mother die. I see them pop off every day in the Mater and Richmond and cut up into tripes in the dissectingroom. It's a beastly thing and nothing else. It simply doesn't matter. . . . To me it's all a mockery and beastly. Her cerebral lobes are not functioning. (*U,* 1.204–11)

We witness Stephen's dissatisfaction with Mulligan as his guide in his hopeful response to the old milkwoman in Telemachus: "old and secret she had entered from a morning world, maybe a messenger," he thinks, and repeats to himself "a messenger from the secret morning" (*U,* 1.399–406). Yet Stephen's confusion and general defensiveness prohibit any interaction: "to serve or to upbraid, whether he could not tell: but scorned to beg her favour" (*U,* 1.406–7). His telegram to Mulligan, revealed in Scylla and Charybdis, canceling their appointment at the pub, where Stephen of course would be doing the buying, reflects a short-lived attempt to reject the messenger of the shadow as does his Shakespeare theory. However, Mulligan reclaims possession of his fallen fledgling. As they depart the library, Bloom passes between them, a foreshadowing of the eventual sundering of Stephen from the bondage of his shadow and the replacement of Mulligan with Bloom as messenger. As Bloom passes, Mulligan sarcastically refers to him as "the wandering jew" (*U,* 9.1209). Jung refers to the lore of Mercurius in which he is often compared to Elijah and Moses, two figures with whom Bloom is frequently associated, and is depicted as a wanderer in the guise of a stranger who confronts the individual directly, a function that Bloom will fulfill for Stephen in Circe.[23] Mercurius is also hermaphroditic,[24] reminding us of Bloom's androgynous personality traits and of his characterization as the "new womanly man" in Circe. Mulligan unwittingly is realizing the role of the Hebraic name which he assigns himself, Malachi having foretold the second coming of Elijah (Malachi 4:5).

Bloom assumes the function of Mercurius for Stephen after passing through his own initiation into the dark reaches of his shadow self in Circe. Budgen speaks of Joyce's "intention of magical evocation" in Circe, and throughout the episode discrete identities are relaxed so that, in Yeats's words, "many minds can flow into one another." Bloom speaks of things about which he could not possibly have any personal knowledge. For example, during the Wandering Rocks episode, Stephen finds the eighth and ninth books of Moses, written by Moses the magician rather than Moses the lawgiver, in a bookstall and reads a line containing the word "Nebrakada" that Bloom speaks in two fantasies in Circe. That the origin of this reference is from a magical text is especially significant in revealing Joyce's concerns, although obfuscated, for ideas that run contrary to Aristotelian rationality.

Early in the episode, Bloom encounters a "sinister figure" "injected with dark mercury" who offers him a password. I take "sinister" to refer to its Latin meaning, "left" or "left-handed," thereby suggesting inversion as direction in keeping with the idea of finding illumination in the darkness of the psyche.[25] That the figure is injected with dark mercury suggests an association with the archetypal Mercurius, and the fact that he gives

Bloom a password suggests the mythological Hermes, the messenger of the gods. It was Hermes who gave Odysseus moly to protect him from the spells of Circe, and Bloom, upon requesting the return of his potato—his moly—from Zoe, states that "there is a memory attached to it" (*U,* 15.3520). In a letter to Budgen, Joyce writes "Hermes—god of signposts—point at which roads parallel merge and roads contrary also" (*Letters,* I, 147–48), and Joyce alludes later in "Circe" to Hermes Trismegistus—"Occult pimander of Hermes Trismegistos" (*U,* 15.2269).

Bloom also acquires attributes of Mercurius through his association with Haroun al Raschid, a shaman-like figure who appears in the dream shared by Stephen, Bloom, and Molly, and with whom Bloom is twice identified in Circe (*U,* 15.3113, 15.4325). The dream occurs on the previous night, a Wednesday, the day with which Mercury is associated. In Stephen's recounting of the dream, Haroun offers him a melon (*U,* 3.368), a round fruit that suggests possible wholeness and artistic fecundity. For Stephen, Bloom represents a direction out of his self-contained thoughts into an interaction with a world that could give his artistic impulses depth and validity. For Bloom, Stephen exhibits the possibility of an introspective confrontation with a mode of living that has been gradually slipping into vacuity. Thus, the conjunction of contraries basic to alchemical theory is enacted within the psychological design of the novel. In Circe, Bloom's and Stephen's faces merge in the mirror with that of Shakespeare. In Ithaca, a "keyless couple" (*U,* 17.81), they discuss the similarities of the Hebrew and Irish languages and peoples, and Stephen leaves Bloom's house playing a Jew's harp. They also urinate together while simultaneously observing a shooting star. Evidence for the unconscious mingling of thoughts between the two characters that occurs throughout *Ulysses* suggests that the borders of personality are relaxed so that the two merge, becoming "Stoom" and "Blephen" (*U,* 17.549–51). At one juncture, we observe them looking into each other's faces to see mirrors of their own: "Silent, each contemplating the other in both mirrors of the reciprocal flesh of theirhisnothis fellowfaces" (*U,* 17.1183–84).

Buck Mulligan's last appearance as Mercurial Mulligan occurs in Circe in the same scene in which Stephen rejects the guilt he feels for his mother's death. Claiming "cancer did it, not I" (*U,* 15.4187), he renounces his bondage to his mother's ghost as well as his servitude to the *dio boia* of his intellect and, by implication, Mulligan's world view as his guide to life. Bloom, who has followed him to Nighttown out of a paternal concern and has undergone his own dark night of the soul while there, rescues him at the conclusion of the episode and assumes his position on the naturalistic as well as the symbolic level as Stephen's guide through the exhausted prose of Eumaeus to the safety of Ithaca and potential resurrection. In doing so, Bloom actualizes a vignette that Stephen imagines in Aeolus, strangely out of context among the chatter of machines and newsmen:

> Messenger took out his matchbox thoughtfully and lit his cigar.
> I have often thought since on looking back over that strange time that it was that small act, trivial in itself, that striking of that match, that determined the whole aftercourse of both our lives. (*U,* 7.762–65)

Having brought Stephen home with him, an event that, at least on a symbolic level, functions to "determine the whole aftercourse of both [their] lives," Bloom kindles a fire in the hearth by lighting "at three projecting points of paper with one ignited lucifer match, thereby releasing the potential energy contained in the fuel" (*U,* 17.130–32). The lucifer match again associates Bloom with Mercurius and the event epitomizes Bloom's fraternity and serves to release a similar "potential energy" in Stephen. Stephen thinks "of others elsewhere in other times who, kneeling on one knee or on two, had kindled fires for him" (*U,* 17.135–36). The kindling of fires seems to serve as a touchstone in Stephen's mind for acts of kindness and for events of joy and pathos that constitute human interaction. That Stephen was affected by these events and that he evidences a sense of empathy regarding them seems to point to a release within him of a dimension of his personality previously held in bondage by his defensive self-involvement. As Mercurius, Bloom offers the purifying fire necessary for his transformation.

Molly as moon symbol and "the heaventree of stars" (*U,* 17.1039) as the white tree with silver apples offer representations of alchemical albedo in Ithaca. While presenting psychological implications for Bloom and Stephen, they also help Joyce to expose the limitations of empiricism as a mode of living. "The heaventree of stars" presents an alternative to the earthbound analytical bias offered by the narrator and links a relativistic perspective with the already established psychological one so that we may see a growth in Stephen's and Bloom's abilities to accept the mutability and incertitude that has so threatened them. Joyce's continual references to the shifting positions of the stars and planets, his insistence on the cosmic level, reinforces the incertitude to which Bloom must expose himself. He must also consciously react to preserve his life by not acquiescing to the void that the narrative point of view promulgates. Molly remains his "goldseam of inexhaustible ore" (*U,* 17.1753), an implicit reference to the aforementioned passage in Sirens, from whom he might continue to mine the light that his values radiate and avoid slipping into the detached cynicism reflected in so many of the self-defeated characters with whom he has come into contact.

Frequent references to the moon in Ithaca coincide with the archetypal feminine influence of Molly, ever present as a dominant undercurrent during the preceding action of *Ulysses,* which now presides over the communal micturition of Bloom and Stephen.[26] She remains a recumbent female shadow toward which Bloom and Stephen gaze while the empirical narrator measures the trajectories of their urine. That her form is indistinct is appropriate in that the events of the day indicate that a change must take place in the way that she and Bloom relate to each other and the direction that this change will take is as yet undetermined. For Stephen, she is a mystery with whom Bloom has attempted to coax him into residence in his home and, although he rejects that attempt, it is mystery and the feminine creative force that give life to Stephen's art. As Gea-Tellus (*U,* 17.2313), the fleshy spheres of her buttocks will telescope Bloom, as Odysseus returned home, from the cosmic back to the earthly realm while focusing his attention on the central object of his turbulence and of his well-being.

As Bloom climbs into bed with Molly and offers a truncated account of his day before drifting off to sleep, "the upcast reflection of a lamp and shade, an inconstant series of concentric circles of varying gradations of light and shadow" (*U,* 17.2300–2301) moves on the ceiling above them. The macrocosmic perspective inherent in references to the night sky has been reduced to the microcosmic interior shelter of the Bloom's bedroom. The objective determinism of the narrative point of view gives way to the relativistic subjectivity implicit in the words "inconstant" and "unvarying." The light of the conscious mind and the shadowy realm of the unconscious are symbolized by the gradations of light and shadow on the ceiling. That they exist as concentric circles suggests that a sense of wholeness and interdependent balance has been achieved between them.

Joyce called Penelope his "final amplitudinously curvilinear episode" (*Letters,* I, 164), and stated it "has no beginning, middle or end" (*Letters,* I, 172). "It begins and ends with the female word yes," he wrote (*Letters,* I, 170), and the final "yes" also serves as a mirrored distortion of the word "stately" which begins the book. Indeed, Joyce assigned infinity as the time for the episode in his schemas. The circularity of Penelope suggests the abolition of time offered by the transformative powers of the Philosopher's Stone. Molly's half-conscious rambling monologue, though full of rational contradictions, establishes a protean character who resolves the psychological tensions of the novel and transforms personal fragmentation into collective unity.

Penelope demonstrates the potentialities of Stephen and Bloom through Molly by implicitly suggesting her capacity to compensate for their limitations. In her fantasized love affair with Stephen, Molly thinks "I can teach him the other part Ill make him feel all over him till he half faints under me" (*U,* 18.1363–64). It is "the other part," the physical realm, that Stephen needs to attend to. While an affair between Stephen and Molly would realistically be a disaster, it is significant on the level of the psychic wholeness that *Ulysses* generates from the Bloom-Stephen-Molly relationship that Molly instinctively intuits the source of Stephen's psychological depletion. Although she adapts this information to the immediacy of her own aroused condition on the naturalistic level, her directness and positive associations with nature exist as a balance and symbolic corrective to Stephen's convoluted theorizing and general apprehension regarding the processes of life.

Molly also offers a means of psychological rectification for Bloom's escapist habits of mind. Her adultery forces Bloom to search his soul and to begin to make some active determinations regarding his life. In doing so, Molly has confronted Bloom with a trial through which he can no longer circumvent responsibility and, ultimately, transformation.[27]

During the course of the episode, Bloom undergoes a transformation in Molly's affections. While we experience no "Circe" with Molly, we might project her sexual encounter with Boylan as a similar purgative, the radical nature of which now permits her access to her long-dormant self. Her references to her sexual tryst with Boylan acquire bestial connotations while her memories of Bloom's love-making grow increasingly tender: "I liked him because I saw he understood or felt what a woman is" (*U,* 18.1578–79). Her last reminiscence further reflects the circularity of the episode in recalling her first act of love-making with Bloom coupled with his proposal of marriage in the sunlight on Howth.

References to the sun, the symbol of the Philosopher's Stone, occur with increasing frequency in the closing pages of Penelope. Molly remembers Bloom telling her on their excursion on Howth, "the sun shines for you" (*U,* 18.1578), an unconscious intuition of her transformative powers. The link between the sun and Molly's continual references to nature also help to underscore the Hermetic correspondence of heaven and earth. Nature seems to serve as a touchstone for Molly to which she returns to soothe her agitation and by which she judges between right and wrong. She thinks often of the sea, the primal source of life, and delights in seasonal changes, representing transformation and renewal. Joyce wrote in his notesheets for "Penelope," "MB = spinning Earth,"[28] and through Molly he employs the Hermetic conception of nature's capacity to lead man out of logical entanglements through fresh observation.[29] Molly proclaims, "theres nothing like nature" (*U,* 18.1558–59), and reinforces *Ulysses*'s condemnation of those who negate mystery and interpret life in a rational but mechanical manner: "as for them saying theres no God I wouldnt give a snap of my two fingers for all their learning why dont they go and create something" (*U,* 18.1563–65). Her denunciation concludes with "they might as well try to stop the sun from rising tomorrow" (*U*, 18.1571), an implicit affirmation of the cyclical quality and healing potential of transformation.

When aligned with the points of view of Stephen and Bloom, Molly's candor and femininity contribute proportion and complete the mind of *Ulysses.* Set on the edge of night and approaching the shadowy dawn while governed by the glow of the moon, "Penelope" unifies the light, dark, and shadow imagery of *Ulysses* as it completes the psychological conditions necessary for the rebirth of the self in its three primary characters. Expressing multitudes and containing opposites, Molly's inclusive contradictions reflect the conjunction of opposites that are at work in every phase of the novel, seeking totality rather than fragmentation and affirmation rather than negation. Past merges with present as we observe Molly's daylight memories in the night of her bedroom while she and Bloom lie head to foot, all inclusive in their unified circularity.

My aim throughout this essay has been to respond to the subtlety and depth of the texture of *Ulysses* while employing a methodology that both elucidates and embraces its values. Alchemy affords access to the theme of transformation which fuses the naturalistic and symbolic impulses of the novel, and functions metaphorically to suggest the Hermetic principles that inform its psychological and moral infrastructure. Joyce attempts to restore the link in the chain of being between microcosm and macrocosm that was broken by overreliance on rationalism in the Western intellectual tradition. In doing so, he recalls another writer with a mind attuned to mystery and psychological nuances. In Dostoevsky's *The Brothers Karamazov,* Alyosha experiences a crisis of belief in which he comes close to losing his faith due to the decay of the corpse of his mentor, Father Zosima (a name curiously similar to that of the Gnostic alchemist, Zosimos). During his dark night of the soul, Alyosha begins to suspect that the world is a mere physical system. His subsequent relief and ecstasy are epitomized as he stares at the stars and feels that "there seemed to be threads from all those innumerable worlds of God linking his soul to them."[30]

Notes

1. William York Tindall, "James Joyce and the Hermetic Tradition," *Journal of the History of Ideas* 15 (1954): 23–29. More recent articles that have considered this aspect of *Ulysses* include Norman Silverstein, "Bruno's Particles of Reminiscence," *James Joyce Quarterly* 2, 4 (1965): 271–80; Craig Carver, "James Joyce and the Theory of Magic," *James Joyce Quarterly* 15, 3 (1978): 201–14; John Rickard, "Isis on Sandymount," *James Joyce Quarterly* 20, 3 (1983): 356–58, and John Rickard, "Philotheology in Mecklenberg Street," *James Joyce Quarterly* 23, 1 (1985): 80–82. Barbara DiBernard has written a book entitled *Alchemy and Finnegans Wake* (Albany: State University of New York Press, 1980); however, her book does not dwell on the psychological analogue that is the focus of this essay.

2. Frank Budgen, *James Joyce and the Making of Ulysses* (Bloomington: Indiana University Press, 1967), 13–14.

3. One might project that as he matured and his sense of humor with him, Joyce would probably have respected Yeats's lack of fanaticism regarding magical practices. George Russell (A.E.) relates a story of how he watched Yeats walking up and down a room holding a sword and repeating incantations; every time he passed a bowl of plums, Yeats took one. Russell chastised him, "really Yeats, you can't evoke great spirits and eat plums at the same time"; quoted in Henry Summerfield's biography of Russell, *That Myriad-Minded Man* (London: Colin Smythe, 1975), 27.

4. W. B. Yeats, *Essays and Introductions* (New York: Macmillan, 1961), 28.

5. *The Workshop of Daedalus: James Joyce and the Raw Materials for* A Portrait of the Artist as a Young Man, ed. Robert Scholes and Richard M. Kain (Evanston, Ill.: Northwestern University Press, 1965), 63–64.

6. Stuart Gilbert, *James Joyce's Ulysses* (New York: Vintage, 1958), 47.

7. Tindall, "James Joyce and the Hermetic Tradition": 28–29.

8. Joyce indicates awareness of this work in a letter to Frank Budgen written in December 1919, *SL,* 244.

9. In addition to Silverstein's "Bruno's Particles of Reminiscence," see Elliott B. Gose, Jr., *The Transformation Process in Joyce's Ulysses* (Toronto: University of Toronto Press, 1980). The best book on Bruno's philosophy is still Frances A Yates, *Giordana Bruno and the Hermetic Tradition* (Chicago: University of Chicago Press, 1964).

10. In addition to the book on Bruno, see Yates's *The Art of Memory* (Chicago: University of Chicago Press, 1966), *The Rosicrucian Enlightenment* (Boulder, Colo.: Shambhala, 1978), *Theatre of the World* (Chicago: University of Chicago Press, 1969), and *The Occult Philosophy in the Elizabethan Age* (London: Routledge and Kegan Paul, 1983).

11. For the history and philosophy of alchemy, see John Read, *Prelude to Chemistry* (New York: Macmillan, 1937); Arthur John Hopkins, *Alchemy: Child of Greek Philosophy* (New York: Columbia University Press, 1934); E. J. Holmyard, *Alchemy* (Harmondsworth, Middlesex: Penguin Books, 1957); Arthur Edward Waite, ed., *The Hermetic Museum, Restored and Enlarged* (London: James Elliott, 1893); and Mircea Eliade, *The Forge and the Crucible: The Origins and Structures of Alchemy* (New York: Harper & Row, 1971).

12. See Read, *Prelude to Chemistry,* 120.

13. M. Esther Harding, *Psychic Energy* (Princeton: Princeton University Press, 1963), 442.

14. Carl Gustav Jung, *Aion, Collected Works,* vol. 9, no. 2 (Princeton: Princeton University Press, 1959), 8–10.

15. Jung, *Letters,* vol. 1, ed. Gerbard Adler with Aniela Jaffe, trans. R. F. C. Hull (Princeton: Princeton University Press, 1973), 206.

16. In *Collected Works* (Princeton: Princeton University Press) see *Psychology and Alchemy,* vol. 12 (1968); *Alchemical Studies,* vol. 13 (1970); and *Mysterium Coniunctionis,* vol. 14 (1970). For a study of the psychological implications of alchemy by a disciple of Jung's, see Marie-Louise von Franz, *Alchemical Active Imagination* (Irving, Tex.: Spring Publications, 1979). The title of my essay is derived from Jung's *Mysterium Coniunctionis.*

17. Yeats, "The Circus Animals' Desertion," *The Collected Poems of W. B. Yeats* (New York: Macmillan, 1972), 336. Another appropriate example would be from "Crazy Jane Talks with the Bishop":

> Love has pitched his mansion in
> The place of excrement;
> For nothing can be sole or whole
> That has not been rent
> (*Collected Poems,* 255)

18. Jung, *The Archetypes and the Collective Unconscious, Collected Works,* vol. 9, no. 1 (1969), 75.

19. For attempts to reinstate this denigrated line of thought, see Frances Yates, *Rosicrucian Enlightenment* and *Occult Philosophy,* and James Olney, *The Rhizome and the Flower:*

The Perennial Philosophy—Yeats and Jung (Berkeley and Los Angeles: University of California Press, 1980).

20. See Robert D. Newman, "The Shadow of Stephen Dedalus," *Journal of Evolutionary Psychology* 2, 3, and 4 (1981): 112–24.

21. See Stanley Sultan, *The Argument of Ulysses* (Columbus: Ohio State University Press, 1964), 337–38.

22. Jung, *Alchemical Studies, Collected Works,* vol. 13, 244–48.

23. Marie-Louise von Franz, *C. G. Jung: His Myth in Our Time* (Boston: Little, Brown, 1975), 214–15.

24. *Alchemical Studies,* 217–20.

25. See Newman, "The Left-Handed Path of 'Circe,' " *James Joyce Quarterly* 23, 2 (1986): 223–27 for a fuller development of the references to left-handedness in Circe.

26. Mark E. Littmann and Charles A. Schweighauser, "Astronomical Allusions, Their Meaning and Purpose, in *Ulysses,*" *James Joyce Quarterly* 2, 4 (1965): 238–46 offers the most detailed information on the astronomical references in *Ulysses.*

27. In this sense, Molly functions as the anima that Erich Neumann calls "the vehicle par excellence of the transformative character . . . as in countless fairy tales [it] confronts the ego hero with a 'trial' that he must withstand," *The Great Mother* (Princeton: Princeton University Press, 1963), 33–34.

28. Phillip F. Herring, *Joyce's Notesheets in the British Museum* (Charlottesville: University Press of Virginia, 1972), 515.

29. See Joseph C. Voelker, " 'Nature it is': The Influence of Giordano Bruno on James Joyce's Molly Bloom," *James Joyce Quarterly* 14, 1 (1976): 39–47.

30. Dostoevsky, *The Brothers Karamazov* trans. Constance Garnett (New York: W. W. Norton, 1976), 340.

The Other of *Ulysses*

SHELDON BRIVIC

The Author as Superego

Hugh Kenner, in his *Ulysses,* directs our attention to "the mind of the text."[1] To be a mind, this evasive entity must be alive and have an identity, either Joyce's or someone else's. This essay will show how Joyce gives life to his work by infusing his own identity into it as an id entity, a being organized below the level of consciousness. Every author must provide depth for his characters from a source beyond consciousness if they are to resemble people, for people are constantly receiving impressions and images within their minds that they cannot understand or predict. Joyce recreated this psychic influx with phenomenal success: the characters and objects of his world are constantly being bombarded with surprising phrases and turns of style. To generate this vitality, Joyce had to project himself as a series of authorial personalities that were designed to react with each other within, above, and below the conscious discourse of the text. By doing so, he synthesized the complex structure of the unconscious, and I will attempt here to use the theories of Freud and their elaboration by Jacques Lacan to describe the basic elements of this structure as it operates in Joyce.

The basis of the narrative agencies that Joyce projects in his work is the Joycean personality that is withheld from his creatures, and so constitutes the unreachable otherness out of which they spring, the unknown that defines and energizes them. This authorial otherness is connected to the work by a generative transformer that uses the structure of the author's unconscious to arrange the personality of the work as a group of interacting forces that are expressed as characters, themes, and techniques. My central subject is this transformer, and while it partly resembles what David Hayman calls the arranger in *Ulysses,*[2] I hope to show that it has more than one aspect.

The Freudian term that fits this device connecting the unarticulatable mind of the author with the articulated text is the superego. Best known as a device for exerting moral control over thoughts, the superego, as I will show, was actually described by Freud as a compound structure that served as the main link between the unconscious and consciousness. By relating the conscious mind of the text to an unconscious that must be provided from outside the logic of that consciousness, this superego functions as the substance wherein text and author are consubstantial. It is not the only mode of connection between the author and his work, but it is one of the most powerful and mysterious ones. Every author serves as superego for the mind of his fiction, but variations in narrative technique will require modifications in the Joycean structure I am examining here.

The concept of the superego was a late addition to Freud's theory, and he had only begun to clarify it at the time of his death.[3] It is commonly thought of as a father's voice that has been internalized as conscience, but it turns out to have both paternal and maternal aspects, and both of these operate in Joyce's relation to his texts. I will here be tracing Freud's most comprehensive indications of the structure of the superego and relating this structure to the theories of Lacan. The synthesis of Freud and Lacan thus formed will serve to define the connection between Joyce and his work.

To understand the operation of the Joycean superego as a framer of narrative, we must see the mind of the text as made up of several forces that interact as distinct personalities. The idea of a mind containing a group of personalities is most often associated with Jung and his archetypes. Lacan, however, reminds us in "The subversion of the subject and the dialectic of desire in the Freudian unconscious" that it was Freud who subverted the traditional unity of the subject by showing that the mind is made up of interacting forces. One reason Lacan is rich in literary implications is that he translates Freud's concepts into linguistic terms. When he speaks of the signifier here, he refers to conscious discourse and its determinants (the text), so that the term is in effect his equivalent for *personality:* "the signifier is constituted only from a synchronic and enumerable collection of elements in which each is sustained only by the principle of its opposition to each of the others."[4]

Personality can exist only as a group of opposed forces, and Lacan presents his own diagrams of such groupings in the form of four graphs in this article. Moreover, he sees the interacting functions of these graphs as people when he identifies them with Shakespeare's characters in "Desire and the Interpretation of Desire in Hamlet."[5] And when we return to Freud after reading Lacan, we may be especially prone to notice that Freud repeatedly represents the dependent relations of the ego to the other parts of the mind in terms of a group of people interacting in a dramatic scene:

> Helpless in both directions, the ego defends itself vainly, alike against the instigations of the murderous id and against the reproaches of the

> punishing conscience. It succeeds in holding in check at least the most brutal actions of both sides. . . .[6]

How can these functions have these feelings and take these actions on a scale ranging from mild to brutal, playing their roles in the plot of neurosis, without having personalities of their own? Helplessness and defense, murderous instigation and punishing reproach—these attitudes can only resemble themselves by being attached to living persons, and they clearly represent different personal interests here.

Stephen Dedalus argues in Scylla and Charybdis that Shakespeare's personality is defined in his work by a familial pattern of connected characters, the eternal triangle of usurpation. Because for Stephen the subject is constituted by a dialectic of desire, the connections between his Shakespeare's characters are relations between the parts of the mind of the creator consubstantial in his work. A similar model applies to *Ulysses* not only through the relations between characters, but also through their relation to the mind of their author.

Father William T. Noon, in *Joyce and Aquinas,* says that Joyce, in his use of theology, tended to put the artist's unconscious in the position of God.[7] In Joyce, as in Christian tradition, created beings are barred from direct knowledge of their creator and may see only symbols of him. This pattern corresponds to Lacan's concept of the barred subject. Lacan's subject—which corresponds to Freud's unconscious, especially the main component of the unconscious, the id—is the inner level of the individual that can never be known. Though Joyce's authorial subject is barred from direct perception by his characters, nevertheless each fictional personality is defined by the Joycean substratum out of which it comes and into which it is inherently aimed at returning.

One of Lacan's best-known precepts is that the structure of the unconscious is the structure of language, and it may be said that for Lacan, personality is made of words.[8] Moreover, one's personality is always an imaginary construct, for it is based on one's perception of how others see one, and this is always a distortion.[9] Therefore, the fact that Joyce's characters are imaginary constructions of language does not prevent them from being full Lacanian personalities. Joyce constitutes life for these personalities by informing them with his will or desire through a structure that resembles the Lacanian graph and the Freudian apparatus at the same time that it acts as the metaphysical machinery of his authordox theology. His relation to his linguistic creation may be comprehensively expressed by saying that he constitutes the superego for each of his characters and for the mind of the work itself.

The value of the term *superego* lies in its ability to accommodate in a functional entity all of Joyce's three main metaphors for the artist: the artificer, the father, and God. The superego as artificer acts as a conduit that transmits into form the formless energy of the id that precedes articulation. It is a voice of parental authority that acts as mediator between the id and the ego. Thus, by organizing techniques and instilling motivation, it provides Joyce's creatures with their only access to both the psychological unconscious and the metaphysical ground of being. These are things Joyce has to feel for them. The superego represents for the conscious mind the sense of otherness within, or the sense of an otherness outside that corresponds to the interior one; this is what Lacan refers to as the Other. The superego that is shared between the author and his creations serves to connect them to levels beneath the surface of Joyce's personality without which they, as verbal constructs, can have no unconscious.

The most active role of the superego in mental life is its command of the narrator or narratizing power of experience. Freud finds

> that very powerful mental processes or ideas . . . can produce all the effects in mental life that ordinary ideas do (including effects that can in their turn become conscious as ideas), though they themselves do not become conscious. (*Ego,* 14)

His system sees all conscious images as shaped by unconscious forces. The central organizing principle through which these forces reach consciousness is the superego, which Freud describes as the nucleus or innermost core of the ego.[10] He says that the superego, which is further from consciousness than the ego, can represent the id to the ego (*Ego,* 49). Apparently, the formless contents of the id can only reach consciousness by being put into language through the control of the superego. The superego tends to manifest itself to consciousness as a voice, and Otto Fenichel describes it as having special power over verbalization: " . . . a person's relation to language is often predominantly governed by superego rules."[11]

Freud did not designate a location for the superego on his topography of the mental apparatus until *New Introductory Lectures on Psychoanalysis* (1933). Here he presents the superego as a passage extending downward into the id and upward into the ego on the opposite side of the apparatus from repression (see fig. 1). Except for this channel, the unconscious on the bottom is barred from the preconscious above it by two dotted lines.[12] This diagram seems to confirm that the superego is the only route of access to the unconscious, and it seems likely that this route is the one by which feelings are transformed into language.

If the superego transforms what is unconscious into words, then it plays a central role in Lacan's system, which emphasizes the idea that what is outside language is unknowable. The articulation of unconscious impulses

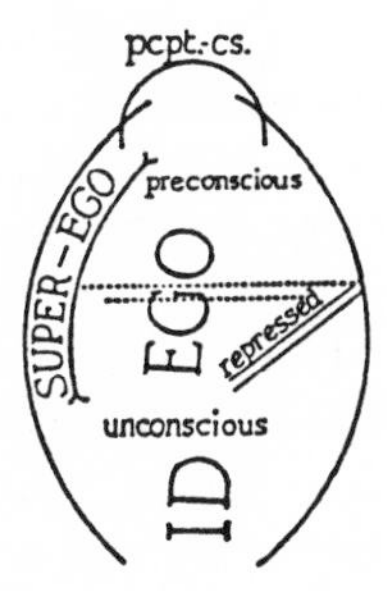

Figure 1. Freud's sketch for the structural relations of the personality, from *New Introductory Lectures in Psychoanalysis.*

as discourse is the function performed by the apparatus represented by the several versions of the graph presented by Lacan in "The subversion of the subject." Lacan says of this graph, "It will serve here to show where desire, in relation to the subject defined in his articulation by the signifier, is situated" ("Subversion," 303). Like the mechanism of Lacan's graph, the superego apprehends and conditions the substance of self-knowledge that is the basis of rational discrimination.

Moreover, Freud identifies the censorship of dreams as a function of the superego.[13] This agency, then, is the basic shaper of both the stream of consciousness and the distortion of dreams, mediating the apprehensible forms of both the inner world and the outer one. Lacan does not use the term *superego,* but he maintains that the basic forms of all human perceptions are shaped by an irrevocable sense of loss that is essentially sexual.[14]

Joyce corresponds to this shaping function of the superego for his characters insofar as he organizes their inner and outer worlds by knowing intuitively what is right for them. In certain respects, he knows what they desire better than they do, but he also knows that they can't be allowed to have it. These two kinds of knowledge—knowledge of the aim of desire and of its impossibility, both withheld from the characters—indicate the two main aspects of the superego as ideal and threat. Joyce's operation as superego, however, goes beyond any definable knowledge in order to serve as the source of life for his creation. He must provide a substructure of interacting forces that conditions every point of the text from several directions at once to fill it with vital tension.

The Marriage of Speaking and Hearing

Emphasis on the paternal aspect of the superego, an aspect enhanced by patriarchal culture, has obscured the fact that Freud described the superego as containing two sexes, yet its bisexual nature is essential to its narrating power. The forerunner of the superego in the toddler is the ego ideal, which Fenichel describes as "an 'inner mother,' threatening a possible withdrawal of affection." The oedipal stage brings about the dominance of the paternal authority that completes the superego. The ego ideal, however, remains present, and the two sides of the superego stay "as intermingled as were the protecting and threatening powers of the parents."[15] One can't protect without potentially threatening, and a threat usually offers possible protection.

In *The Ego and the Id* Freud says that the ego is constituted by a series of identifications, and that the earliest and strongest of these make up the superego, which tends to include the unconscious portion of the ego, and which is composed primarily of maternal and paternal identifications *"in some way united with each other"* (*Ego,* 34, Freud's italics). This image of internal coition represents the core of the narrative activity of the mind. In the act of writing, the most basic identifications involved are polarized as active and passive because the writer enters his work by being able to speak, and his speech is always a relation of a speaker to a listener in his mind.

Joyce's interior monologue techniques turn from the tradition of narrative spoken or written to another person in order to emphasize the fact that all discourse begins by being addressed by one aspect of the mind to another. All stream of consciousness discourse is motivated by loss. In *Ulysses,* it is motivated most immediately by Stephen's loss of his mother and by the Blooms' partial loss of each other. But everyone who speaks in his mind is addressing someone who is not there—and internal speech, or thought, is much more frequent than external speech and may be the basis of the latter.

Bloom, in Sirens, thinks, "Thou lost once. All songs on that theme" (*U,* 11.802), and Stephen, in *Portrait,* defines the lyric as "the simplest verbal vesture of an instant of emotion" (*P,* 214), or a direct expression of the self. The purest expression of the self is a sense of loss, and this is one reason Lacan insists that the subject is always based on a sense of being cut off.[16] In Freud, the identifications that make up the ego are motivated by separation from the persons identified with, so that we form our personalities by a series of losses (*Ego* 28–29).

In the world Joyce came from, the most essential loss was supposed to be the separation from God. People were supposed to talk to God and take him into themselves, and Joyce, as the *Portrait* indicates, did this passionately as an adolescent. In the world he went into, the world of his work, the great basic loss is the loss of Joyce. No matter what relatives, friends, enemies, spirits, or self-images the characters may address in their minds, they are always talking to Joyce. Every loss is a gain for the mind because it generates new identifications that expand the personality, and the intercourse between Joyce and his creatures is the predominant source of their lives. It is a communion in which Joyce plays both masculine and feminine roles, both giving and receiving.

If such interaction between poles of the mind has the power to create life, it must be what one of Faulkner's characters, speaking of storytelling, refers to as a "happy marriage of speaking and hearing."[17] The basic hermetic doctrine that "no creation, physical, mental or spiritual, is possible without" the operation of "the principle of gender" is a pervasive assumption in Joyce's work.[18] Regarding every mental impulse in Brunonian terms as constituted by reaction to its opposite, he thought of what Stephen calls "artistic conception, artistic gestation and artistic reproduction" (*P*, 209) as a process of interaction between masculine and feminine principles in the artist's mind. Therefore all of Joyce's narrative is thought of as resting on a feminine substratum. In *Portrait,* for example, Stephen is shown conceiving a poem: "In the virgin womb of the imagination the word was made flesh. Gabriel the seraph had come to the virgin's chamber" (*P*, 217).

The poem Stephen writes in *Ulysses* focuses on his vision of a male vampire kissing a woman: "He comes, pale vampire . . . mouth to her mouth's kiss" (*U*, 3.397). This has overtones both of the death of Stephen's mother at God's lips and of the primal scene of intercourse between father and mother. Stephen elicits the poem from the stream of his consciousness by halting the flow of his thoughts: "Put a pin in that chap, will you?" (*U*, 3.399). The writing of the poem is thus parallel in function to the "elementary cell" of Lacan's first graph, "the 'anchoring point' *(point de capiton),* by which the signifier stops the otherwise endless movement *(glissement)* of the signification" ("Subversion," 303).

Lacan's first graph of the forces that articulate conscious discourse, like his other versions of the graph, consists basically of two opposed movements (see fig. 2). There is an arc-shaped vector moving clockwise and a hook-shaped vector moving counterclockwise and crossing the arc at two points. The arc represents the endless movement of the signifier toward the signified; that is, our words keep trying to express the truth of their subjects, but they never get there. The hook goes in the opposite direction, and on the second version of the graph, the first point at which the hook crosses the arc is labelled "O," while the second point of crossing is labelled "s(O)." I believe this means that the hook moves from the Other, which is so rich with suggestion that it cannot be expressed, to the statement of the Other, which pins down the Other, reducing it to an inadequate representation. Therefore the arc moves toward uncertainty and represents the drive of language to express the ineffable, while the hook moves toward certainty and represents the tendency of language to trap or enclose meaning. They may be compared to speaking and hearing respectively, and as impulses crossing in opposite directions, they may also be compared to traditional sexual roles.

Moreover, from a Lacanian perspective, the vampire and the woman in Stephen's vision may be seen respectively as the signifier and the signified. When the signifier (which Lacan tends to see as a phallus)[19] makes contact with the signified, the latter dies. The soul of the artist, which Joyce consistently represents as a woman *(anima),* is the signified in this arrangement, and it dies by being transformed into the signifier of the work. Stephen, however, is trying to escape this morbid vision of the sex act and perhaps also of the act of writing; and Joyce's effort was to bring what had been sacrificed for the work back to life in that work.

Joyce's most advanced representation of the relation of the artist to his work appears in the lesson chapter (II.2) of *Finnegans Wake*. Here the emanation of the author into his work is depicted in images based on the kabbalistic model for the creation of the world: an unknowable God projects himself toward existence by dividing his original unity into a series of ten subordinate beings. In Joyce's version, the first two of these beings are husband and wife: "Ainsoph, this upright one, with that noughty besighed him zeroine" (*FW,* 261.23).[20] Throughout the *Wake,* starting with the first chapter, HCE generates the other members of the family out of himself, usually starting with ALP; and throughout the *Wake* the full reality of HCE is said to lie in a prior existence as Finn rather than being present in the *Wake*'s dream world.

The structure of the Joycean superego as an intercourse between mother and father imagoes energizes the characters and provides them with an amplitude of signification. They can only have access to feelings beyond logical construction, or to the sliding of the signifier away from fixed meaning, insofar as Joyce provides them with depth from his own unconscious. The generative heart of Joyce's experimental technique is

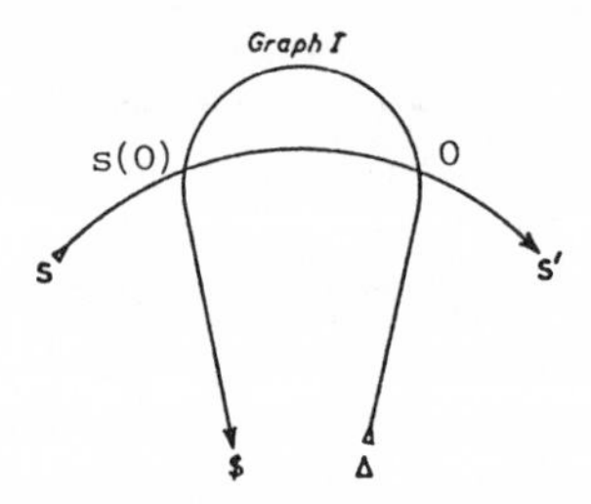

Figure 2. Lacan's first graph from "The subversion of the subject and the dialectic of desire in the Freudian unconscious." Note: The labels "O" and "s(O)" have been given for the two crossing points here although they do not appear until Lacan's "Graph II."

not a matter of theory, which serves to enclose its subject, but of feeling, which leads beyond itself. The unconscious can never be created by theory, but only restricted by it.

The basic dynamic model charging the being of Joyce's creatures combines a masculine threat *(animus)* and a feminine attraction *(anima).* As often happens, the Jungian system is congruent with the Freudian here.[21] In *Joyce Between Freud and Jung* I showed in detail how the minds of Stephen and Bloom are constantly moving back and forth between images of threat and images of attraction. I also explained why proximity to one pole would arouse fear (of the *animus*) or guilt (for approaching the *anima*), and so propel the mind back towards the other pole.[22]

A particularly strong example of the elementary dynamic context of Joycean personality appears at the crucial juncture just before Stephen loses his virginity in *Portrait*. His desire appears as an incubus driving him forward: "His hands clenched convulsively and his teeth set together as he suffered the agony of its penetration" (*P,* 100). Stephen's assertion of masculinity not only pushes forward toward the maternal figure of the prostitute, but is pushed from behind by the paternal threat, which, however perverse its manifestations, tends to be equatable with a fear of not measuring up to other men.

Similarly, Bloom has not only Molly on his mind, but the demonic Blazes Boylan; and while the image of Boylan should deter Bloom from doing what he does, in fact this image is part of the mechanism that keeps him on his course. His need is such that he cannot resist the dynamism of evil: in Hades, he thinks to himself, "Fascination. Worst man in Dublin" (*U,* 6.202) and though he attributes this fascination to Molly, he is clearly not free from it himself. His superego is so strong that he enjoys being abused by it. This is Joyce's ironic version of what some psychologists refer to as being "well-adjusted."

Bloom represents an attitude and a phase of life in which holding back is more profitable than action. Insofar as he is primarily a father, his potential for psychic development relates to others more than to himself. When Stephen moves toward his *anima,* temptress and muse, he is developing his own soul; but Bloom, by allowing himself to be invaded by the *animus,* the competing male, operates creatively on Molly and Stephen, expanding himself through them. He sacrifices himself for Molly through cuckoldry to revive her love, and his unselfishness to Stephen allows the young man to accept the idea of fatherhood—a crucial step toward the maturation of the artist and the creation of *Ulysses.* Stephen observes in Scylla and Charybdis that the son's "growth is his father's decline" (*U,* 9.856); likewise, the decline of the father propels the development of the son. On this fundamental level, the living father is an imperfect form of the dead father, the definitive form of paternity that is enshrined in the superego.

The common or familiar nature of many of Bloom's ideas indicates his alignment with the superego. In its punitive aspect, the superego is an agency of social conformity that tends to be substantially shared by large numbers of people. Yet the form that the superego takes in relation to the other parts of the mind must be unique for each individual and for each moment of each individual. Joyce achieves this effect by applying a combination of constant innovation and masterful control to the elements that are submerged at various levels beneath the surface of language. He uses the opposing forces on Lacan's graph to control and vary the interplay of speaking and hearing.

Bloom is so well adjusted, so good at accommodating his guilt rather than fighting it, that his greatest pleasure and excitement lie in entering the minds of others while effacing himself. He does this on the numerous occasions on which he returns a mild reply to insults, thinking "Be sorry after perhaps when it dawns on him" (*U,* 6.1031). This is a very common pattern in life, though no one accepts insults in quite the same ways that Bloom does. He is after all an original as the first major figure in English literature to demonstrate this pattern.

Bloom may also be entering the mind of another while effacing himself in Nausicaa, for Joyce is reported to have suggested that Gerty MacDowell's monologue is at least partly a projection of Bloom's.[23] Bloom certainly follows the pattern of self-transfer when he is imagined watching Blazes and Molly in Circe: "Show! Hide! Show! Plough her! More! Shoot!" (*U,* 15.3815). Virtually all of the channels of Bloom's desire—cuckoldry, masochism, fetishism, coprophilia, and love for daughter—emphasize the negation of personality. This mounting obliteration is related to Bloom's being past the middle of life: " . . . from existence to nonexistence gone he would be by all as none perceived" (*U,* 17.68–69). While Stephen is asserting himself by opposing the superego, Bloom is lapsing into its otherness.

On the other hand, a person's weakness may give him strength by helping him to relate to another person, and Bloom's self-sacrifice may prove fruitful through his relations to Stephen and Molly. Molly, in particular, seems determined as the book ends to give Bloom a great deal of the kind of sexual stimulation that she knows will excite him (*U,* 18.1520–38). This stimulation is largely a matter of anal imagery, and the part of her that he usually makes love to is her "bottom" (*U,* 18.53,77). Yet it is possible that with her interest in vaginal intercourse recently stirred up, she may succeed in situating him in the haven from which he has been exiled for a decade. The superego of the book, however, maintains an essential realism by not permitting this ideal possibility to be actualized.

Although it is the superego that exiles all of Joyce's characters, it is also the superego that allows them to be created by defining them. As an internalized parental power, the superego can motivate restriction only by sustaining the assurance that sacrifice will lead to reward. Just as the superego is not only masculine, but feminine, so, as the source of all guilt and beauty, it provides not only terror, but delight. Freud designates these two aspects by his two names for it, which he often uses without distinction in *The Ego and the Id, superego* (*über-ich*) and *ego ideal* (*ichideal*).

Freud says that "the moral and aesthetic trends in the ego" instigate repression (*Ego,* 35), and that "the ego ideal answers to everything that is expected of the higher nature of man" (*Ego,* 27). All beauty is perceived through the superego because in order to become conscious, the feelings in the unconscious must be articulated in language, whether this language is a dictionary language or merely a set of discriminations. We may think we feel pure pleasure, but as soon as we become conscious of it, it has been idealized by the superego.

The shame of the superego and the bliss of the ego ideal correspond to that inseparable pair, taboo and totem, the vile and the sacred, or what is beneath the parenthesis of consciousness and what is above it. Metaphysically, they correspond to alpha and omega, the prior cause and the ultimate goal. These functions exist for the characters of *Ulysses* and their world only insofar as Joyce provides them; and he does so by projecting his mind into his work as a dynamic structure that allows him to convey his vital energy into his world.

The Intersaid

The idea that the unconscious cannot reach consciousness without being transformed by the superego is one of the bases of Lacan's concept of the barred subject. He speaks of "the Other as previous site of the pure subject of the signifier" ("Subversion," 305). This means that when we try to look at the subject, it is gone, but we can see where it used to be by looking at otherness, what is unknown to us and unexpected. Thus, the barred subject Joyce constitutes for his work is objectified for his characters and for his readers as the Other. The activity of the author is manifested every time a word or sign appears that is not expected, that does not come from what has been established, but from outside.

Each of the protagonists, Stephen and Bloom, represents the Other for his opposite. Each is the source of creation for the other in that they are created for the purpose of meeting. The plot of the novel is a series of events in which they confront each other with new possibilities of personal development. The depth of their relationship flies in the face of convention, for on the surface they hardly know each other. Yet the general organization of *Ulysses* makes it obvious that the depth of their relationship constitutes the soul of the book. This depth is based on a sense of otherness. It manifests itself to the protagonists in a sense of being outside the ordinary world, a sense which dominates the second half of the book from Oxen of the Sun onward as the factual world of Bloomsday is overshadowed by stylistic distortions. The antirealistic effects of the parodies of Oxen, the fantasies of Circe, the self-defeating clichés of Eumaeus, and the interstellar atmosphere of Ithaca tend to shift the action from the real world into a cosmic perspective, but this perspective has been in the background all along.

All of the characters in *Ulysses* partake of a collective unconscious because Joyce constitutes for them the numerous images that they cannot consciously derive. The book emerges from this mental totality when it begins in a tower that is referred to as an "omphalos" adjoining the sea that ended *Portrait*. In Proteus, Stephen conceives of a navel cord that extends into the distant past, and it may be that the navel of the text is connected to the unconscious that precedes it, the Joycean mental world into which Stephen set out at the end of *Portrait*.

In the Telemachia, the narrative moves into Stephen's mind to discover progressively the depth of his need, the Joycean substratum that connects him to Bloom. "What is that word known to all men?" (*U*, 3.435) he asks the ghost of his mother, a representative of the superego. In Scylla and Charybdis, he identifies this word as "love."[24] Bloom should be able to convey this word, for he is the only figure in possession of love whom Stephen encounters in *Ulysses*, and he is filled with common knowledge. Yet the "word known to all men" should not be taken as a simple entity, for Stephen asks his mother the same question again after he has supposedly answered it: he does this in Circe as she is trying to make him submerge himself in the Father by repenting (*U*, 15.4192). Here she drives him into a confrontation that ends up attaching him to Bloom, thus revealing the superego as fate. The idea of the "word known to all men" is not completed.

It is conceivable that Bloom is referred to by the missing white corpuscles (leucocytes) of Buck Mulligan's Eucharist on the first full page, for Bloom is later referred to as "leucodermic" (*U*, 17.785). At any rate, once Stephen's need has been unfolded, we find that Bloom has been going on simultaneously answering it. The "urinous offal" Stephen thinks of at the end of his episodes (*U*, 3.479–80) is followed by the kidneys on Bloom's mind at the start of his, and these characters are connected throughout the book by scores of synchronicities—coincidences and thoughts that are shared without being perceptibly communicated.[25]

When these connections are perceived, they lift the reader out of the naturalistic world the characters inhabit into the superego or ego ideal of the book—Freud uses the two terms interchangeably because, as Fenichel points out, they are inseparable. When, on the other hand, the differences between the characters are emphasized, the empirical reality of Bloomsday under the superego comes to the fore. Wandering Rocks elaborates the breadth of the field separating the protagonists in order to create the most concrete vision of the city in the book. After this, the objective world is increasingly subordinated to a Joycean world of style as the protagonists move toward communion with each other.[26] This communion will constitute their first cause, the artist as mature man who results from Bloom's influence on Stephen. Therefore the increasing intervention of the author through stylistic complexities represents a major psychic reality of the book, the growth of Joyce's mind. The individual streams of consciousness of the protagonists rarely appear to be unmediated after Nausicaa. The narrative comes to be dominated by a series of narrators who represent something larger than the individuals.

What the Linati schema refers to as the "fusion" of Stephen and Bloom is signaled through the "infusion" and "diffusion" (*U,* 17.357–58) of the cocoa they share.[27] The episode in which they clinch this fusion, Ithaca, takes the form of questions and answers. The Catechism, on which it is based, presents a youth or novice asking a priest or adept for spiritual knowledge, and therefore its form embodies the relation between son and father.[28] Just as the cosmic but detailed narrative of Ithaca exists only through the difference between question and answer, so Stephen, in Scylla and Charybdis, argues that the universe is founded on the void that constitutes the relation between father and son (*U,* 9.840–41). One implication of this fundamental analogy is that all knowledge rests on the relation between what is known (the father) and what is not known (the son). Once knowledge settles into being known, it stops having a living relation to the ungraspable reality of flux and becomes opposed to the activity of knowing. The universe is built on what we know, but the reality of the universe comes home to us when it violates our principles and makes us realize that it is more than our fantasies about it. Therefore the reality of knowledge is situated in the gap between the incommensurable categories of what is known and what is not known. It is in this gap that Joyce operates as author.

The universe of the example of artistic creation that Stephen concentrates on, *Hamlet,* is certainly built on the void between father and son. The action of the play begins with the apparition of the ghost of the father, and at the end, when father and son are atoned, the ghost must leave the world and that world comes to an end as the drama is completed. Every action in the play is an expression of the mystery of uncertainty that connects the son to the father. Joyce's central model of the artist as superego is Stephen's vision of Shakespeare playing the ghost in Hamlet. This godlike father spirit operates as a function of his son's personality to shape the action and to give his son access to guilt and glory.

Freud says that the relation of the superego to the ego is that of father to son.[29] This reinforces the notion that the active perception of reality depends on the difference between an established view and a new one. Thus, for Freud, human perception expresses not a single agent, but a simultaneous combination of agents, and the same is true of discourse, which expresses the superego and the ego at once. Lacan expands on this idea in "The subversion of the subject," where he speaks of "the right way to reply to the question, 'Who is speaking?', when it is the subject of the unconscious that is at issue." The speaker is a space between persons, an idea that receives indirect confirmation from the recent findings of experimental psychologists that the two lobes of the brain, which work together in normal consciousness, have completely different personalities.[30] Lacan replaces the unified classical subject with a divided Freudian subject:

> the place of the 'inter-said' *(inter-dit),* which is the 'intra-said' *(intra-dit)* of a between-two-subjects, is the very place in which the transparency of the classical subject is divided and passes through the effects of 'fading' that specify the Freudian subject by its occultation by an ever purer signifier. . . . (299)

In *Ulysses,* where Stephen is generally seen with Bloom's compassion and Bloom is generally seen with Stephen's irony, what is usually speaking at any point is neither Stephen nor Bloom, but a combination of the two. This combination is both inter-said, because it lies between two characters, and intra-said, because it expresses parts of one mind. This mind is constantly expressed on several levels at once by the linguistic multivalence of the text, which involves several different voices speaking at once in each word. It is the mind of Joyce that speaks in this multivalence. It speaks out of its own deep division to specify the subject "by its occultation by an ever purer signifier," the Joycean superego that complicates the text.

Ithaca emphasizes the origin of its discourse in a source beyond any specific identity: not only its use of inquiry, but its cosmic context and its infinite regresses into detail serve to evoke an interdicted substratum or a margin beyond the known. The mind approaches sleep by withdrawing from consciousness, and Bloom's devotion to matter and his faith in nature are presented as obeisance to a power beyond his knowledge. The symbol of this unconscious power is Molly, whom he uses to represent the world as benevolent. He elucidates for Stephen "the mystery of an invisible person, his wife . . . denoted by a visible splendid sign, a lamp . . ." (*U,* 17.1178).

A few pages after this description of Molly as the Holy Ghost, the "mystery of an invisible person" who completes the father and the son,[31] Bloom evokes the masculine side of his deity as he wonders if he should wait to be inspired by the rebirth of the sun, "the visible diffusion of the light of an invisible luminous body" (*U,* 17.1266–67). The sun was associated by Stephen with Shakespeare as the artist who returns in his work (*U,* 15.2118). The superego resembles God in being invisible or submerged from consciousness, and in being the source of religious values; and like God, it appears indirectly through whatever is beautiful and terrible. Another parallel between the superego and the traditional concept of God is that the ego requires the love of the superego to live (*Ego,* 58).

Molly and the sun both represent invisible powers, the unconscious and the first cause respectively. These powers are manifested constantly in the form of synchronicities and other departures from established styles or systems of reality. Such surprising connections, stylistic devices, external references, and enigmas seem to have no cause in the naturalistic world of the novel, yet they may add to its realism. For it may be that people are constantly creating new connections, styles, references, and enigmas in their lives without being aware of it. These unassuming innovations follow internal ordering principles unknown to intentional awareness.

These surprising connections that originate in orders outside the ordinary reality of Bloomsday serve to expand that reality beyond systematic theory. Because these infusions of vitality cannot come from the created world, their motivation must come from Joyce. He must personally generate the desire and being necessary to save his world from death. Joyce as a generating power is not only manifested every time we grow aware of his virtuosity, his use of structure, his allusions, and his self-reflexive references; he is also, like the family members of the *Wake,* visible in the landscape, the seascape, and the skyscape.

Joycean Topography

Freud found the unconscious to be manifested in mistakes because such actions are situated at the edge of perception. Because they are hard to perceive, distant views are like phenomena experienced in semi-conscious states in that they represent the margin or level of being that precedes rational articulation. Therefore, Joyce's relation to his work is represented not only by the depths and surfaces of his style, but by his images of the margins of landscape: the sea, the sky, and the earth. In *Joyce the Creator,* I describe how Joyce speaks as "the sea's voice" (*U,* 9.479) in *Ulysses.*[32] A few points can be added to that argument. First, the sea, from which Stephen seems to receive his vocation when he hears "a voice from beyond the world" in *Portrait* (*P,* 167), is located within his mind in the first chapter of that novel. At the start of the following paragraph, Stephen is awake; at the end, he is dreaming of a dead father figure, Parnell's body being borne on a ship into Dublin Bay. This body of water, which is referred to here as "the sea of waves," is to inspire Stephen with vision again and again in this novel and in *Ulysses,* where it also inspires Bloom:

> How pale the light was at the window! But that was nice. The fire rose and fell on the wall. It was like waves. Someone had put coal on and he heard voices. They were talking. It was the noise of the waves. Or the waves were talking among themselves as they rose and fell. (*P,* 26)

As he enters the depths of his mind, the waves are heard speaking as a multitude. This incoherent swarming of voices on the inner level of his mind is the same liquid multitude Stephen hears when his desire presses him in the second chapter:

> a presence subtle and murmurous as a flood filling him wholly with itself. Its murmur besieged his ears like the murmur of some multitude in sleep; its subtle streams penetrated his being. His hands clenched . . . as he suffered the agony of its penetration. (*P,* 100)

This murmuring flood is the irruption of the id, the multitudinous, disordered flowing of forms that precedes articulation; but the id can only be perceived as having a definite form when it is channeled through the superego. Insofar as the words of this flood are heard, or insofar as the irruption is focused or pointed enough to propel motivation, the superego shapes the unconscious.

The other example of water imagery I want to discuss is anticipated in Scylla and Charybdis when Stephen predicts his own redemption and gives the unknown word the name of love in the course of an account of Shakespeare as cuckold that prefigures Bloom. Stephen asks, "What softens the heart of a man, Shipwrecked in storms dire, Tried, like another Ulysses, Pericles, prince of Tyre?" and answers, "A child" (*U,* 9.406). Jung tells us that the child saved from the sea may symbolize a new idea delivered from the unconscious.[33] In this case, the idea beginning to emerge from the Joycean unconscious must be the conception of *Ulysses,* the novel that will unite Stephen and Bloom. Of course Stephen does not know what he is predicting when he predicts Bloom or speaks of reconciliation or of the artist who becomes his own father consubstantial in his work. He only knows that his version of Shakespeare is for him an uncanny revelation of the mysteries of fate and desire. But the mind of the text has to know what he is predicting in order to represent not only his surface experience, but the great potential in his depths.

When the symbolic child that Stephen predicts appears in the form of

Rudy Bloom as a possibility, or what Rudy might have been, at the end of Circe, both Stephen and Bloom are murmuring of the sea. Stephen "murmurs" Yeats's "Who Goes with Fergus?" while Bloom "murmurs" lines of unknown origin: " . . . a cabletow's length from the shore . . . where the tide ebbs . . . and flows . . ." (*U,* 15.4953–54, Joyce's ellipses). Their minds are both focused on the distant depths of the "white breast of the dim sea" because they are in touch with the psychic potential that unites them.

The main topographical image of Joyce as superego that I want to concentrate on here is that of the sky.[34] The first striking indication of a connection between Stephen and Bloom is the cloud they both notice over the sun in the first of their simultaneous opening episodes. Focusing their attention on the sky, the cloud evokes for both a sense of horror associated with an aging female: Stephen thinks of his mother on her deathbed and Bloom sees "a bent hag" on the street (*U,* 1.248, 4.224). The stricture of the superego gives both men visions of the ego ideal, which both perceive in terms of the loss of a mother.

Moreover, both men think here of a body of water associated with death: Stephen sees Dublin Bay as "a bowl of bitter waters," while Bloom thinks of "poisonous" waters and "a dead sea." Weldon Thornton points out that "bitter water" is used to curse unfaithful women in Numbers 5:18,[35] and this suggests that both men are thinking of infidelity. After the cloud passes, both men perceive "warm running sunlight" (*U,* 1.283, 4[illegible]40). As a signal from the Father-God, the cloud makes Stephen think of his mother's death, for which he constantly blames "the Universal Husband" (*U,* 14.1319).

Stephen later feels (*U,* 17.40) that this cloud came back and caused his collapse in Nighttown (see *U,* 15.4661, 4669), showing that he thinks of it as a permanent threat. He refers to it as "at first no bigger than a woman's hand" (*U,* 17.42), a reference to I Kings 18:44, where "a little cloud" is a sign of God's threatening. In Scylla and Charybdis, he says that "the signature" of Shakespeare's initial appeared among the stars at his birth (*U,* 9.931). He is in the habit of seeing the sky as a field on which divine messages appear.

In Ithaca, where they come closest to Joyce, Stephen and Bloom study the sky, seeing a shooting star that passes from the Lyre to Leo (*U,* 17.1211). We study the sky at night because at this time we can see outer space, whereas during the day we can only see our own atmosphere. This underlying sense of being lost in space may be one reason we are further from our conscious minds at night. This tendency is paralleled by the increasing stylistic complication in the second half of the novel, which shifts our focus to something within or behind or beyond or above the action: the mind of the artist.

The cosmic perspective that accompanies the opening of the mind beyond daylight logic is a scope that allows the deity in Joyce to flex his muscles. The immanent and transcendent (or below and above) aspects of the Joycean superego are suggested and united when he reaches outward to the outer limits of the universe and then inward to the tiniest part of a quark (*U,* 17.1042–69). Joyce may have been the first writer to focus as sharply as he does on such tiny units of matter, though it wasn't until the *Wake* that he coined the noun *quark* (*FW,* 383.1).[36] If the inner space in this passage is uniquely Joycean, it is important to remember that no matter how far one follows these meditations of Bloom's into outer space, one must always remain within Joyce's mind, the framer of the vision. Joyce binds inner space and outer space together by the daring assumption, probably inspired by Giordano Bruno,[37] that the entire universe is contained within the subquark, and an infinite number of cosmoses in the mind. This recognition leads to the *Wake,* which portrays the entire universe as contained within a letter that may be no more than a single alphabetical character.

For Bloom, as Joyce clarifies his thinking and thinks through him to complete his thought, the stars represent in their remoteness what Lacan calls the barred subject—the inability of the mind to know its own truth, which Lacan sees as the starting point of consciousness. As I have suggested, the barred subject tends to be objectified as the Other, so that the more one sees of otherness, the more one sees of subjectivity:

> That it was not a heaventree . . . not a heavenman. That it was a Utopia, there being no known method from the known to the unknown: an infinity renderable equally finite by the . . . apposition of one or more bodies equally of the same and of different magnitudes: a mobility of illusory forms immobilised in space, remobilised in air: a past which possibly had ceased to exist as a present before its probable spectators had entered actual present existence. (*U,* 17.1139–45)

Bloom agrees with Einstein that all motion is relative, the "apposition of one or more bodies." Therefore the universe we imagine to be standing still must from other viewpoints be moving. Its "mobility," by evoking Aristotle's definition of the soul in *De Anima* as a source of motion, ultimately suggests that the universe is part of a larger being, the being against whose parts it defines its motion. This being has absolute authority over the Joycean speaker because that speaker is a part of him. Nevertheless, like God, or the author to his characters, or one's parents, or one's unconscious, it can never be known. We may live in its projected light after it has ceased to exist, as Joyce's characters continue to partake of constantly changing manifestations of his creativity. We are doomed to apprehend this barred subject only indirectly as a relation among parts, an intertextuality. Yet we can never stop looking for it, and we can never see anything else but fragments of it. This is made clear by Lacan's definition of language: "a signifier is that which represents the subject for another signifier" ("Subversion," 316). Lacan understands that words always describe an unreachable totality.

If all perception is perception of something absent, then the real nature of perception may be seen most clearly in starlight, for starlight makes things seem unreal or dream-like, suggesting a photographic negative or an anti-world. This is why Bloom reflects that his visual field, what Stephen calls the diaphane, consists of light waves that come from an unknowable source. Our field of perceptions is illusory in the sense that we can never see where it actually comes from, any more than we can look at the sun. What we can see of its external sources is at the mercy of internal sources we can scarcely comprehend. Nevertheless, Bloom grants this field "esthetic value" in view of "reiterated examples of poets in the delirium of the frenzy of attachment or in the abasement of rejection invoking ardent sympathetic constellations or the frigidity of the satellite of their planet" (*U,* 17.1147–50).

Bloom's vision of heaven has its earthly implications, for Joyce refers to a woman's buttocks in this episode as "a bispherical moon" (*U,* 17.1996), and in Circe, Bloom says, "I have paid homage on that living altar where the back changes name" (*U,* 15.3405–6). His devotion to this orb, the center of his materialism, is quite intense. If we can only perceive through the energy of our desires (however that energy may be organized), then Bloom may be said to see very little but moonlight, however that light may be reflected, so that psychologically his sun reflects his moon.

Bloom is aware that though all we can see are moonbeams, these illusions are the sources of our highest values. In the above passage (17.1147–50), these values are erotic. Lacan holds that images gain their value through their association with language, and the truth is, as Lacan's definition of the signifier suggests, that all of the traditional words of language originally owed *their* validity to the concept of God. Though we can never know the author of our thought, still every term for him, or her, is a term for our mind, Psyche. We create ourselves by creating her, and see our beauty in her, as Bloom suggests when he considers the theory that the moon influences events on earth:

> It seemed to him as possible of proof as of confutation and the nomenclature employed in its selenographical charts as attributable to verifiable intuition as to fallacious analogy: the lake of dreams, the sea of rains, the gulf of dews, the ocean of fecundity. (*U,* 17.1153–56)

Bloom's religious devotion to materialism is often used to demonstrate that science, like religion, is a means of projecting the human mind on the cosmos. Thus, for example, he claims that the movements of the heavens are caused by magnetism and then equates magnetism with sexual desire: "Back of everything magnetism. . . . Woman and man that is" (*U,* 13.987–93). The belief that the universe is run by desire is quite valid in a universe run by Joyce's mind.

The labels we pin on the heavens are arbitrary, as are those we affix on parts of the mind, for the signifier and the signified are sundered. Nevertheless, by mapping out a language, we give ourselves a system of discriminations that unfolds the subject to express our feelings. In this sense—which is essentially poetic because it involves the creation of new verbal connections—we are able to partake of heaven, for in imagining our minds, we create them, assuming a divine role or joining the activity of our author. And though Joyce's presence in his world is no more graspable than the presence of God, yet that presence unfolds itself in language to give that world reality.

The Great Reservoir of Libido

At the end of his narrative life, Bloom completes his movement toward the Other by lapsing into the womb of the unconscious. His career as a signifier done, he is returning to Joyce's mind. He does so through the black dot at the end of Ithaca, which represents the aperture at which he locates his personal god (*U,* 17.2332). This spot represents Molly's genitals in general, but probably her anus in particular. This was the center of Bloom's attention when he kissed her buttocks two pages earlier "in their mellow yellow furrow, with obscure prolonged provocative melonsmellonous osculation" (*U,* 17.2242–43). This spot may be linked to his superego because it is for him the center not only of transcendent bliss (the ideal), but also, as he demonstrated in Circe (*U,* 15.3057), of maximum shame and guilt.[38] It is through this point, this passageway into the interior, that he dies and is reborn; and the operator of this passage in his mind is the superego, the internal force of his Joycean deity, which acts as father in death and mother in rebirth.

In the last paragraph of Ithaca, syntax and logic disintegrate as Bloom enters the womb of sleep, where he will float in the unformed primal matter of language. Here in the murmuring sea of the unconscious, he merges with all possibilities, squaring the circle "in the night of the bed of all the auks." Bloom joins the metonymous series of variations on "Sinbad the Sailor," which changes its simple alphabetical nature toward the end to indicate that it could go on forever. This series of adventurers represents every possible impulse that exists in the id or the barred subject prior to formulation. This realm can only be perceived as it is distorted by language, and so it can reach the text only through the imposition of Joyce as superego.

If Joyce suggested to Power that Gerty MacDowell's monologue is a projection of Bloom's, then it may also be that Molly's monologue is at least partly an expression of Bloom's unconscious.[39] The thoughts of both women could exist as independent entities and yet reflect Bloom's ideas and psychic functions as easily as Stephen reflects Bloom's ideas and functions throughout the book. The distinction between the functions of the two women with relation to Bloom is that Gerty represents Bloom's unconscious from the point of view of his waking mind, while Molly represents the full release of the unconscious in sleep. Gerty, subjected to rational control, is an object limited by the constriction of Bloom's superego to the repressive dallyings of perversion. Molly, on the other hand, exceeds ordinary humanity in her latitude because she is a subject. In fact, she is the subject of Bloom's life in several ways, and this may explain why she is barred. It is ultimately not only her, but himself that he desires too deeply for possession.

As an embodiment of subjectivity, Molly represents the endless sliding of the signifier by her use of language.[40] Joyce was well aware that the meaning of every word is determined by its position in a sentence. No word thought by Molly, however, has a position in a sentence. Though her phrases and clauses often seem clear, they all ultimately lack the context that would finalize them, and this often adds to their lyrical suggestiveness. In many cases her words shift their context as they are in progress, changing their orientation from a prior referent to a subsequent one. The italicized words in the passages below are elementary examples of this pattern. Each of these words starts out connected to the words before it, but ends up being attached to the ones that follow:

> telling me all her ailments *she had* too much old chat in her (*U*, 18.7)

> I had everything all to myself *then a girl* Hester we used to compare our hair (*U*, 18.637)

> I hate people that have always their poor story to tell *everybody* has their own troubles (*U*, 18.725)

These are the simplest kinds of examples of the shiftings that go on constantly on various levels of Molly's discourse of the Other. Many such words could be "cleared up" by punctuation, but of course the point is that they are not. In fact, every word we use does change in transition from its past context to its future one, but we are trained to think of sentences as static structures. By liberating verbal units from containment by sentences, Molly reveals the constant sliding or dynamic interplay of language that corresponds to the actuality of feeling, the source from which language comes and toward which it aims.

Molly's syntactical shifting, combined with her tendencies to contradict herself and to confuse references to persons and times,[41] tends to cause her language to be internal because it blurs external context. This is a step toward the pure language of the *Wake,* which reduces referentiality to an archetypal aura. Of course, Molly does convey a good deal of information reasonably clearly: her shifting effects are only a margin or horizon of her discourse. I believe, however, that this shifting area of her thinking is the part that Bloom promotes by sacrificing himself to the world in order to maintain the flow of her feelings.

The freedom from definition that Bloom supports in Molly provides him with a transcendent source of motivation, a haven of flowing possibilities outside the world of fact. When Molly says, "Theyre all mad to get in there where they come out of" (*U,* 18.806), she recognizes herself as alpha and omega, the origin and goal of all desire and therefore of all discourse. Freud repeatedly maintains that the primary focus of desire is one's own id, and that other objects of desire are like pseudopods of an amoeba, temporary extensions of a fundamental and abiding narcissism. He also says that narcissistic qualities are highly attractive erotically because the lover makes contact with his own narcissism through that of his beloved.[42]

In relating to Molly, Bloom enlarges her center to include everything. The multiplicity of her sympathy, sensitivity, and perspective—indeed, the multiplicity of her truth—locates her outside the control of the superego, outside the narrative, and within the Other itself. If Joyce is associated with two of the topographical limits of existence, the sea and the sky, Molly is linked to him by being associated with the third limit, the earth. In a letter of 8 February 1922 to Harriet Shaw Weaver, Joyce said of Penelope, " . . . I tried to depict the earth which is prehuman and presumably posthuman" (*Letters,* I, 180). This aim is typical of Joyce's constant striving in *Ulysses* to express points of view that are more than human, that are in fact divine.

The Structure of the Superego

The empirical reality of Bloomsday Dublin, which I described earlier as constituted by the separation of Stephen and Bloom, is a function of the strict aspect of the Joycean superego. This agency is at its strictest in *Dubliners* (which places greatest emphasis on the harshness of actuality) and relents progressively through Joyce's career. The other aspect of the superego, the ego ideal, which is associated with the mother imago, gains ascendency as the canon advances. Though this aspect represents the id, it has to be seen as part of the superego, for it represents in words something outside form or signification. Moreover, mercy and severity are aspects of the same continuum.

In the structure of the superego, then, the feminine part is closer to the id, while the masculine part is closer to the ego. This corresponds to a pattern in the Kabbalah called emanation, which Joyce used in the *Wake* and was probably aware of when he wrote *Ulysses.* Emanation is the mode of projection of mental beings or *sephiroth* by which God's mind enters its creation. In *Isis Unveiled,* Madame Blavatsky says, "When Sephira emerges like an active power from within the latent Deity, she is female; when she assumes the office of a creator, she becomes male; hence, she is androgyne."[43] According to this scheme, Joyce as a male writer must move toward his feminine part in order to recreate the powers of God, and this statement applies to the operation of the complex superego.

The projected feminine receptivity that draws the artist into his work may be called the muse, the term Kenner uses for the narrator of the last two episodes of *Ulysses.*[44] Joyce's entire career represents a steady movement away from the outer level of harsh reality toward this inner level of dream. The muse acts in opposition to the organizing or restricting force of the superego to constitute or liberate the designer of new systems of style, which Hayman calls the arranger. While the arranger is manifested as a controlling force from outside the text, the muse appears when the richness of the text leads the mind to contemplate a creative force acting through it. The muse operates the function that opens up from inside to expand the created world. It expresses what Erik Erikson calls the feminine power of inner space, and it also expresses the interior nature of the earth.[45]

The muse is present in the feminine aspect of the sea, the Other through which Stephen expands toward his vocation. Therefore his thoughts of the feminine aspect of the sea draw him toward this function of his creator. A good example occurs in Telemachus when Stephen thinks of Yeats's line "white breast of the dim sea" (*U,* 1.244). This is the line he later recites unconsciously to give Bloom the vision of the sea that precedes the apparition of Rudy. In Telemachus, Stephen is watching the wind rippling the sea, a symbol of the contact between spirit and matter or God creating the world. He thinks of the rhythm of the words he speaks, and the fullness of its beauty generates the thought of an invisible maternal creative power implied by this rhythm: "The twining stresses, two by two. A hand plucking the harpstrings merging their twining chords" (*U,* 1.245–46). The image of a hand without a body implies an agency beyond Stephen's world, but this agency operates on that world not by controlling it, but by caressing it to draw it forward to expansion.[46]

When an image of maternal attraction appears in the mind of the text, it tends to be followed by a paternal threat, and the "wavewhite" words are followed immediately by the cloud over the sun that reenacts the death of May Dedalus by shadowing the bay. This is the harsh side of the superego that enforces the limits of naturalism and skepticism. But this side is incapable of existing or motivating narrative without the ego ideal to draw it forward. The constant back-and-forth interplay between the terrible and beautiful aspects of the superego is the dynamic rhythm in which the narrative breathes.

While I am not able to pursue a survey here, I believe that every writer operates as a superego for his creatures, not only by judging their sexual and moral activities, but by giving them being from a level below consciousness. This animation flows from the author's depths to motivate the characters in several directions at once, making them subject to a larger life behind, above, beneath, and beyond them. Moreover, I believe that writers who try to eliminate their own intervention and authority and to be objective are really emphasizing the masculine and constricting side by suppressing their feelings. They end up in effect binding their characters to a harsh, inhuman superego because theories cannot provide life to their subjects without personal intervention.

Joyce, of course, does engage in such deconstruction of the metaphysical basis of personality, but it is only one side of his narrative activity. He does it in order to reconstruct a larger composite personality that is more personal, more complex, and more deeply metaphysical because it is based on a more rigorous analysis. His figures of the mind are constituted in the amplitude of their mental beings by reflecting the otherness that he provides for them with corresponding richness.

Notes

1. Hugh Kenner, *Ulysses* (London: Allen and Unwin, Unwin Critical Library, 1980), 112. Kenner says he got this idea from Bruce Kawin, author of *The Mind of the Novel: Reflexive Fiction and the Ineffable* (Princeton: Princeton University Press, 1982).

2. The arranger selects and organizes technical frameworks for different parts of the novel. What I am concerned with here is the complex motivation behind this function. See David Hayman, Ulysses: *The Mechanics of Meaning,* 2d ed. (Madison: University of Wisconson Press, 1982), 88–104.

3. The concept of the superego was prefigured by that of the ego-ideal in "On Narcissism: An Introduction" (1914), in *The Standard Edition of the Complete Psychological Works of Sigmund Freud,* trans. James Strachey et al., 14 (London: The Hogarth Press, 1961): 93–97. The term *superego* was introduced and given its most extensive treatment in *The Ego and the Id* (1923), in *Standard Edition,* 19 (1961): 28–39, 48–59. Important additions to the theory of the superego appeared in *Inhibitions, Symptoms and Anxiety* (1926), in *Standard Edition,* 20 (1959): 115–40; "Humour" (1927), in *Standard Edition,* 21 (1961): 161–66; and *New Introductory Lectures on Psychoanalysis* (1933), in *Standard Edition,* 22 (1964): 28, 62–67, 78–79, 109–10.

4. Jacques Lacan, "The subversion of the subject and the dialect of desire in the Freudian unconscious," in *Écrits: A Selection,* trans. Alan Sheridan (New York: W. W. Norton, 1977), 304. Further references to pages of this essay will appear in parentheses preceded by "Subversion."

5. Lacan, "Desire and the Interpretation of Desire in Hamlet," in *Literature and Psychoanalysis: The Question of Reading: Otherwise,* ed. Shoshana Felman (Baltimore: Johns Hopkins University Press, 1982), 11–52. Early in this essay, Lacan identifies Hamlet with the pure signifier, Gertrude with the Other, and Ophelia with the object. He says little about the role of the elder Hamlet, which I will take up below.

6. *The Ego and the Id,* 53–54. The fifth chapter of this study, "The Dependent Relationships of the Ego," 48–59, is especially rich in interior drama. Future references to pages of this work will appear in parentheses preceded by "Ego."

7. William T. Noon, *Joyce and Aquinas* (New Haven: Yale University Press, 1957), 135.

8. Lacan, "The agency of the letter in the unconscious or reason since Freud," in *Écrits,* 147ff.

9. This idea of Lacan's is explained effectively in Juliet Mitchell, *Psychoanalysis and Feminism* (New York: Vintage Books, 1975), 39–41.

10. Freud, "Humour," 164. This essay says that humor is a function of the superego.

11. Otto Fenichel, *The Psychoanalytic Theory of Neurosis* (New York: Norton, 1945), 107. Fenichel is here citing Otto Isakower, "On the Exceptional Position of the Auditive Sphere," *International Journal of Psychoanalysis,* 20 (1939): 340–48. As an internal voice, the superego has a special relation to narrative.

12. *New Introductory Lectures on Psychoanalysis,* 78–79.

13. *New Introductory Lectures,* 28.

14. Lacan, *The Four Fundamental Concepts of Psycho-Analysis* (New York: W. W. Norton, 1981), 72–103. In this discussion of visual imagery, Lacan argues that such elements as depth and perspective are organized by the need to control desire.

15. Fenichel, *Psychoanalytic Theory,* 102, 106.

16. "The *objet a* is something from which the subject, in order to constitute itself, has separated itself off as organ" (*Fundamental Concepts,* 103). The *"a"* of *"objet a"* stands for *autre.*

17. William Faulkner, *Absalom, Absalom!* (New York: Random House, 1936), 316.

18. Three Initiates, *The Kybalion: A Study of the Hermetic Philosophy of Ancient Egypt and Greece* (Chicago: Yogi Publication Society, 1912), 40. It is not likely that Joyce read this work, but in the last section of this essay, I quote a similar idea from a work by Madame Blavatsky that Joyce was familiar with.

19. "The signification of the phallus," in *Écrits,* 281–91.

20. See Brivic, "The Mind Factory: Kabbalah in *Finnegans Wake,*" *James Joyce Quarterly* 21 (Fall 1983): 7–30.

21. Jung sometimes gives the impression that the male unconscious is composed entirely of the anima, the female image in which a man projects his desires, while the female unconscious is composed entirely of animus, the male image in which she projects hers. But he suggests at other times that each of these sides is dominant rather than exclusive and that both sides are needed for completion. See C. G. Jung, *Aion: Researchers into the Phenomenology of the Self,* ed. Sir Herbert Read *et al.,* trans. R. F. C. Hull, *Collected Works,* vol. 9, no. 2 (Princeton: Princeton University Press Bollingen, 1959), 11–22, especially the last page.

22. Sheldon Brivic, *Joyce Between Freud and Jung* (Port Washington, N.Y.: Kennikat Press, 1980), 21–61.

23. Arthur Power asked Joyce what happened between Bloom and Gerty, and Joyce said, "Nothing happened between them . . . . it all took place in Bloom's imagination." Power, *Conversations with James Joyce* (London: Millington, 1974), 6, 32. Presumably this includes Gerty's fantasies about Bloom. A suggestive demonstration that Gerty is partly a projection of Bloom appears in John Gordon, *James Joyce's Metamorphoses* (Dublin: Gill and Macmilan, 1981), 75–80.

24. The line "Love, yes. Word known to all men" (*U,* 9.429) does not appear in editions of *Ulysses* before Gabler's.

25. Synchronicity is defined by Jung, "Synchronicity: An Acausal Connecting Principle,"

in *The Structure and Dynamics of the Psyche, Collected Works,* vol. 8 (1960), 419–519. I discuss Joyce's use of synchronicities in *Between Freud and Jung,* 168–182. A list of about 150 synchronicities appears as an appendix to Brivic, *Joyce the Creator* (Madison: University of Wisconsin Press,1985), 145–153.

26. A fine account of how the styles of *Ulysses* progressively come to dominate the action appears in Karen Lawrence, *The Odyssey of Style in* Ulysses (Princeton: Princeton University Press, 1981). I differ with Lawrence in my emphasis on the ways in which the styles express Joyce.

27. The Carlo Linati schema appears in Richard Ellmann, *Ulysses on the Liffey* (New York: Oxford, 1972), after 187. The original schema is in Italian.

28. Although the catechism takes the form of questions asked by someone who doesn't know to someone who does, in practice it is often the priest who asks and the youth who must feed back the answers; but this does not impair the father-son relationship, for fathers often train their sons by letting the youths pretend that they are men.

29. Freud, "Humour," 164.

30. See Julian Jaynes, *The Origin of Consciousness in the Breakdown of the Bicameral Mind* (Boston: Houghton Mifflin, 1976), 100–25.

31. Robert Richard Boyle, S.J., explains Molly's role as Holy Ghost in "Worshipper of the Word: James Joyce and the Trinity," in Edmund L. Epstein, ed., *A Starchamber Quiry: A James Joyce Centennial Volume, 1882–1982* (London: Methuen, 1982), 139.

32. See chap. 5, "The Sea of Joyce," in *Joyce the Creator,* 84–102.

33. Jung, "The Psychology of the Child Archetype," in *The Archetypes of the Collective Unconscious, Collected Works,* vol. 9, no. 1, 167.

34. After reading a draft of this essay, Robert D. Newman suggested that the sea tends to function as the id, and the sky, as the superego.

35. Weldon Thornton, *Allusions in* Ulysses: An Annotated List (Chapel Hill: University of North Carolina Press, 1968), 16.

36. Of course, Joyce had no way of knowing the use that *quark* would be put to by physicists, but he liked to believe in his powers to predict and name.

37. Bruno's idea that "all things are in all things" appears in J. Lewis McIntyre, *Giordana Bruno* (London: Macmillan, 1903), 126, a book Joyce reviewed. On the other hand, the idea that the tiniest particle contains a universe may have been current among scientific or theosophical writers by the twentieth century. "The cosmic character of the 'smallest' particle of matter" is developed in Thomas Mann, *The Magic Mountain* (1924), trans. H. T. Lowe-Porter (New York: Alfred A. Knopf, 1955), 284.

38. One reason that this aperture should connect Joyce to his work is indicated when Lacan explains his title in *Fundamental Concepts,* 5. He says that in the Kabbalah the *fundamentum* is the locus of divine manifestation.

39. Joyce's reference to Penelope as the "countersign to Bloom's passport to eternity" suggests that she expresses the other side of his value. Frank Budgen, *James Joyce and the Making of* Ulysses (Bloomington: Indiana University Press, 1960), 264.

40. Colin MacCabe, *James Joyce and the Revolution of the Word* (London: Macmillan, 1979), 49–51, 104–5, et al., uses Lacan's ideas to argue that Joyce strove throughout his career to release words from fixed meanings because the fragmentation of fixed reality allows the feminine force of desire to speak.

41. See James Van Dyck Card, "'Contradicting': The Word for Joyce's 'Penelope,'" *James Joyce Quarterly* 11 (Fall 1973): 17–26.

42. Freud, "Narcissism," 75, 89. The image of pseudopods recurs in *Ego,* pp. 63–65.

43. Hilda Petrovna Blavatsky, *Isis Unveiled: A Master Key to the Mysteries of Ancient and Modern Science and Theology* (1877: rpt., Los Angeles: Theosophy Company, 1975), 2:267. Joyce referred to this work many times.

44. Kenner, *Joyce's Voices* (Berkeley and Los Angeles: University of California Press, 1978), 95–98. A muse tends to represent pure beauty, and both of the final episodes are heavenly.

45. Erik H. Erikson, *Identity: Youth and Crisis* (New York: W. W. Norton, 1968), 261–94.

46. This passage was pointed out to me by David Bloom, who suggested many of the best points in this article. Jeanne Gibbs points out Leopold Bloom's equivalent, which does seem to control: "Lady's hand" (*U,* 5.113). Thanks also to Elliott Gose.

The Coincidence of Contraries as Theme and Technique in *Ulysses*

ELLIOTT GOSE

I

The coming together of seeming opposites forms an important pattern of construction in *Ulysses*. Such a pattern is arguably present in all episodes but is more obvious in some than in others. Based on the coinciding of opposing principles or points of view, the pattern involves a convergence frequently associated with a chiastic mirror reflection. Very evident as stylistic opposition in double-narrator episodes such as Cyclops and Nausicaa, the pattern also appears in the balanced structure of such major episodes as Circe and Ithaca. This opposition-resolution pattern may even be applied to *Ulysses* as a whole.

The notion that all contraries finally coincide was an integrating element in the philosophy of Giordana Bruno and obviously made an impact on Joyce during his early allegiance to the Renaissance Italian philosopher and heresiarch. That allegiance, known to date from Joyce's university days, is evident in his 1903 review of Lewis McIntyre's excellent book on Bruno (*CW*, 132–34; see also *JJII*, 59–60). More than twenty years later, as he began *Finnegans Wake*, Joyce was still praising Bruno, characterizing the coincidence of contraries as "a kind of dualism—every power in nature must evolve an opposite in order to realise itself and opposition brings reunion etc etc." Later, after recommending McIntyre's book, Joyce made a revealing statement: While confessing that he was using Bruno's coincidence of contraries and Vico's cyclic theory of history "for all they are worth," he insisted, "I would not pay overmuch attention to these theories, . . . but they have gradually forced themselves on me through circumstances of my own life" (*Letters*, I, 224–25, 241). Clearly, Joyce found the ideas more than merely useful; they had become personal beliefs. This intellectual-emotional incorporation of theory through experience helps explain the fact that Bruno's coincidence of contraries informs both the theme and the structure of *Ulysses*.

As described by McIntyre, Bruno's doctrine asserts "the unity and coincidence of all differences."[1] For instance, "the 'principle' of corruption and of generation is one and the same. The end of decay is the beginning of generation; corruption is nothing but a generation, generation a corruption."[2] This opposition and others like it may be discerned in the commonplaces that flow through the mind of Leopold Bloom. The most striking examples of the coincidence of contraries early in the novel occur in Hades. They are tied to the version of the theme derisively enunciated later by Lynch: "Extremes meet. Death is the highest form of life" (*U,* 15.2098). The word "extremes" appears nowhere else in the novel, but the singular "extreme" does appear earlier. In Hades it carries something of Lynch's sense in Bloom's mind:

> Our Lady's Hospice for the dying. Deadhouse handy underneath. Where old Mrs Riordan died. . . . Nice young student that was dressed that bite the bee gave me. He's gone over to the lying-in hospital they told me. From one extreme to the other. (*U,* 6.377–82)

The intern's shift from the hospice deadhouse to the maternity lifehouse is one of several instances that enter Bloom's mind during the funeral episode. He remembers Molly asking for intercourse: "Give us a touch Poldy. God, I'm *dying* for it. How *life* begins" (*U,* 6.80–81, emphasis added). The closest to Lynch's formulation comes to Bloom's mind in the cemetery: "Whores in Turkish graveyards. . . . Love among the tombstones. . . . In the midst of death we are in life. Both ends meet" (*U,* 6.757–59). I take "both ends" to refer to the end of life, first as aim (procreation) and second as conclusion (death). "Both ends meet" is copulative as well as conceptual.

One of Bruno's own examples of the coincidence of contraries occurs to Bloom while he is at the chemist's: "Poisons the only cures" (*U,* 5.483).[3] Earlier, on his way to the outhouse, Bloom thinks "Dirty cleans" (*U,* 4.481). Later in "Nausicaa," he speculates on a virgin's desire: "I'm all clean come and dirty me" (*U,* 13.797), a neat reversal of the earlier perception.

Although the appearance of the coincidence of contraries can easily be demonstrated thematically in the early episodes, Joyce's application of this principle to the technique of these episodes is not as evident.[4] Yet several critics have laid the groundwork for such an analysis in discussing different episodes in the second half of the novel. After some comments on Aeolus, I shall be offering a brief survey of approaches which suggest the coincidence of contraries in Penelope, Nausicaa, and Cyclops. I shall then discuss in more detail how Bruno's thesis operates in Scylla and Charybdis before offering some comments on the structure of the novel as a whole.

The first obvious example of stylistic contraries can be found in the seventh episode, Aeolus, in the opposition of the headlines to the narration. The narrative strives for continuity; the headlines isolate parts and fragments. The narrative has a story to tell. The headlines interrupt it with self-important commentary, sometimes formal, pompous, allusive, alliterative. Thematically this opposition is paralleled by the first appearance in the same episode of Bloom and Stephen. Since they do not actually meet, neither the thematic nor the technical contraries can be said to coincide yet. How might they if they did? Visually, they will sometimes coincide in a mirror, as Stephen and Bloom do in Circe. In fact, the convergence of opposites will often be accompanied by what might be called a mirror reversal. For instance, Diane Tolomeo has argued that the eight sentences that make up Penelope are so structured.[5] As Tolomeo demonstrates, Molly's last four sentences can be seen as a mirror version of the first four. In support of her contention for Penelope, Tolemeo reproduces a numerical symmetry Joyce toyed with in his notes for Ithaca:

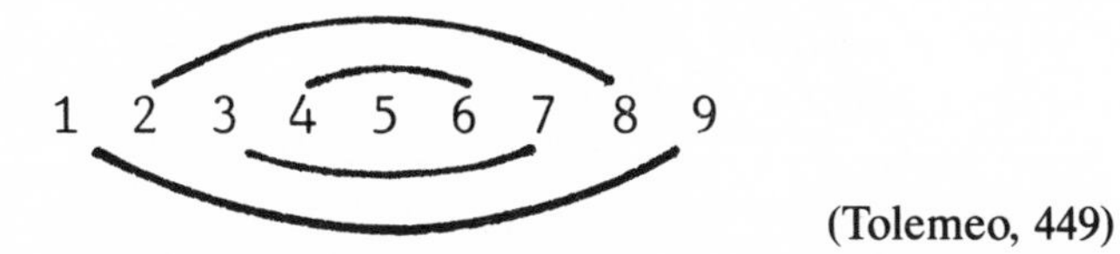

(Tolemeo, 449)

In contrast to this odd-numbered diagram with "5" as a centerpoint, Penelope with its even-numbered eight parts has, in Tolemeo's view, a balancing without a centerpoint. As we shall be noting presently, the nineteen parts of Wandering Rocks have also been asserted to have a chiastic structure, one more like the odd-numbered diagram above. I shall be suggesting that Joyce used the chiastic or mirror form in yet different ways in other episodes. In those I discuss, it will usually be signalled by characters entering (or exiting or fusing), often dividing an episode in half, as Mulligan's entry does Scylla and Charybdis, or dividing it in four, as I shall argue (in Part II) Circe and Ithaca are divided.

Halfway through many of the later episodes there is a crossover to an opposite involving a reciprocal exchange, if not a mirror reversal. Such an exchange or reversal is noticeable in both the Nausicaa and Cyclops episodes. In Nausicaa, the contraries are Gerty's sensibility and Bloom's. Similarly, Cyclops has an "I" narrator and his contrary, a series of inflated, interrupting voices. This formal similarity has led Fritz Senn to characterize the structure of these two episodes as "bi-polar."[6] This term could also be applied to the headlines and narrative text of Aeolus, as well as to the question and answer method of Ithaca. The questions of Ithaca in this view call forth the answers, but the answers often contend with the question, as when a pretentious question receives only a monosyllabic answer. I believe that this important principle of construction is based on

Joyce's reading of Bruno. In 1912, in an essay on the Renaissance, Joyce cited Bruno as contending "that any power, whether in nature or in the spirit, must create an opposite power, without which it cannot fulfill itself" and adding "that in each such separation there is a tendency towards reunion."[7] I believe Nausicaa embodies a structural reunion, and I shall be showing how Cyclops embodies a coincidence of contraries in theme as well as form. Both episodes demonstrate the possibility of a convergence at the halfway point and actually provide it at the end.

Joyce's "tendency toward reunion" is most clear in Nausicaa because of what Senn calls its "evident antithetical symmetry." Behind the obvious contrasts of Gerty's section with Bloom's, he notes that the two halves are actually dovetailed in an intricate way, "separated by a definite, and yet joined by a gliding transition." While still in Gerty's mind, we are told that the stranger to whom she has been exhibiting herself is Bloom. As Senn points out, the tone and style temporarily become his before we have left Gerty's section. Similarly, Bloom's own monologue is interrupted by passages that are close to the style associated with hers ("reverting to the novelette manner" as Senn puts it.)[8] At the very end of the episode, the dominant narrative modes are reunited by means of a clock chiming, as Gerty's point of view is explicitly reintroduced. This reunion pattern of a mid-point crossover of styles and an end resolution of them is also evident in the Cyclops episode.

In investigating the bi-polar structure of Cyclops, another critic, Mary Beth Pringle, has discovered that halfway through Joyce violates the dialogue conventions he has set up for the narrative voices.[9] What Pringle demonstrates is a crossover of established conventions, a coincidence of contrary techniques and styles which suggests that perhaps the seeming opposite voices of back-biting narrator on the one hand and pretension-exposing interruptor on the other may finally converge. As in Nausicaa, such a convergence does take place at the end of Cyclops when the inflationary voice works itself up to an apocalyptic celebration of Bloom as Elijah, only to be brought down to earth by two concluding lines in the reductive, colloquial style of the cynical narrator.

> And they beheld Him even Him, ben Bloom Elijah, amid clouds of angels ascend to the glory of the brightness at an angle of fortyfive degrees over Donohoe's in Little Green street like a shot off a shovel. (*U,* 12.1915–18)

Most critics see the final deflationary particulars as undercutting the pretensions of the previous biblical tone. In this reading, the narrator who has been interrupted so often and so devastatingly throughout the episode could be seen as finally getting his own back, turning the tables on the omniscient parody voice to deflate it. But what I am suggesting is more a balancing of tones, a final convergence which demonstrates that the narrator's cynical view and the inflated ones that match it are equally limited. Or, to put it more positively, this convergence represents that reunion which Joyce, as Brunian stylist, here brings to triumphant and comic consummation.[10]

This balancing is also evident in the thematic coincidence of contraries at the end of the episode. Bloom has finally answered the Citizen's anti-Semitic hostility with a defense that concludes "Christ was a jew like me" (*U,* 12.1808–9). The Citizen responds with his own unconscious bringing together of opposites: "By Jesus . . . I'll brain that bloody jewman for using the holy name" (*U,* 12.1811). Bloom of course has not sworn at all. Just as biblical and everyday language coincide at the end of the episode, so here Jesus and Christ (the secular and the holy name) come together. Other opposites also move toward coinciding. Remembering Joyce's care in connecting Bloom with both Moses and Christ elsewhere in the novel, we could take the Citizen's "Jesus" as an unintended tribute to Bloom. Similarly, we could take Bloom's uncharacteristically aggressive response to the Citizen as an unintended tribute to his Cyclopean forthrightness. As opposites, Bloom and the Citizen had earlier upheld love and hate respectively. In McIntyre's formulation, this opposition is one of the most plausible forms of contraries coinciding:

> In substance and in root, . . . love and hate, friendship and strife, are one and the same thing. . . . There is but one potency of two contraries, because contraries are apprehended by one and the same sense, therefore belong to the same subject or substrate. (*Giordano Bruno,* 177)

This substrate we might name *passion,* love and hate being the positive and negative poles which tend to converge.

The end of Cyclops thus provides in its resolution of both theme and technique a coincidence of the contraries established during the episode. It is no coincidence that the pattern I have just traced in this episode and in Nausicaa should be most easily illustrated from the second half of the novel. The two episodes which I shall be considering in Part II (Circe and Ithaca) come from that half. But the pattern can also be discerned in the first half of the novel.

In Scylla and Charbydis, Stephen makes several assertions about Shakespeare that seem to be projections of his own sense of alienation but that also refer to known preoccupations of Joyce. Where Joyce had written in 1912 that in each "separation there is a tendency toward reunion," he has Stephen say of Shakespeare in 1904, "where there is a reconciliation . . . there must have been first a sundering" (*U,* 9.334–35). In this reversal of emphasis lies one of the key differences between Joyce, who had reconciled himself to the Dublin of his youth, and Stephen, whose need to leave Dublin conditions his focus on sundering. The second time Stephen makes his remark, it is in response to Best's conventional assertion that Shakespeare's last plays breathe "the spirit of reconciliation" (*U,* 9.396). I find the same spirit in much of *Ulysses,* particularly the last two episodes. Whereas Stephen's emphasis is on contraries and separation, Joyce's includes coinciding or reunion.

On the other hand, Stephen's insistence on sundering leads to the theme of exile which was important to Joyce as well. Speaking of Shakespeare, Stephen insists that "the note of banishment, banishment from the heart, banishment from home, sounds uninterruptedly" (*U,* 9.999–1000). There follows a portentous and enigmatic statement: "It doubles itself in the middle of his life, reflects itself in another, repeats itself, protasis, epitasis, catastasis, catastrophe" (*U,* 9.1002–4). "It" must refer to *banishment,* and "his life" must be Shakespeare's. But pronoun identification only sets the terms of the actual difficulty, matching biographical incidents with dramatic categories. In attempting to impose a classical dramatic structure on Shakespeare's life, Stephen offers four Greek terms but only three biographical incidents. Two sentences farther on, however, he says, "But it was the original sin that darkened his understanding, weakened his will" (*U,* 9.1006–7). That original sin was Shakespeare's seduction by Anne Hathaway (*U,* 9.257). It corresponds to protasis (the proposition or introduction). I see his leaving Avon and Anne as part of the introduction, banishment from heart and home being two manifestations of the basic condition. The mid-life doubling takes place in London when Shakespeare is doubly betrayed, by the dark lady and the lord he also loved (*U,* 9.657–58); this incident corresponds to epitasis or that which follows. I take "reflects itself in another" as Anne's adultery with Shakespeare's two brothers, Richard and Edmund, (*U,* 9.963, 997–99); since this is the incident Stephen has been emphasizing, and the one that leads into the banishment discussion, this second double betrayal fits well as the catastasis or climax. And the catastrophe or final repetition would be that "banishment from the heart" of Anne which Stephen sees in Shakespeare's last will. "It is between the lines of his last written words, it is petrified on his tombstone under which her four bones are not to be laid" (*U,* 9.1009–11).

Behind Stephen's intent lies Joyce's: I believe the biographical sequence is reflexive and represents one way of understanding the aesthetic of *Ulysses.* What it describes is chiasmus, the rhetorical doubling through reversal of two clauses or actions. The notion of mirroring is implicit in both chiasmus and in "doubles itself . . . reflects itself." Chiastic mirroring is evident in the four-part banishment sequence: Shakespeare, alienated, leaves Anne (protasis); Shakespeare is betrayed by dark lady and dear lord (epitasis)—midpoint—Shakespeare is betrayed by Anne and his brothers (catastasis); Shakespeare, alienated, leaves Anne (his second-best bed, dies) (catastrophe). As we shall see in Part II, Circe is structured on the same principle, reversing itself at its midpoint. There is also a sense in which the novel reverses itself at its halfway point, the end of this ninth episode. As a group, the last nine episodes are often seen to be in opposition to the first nine. I shall return to this question presently.

The best-known example of chiasmus in *Ulysses* comes on the first page of Aeolus, the episode that Joyce devoted to rhetoric and its tropes. There he presented two sentences about barrels rolled on a brewery float, the second sentence simply reversing the order of most of the phrases in the first. In this same episode, however, Joyce provided a briefer and more characteristic example of chiasmus, one that better illustrates the coincidence of contraries. Stephen thinks, "Poor Penelope. Penelope Rich" (*U,* 7.1040). The second statement does repeat the first in reversed order, but in pairing Rich and Poor, Joyce was substituting an opposite for the identity of a conventionally reversed phrase. Such an adaptation of chiasmus is characteristic of Joyce's use of the device in the structure of Ulysses.

Stephen's later development of the Penelope reversal fits into the doubling theory that he enunciates in the library. He suggests there that "lady Penelope Rich" was Shakespeare's lover (*U,* 9.638–9), a speculation made by several nineteenth-century Shakespearean commentators who tried to link the two through the sonnets.[11] Shortly after, Stephen refers to Anne Hathaway as "poor Penelope in Stratford" (*U,* 9.649). The asserted liaison with Penelope Rich is part of that banishment from heart and home which estranges Shakespeare from his wife, as Ulysses is kept from Penelope by his seven years with Calypso. In Elizabethan England, one Penelope is rich in having a husband and a lover, the other is poor in lacking even her husband (until like Molly-Penelope, she also commits adultery). As already indicated, Shakespeare's "banishment from the heart" expresses itself in that which follows in London, but then it "reflects itself" in the climax of Anne's adultery. The connection of the verb "reflects" with adultery makes all the more appropriate the appearance of Shakespeare's face crowned with cuckold's horns in the mirror at the turning point of the chiastic structure of Circe. Not only there but in Eumaeus and Ithaca, Stephen will see himself in Bloom, find himself reflected in his contrary.[12] Similarly we could say that Bloom, "in the middle of his life," will see his double in Stephen. Both Bloom and Stephen are banished from the heart and self-banished from the home on 16 June 1904.

Stephen's statement about the dramatic curve of Shakespeare's life can thus be applied to both the theme and the structure of *Ulysses.* I have indicated how Penelope, Nausicaa, and Cyclops can each be said to double itself in the middle of its "life," by means of a structural or stylistic reversal. The same is true of Scylla and Charybdis. The end of the episode offers a low-key thematic resolution of the opposition Stephen Dedalus senses from Buck Mulligan: "My will: his will that fronts me. Seas between. A man passed out between them, bowing, greeting" (*U,* 9.1202–3). The man is Bloom, here Ulysses passing between Scylla and Charybdis. Although Stephen earlier demonstrated his allegiance to Aristotle (the Rock in Joyce's schema for the episode), at this point Stephen is to be taken as Charybdis not Scylla. The reason is that there has been a reversal halfway through the episode, and Stephen is strongly affected by it.

Joyce connected Charybdis, the whirlpool, with the mysticism of Plato. A.E. voices that position best in the first half of the episode, but he has left by the time Mulligan appears. In fact, as Robert Kellogg notes in his perceptive discussion of Scylla and Charybdis, the entry of Mulligan provides an entr'acte which signals a "shift of various sorts, philosophical and tonal."[13] Kellogg is referring to the one-word paragraph, *"Entr'acte"* (*U,* 9.484), which actually locates the mid-point shift in technique for the episode. After it the dramatic mode becomes pronounced, with a cast of characters (*U,* 9.1180–89) and dialogue (*U,* 9.684–706, 893–934), not to mention a line of music (*U,* 9.499). But the tonal change is equally important, as Kellogg indicates: "Stephen's thoughts [pivot] from an energetic rebuttal of ideas and opinions expressed by rather faintly drawn characters to a defensive stance against the hilarious blasphemy of his charming enemy," Mulligan.[14]

Another of Kellogg's observations provides for the clue for our understanding of an equally important shift, that of the oppositions pointed to by the Homeric parallels: "As Stephen mocks Russell's mysticism Mulligan mocks Stephen's."[15] In other words, early in the episode Stephen played Aristotle to the Platonic views of Russell (A.E.), who asserted that "the words of Hamlet bring our minds into contact with the eternal wisdom, Plato's world of ideas" (*U,* 9.51–52). But now, with an exchange of opposites, Stephen must face a materialist instead of an idealist. In that sense, Mulligan stands for the Rock of sensuality, while Stephen reverses himself, defining fatherhood as a "mystical estate" and insisting that the Church was founded not on the rock, Peter, but on incertitude and "the void" (*U,* 9.842). Depending entirely on whom he is opposing, Stephen is capable of swinging around from one line of argument to its exact contrary.

Such reversals, while quite compatible with the dialectic to which Stephen claims allegiance (*U,* 9.23–25), allow the reader to see that argument may have less to do with logic than with a need to oppose. The way is thus prepared for Bloom as the Ulysses who steers between conflicting forces, a good omen appropriate to the conclusion of this episode that completes the first half of the novel. Although during the second half, Bloom will be forced into opposition in Cyclops, he will ultimately transcend the apparent opposites of this world and achieve a balanced internal unity based on the coinciding of contraries.

When Joyce finished writing Scylla and Charybdis, he indicated on the manuscript his awareness of having completed the first half of *Ulysses*. In October of 1920, Joyce thought of introducing an "*Entr'acte* for *Ulysses* in middle of book after 9th episode Scylla and Charybdis *[sic]*. Short with absolutely no relation to what precedes or follows like a pause in the action of a play" (*Letters*, I, 149). Joyce had already finished Wandering Rocks at this time, but it can itself be taken as an entr'acte. Though not short and bearing some "relation to what proceeds and follows," Wandering Rocks is the only episode not modeled on one in the *Odyssey* and the only one not focused largely on one of the three major characters. Rather, it takes the reader into the minds of a number of characters in a series of vignettes. But this continuation of the technique of the first half of the novel is violated by the bald insertion into most sections of at least one sentence from some other section. In short, this episode is full of crossovers, narrational disruptions which foreshadow what we have seen as an insistent stylistic device of the later episodes.

Wandering Rocks has also been viewed in a manner even more germane to my analysis. Leo Knuth points not only to the number of references to mirrors in the episode, but to several incidents involving the "bilateral symmetry" of two gestures or events that mirror one another. He believes that Wandering Rocks is built on a chiastic structure, similar to the one Tolomeo outlined for Penelope.

> A kind of mirror symmetry of the entire episode appears to emerge when we allow the mirror line to coincide with the central section [the tenth of the nineteen that make up the episode]. The second half of the chapter repeats certain themes, motifs or objects of the first half in inverse order.[16]

He connects such bilateral symmetry with classical notations for ten, Roman *X* or Greek *chi;* in fact, he perceives a cross pattern involving Bloom and the routes of Father Conmee and the Viceroy.

Such critical ingenuity tempts one to look for bilateral symmetry in the structure of *Ulysses* as a whole. I shall resist that temptation.[17] There is, however, a more general sense in which a symmetrical design is apparent in *Ulysses* as a whole. The second half of the novel is frequently seen to mark a turn away from character-oriented interior monologue toward an opposed technique-oriented concern with formal values. In the last nine episodes, the personal styles of Bloom and Stephen are generally replaced by a seemingly arbitrary series of impersonal styles, yet Penelope concludes the book with the only unmediated stream of consciousness Joyce provided. Thematically, Molly's thoughts resolve many of the difficulties raised earlier by Stephen and Bloom's male consciousness. I am, in other words, suggesting for *Ulysses* as a whole a version of the structure I have been developing for a number of the individual episodes: a stylistic and thematic statement in the first half, a counterstatement in the second, and a reconciliation of these opposites at the end.

Placing the reader in Molly's mind, the last episode moves back toward the single-character interior monologues of the first six episodes. As stream of consciousness, Penelope lacks the authorial scene setter who provided an opposing voice to those early episodes. Instead, Molly's consciousness contains a self-generated set of oppositions. Her self-contradictions (well catalogued by James Card)[18] were long seen as proof of her hopelessly limited personality. Recently, however, they have been advanced by Joseph Voelker as an indication of her largeness of nature. He makes a compelling case for taking her as the embodiment of Bruno's conception of nature as the coincidence of contraries.[19] In this sense, she could be seen as subsuming all the opposites of the novel in her grand naturalness. Even in calling Ithaca the final episode and Penelope only a coda to the completed narrative, Joyce felt compelled to add that Molly provided "the indispensble countersign" on "Bloom's passport to eternity" (*Letters,* I, 160): sign and countersign are opposites leading to recognition and incorporation.

Many contraries coincide in various episodes from the second half of the book. It is in these most technique-dominated episodes that we find a somewhat obscured but definite, if unexpected, coming together of characters—Bloom and Simon Dedalus in the "Siopold" of Sirens (*U,* 11.752), Bloom and his opponent the Citizen through the spoken Christ at the end of Cyclops, and Stephen and his opponent Private Carr when the soldier strikes the poet near the end of Circe;[20] most importantly Bloom and Stephen, not only in Lynch's scornful "Jewgreek is greekjew" during Circe (*U,* 15.2097–98), but also in the Stoom and Blephen of Ithaca (*U,* 17.549, 551). In the second half of this paper, I shall investigate some of these convergences, with a shift in focus from style to narrative structure as I consider the form Joyce gave to the Circe and Ithaca episodes.

II

Having outlined the coincidence of contraries as underpinning for a number of specific episodes and in general terms for *Ulysses* itself, I now propose to establish it in detail for two of the most important episodes.

Circe is a meeting place for all the characters, objects, motifs, and forces that appear in the book as a whole. Because of its dramatic expressionism, its swiftly shifting fantasy scenes, it has the seeming incoherence of a dream. As usual, however, Joyce has imposed complexity on a basically simple structure. The scenes are grouped into three sections: those at the beginning outside the brothel, those inside it in the middle section, and again those outside it at the end. The first section is concerned mainly with Bloom, the second with both Bloom and Stephen, and the third mainly with Stephen. There are thus two significant threshold crossings, Bloom's entry into the brothel and Stephen's exit from it: between them comes a point of reversal in which a mirror facilitates the shift of focus from Bloom to Stephen. Joyce's concern with the mirror as a structuring device is more pronounced in this episode than in any other. In the British Museum notes for *Ulysses,* Joyce wrote, "In mirror left hand is right."[21] Circe provides a number of character and thematic alignments based both on the mirror and on right and left. I shall begin with the importance of threshold crossings and what they separate.

Joyce highlighted the dividing line between Bloom's experience outside and inside the brothel. Zoe, one of Bella Cohen's prostitutes, has come out to entice Bloom into the house. When she leads Bloom to *"the doorway,"* he *"trips awkwardly."* After she steadies him, he still *"stands aside at the threshold"* (*U,* 15.2027), insisting that she go first. *"(She crosses the threshold. He hesitates. She turns and, holding out her hand draws him over. He hops . . . ,"* *U,* 15.2031–32). Outside we see Bloom mainly as a public political figure; inside we see his hidden sexual inclinations being indulged. The sado-masochistic rites with Bella Cohen constitute Bloom's actual encounter with Circe. Similarly, outside the brothel, Bloom is associated with the right, inside it with the left. When Zoe tries to excite him on the street by putting her hand on his left thigh, he tells her his testicles are "on the right" (*U,* 15.1301). Shortly after, while being sworn in as a ruler in a fantasy, he places *"his right hand on his testicles"* (*U,* 15.1484). But inside the brothel, he advances his *"left foot"* to ward off an evil influence (*U,* 15.2723). Then when he begins to fall under the spell of Bella, she tells him "Slide left foot one pace back! You will fall" (*U,* 15.2848). Bloom's crossing the threshold of the brothel can thus be taken as a kind of through-the-looking-glass reversal.

Certainly once Bloom has crossed, Joyce presents the reader with a series of doubles as if to emphasize the split. Bloom's alter ego, Henry Flower, emerges *"from* left *upper entrance with two gliding steps"* (*U,* 15.2478, emphasis added). Two pages later we see Stephen split into Phillip Drunk and Phillip Sober. And soon Stephen appears as *"Simon Stephen cardinal Dedalus"* (*U,* 15.2654), a persona who combines characteristics of the son and the father. This character *"looks at all for a moment, his right eye closed tight, his left cheek puffed out*" (*U*, 15.2668–69). I take this distortion to indicate the dominance of sensual left over insightful right in this episode. The illicit society of Nighttown is matched by the physical distortions in Joyce's descriptions and the distorting mirror effect of his form.

An explicit mirror is the focus for the key reversal in the episode. Lynch says, "The mirror up to nature" (*U*, 15.3820) and immediately the stage directions respond.

> *(Stephen and Bloom gaze in the mirror. The face of William Shakespeare, beardless, appears there, rigid in facial paralysis, crowned by the reflection of the reindeer antlered hatrack in the hall.)* (*U*, 15.3821–24)

Up to this merging in the mirror, the main phantasmagorias have concerned Bloom; after it they concern Stephen. Shakespeare's paralytic speech to Stephen—"Weda seca whokilla farst" (*U*, 15.3853)—is a distorted version of Stephen's earlier quotation (*U*, 9.679) of the player Queen's protest, "None wed the second but who killed the first" (*Hamlet* 3.2). Unlike Bloom, who has faced and accepted adultery, Stephen, as we saw in his discussion of Shakespeare, is still tied to it (like Hamlet) by fascination and loathing. Shakespeare's tag line is thus a proper prologue to Stephen's phantasmagoria which works up to the confrontation with his mother, climaxed by his defying her with his stick and terrifying the whores before he rushes outside in this second emphasized boundary crossing. "*Stephen . . . flies from the room, past the whores at the door*" (*U*, 15.4255). But the real dramatic emphasis falls on another threshold, one more consonant with Stephen's preoccupation. "*He lifts his ashplant high with both hands and smashes the chandelier. Time's livid final flame leaps . . .*" (*U*, 15.4243–44). This private movement toward apocalypse prepares us for Stephen's subsequent similar public experience. Like Bloom's, Stephen's experiences inside the brothel are private and domestic, while those outside concern public social matters. But the order is reversed. The literal mirror scene thus divides the episode chiastically into experiences which have a bilateral symmetry: Bloom outside (public fantasy), Bloom inside (private fantasy)—mirror scene—Stephen inside (private fantasy), Stephen outside (public fantasy).

After Stephen is challenged by Carr outside, we witness preparations for a battle and the celebration of a black mass during which the coincidence of contraries becomes evident. In the multiple duels whose opponents are named in the stage directions for the battle, we find Irishmen opposing each other. Toward the end of the list, the opponents represent quite clearly a converging of opposites: "*John O'Leary against Lear*

O'Johnny, Lord Edward Fitzgerald against Lord Gerald Fitzedward, The O'Donoghue of The Glens against The Glens of the O'Donoghue" (*U*, 15.4685–88). These mirror images lend themselves to a vision of the historical Ireland whose left and right hands have often combatted each other.

The reference to glens is immediately followed by a stage direction for their opposite, "an eminence," preparing for a reversal from war to religion. The two celebrants of the Black Mass represent the merging of Catholic and Protestant:

> *Father Malachi O'Flynn in a lace petticoat and reversed chasuble, his two left feet back to the front, celebrates camp mass. The Reverend Mr Hugh C Haines Love M.A. in a plain cassock and mortarboard, his head and collar back to the front. . . .* (*U*, 15.4693–97)[22]

The most obvious conjunction of opposites here is "Haines Love," i.e., Hate-Love. As suggested earlier, this conjunction is one of Bruno's most compelling examples of the coincidence of contraries. The Black Mass itself is a reversal, for which the clergymen's names and garb make them appropriate celebrants.

THE VOICE OF ALL THE DAMNED

Htengier Tnetopinmo Dog Drol eht rof, Aiulella!

(From on high the voice of Adonai calls.)

ADONAI

Dooooooooooog!

THE VOICE OF ALL THE BLESSED

Alleluia, for the Lord God Omnipotent reigneth!

(From on high the voice of Adonai calls.)

ADONAI

Goooooooooood!

(*U*, 15.4707–16)

Joyce here adds the Black Mass to that pattern of reversals and of oppositions which turn out to be identical. Stephen, who earlier feared pain from both God and His chiastic this-world embodiment, dog, is about to provoke an attack on himself. Joyce had told Frank Budgen that body and mind were the same thing; like Bruno he acknowledged "god to be in things, and Divinity to be latent in Nature."[23] The lesson that Stephen has yet to learn is to accept rather than combat. To combat is to meet in violence that contrary with which one should merely coincide.

After he is knocked down, Stephen is of course rescued by Bloom, who has accepted his internal contraries (male-female, masochist-sadist, adulterer-cuckold). As a result, when Bloom and Stephen are reunited, Bloom is rewarded by a feeling of at-one-ment with his dead son, Rudy. Equally important, I discern in this episode the same pattern outlined earlier for other episodes: first, a midpoint crossover (the shift of our attention from Bloom to Stephen signaled by their coalescing images in the mirror) and second, a final convergence (in their reunion at the end).

The mirror duplications and distortions make clear the importance of structural chiasmus in Circe. The groundwork for the symbolic prominence of distorting mirrors was laid in the very first episode of the novel. On hearing the history of Mulligan's shaving mirror, Stephen complains that "it is a symbol of Irish art. The cracked lookingglass of a servant" (*U,* 1.146). Mulligan, basically an establishment man, can use the mirror to demonstrate his integration with this world: "He swept the mirror a half circle in the air to flash the tidings abroad in sunlight now radiant on the sea" (*U,* 1.130–31). As self-appointed priest, he has solved easily and superficially the problem of right relation to light, a problem that will bother Stephen through the novel.

Stephen voices the problem in personal terms to Haines, claiming that as an Irishman he is the servant of two masters, England and Rome (*U,* 1.643–44). Joyce had faced the same problem, but by the time he began writing *Ulysses* he had been an exile for ten years and had gained a perspective on both empire and religion. He was able to hold up to Dublin a mirror which was not cracked but was Irish in offering both a realistic and an exaggerated view of the world that shaped him. Joyce's distortion, as we have seen it in Circe, contains the kind of truth he strove to embody, in an art that incorporated the insights of philosophy, theology, and psychology. The first two of these three are evident in Stephen's attempts to find a liberating perspective. Joyce signaled his psychological intention in Circe when Bloom first appeared. "A concave mirror at the side presents to him lovelorn longlost lugubru Booloohoom. . . . but in the convex mirror grin unstruck the bonham eyes and fatchuck cheekchops of jollypoldy the rixdix doldy" (*U,* 15.145–49). Concave and convex, these mirrors introduce two contrasting views that will be developed in the episode, of Bloom as adult and as child, as sad and as happy. These contrary moods will coincide in our response of sympathetic laughter at

Bloom as omnipotent child and unharmed victim of his own fantasies. These mirrors thus anticipate Joyce's aim of holding the distorting mirror up to give an unreal but true picture of Bloom's inner nature.

In Circe Joyce used the insights of depth psychology to shape his art; Stephen uses philosophy and theology to work toward a similar position. Lacking worldly power and skeptical of received opinions, Stephen tends to associate himself with heresiarchs or Middle-East philosophers. In Nestor, he thinks of Averroës and Maimonides, "dark men in mien and movement, flashing in their mocking mirrors the obscure soul of the world, a darkness shining in brightness which brightness could not comprehend" (*U,* 2.158–60). Like Joyce's art, the mirrors mock those who identify with worldly light, presumably because they cannot understand darker truths. Since Bloom is called a dark man, and compared to Moses, his climactic fusion with Stephen in the mirror and their reunion outside the brothel can be seen as offering Stephen a chance to gain the shining darkness he earlier admired in the philosopher Moses Maimonides.

Lynch's Aristotelian introduction of the fusion scene, "The mirror up to nature," certainly mocks Stephen. Equally important, as a mimetic rubric introducing a completely unrealistic incident, it should cause the reader to ask what nature is supposed to mean if the mirror reflects two living Dublin faces a historical English face (not to mention its presenting the figurative image of a cuckold's horns as a reflection of the literal hatrack). In other words, how far are we from Aristotle?[24] Because of its dramatic form, Circe could be said to emulate the genre Aristotle considered highest in its imitation of an action from nature. In fact, of course, this episode mirrors less outer actions than inner feelings. As several critics have shown, Joyce has not simply given us each character's hallucination; he has rather left even subjective representation behind. Here as elsewhere in the second half of the novel, he has mocked the conventions of fiction.

The convergence of Stephen and Bloom is intensified in Ithaca. In the Linati scheme for this episode, one of the key words under "Technique" is *fusion.* A phrase to describe this process can be found on *U,* 17.769: "mutual reflections merge." In context the reflections are Stephen and Bloom's continuing thoughts, but the episode itself is told in a style that combines opposites, "jocoserious" (*U,* 17.369); it also offers occasions when mirror reflections merge. Besides the "Stoom . . . Blephen" (*U,* 17.549–51) convergence already mentioned, their union is again suggested through the figure of Shakespeare, connected this time with a cosmic event:

> the appearance of a star (1st magnitude) of exceeding brilliancy dominating by night and day (a new luminous sun generated by the collision

> and amalgamation in incandescence of two nonluminous exsuns) about the period of the birth of William Shakespeare. . . . (*U,* 17.1118–22)

Aided by Joyce's note for the episode, "SD & LB a double sun" (*Notebooks,* 455) and by the pun "exsun," we can see that, though Stephen and Bloom do not shine separately, when their traits coalesce, a harbinger of Shakespearian genius will appear. Two pages later the fusion finally takes place directly: "Both then were silent? Silent, each contemplating the other in both mirrors of the reciprocal flesh of theirhisnothis fellowfaces" (*U,* 17.1182–84). This at-one-ment through mutual mirroring is an actualization of an earlier, more tentative and theoretical recognition: "—*Ex quibus,* Stephen mumbled in a noncommittal accent, their two or four eyes conversing, *Christus* or Bloom his name is or after all any other, *secundum carnem"* (in Eumaeus, *U,* 16.1091–94). In Ithaca the recognition is directly *sedundum carnem,* as Stephen experiences "the reciprocal flesh" of Bloom. Since "reciprocal," it is appropriately "theirhisnothis": their as belonging to both, "hisnothis" as the individual transformed.

The midpoint of Ithaca may be determined in the same way as that of Circe, by noting exits and entrances, threshold crossings. As in Circe, the action in this episode divides into four sections, connected with the four settings in the episode. It begins with Bloom's walking Stephen to Eccles St. and getting him inside. The second section includes all that happens while the two are in Bloom's house. The third section is set in the garden and concludes with Stephen's departure and Bloom's reentry into his house. The fourth section is set in various rooms of the house and concludes with Bloom's falling to sleep in bed with Molly. By this division, the halfway point of the episode comes when Bloom and Stephen leave the house for the garden. As in Circe the boundary crossings that precede and follow this midpoint are also strongly emphasized: Bloom's difficulty in gaining initial entry to his house and, as Stephen leaves later, their shaking hands at the garden door (while "on different sides of its base," *U,* 17.1221).

As indicated earlier, the question-and-answer form of Ithaca gives it a bipolar structure comparable to the headline and story form of Aeolus and the alternating narrators of Cyclops. Like those two episodes, Ithaca draws much of its humor from the resultant stylistic contrasts. Unlike Cyclops, however, Ithaca does not offer significant stylistic reversals in its midpoint crossover and final convergence scenes. The crossover when Bloom and Stephen leave the house is given as a simple exchange: "For what creature was the door of egress a door of ingress? For a cat" (*U,* 17.1034–35). This cat had earlier been compared to Milly (*U,* 17.890–92). The presence of two females inside is balanced by two males outside. A possible convergence is suggested when Bloom tries to interest Stephen in

Molly with the possible goal of linking him with Milly (*U,* 17.940–42). But I shall be arguing that the important convergence of male and female characteristics takes place within Bloom.

Whereas in Circe the midpoint crossover involved a convergence of two images in a mirror, in Ithaca, there is a physical threshold crossing that is ceremonial—in Joyce's words, an "order of precedence" for "the exodus from the house of bondage" (*U,* 17.1021–22): Bloom with a lighted candle and Stephen with a deacon's hat on his ashplant. Their action is accompanied by the silent intoning of a "commemorative psalm," the 113th in the Vulgate version, "When Israel went out of Egypt." Critics have found two allusions to Dante in this scene, one to the *Divine Comedy* and one in the reference to the psalm, since it was the occasion for Dante's well-known explication of the four levels of literary meaning. We may apply two of these meanings to suggest the convergence of Bloom's literal exit with an anagogical level: the passage of the soul from bondage to liberty. The allusion to the *Divine Comedy* at the midpoint of Ithaca is appropriate as a prelude to a view of the heavens and an impersonal elucidation of the relation of earthly difficulties to cosmic patterns. (Similarly, the invoking of Shakespeare at the midpoint of Circe was appropriate for an episode in dramatic form which offered a modern version of the bard's penetrating insight into human irrationality.)

The intoning of the particular psalm that accompanies Bloom's crossing of a threshold calls attention to the Jews' leaving Egypt. Bloom as a modern Moses is thus involved in an external historical convergence as well as an internal symbolic one. He has in addition come to embody opposites more obviously in need of reconciliation. For instance, a sense of Bloom as himself a coincidence of male and female contraries is evident in the evocation of "his firm full masculine feminine passive active hand" (*U,* 17.289–90). Bloom's full humanity means his nature must include masculine and feminine, active and passive, literal and symbolic, Jewish patriarch and Irish ad canvasser, as well as right and left, body and mind, and so forth.

To begin moving toward a conclusion, I would assert that Joyce's goal was to develop fully the qualities not only of his main character but also of each episode. One result was his use of mirror opposites both for thematic resonance and for structural articulation. Thus the rock of Aristotelian dogma and the whirlpool of Platonic mysticism suggested themselves as the complementary, contending-yet-interchangeable forces of Scylla and Charybdis. In Nausicaa, Gerty's sentimentality and Bloom's worldliness are equally isolating and converge in the exhibitionism-masturbation scene at which the narrative crosses over. In Cyclops, the barfly narrator's cynical undercutting of everyone he presents is matched by the intervening voices which remorselessly inflate every situation they conjure up. The result should be to cause doubt whether the animus generated by the narrator's seeing through every one is distinguishable from the leveling naïveté of the interruptions. In Ithaca Joyce returned to a constantly alternating (question and answer) structure, the midpoint being a symbolic exodus, the second of three boundary crossings. In Circe, the crossover point is connected with a fusion, the chiastic reflection "Jewgreek is greekjew" (*U,* 15.2097–98) in an actual mirror.

The mirror exists not just as a motif in *Ulysses* but also, I indicated earlier, as a symbol of Joyce's complex art, particularly as a means of structuring many of the episodes. The influence of Bruno is also evident in this choice of symbol. In the chapter "The Infinite Universe: The Mirror of God," McIntyre quotes Bruno's advice that man should "turn his eyes to the heavens and the worlds; there is spread before him . . . a mirror, in which he may . . . contemplate . . . the reflection of the highest good."[25] Or from a slightly different point of view in a brief later paraphrase by McIntyre, "Nature is God in things, His infinite mirror, the *explicate* unfolded, extended, immeasurable world, and He is *implicitly* everywhere in the whole."[26] Thematically, Joyce certainly adopted the premise that the divine is reflected in the world, as can be seen in Ithaca, where one of the answers refers to Bloom hearing Stephen's "retreating feet on the heavenborn earth" (*U,* 17.1243). Structurally, Joyce seems to have built several of his episodes as mirrors, partly to show how one contrary reflects its opposites, but also to demonstrate that in his universe there is an order which reflects its principle of construction. It is an order explicitly unfolded as each episode develops, but on closer examination it also contains its creator implicitly within it, as the organizer who plants clues which enable the wary reader to discover that conventional ideas of order are inadequate, that contraries do finally coincide, that all is thus mysteriously and immeasurably one. As Bruno put it in *The Expulsion of the Triumphant Beast,*

> we see that all Deity finally reduces itself to one source, just as all light is reduced to the first and self-illuminated source, and images that are in mirrors as diverse and numerous as there are particular subjects are reduced to their source, the one formal and ideal principle. (240)

Just as each image in *Ulysses* might be said to mirror some other in a symbolic network which gives the novel its incredible complexity, so all can be reduced to one source, the mind of their creator, and can be seen as illustrations of a formal principle. In *Ulysses* Joyce brought seeming incompatibles together in a resolute embodiment of powerful contraries which fulfill themselves by virtue of their tendency to reunite.

Notes

1. J. Lewis McIntyre, *Giordano Bruno* (London: Macmillan, 1903), 176. He there mentions that Bruno got the idea from Nicholas of Cusa.

2. Ibid., 177. As Richard Ellmann has pointed out, Joyce used this particular version of the coincidence of contraries dialetically to integrate Stephen's views and Bloom's in the first six episodes of the novel. Cf. *Ulysses on the Liffey* (New York: Oxford University Press, 1973), 58–61. Hereafter cited as *Liffey*.

3. As McIntyre puts Bruno's belief, "Poison gives its own antidote, and the greatest poisons are the best medicines," 177.

4. But the reader's necessary awareness of at least two voices or perspectives in the earlier episodes is demonstrated in convincing detail as anticipating the stylistic shifts of the second half of the book by Jean Paul Riquelme in *Teller and Tale in Joyce's Fiction* (Baltimore: Johns Hopkins University Press, 1983). "Because of the book's stylistic fluctuations, we sense its double vision even in the first six episodes. We perceive Bloom both as a presence and as the effect of the teller's stylistic manipulations" (181). While putting the case for "Oscillating Perspectives" (his subtitle), Riquelme also acknowledges the convergence of perspectives.

5. In "The Final Octagon of *Ulysses," James Joyce Quarterly* 10 (Summer 1973): 439–53.

6. In his chapter on this episode in Clive Hart and David Hayman eds., *James Joyce's* Ulysses (Berkeley and Los Angeles: University of California Press, 1974), 297.

7. Louis Berrone, "Two James Joyce Essays Unveiled," *Journal of Modern Literature* 5 (February 1976): 15.

8. Senn, 297, 303–4.

9. Pringle has established that the narrator of Cyclops, an anonymous barfly, is interrupted thirty-three times by the ironic inflating commentator. Pairing segments of narration with parodies of it, we would expect the midpoint to be in the seventeenth pair. In fact, Pringle has discovered that Joyce's violation of the conventions of each voice takes place not only at the seventeenth but more noticeably at the thirteenth and fifteenth parts. Cf. "Funfersum: Dialogue as Metafictional Technique in the 'Cyclops' Episode of *Ulysses," James Joyce Quarterly* 18 (Summer 1981): 402–4.

10. Joyce achieves a similar but more subdued effect later in the novel in another description of Bloom which puts the mundane details first and ends the paragraph with elevated rhetoric. Bloom "proceeded towards the oriental edifice of the Turkish and Warm Baths, 11 Leinster street, with the light of inspiration shining in his countenance and bearing in his arms the secret of the race, graven in the language of prediction" (*U*, 17.338–41). Here the coincidence of contraries is nicely focussed on the word "race" which functions as the mundane horse race whose winner Bloom has unknowingly foretold and the Jewish race through which he is connected with the Moses who received inspiration on Sinai (see *U*, 7.867–69 for the passage Joyce is alluding to).

11. This point is annotated by Don Gifford and Robert Seidman in *Notes for Joyce: An Annotation of James Joyce's Ulysses* (New York: E. P. Dutton, 1974), 185–86.

12. In a stimulating essay, "The Structural Rhythm of Ulysses," *Twentieth Century Literature* 30 (Winter 1984): 404–19, Mack Smith uses musical terms quite compatible with my Brunian thesis to demonstrate how Stephen and Bloom as opposites function in the novel's sonata form of "introduction—conflict—resolution" (410).

13. In his chapter on this episode in the Hart and Hayman collection, 151.

14. Ibid.

15. Ibid.

16. Leo Knuth, "A Bathymetric Reading of Joyce's *Ulysses,* Chapter X," *James Joyce Quarterly* 9 (Summer 1972): 413.

17. The immediate problem with a chiastic pairing comes from Joyce himself. He indicated on the scheme he gave Gilbert that although the techniques of the first three and the last three episodes were to be paired, the order was consecutive, not reversed: 1 "Narrative (young)" and 16 "Narrative (old)"; 2 "Catechism (personal)" and 17 "Catechism (imper-

sonal)"; 3 "Monologue (male)" and 18 "Monologue (female)." His pairing is certainly of contraries and may be a clever after thought (the early Linati scheme is different), but it certainly seems to rule out any intention of creating an inverse ordering of episodes.

18. James Van Dyck Card, "Contradicting: The Word for Joyce's 'Penelope'," *James Joyce Quarterly* 11 (Fall 1973): 17–26.

19. Joseph Voelker, "Nature it is: The Influence of Giordano Bruno on James Joyce's Molly Bloom," *James Joyce Quarterly* 14 (Fall 1976): 42–43.

20. Carr is an alter ego for Stephen, as I point out in *The Transformation Process in Joyce's* Ulysses (Toronto: University of Toronto Press, 1980) 128–29.

21. Philip Herring, ed., *Joyce's* Ulysses *Notesheets in the British Museum* (Charlottesville: University of Virginia Press, 1972), 136. Hereafter cited as *Notebooks.* For further ramifications of a right-left, male-female pattern in "Circe," see my article, "Joyce's Goddess of Generation" in *James Joyce The Centennial Symposium* (Urbana: University of Illinois Press, 1986).

22. O'Flynn and Haines represent several contraries. As Robert Adams points out, oddities in their description mean that "one man looks forward and walks backward, the other looks backward and walks forward," *Surface and Symbol: The Consistency of James Joyce's Ulysses* (New York: Oxford University Press, 1964), 30.

23. Giordano Bruno, *The Expulsion of the Triumphant Beast,* trans. Arthur Imerti (New Brunswick, N.J.: Rutgers University Press, 1964), 237.

24. Brook Thomas takes a different approach to the same question in *James Joyce's* Ulysses: *A Book of Many Happy Returns* (Baton Rouge: Louisiana State University Press, 1982), 45–52.

25. McIntyre, *Giordana Bruno,* 181.

26. Ibid., 315.

Art and History: Stephen's Mirror and Parnell's Silk Hat

MICHAEL H. BEGNAL

Stephen Dedalus, in the Telemachiad, sets two problems which are central to the thematic development of *Ulysses*. On the top of the Martello tower, confronted by his own frowsy image in Buck Mulligan's shaving mirror, he declares: "It is a symbol of Irish art. The cracked lookingglass of a servant" (*U,* 1.146). Whatever the state of the Celtic Renaissance, it holds no promise for this aspiring young writer. Later on, in response to the platitudes of Mr Deasy who must advise before he will pay his youthful teacher's salary, Stephen will reply that: "History . . . is a nightmare from which I am trying to awake" (*U,* 2.377). Art and history will bedevil Dedalus throughout the novel, and Stephen's views of them provide the bars to life and experience which trap him within his own intellectual prison.

Indeed, these are only a couple of the dreams that trouble his waking sleep. In his own inimitable way, Leopold Bloom is also concerned with art and history, and ultimately it is his ability to circumvent and resolve the dangers of this cultural Scylla and Charybdis that endows *Ulysses* with much of its resolution. After all, as even Lenehan has been able to recognize: "He's a cultured allroundman, Bloom is. . . . There's a touch of the artist about old Bloom" (*U,* 10.581). When questioned by the First Watch in Circe about his profession or trade, Bloom will answer: "I follow a literary occupation, author-journalist" (*U,* 15.802), though later Philip Beaufoy will assert that he is: "A plagiarist. A soapy sneak masquerading as a *littérateur*" (*U,* 15.822).

Joyce's investigations into the state and function of contemporary art return continuously to the symbol of the mirror, and it is significant that only rarely do these recurrences of the mirror imagery concern Stephen Dedalus. He sets up the symbol, and then it deserts him. As an artist it is probably fair to say that, up to the point of 16 June 1904, he is a distinct failure. Granted he is only twenty-two years old, but he has published nothing, and, if for no other reason than that, he is not to be included in A.E.'s forthcoming collection of the verses of fledgling Irish poets. Ironically, even Mulligan will have a place. Stephen's pallid and stilted villanelle in *A Portrait of the Artist as a Young Man* is just as ineffectual as the vampire lover lyric which he has unconsciously lifted from Douglas Hyde's *Lovesongs of Connacht: "On swift sail flaming/From storm and south/He comes, pale vampire,/Mouth to my mouth"* (*U,* 7.522). His artistic attempts are still rough drafts, whether they be the Nuncle Richie Goulding daydream with pretentious Elizabethan flourishes, or the critical novelette on the life of William Shakespeare that sprawls across the chapter which takes place in the National Library. Buck Mulligan's alternative offering: *"Everyman His own Wife/or/A Honeymoon in the Hand/(a national immorality in three orgasms)"* (*U,* 9.1171) caps the section, and it is probably just as nationally relevant as is Stephen's production.

The art of Dedalus is still bound up in the sterility of his own consciousness, and it is not totally immune to the leer and snicker of Mulligan's melodrama. *A Pisgah Sight of Palestine or the Parable of the Plums* in form suggests a short story which could have been edited out of Joyce's own collection, as he notes in Stephen's preparatory introduction to the tale: "Dubliners" (*U,* 7.922). But no epiphany is offered here. The story's masturbatory theme, with its mock juxtaposition of the diminished digits of the frisky frumps and the mighty fingers of the statue of Lord Nelson, the "Onehandled adulterer" (*U,* 7.1019), hearkens back to Stephen's morbid meditation on abortion and miscarriage earlier on the strand when he had sighted the two midwives. While at least Garrett Deasy's letter on hoof and mouth disease has a form and a function, and will even see print that very day, Stephen's little tale is only half listened to by Dubliners hurrying to the pub for a drink. Dedalus continues to wallow in his own malaise. The problem here is that his art is egotistic, confessional, and obsessively introspective. When Stephen looks into the mirror of art he sees a foreigner, a stranger: "Who chose this face for me?" (*U,* 1.136), and it is obvious that he cannot be at ease with himself. His clever bon mot, derived from the servant Ursula's lookingglass, will be transformed ultimately into a commodity to be sold to the Englishman Haines for his collection of Irish folklore.

Even the aphorism itself is not completely original, since it is stimulated in Stephen's mind by Mulligan's comment: "The rage of Caliban at not seeing his face in a mirror, he said. If Wilde were only alive to see you" (*U,* 1.143–44). The reference, of course, is to the preface to *The Picture of Dorian Gray,* where Wilde describes the angry reaction as: "The nineteenth century dislike of Romanticism is the rage of Caliban not seeing his own face in a glass,"[1] an apt tie to Dedalus. Just before this pronouncement, Wilde states, in an attempt to specify what art does, if not what it is: "The nineteenth century dislike of Realism is the rage of Caliban seeing his own face in a glass." So far, so good; both Romanticism and Realism could not satisfy the reader-Caliban of the last century, but we need to go further into the preface, to what Wilde sets up as the essential function of art in the modern age. "It is the spectator, and not life, that art really mirrors."[2] The primary purpose of the work of art is specification, and thus the reader must glean from the work whatever individual insight he or she can.

Joyce seems to be following Wilde's lead. In the world of most of the characters of *Ulysses,* art cannot move the spectator to see himself, since it is all either disconnected from experience, as in Stephen's unsuccessful attempts, or totally unrealistic like the mystic gibberish of A.E.'s poetry. Irishmen are unable or unwilling to confront themselves, so that art will remain inoperative until they do. Joyce then is placing a strong emphasis upon the spectator, upon the act of looking and attempting to understand. In Stephen's mind, the mirror is cracked, shattered beyond repair, but Bloom must deal with his own image almost everywhere he looks. Joyce's use of the mirror metaphor, in relation to both Bloom and Dedalus, helps to clarify the comment that *Ulysses* is making on the dissociation of experience and insight that characterizes the modern world. Bloom does not know much about art, but in his striving for self-knowledge he comes to represent the kind of spectator for which both Wilde and Joyce were looking. Joyce said that contemporary literature: "speaks of what seems fantastic and unreal to those who have lost the simple intuitions which are the tests of reality" (*CW,* 81), and in Bloom Joyce seeks to describe just what those all-important simple intuitions are.

One of the most significant references in *Ulysses* tying Stephen to mirrors is in relation to his guilt over his mother's death: "Mother's death bed. Candle. The sheeted mirror" (*U,* 9.221), where obviously his reflection and that of his mother cannot appear together. He has been avoiding his agenbite of inwit for many days before this one. In this case, he deflects the consequences of being a spectator, of looking at himself directly. Certainly, as well, we need to examine the essential spectator in the mirror, the Leopold Bloom whom Alexander J. Dowie dubs: "Caliban" (*U,* 15.1760) in the Circe chapter, thus establishing again the connection to Wilde. Bloom is Joyce's new Caliban, not so much a monster as an innocent who is learning to deal with his own face in life's glass. How Bloom is a spectator, and how he deals with mirrors and with everyday experience, moves us much closer to a Joycean version of the complexities and possibilities of art. For Bloom, to be a spectator is not simply to be a passive observer, but rather to accept a cavalcade of co-actors, the multiplicity of his own personality, as all part of his own image.

When Stephen and Bloom gaze into the mirror in Bella Cohen's whorehouse near the end of Circe, a situation precipitated by the crude

Lynch who holds: "The mirror up to nature" (*U,* 15.3820), they do not see themselves, but instead, first of all, the: *"face of William Shakespeare, beardless . . . crowned by the reflection of the reindeer antlered hatrack in the hall"* (*U,* 15.3821). This young Shakespeare, with his strong overtones of cuckoldry, completely ignores Dedalus, and calls out to Bloom: "Thou thoughtest as how thou wastest invisible. Gaze" (*U,* 15.3827). As the mirror transforms itself, it displays an image of the bearded face of Martin Cunningham, whom Bloom had equated with Shakespeare for the lawyer's humanity and compassion on their drive out to Paddy Dignam's funeral. Bloom had mused: "Sympathetic human man he is. Intelligent. Like Shakespeare's face" (*U,* 6.344–45). Though later in the Ithaca chapter we are told that many times had Bloom perused the plays of the Bard for the solutions to life's problems without very much success, it is not Shakespeare who is important here. Bloom is observing two versions of himself, youth and age telescoped together. Shakespeare equals Bloom plus Stephen. If the art of *Ulysses* is a mirror that reflects the self, then its function for Joyce is to encourage the individual to accept the self. As readers we may see ourselves in Bloom looking at himself. Ironically enough, artistic vision in *Ulysses* is to be granted to the bourgeois and oftentimes silly Bloom because, when he holds the artistic mirror up to nature, he can perceive the life that is so abundant around him. Stephen, unfortunately, would-be artist, is afraid of the mirror which would reveal to him all that he hopes to avoid in his consciousness.[3]

Whereas Stephen conceives of his mirror in typically pretentious terms, and abhors it as much as he abhors water, Bloom is almost literally surrounded by such imagery throughout the novel. He associates his daughter with his reflected gaze: *"O, Milly Bloom, you are my darling. / You are my lookingglass from night to morning. / I'd rather have you without a farthing / Than Katey Keogh with her ass and garden"* (*U,* 4.287–90). He amusedly recalls the evening when Milly discovered that Professor Goodwin had placed a mirror inside his hat, the better to see up the dresses of the women with whom he sat. All mirrors are not necessarily aesthetic. Bloom does his Sandow's exercises in front of a mirror, is accused by Bello in Circe of posing in front of a mirror in his wife's underclothes, and he remembers Molly the night before: "The mirror was in shadow. She rubbed her handglass briskly on her woolen vest against her full wagging bub. Peering into it" (*U,* 4.531–32). Mirrors seem to leap out at Bloom, and, no matter how much he might wish to avoid his situation, to suppress it, his reflected image thrusts itself into the foreground. Indeed, occasionally he must deal with magical mirrors which change and metamorphose his image, splitting it, shattering it, and putting it all back together again.

As Bloom walks along the beach, after his encounter with Gerty Mac-

Dowell, he ponders his own spiritual development and the possible conclusion of the statement of his ongoing self-evaluation: "I AM A" (*U,* 13.1258–64). While earlier on the same spot Stephen Dedalus viewed nature as an incomprehensible text *out there:* "Signatures of all things I am here to read, seaspawn and seawrack, the nearing tide, that rusty boot" (*U,* 3.2–3), Bloom again turns inward: "Tide comes here. Saw a pool near her foot. Bend, see my face there, dark mirror, breathe on it, stirs. All these rocks with lines and scars and letters. O, those transparent!" (*U,* 13.1259–62). Transparent "what" we never know, and certainly Bloom does not complete his first sentence either, but he seems to be focussing on the right subject, himself. Perhaps even a short story might come out of it: "See ourselves as others see us. . . . Ask yourself who is he now. *The Mystery Man on the Beach,* prize titbit story by Mr Leopold Bloom" (*U,* 13.1058–60). Of no use would be George Russell's amorphous statement: "Art has to reveal to us ideas, formless spiritual essences" (*U,* 9.48–49).

Bloom can turn himself into a mirror, and the young-old Shakespeare in Circe has been anticipated by a moment in Oxen of the Sun: "No longer is Leopold, as he sits there, ruminating, chewing the cud of reminiscence, that staid agent of publicity and holder of a modest substance in the funds. . . . He is young Leopold. There, as in a retrospective arrangement, a mirror within a mirror (hey, presto!), he beholdeth himself" (*U,* 14.1041–45). Such mirroring, a fusion of the past and present, is itself a kind of art which offers Leopold Bloom as its central protagonist: "But hey, presto, the mirror is breathed on and the young knighterrant recedes, shrivels, dwindles to a tiny speck within the mist. Now he is himself paternal and these about him might be his sons" (*U,* 14.1060–62). As a final example of such coming together, he is once again reflected and split into two as he hastens into Nighttown: *"A concave mirror at the side presents to him lovelorn longlost lugubru Booloohoom . . . but in the convex mirror grin unstruck the bonham eyes and fatchuck cheekchops of jollypoldy the rixdix doldy"* (*U,* 15.145–49). One thinks perhaps of Giordano Bruno and his coincidence of contrarieties. There are no cracks in Bloom's mirrors, and his multiple images combine into oneness, a vision of the spectator which Wilde offers as the truly significant function of art.

Bloom without doubt has tried his hand at the literary game, as he might say, and he still has quasi-literary aspirations. As he sits in the outhouse reading *Matcham's Masterstroke,* he considers the possibility of a sketch to illustrate some likely proverb or a realistic piece based on the notes he jotted down on his shirt cuff as Molly was dressing. Whether or not his magnum opus will ever come to pass, his final act in the backyard exemplifies a perfect incorporation of art's aesthetic pleasure and utilitarian function: "He tore away half the prize story sharply and wiped himself with it" (*U,* 4.537). Not only does Bloom resemble Lord Byron in Molly's opinion (and he has presented her with a volume of the poet's work as a gift), but he, "potential poet," wrote his first original verse at the age of eleven:

An ambition to squint
At my verses in print
Makes me hope that for these you'll find room.
If you so condescend
Then please place at the end
The name of yours truly, L. Bloom.
(*U,* 17.396–401)

Eleven years later, on Valentine's Day, the now "kinetic" poet sent Miss Marion Tweedy the following acrostic:

Poets oft have sung in rhyme
Of music sweet their praise divine.
Let them hymn it nine times nine.
Dearer far than song or wine,
You are mine. The world is mine.
(*U,* 17.412–16)

If nothing else, the poems are mirrors of Poldy. Certainly Stephen Dedalus would feel nothing but scorn for such attempts, but Joyce is more tolerant of what Bloom sees as art and what he does with it. Even Molly can appreciate him, and she is something of a potential writer herself: "I declare somebody ought to put him in the budget if I only could remember the 1 half of the things and write a book out of it the works of Master Poldy yes" (*U,* 18.578–80). Bloom may not look a bit like Byron, and undoubtedly he will not write *Don Juan,* but his artistic consciousness has its roots in the real and the actual, and even his Valentine verse carries more impact than Stephen's villanelle. Molly may have betrayed Bloom, but she still can see his worth: "[Boylan] slapping us behind like that on my bottom because I didnt call him Hugh the ignoramus that doesnt know poetry from a cabbage" (*U,* 18.1369–71).

Bloom, in other words, transforms art into life, and it is in this way that he transcends Stephen's dilemma. In the garden outside 7 Eccles Street, they make a wordless farewell: "Silent, each contemplating the other in both mirrors of the reciprocal flesh of theirhisnothis fellowfaces" (*U,* 17.1183–84). Perhaps this is the resolution of Stephen's cracked looking-glass and young-old William Shakespeare. Perhaps the human eyes have it. All that is left now for Bloom to do is to take stock, and this he does, reading in the book of himself. His final image in a mirror has come together in the parlor of his house, and it simply represents his totality: "What composite asymmetrical image in the mirror then attracted his attention?/The image of a solitary (ipsorelative) mutable (aliorelative) man" (*U*, 17.1348–50). Though momentarily solitary, it is most important that Bloom is mutable, and again a mirror has accomplished a totality, as we are told that Poldy, from infancy to maturity, resembled his mother and, from maturity to senility, his father. It seems finally fitting that even here Bloom will turn for consolation to art, at least what he considers to be art: "The candour, nudity, pose, tranquility, youth, grace, sex, counsel of a statue erect in the centre of the table, an image of Narcissus purchased by auction from P. A. Wren, 9 Bachelor's Walk" (*U*, 17.1427–29). Bloom has not fallen in love with his own image, as did the youth from mythology, but he has learned that the answers to his questions will only come through his studying of himself. Just as the statue is erect, so too will Bloom become at the end of this chapter. This is art to Bloom, as it is perhaps to Joyce himself, and certainly it is not the cracked lookingglass of a servant.

If art has proven to be an impasse for Stephen Dedalus, then history is a quagmire. To him, history makes no sense, and, even though he teaches it in the Nestor chapter, he defines history as nothing more than chaos, death, and confusion: "Jousts, slush and uproar of battles, the frozen deathspew of the slain, a shout of spearspikes baited with men's bloodied guts" (*U*, 2.316–18). Stephen cannot awaken from his own nightmare because, for him, history remains totally disconnected, a meaningless progression of names, dates, and places. Rather than being used as a key to an understanding of human experience, man's chronicle becomes manipulated as an excuse or a platitude, much as Haines brushes aside three hundred years of British imperialism with: "We feel in England that we have treated you rather unfairly. It seems history is to blame" (*U*, 1.648–49). For Irishmen: "history was a tale like any other too often heard, their land a pawnshop" (*U*, 2.46–47), and Mr Deasy will go so far as to locate the cause of all the trouble in the creation of woman. In his opinion, it was woman who brought sin into the world, thus setting up the eternal struggle between Christianity and evil: "All human history moves towards one great goal, the manifestation of God" (*U*, 2.380–81).

None of this, of course, is of any help to Dedalus: "Liquids I can eat, Stephen said. But O, oblige me by taking away that knife. I can't look at the point of it. It reminds me of Roman history" (*U*, 16.815–16). The death of Parnell, the Phoenix Park murders, Cain's killing of Abel, the assassination of Julius Caesar are all points on an undecipherable compass. While Mulligan looks to the past effetely and naively, proposing to Stephen that they Hellenize the Irish island, Myles Crawford, citing Ignatius Gallaher's coup as a reporter, plumps for the present of journalism: "—History! Myles Crawford cried. The Old Woman of Prince's street was there first" (*U*, 7.684–85). The intellectualization of history is a misunderstanding of life, a fallacy of the academy, as earlier Joyce had stated in 1902 in his first essay on James Clarence Mangan: "No doubt they are only men of letters who insist on the succession of the ages, and history or the denial of reality, for they are two names for one thing, may be said to be that which deceives the whole world" (*CW*, 81).

Perhaps because Bloom has been an actual part of history within this fiction, has had dealings with the likes of Arthur Griffith and Charles Stewart Parnell, he approaches it in a totally different way from Stephen. Bloom humanizes history, makes connections, just as he humanizes art. From his point of view, human history is family history, and it is on this level of apprehension that it can make sense. History for this Irish Jew is memory, whether it be the painful recollection of his father's suicide or of Rudy's death in infancy, or the happy thoughts of making love with Molly on the Hill of Howth and the early days of their marriage: "Pleasant evenings we had then. Molly in Citron's basketchair" (*U*, 4.206–7). In the Ireland of *Ulysses* history usually means a backward look at the past and its destruction, exemplified by the Citizen's ranting on in Barney Kiernan's pub: "he starts gassing out of him about the invincibles and the old guard and the men of sixtyseven and who fears to speak of ninetyeight and Joe with him about all the fellows that were hanged, drawn and transported for the cause by drumhead courtmartial" (*U*, 12.480–83).

All of this jumble leads to the blowup in Bloom's confrontation with the Citizen and his cronies, where Poldy strips the abstractions from history in a direct and simple way. "Persecution, says he, all the history of the world is full of it. Perpetuating national hatred among nations" (*U*, 12.1417–18). This may be something of a redundant description of Stephen's bad dream, but Bloom is able to dispel the shadow of the quandary quite completely.

> But it's no use, says he. Force, hatred, history, all that. That's not life for men and women, insult and hatred. And everybody knows that it's the very opposite of that that is really life.
> —What? says Alf.
> —Love, says Bloom. I mean the opposite of hatred. (*U*, 12.1481–85)

The past to Bloom, to Joyce, is something which is only relevant as it sheds light on the present, as it makes clearer the basic patterns of existence which are common to all people in all ages. Bloom is wide awake; history should not be violence. "How can people aim guns at each other? Sometimes they go off" (*U*, 13.1193–94). History should be instead a portal of discovery into the problems and complexities of the present.

History has taught Bloom that everything is part of the same archetypal process, that time is a cyclical pattern rather than a horizontal continuum—history repeats itself. Thus, just as he has been both young and old in his various mirrors, he sees his wife and daughter in exactly the same way. His knowledge and memories of Molly: "lieutenant Mulvey that kissed her under the Moorish wall beside the gardens. Fifteen she told me. But her breasts were developed" (*U,* 13.889–90), find a parallel in what he can foresee for Milly: "Fifteen yesterday. Curious, fifteenth of the month too. . . . A soft qualm, regret, flowed down his backbone, increasing. Will happen, yes. Prevent. Useless: can't move. Girl's sweet light lips. Will happen too" (*U,* 4.415–49). History for Bloom is not vague and amorphous, but something that fits together and leads finally to comprehension of the self. "June that was too I wooed. The year returns. History repeats itself. . . . So it returns. Think you're escaping and run into yourself. Longest way round is the shortest way home" (*U,* 13.1092–111). No student of Vico or Spengler, Bloom personalizes history and becomes an active participant within it. Stephen dreams, but Bloom will act.

And, as was mentioned before, Bloom has had his own contact with what might be called the textbook aspect of history. He has met Parnell, Stephen's "our dead king." In the Eumaeus chapter, amid the seafaring yarns and the tall tales of the sailor W. B. Murphy, the talk turns to Charles Stewart Parnell. There is no outright fact here, however, since the Chief is reduced to rumor and fantasy: he is not dead, for the coffin is filled with stones; he fled to South Africa and assumed the identity of the Boer general DeWet; he will appear once again in the time of Ireland's greatest need, like King Arthur or Robin Hood. But Bloom has had the honor of returning to Parnell his silk hat, which was knocked from his head in the midst of a riot outside the newspaper offices of the *Insuppressible* or the *United Ireland,* he is not really sure which. Interestingly enough, as Bloom muses, Parnell emerges not as a "historical personage," but as an actual person who has had common, human, social contact with Bloom. "And he said *Thank you,* excited as he undoubtedly was under his frigid exterior notwithstanding the little misadventure mentioned" (*U,* 16.1336–38). Bloom may not have his facts completely straight, but he has been involved with Parnell, not in terms of history, but in terms of ordinary politeness. This he can understand, by filtering history through his own human experience.

Curiously, history repeats itself again a few pages farther into *Ulysses,* as Bloom retells the story all over again, this time with stylistic embellishments and many more appropriate details. The description of Parnell is expanded quite a bit: "palpably a radically altered man he was still a commanding figure though carelessly garbed as usual with that look of settled purpose which went a long way with the shillyshallyers" (*U,* 16.1505–7). In the recasting of the narrative, Bloom now receives a dramatic elbow in the stomach from a person unknown, as he struggles in the crowd. Parnell again says thank you: "though in a very different tone of voice from the ornament of the legal profession whose headgear Bloom also set to rights earlier in the course of the day," and now we have: "history repeating itself with a difference" (*U,* 16.1523–26). Bloom is remembering his encounter in the cemetery on the morning of 16 June with John Henry Menton, where his aid had received less than Parnellian politeness. Once again the past has led him back into the present, and Menton's pettiness is contrasted with Parnell's largesse.

On another level, this is history with a difference because, of course, literally it is not history at all. Just the same, the insistence on the facticity of the episode, first: "in point of fact" (*U,* 16.1335) and then: "as a matter of strict history" (*U,* 16.1514), goes a long way toward intermingling the Bloomian conceptions of art and history. Here it is difficult to say which is which. (Brook Thomas objects that: "he [Joyce] cannot have a fictional character meet an important historical character and claim the meeting to be history without the reader's hedging" (113) but actually we do not hedge at all because we realize that we are in the middle of a novel. We do not quibble that Alice could not fit down a rabbit's hole, nor that Lilliputians do not exist. In the Library, in Scylla and Charybdis, we have already met the real Eglinton, Best, and A.E.) To complicate matters even further, however, this is art within art, or a fiction of Bloom's within a fiction of Joyce's. As Bloom goes over the incident the second time, he fills in gaps of mood and tone, makes things up as he goes along, much like Stephen with the Shakespeare biography. In the process, art and history merge. History, like art, is relative; Parnell is important in the context because he is remembered and created by Bloom, not Bloom being important because he saw Parnell. Both history and art are significant, then, only as one or the other is mirrored in an individual consciousness. As an artist-historian Narcissus, Bloom handles the two entities as lookingglasses which reflect back to him a meaningful image of himself. Everything comes full circle, as Bloom unifies the two ways of looking at experience to produce fiction and a kind of reality that prevail because they are more clearly enunciated and more immediate than anything which might have occurred in documented history.

Thus, it is not that Joyce is rejecting the young and aesthetic Stephen, but rather that he is celebrating the mature and more down-to-earth Leopold Bloom. Concepts existing only as concepts have no real relevance to experience unless they are translated into "real" life. Almost innately, though Bloom may not be completely familiar with their dictionary definitions, he understands art and he understands history because he can see their reflections and their ramifications in the people around him. History repeats itself with a difference, art repeats itself with a difference, and life repeats itself with a difference. In the midst of experience's archetypal sameness, James Joyce frames in Leopold Bloom a portrait of uniqueness.

Near the end of the Ithaca chapter, Bloom, wise old owl, contemplates another wise old owl. "In the mirror of the giltbordered pierglass the undecorated back of the dwarf tree regarded the upright back of the embalmed owl. Before the mirror the matrimonial gift of Alderman John Hooper with a clear melancholy wise bright motionless compassionate gaze regarded Bloom while Bloom with obscure tranquil profound motionless compassionated gaze regarded the matrimonial gift of Luke and Caroline Doyle" (*U,* 17.1342–47). The balance explicit in the syntax of this sentence is implicit in Bloom's explorations of art and history, and of his final feeling of: "equanimity" (*U,* 17.2155) in regard to the events which go to make up 16 June 1904, *Ulysses.*

Notes

1. Oscar Wilde, *The Picture of Dorian Gray* (New York: Dell Publishing Company, n.d.), 5.
2. Ibid., 6.
3. Brook Thomas devotes an entire section to Joyce's mirrors in *James Joyce's* Ulysses: *A Book of Many Happy Returns* (Baton Rouge: Louisiana State University Press, 1982). Since we certainly do not agree on many points, this essay seems to me to complement the insights to be found in his book.

Voices and Values in *Ulysses*

WELDON THORNTON

I

No aspect of *Ulysses* has been more discussed and analyzed in recent years than the styles or voices of the successive episodes.[1] In the process we have learned much about when and how in the composition of *Ulysses* these styles came into being, and our terminology for analyzing modes of authorial presence has been wonderfully refined. We have not, however, reached consensus about the purpose or meaning of these styles in the novel. On the contrary, attention to the styles appears to have widened the rift between those critics who attend primarily to plot and character in *Ulysses,* and those who focus upon technique: several recent critics assert or imply that the technique, the style, is the real "subject" of *Ulysses.*[2]

My aim in this essay is to propose a general thesis about the meaning of these successive styles, and to illustrate this thesis by a reading of the Oxen of the Sun episode. My thesis can be stated briefly. I believe that the "initial style" of *Ulysses* is the normative, authorial style of the novel, the style that expresses the stance of Joyce himself and the underlying values of the novel most clearly and directly, and that the voices of the later episodes represent styles that Joyce wishes to expose as somehow incomplete or mistaken.[3]

My development of this thesis must begin with some discriminations and clarifications. First, by the "initial style" I do not mean simply the speaking voice of the first six episodes. Discussion of the styles of *Ulysses* has been clouded by overemphasis on the "voices" of the novel and by a consequently narrow sense of what constitutes the "initial style." This focus on voices has caused us to attend too narrowly to techniques of presentation and to neglect character, event, structural patterns, and selection/emphasis as basic expressions of authorial presence. And this in turn has led to claims about Joyce's relativism in the novel. Such detailed analysis of point of view and of the psychological status of words and phrases obscures the fact that there is in *Ulysses* a fictive world consisting of far more than the "speaking voice" of each episode, and that here as in all novels, the most basic expressions of authorial presence and of the novel's underlying values are the persons and events and structures of the book. It is, for example, a fact about *Ulysses* that the paths of Stephen and Bloom cross several times during the day; this crossing of their paths is Joyce's doing, and while we may debate its precise meaning, we cannot deny that it is there and that for some purpose Joyce created this set of events rather than another.

It is equally true that the characters, the personalities, of Stephen and Bloom, are expressions of Joyce's authorial purposes and values—as is his decision to make these characters central to the novel rather than, say, Deasy and his wife. And whatever the authority of the "narrative voice" or "arranger" in the later episodes, that authority does not extend to altering Bloom's character in Oxen of the Sun from what it is in Calypso and Lotus-Eaters. We may admittedly have a hard time in Oxen of the Sun making out what Bloom is saying or doing, but when we argue about his words or actions, we are in any event arguing *about Bloom*—about how what he has presumably said or done congrues with his personality as revealed in all other parts of the novel. To my knowledge no critic has yet proposed that Joyce's "relativism" extends to his rendering the personalities of "Stephen" or "Bloom" in any of the later episodes *discontinuous* with those personalities elsewhere in the novel.[4]

So firm and stable is the fictive world that Joyce creates in *Ulysses* that some important events occur either "offstage" or in the interstices of the narration. We may not be certain how the furniture in 7 Eccles Street got moved about during the day—whether by Molly or Boylan or both—but we cannot be content to say that it was not moved (Bloom does find a solid object in an unexpected place), or that it moved itself, or that Stephen Dedalus moved it. And while we may not be able to determine such events with certainty, we do not regard questions about *even those events* as utterly arbitrary. My point, then, is that the most stable and pervasive mode of authorial presence—of *Joyce's* presence—in the novel is not the "speaking voice" of an episode, but the very characters and events and structures themselves. These aspects of the book, directly attributable to Joyce, constitute the substance of the fictive world of *Ulysses,* saving the novel from arbitrariness. They are the real "rock of Ithaca" underlying the other strata of the novel, both in the early episodes, where in my view the voice is "reliable," and in the later episodes, where it is not. In this sense, then, the stability of character and event—of fictive world, in effect—throughout all eighteen episodes is an integral part of the "initial style" that remains firm beneath our feet even after the voice of the early episodes has been obscured by other narrators.

Furthermore, these events and correspondences and especially these characters provide the most pervasive manifestation of the *values* of the novel. I fully agree with Marilyn French that "it is impossible to write a sentence, much less a novel, without making value choices" (*Book as World,* 36), and I concur in her inference of the values of the novel from the characters. (See her discussion of Stephen's intellectual acumen [82] and of Bloom's *caritas* [85].) This is not to say that Joyce presents these values simplistically or unambiguously; it is to say that the fictive world of *Ulysses,* of which James Joyce is the creator, necessarily implies values—Joyce's values. And while the styles of certain of the episodes may *obscure* the characters and events and their implied values, these values remain fundamental to the novel.

Having clarified my view of the "rock of Ithaca" underlying the novel, I want now to elaborate my claim that the "initial style" of the early episodes is the normative, authorial style of the novel—the style to which Joyce committed himself, without any ironic undercutting. For many critics of *Ulysses,* the claim that Joyce stands behind any of the book's styles is suspect, primarily because it runs counter to Joyce's pride in his own protean capacities as a stylist. Surely (their argument runs) Joyce, master of all styles, would never permit himself to be identified with any single style, for such a style, however subtle, would finally be characterizable, and if characterizable, then capable of becoming dated and even of being parodied, and it seems unbelievable that this master parodist should subject himself to parody. Quite likely Joyce did entertain such ideas, and the role of such an un-parodyable Proteus appealed to him. There is, however, evidence within *Ulysses* that Joyce came to realize that even parody, even standing aloof, can be carried too far and will then contravene more important aesthetic and human values.

My hypothesis is that Joyce thought these issues through and came to see that there were three alternatives open to him as a novelist: first, to present his material "objectively"—without any coloring of value whatsoever; second, to assume a relativistic and parodic stance, from which he could expose the insufficiency of others' values and styles without committing himself to any; and third, to ground his novel in certain values that are admittedly less than absolute, fully aware that the style in which he expressed those values would not be objective and thus could be characterized and even parodied. I believe that Joyce recognized the first alternative as impossible, saw the second as undesirable, and thus embraced the third.

Let us briefly examine these alternatives. The impossibility of an objective, value-free work of literature seems to me (and to Marilyn French, above, p. 4) self-evident; values are inherently expressed in the characters the author creates and focuses upon, in the events and situations he creates and emphasizes, and in the structures linking the parts of the work together. As to the undesirability of a relativistic stance, there are several kinds of evidence for that in *Ulysses*. One is that this stance is measured and found wanting in the Cyclops episode. In Cyclops the stylistic mode being explored (and exposed) is parody—a mode that seems to have special appeal for the Irish, in their literature as well as their pub talk. But if we press the question of what the underlying basis or purpose of this parody is—what underlying values the parody is grounded in—we find that there are none, but that we are dealing with a "mad parodist," who parodies all qualities indiscriminately, even heroism or patriotism or love.

This might of course be taken to reflect Joyce's own relativism were it not for another kind of internal evidence—the fact that *Ulysses* does favor certain values over others. Among the values that the novel sanctions are the sincerity and commitment behind Stephen's attempts to find a viable world view, as well as the responsiveness to the world and the openness to experience and concern for others that are such deep features of Bloom's personality (in French's terms, his *caritas)*. Among the qualities that the novel denigrates are the mockery and cynicism exemplified in Mulligan (as well as in the mad parodist of Cyclops), the presumptuous and insular "wisdom" of Deasy, and the purblind chauvinism of the Citizen. Such broad statements about the novel's values do little toward resolving specific textual cruxes, or toward clarifying what tone Joyce evokes toward certain characters (seeing Deasy as pathetic and sententious, for example, does not erode all of our sympathy for the old man), but amidst claims that *Ulysses* intends to be relativistic or value-neutral, such broad statements offer needed guideposts.[5]

And so my view is that in *Ulysses* Joyce does stand behind certain values that, in addition to being expressed in the characters, events, and structures of the novel, are manifested also in the style, the speaking voice, of the first six episodes. I am not, then, claiming that initial style to be either objective or absolute. The style is value-laden in a host of ways, from the choice of situations and perspectives it emphasizes, to the tone and mood that it evokes, to the specific evaluative words (many of them undeniably authorial) used to present the characters and events. Nor is the authorial judgment confined to such implicit devices as selection of perspective or juxtaposition; it emerges as an active quality, enabling, even requiring, us to evaluate Stephen and Bloom and Mulligan. Through this narrative perspective we come to regard Stephen and Bloom with sympathy, but also to realize that they are in their different ways self-indulgent and escapist, and we come to hope that they will face up to their own fears and become what they are capable of becoming. Through this same narrative perspective we see Mulligan as a superficially engaging but shallow and selfish materialist, and later in the novel, we see the destructiveness of chauvinism in Cyclops and of sentimentality in Nausicaa. Thus the "initial style" (including character, event, structure—and voice) offers a normative base that underlies even the later episodes, where the voice becomes aberrant.

The second part of my general thesis is that the voices of many of the subsequent episodes represent styles that Joyce wishes to expose as insufficient or distortive. This is by no means an unprecedented view; several critics have proposed that some parts of the novel involve a narrative persona whose aims and values run counter to those of the novel.[6] But I am making a claim that is at once broader and more specific. In my view the styles in each of the later episodes are the result of a different narrative persona that Joyce permits to take over the *presentation* of the material of each episode. The precise limits of this Presenter's authority are admittedly hard to establish and they vary from one episode to another.[7] These limits can extend to clouding or obfuscating the presentation of the thoughts and dialogue of the character, but they do not extend to liberties with the *events* of the novel or with the *personalities* of the characters or with the *content* of their thoughts or dialogue. My claim, then, is that the narrative voice of many of the episodes of *Ulysses* illustrates some literary mode or theory about language that Joyce does not himself sanction—that in fact he reveals as insufficient or distortive. I make this claim for the "headlines" in Aeolus, for Scylla and Charybdis, for Wandering Rocks, for the first half of Nausicaa, for the parodic voice in Cyclops, and for Oxen of the Sun, Circe, Eumaeus, and Ithaca. The normative narrative style or some recognizable variation of it exists in the first six episodes, in Aeolus apart from the headlines, in Lestrygonians, in the second half of Nausicaa, in the first-person narration of Cyclops, and in Penelope.

Joyce's disdain of some of these styles, or at least his presenting a style to reveal its imperfections, is obvious and has become a matter of general critical assent. It is clear that the "namby-pamby jammy marmalady drawersy"[8] style of Gerty's portion of Nausicaa represents a late-nineteenth-century sentimental style that lures its clientele into what Joyce and *Ulysses* show to be a dangerously simplistic and incomplete view of reality. For while Joyce is himself the "onlie begetter" of these pages, we have no hesitation in saying that he does not "stand behind" them—that they represent a style and a mentality that he judges against.[9] And my present point is unaffected by whether we see this style as Gerty's own narration or that of some persona. Nor does it matter whether we simply say that Joyce is here speaking in an ironic voice. The point is that the prose medium through which the characters and events are presented here is shown by the larger perspective of the novel to be simplistic, distortive, deficient. Another episode in which it appears obvious that Joyce abjures the style and the mentality it reflects is Eumaeus, though the precise status of that style has been clouded by arguments about whether it reflects Bloom's mode of thought or of public expression. But once again, whatever its relation to Bloom's mind (and I think there is none), the style of Eumaeus is an inferior style, and we are to understand that anyone who did think or write in that style would have a depressingly (if not dangerously) distorted view of reality.

But if my claim that Joyce used these styles to expose something he abjures can be accepted for Nausicaa and Eumaeus, most critics would not accept it as a principle applicable as well to Oxen of the Sun and Circe. The consensus about these episodes still seems to be that, whatever is going on there, Joyce stands behind it. The Sirens episode, however, can serve as an example appropriate to my purpose, because we can be quite clear about its stylistic program, and because there has been a considerable shift in critical attitude about whether Joyce himself sanctions this stylistic tour de force. In Sirens, the style emulates musical forms and devices, epitomizing Walter Pater's view that "all art constantly aspires to the condition of music."[10] And the presumption of many early commentators, even those who lamented the effects that this program has on the comprehensibility of the episode, was that Joyce himself agreed with Pater and sanctioned such an exercise.[11] But my contention is that this attempt is not Joyce's but that of the narrative persona, the Presenter, who fails to understand the qualitative differences between these two modes of art and who is oblivious to the confusion that results if literature is made to imitate music. And more recent critics (though not necessarily hypostatizing an Arranger or Presenter) have agreed that Joyce looks askance at this experiment.[12]

The second half of this essay is devoted to an interpretation of Oxen of the Sun, designed to explain what theory of language Joyce is there dramatizing and to show that he does not sanction it. Briefly, my thesis is that the theory of language being exposed there is the idea of "imitative form," proffered by a narrator who mistakenly believes that literary structure can meaningfully be grounded upon a physical process, such as evolution or gestation. My claim is that while the Presenter of the episode takes the theory literally, Joyce shows that such a theory is not simply mistaken, but that it is "idolatrous," in that it would substitute some physical process for *meaning* as the basis of literary form. My claim runs directly counter to the usual assumption that Joyce quite seriously accepted the fetal and evolutionary analogies revealed in his letters and notes. Furthermore, I believe that some comparable case can be made concerning the several "aberrant" episodes or voices that I indicated earlier.[13]

Before turning to a reading of Oxen of the Sun, I must say more about

Joyce's motives for presenting a series of styles that he does not sanction. Aware that he was living in a time of great literary, psychological, and philosophical ferment, when a great host of theories, models, styles were being bruited about, Joyce wished his novel to subsume many of these. One reason for this was Joyce's great versatility and his pride in his ability to reproduce any stylistic mode. But more substantially, Joyce wished to subsume certain of these theories and styles in order to take their measure, to show their insufficiency, and in this sense it is true that the latter half of *Ulysses* is to some extent *about style, about language,* but by this I mean something quite different than what is meant by those critics who regard the book as "self-referential." I believe that these stylistic forays result not from Joyce's having lost interest in the novelistic elements of character and plot, but from his wishing to show us the insufficiency or inappropriateness of these various styles to the underlying subject matter of the novel—something he could not possibly do without a firm substrate of character, plot, and structure that we are then asked to view through the kaleidoscope of less than appropriate styles.[14]

One effect of these stylistic forays, then, is to make us think carefully about the relationships between form and content. The current received ideas hold that there is no possibility of separating content from form and that we cannot speak of one linguistic rendering as more veridical than another—they are simply different. And in our mundane sphere it is true that we have no experience of a subject *an sich*—a subject not embodied in some content. But in *Ulysses* Joyce shows us that while it may not be possible to "produce a subject that exists apart from words" (H. Kenner, *Joyce's Voices,* 52), it certainly is possible for us to *distinguish between* a subject and the language in which it is presented, and it is even possible to say that some modes of language present a given subject more faithfully or more appropriately than others. For example: the initial style of *Ulysses* is a better, a more appropriate, vehicle for the story and the personalities of Stephen and Bloom than is the style of Sirens, or of Nausicaa, or of Oxen of the Sun; and we know this because in those later episodes we experience the difficulties of seeing this story and these characters through these distortive media.

This is not the view of Joyce's purpose that is common among critics today. For most recent critics, Joyce's aim in presenting this array of styles in *Ulysses* is to show us the insufficiency, the arbitrariness, of all styles—even the "normative" initial style.[15] Both Karen Lawrence and Marilyn French argue that Joyce's development from *Dubliners* to *Ulysses* shows his coming to understand that there is no such thing as objective reality, much less a form of language that presents "reality" veridically, and they see this relativism as itself one of the major points of *Ulysses.*[16] I am in partial agreement with this, in that I agree that Joyce came to understand that we human beings have no unmediated access to the *ding an sich* or to "reality." I further agree that Joyce came to see that there is no style, not even the "objective plain style," that can present "reality" directly.

But I differ with these critics about Joyce's response to this realization, and, consequently, about what he is doing in *Ulysses.* For in *Ulysses* at least, if not in "real life," we do have a substrate of novelistic reality available to us in the events and the personalities of the characters, and this reality is far better mediated by some of the book's styles than by others. This, and not the equal arbitrariness of all styles, is the point of his beginning with the normative "initial style" and only later invoking the various distortive styles that force us to peer through them to the bedrock of character and event that persists throughout the book. And almost every critic of *Ulysses,* even those just mentioned, agrees that in the later episodes the reader is trying to see *through* the styles to what is "going on."[17] Yet these critics seem not to see the implications of this formulation—namely that we *do* distinguish between content and form, and that these later styles are less sufficient vehicles of the content of *Ulysses* than the initial style is. (If Joyce had intended truly to illustrate relativism, he might have altered the characters and the plot at every episode, as well as the speaking voice—and by this I don't mean introduce *new* characters, but *change the natures of the ones he had been calling Stephen and Bloom*—that would indeed be relativism.) Again, this is not to say that Joyce naively regarded this initial style as objective or translucent (i.e., nondistortive of reality); it is to say that he chose and developed this style wittingly, in the belief that it was an appropriate vehicle for (not the absolute or inevitable vehicle of) the reality he wished to convey in his novel. Caught in the human predicament of having no access to absolute reality, Joyce made the human decision to take a stand where he was and on what he believed in and hoped for: he set his book in Dublin, not in u-topia, and in it he reveals his preference for *caritas* over selfishness, for responsiveness over solipsism, for honest self-awareness over sentimental self-indulgence—even if these qualities cannot be grounded in any absolute.

I would venture two predictions (or perhaps hopes) about criticism of *Ulysses.* The first is that as we continue to wrestle with these later episodes, especially if we keep before us the question of *why* Joyce is doing all of this, we shall more fully infer that Joyce does not stand behind the styles of these episodes. Already there is a discernible pattern in the critical response to some of the episodes, involving, first, admiration for their virtuosity; second, complaints of some critics that Joyce's flamboyance is not in the best interests of his narrative; third, speculation that Joyce must have been aware of these negative effects; and, fourth, claims that, for whatever purpose, Joyce is in fact "parodying" the narrator's stylistic excesses. It is, though, sobering to realize how largely our evaluation of the various episodes has been influenced by Joyce's own statements, external to the text: the condemnation of the style of Nausicaa is grounded in Joyce's denigration of it (quoted above), while the venerable status of Oxen of the Sun has been maintained by the famous letter to Frank Budgen (quoted below) that appears to sanction the stylistic program of the episode.

My second prediction is that we shall come to see that, while *Ulysses* incorporates a great variety of tones, and specifically a great deal of parody and mockery, the underlying and characteristic tone of the novel is not of mockery but sympathy and tolerance. Consider for example the three major characters. No one could claim that they project ideal personalities: they have their foibles, their flaws, their defensiveness, all of which render them vulnerable to satire or mockery—and each is subjected to demeaning gibes by some member of the Dublin community and in Bloom's case by some narrative persona. But to say that they are not perfect, not absolute, is not to say that we must therefore condemn or mock them, and finally the novel does not do so—its attitude toward Stephen, toward Molly, toward Bloom, is one of deep sympathy and acceptance. I stress this point because some recent works on *Ulysses* conclude (or presume) that Joyce's persistent stance is parody, his tone mockery (e.g., the books of Michael Groden and Karen Lawrence, and to some extent those of Marilyn French and Hugh Kenner). While I acknowledge a great deal of mockery among the characters and voices of *Ulysses* (perhaps a reflection of our deracinated, hyper-intellectual culture), I do not believe that attitude represents Joyce's stance or the novel's.[18]

II

"he sets his mind to sciences never explored before, and alters the laws of nature"
—Ovid, *Metamorphoses,* VIII, 188–89

The Oxen of the Sun has always been one of the most problematic episodes of *Ulysses*—in 1920 Joyce called it the most difficult episode both to interpret and to execute.[19] Its scant action is obscured by its murky, at times opaque, presentation, which apparently attempts to recapitulate the evolution of English prose style. If it requires attention and effort to discern the action of the chapter, it is even more difficult to see the rationale, the purpose, of its mode of presentation. This difficulty stems in part from the complexity and ambiguity of the style itself, but another contributing factor is Joyce's own statement about his aims in this episode, compounded by earlier critics' attempts to vindicate this authorial pronouncement. Joyce's statement occurs in a famous letter to Frank Budgen in March 1920:

> Am working hard at *Oxen of the Sun*, the idea being the crime committed against fecundity by sterilizing the act of coition. Scene, lying-in hospital. Technique: a nineparted episode without divisions introduced by a Sallustian-Tacitean prelude (the unfertilized ovum), then by way of earliest English alliterative and monosyllabic and Anglo-Saxon . . . then by way of Mandeville . . . then Malory's *Morte d'Arthur* . . . then the Elizabethan chronicle style . . . then a passage solemn, as of Milton, Taylor, Hooker, followed by a choppy Latin-gossipy bit, style of Burton-Browne, then a passage Bunyanesque . . . after a diarystyle bit Pepys-Evelyn . . . and so on through Defoe-Swift and Steele-Addison-Sterne and Landor-Pater-Newman until it ends in a frightful jumble of Pidgin English, nigger English, Cockney, Irish, Bowery slang and broken doggerel. This progression is also linked back at each part subtly with some foregoing episode of the day and, besides this, with the natural stages of development in the embryo and the periods of faunal evolution in general. The double-thudding Anglo-Saxon motive recurs from time to time to give the sense of the hoofs of oxen. Bloom is the spermatozoon, the hospital the womb, the nurse the ovum, Stephen the embryo.
>
> How's that for high?[20]

Each of the explicit or implicit claims Joyce makes here has left its mark in critical discussions of this episode. Several critics have attempted to pin down precisely what styles and sources Joyce used, and debated whether he "parodies" them. Joyce's explicit statement that the "idea" of the episode is "the crime committed against fecundity by sterilizing the act of coition" understandably caused some critics to read the episode as an attack on contraception. Perhaps most influential and most problematic have been Joyce's suggestions that the structure of the episode is built upon the physical process of fetal gestation and the historical process of faunal evolution. Several early critics assiduously attempted to show how the structure of the episode is grounded in embryology and evolution, but for others these claims of imitative form have posed serious problems. And one underlying effect of Joyce's pronouncement has been the presumption that the narrative persona of this episode must be identified with Joyce—a presumption that has been doubted by some recent critics but has never been challenged fully and systematically.[21]

But if this chapter has had its defenders and its dedicated explicators, it has also had its detractors, so much so that Marilyn French calls it "the most censured chapter in *Ulysses*" (*Book as World*, 168). And for the most part what the detractors criticized were the same features other critics were laboring to defend—the attempt to show the "evolution" of English prose, or to provide a literary analogue of gestation. Among the most trenchant early criticisms was that of Harry Levin, who, in 1941, said of this episode,

> By this time [Joyce] has abandoned all pretense of adhering to the coign of vantage of certain characters. . . . The clinical small-talk of Stephen's friends, while Bloom awaits the birth of Mrs. Purefoy's child, is reported in language that recapitulates the evolution of English prose, from a primitive ritual to an American revival meeting, and that obliterates the point of the story—when Stephen gives up his key. These parodies, we are admonished, illustrate the principle of embryonic growth. We cannot take this admonition very seriously. To call in so many irrelevant authors as middle term between the concept of biology and the needs of the present narrative is to reduce Joyce's cult of imitative form to a final absurdity.[22]

Levin, then, directly challenges the idea of building a narrative around biological processes, calling it "Joyce's cult of imitative form." I find this criticism, and especially the term *cult,* very perceptive, as my own subsequent interpretation will show.

More recently, critical responses to Oxen of the Sun have undergone a change, with three noteworthy developments. First, in place of the earlier attempts to vindicate Joyce's purported program, there is real skepticism about whether this can be done, at least with any precision. J. S. Atherton, in an intelligent essay that does not simply dismiss Joyce's claims, says, "Indeed I find it impossible to reduce Joyce's details to a consistent pattern."[23] Second, critics now look askance at the earlier assumption that in this episode fertility is an unqualified good. Marilyn French, for example, says "Religious groups have been maintaining for some years that if God ordered increase, contraception is sin, and that is the premise of this chapter. However, this premise is handled ironically and comically as well as seriously" (*Book as World,* 173).[24] Third, and perhaps most important, it has been questioned whether the speaking voice, the narrator, of this episode can be identified with Joyce, and whether the aims and values of this narrator are consistent with those throughout *Ulysses.* As early as 1966 Arnold Goldman observed of this episode that the styles are "the narrator's" and said that "The theory of the 'organic whole' of style and subject will not work for *Ulysses,* whose symbolic dimension (including its 'styles') wars with its human dimension."[25]

I fully agree with these critics' misgivings about the presumed program behind this episode and have already explained my own view that the narrators of each of these later episodes reflect various literary modes or theories that Joyce wished to reveal as mistaken. I want now to propose a reading of Oxen of the Sun that will explain what the narrator's theory is and show how the underlying themes of the episode reveal it to be fallacious. My aim is to present an interpretation that will incorporate the medical setting, the Homeric parallels, the style (including the narrator's aims), and the main themes and motifs of the episode into a coherent unity.

Some critics have ventured broad thematic interpretations of this episode, but there is little agreement among them, and their typical neglect of the style or voice of the episode renders their suggestions less than satisfactory because it perpetuates the dichotomy between style and substance that commentators on this episode have always run up against.[26] The basic problem is in finding some reasonable thematic connection between the themes of this chapter and its mode of presentation. Not that this problem is unique to Oxen of the Sun. It is present to some degree in every episode from Wandering Rocks on, and our general failure to solve this problem suggests that there is some basic point that we are missing—a point having to do with the status of the narrative voice in each of those episodes. For when we do come to understand what these episodes are about, when we come to see their underlying thematic unity, that unity should encompass both style and substance.

In my view, the underlying theme of the Oxen of the Sun episode is idolatry, in several appropriate senses of that term. While this theme is less obvious on the surface than is procreation or gestation, it is more fundamental and comprehensive, enabling us to see implicit links between subject matter and technique and to understand what role the narrator's attempt at imitative form plays in the episode. The act of idolatry involves worship of an object, a physical thing, rather than of the true God who is spirit rather than flesh or icon. Idolatry is a serious offense, a sin, because it reflects the worshiper's confusion about what is real, about the very nature of God. In essence idolatry is present whenever the physical is mistaken for, or given priority over, the spiritual. In terms more appropriate to this episode, it involves a misunderstanding of the proper relationship between man, God, and nature. It involves, in George Herbert's apt phrase, resting in Nature, not the God of Nature.[27]

That this theme is present in the setting and the subject matter of this chapter, in its sub-themes and motifs, can be readily shown; and working from that base we can see as well that idolatry is the underlying issue of the stylistic tour de force of the episode—the grounding of the development of English prose in gestation and in faunal evolution. Let us turn first to idolatry as unifying the various themes and motifs of the episode.

Apropos of the theme of idolatry, one of the most frequent and pervasive topics of discussion among those gathered in the maternity hospital is the nature of God, and this question invokes an array of issues that turn on the relationship between spirit and matter. The young men debate, for example, the precise time when the developing fetus acquires a soul, and, while their tone is mocking, their subject is one that has seriously engaged theologians for centuries. Nor is the subject passé even in our day, though we cast the argument in less overtly religious terms, debating with perhaps even more vagueness than the schoolmen when the fetus becomes a "person," and consequently whether, or when, abortion is murder. Among the other explicitly theological topics broached here are "transubstantiality *oder* consubstantiality" (*U,* 14.308), and the "theological dilemma created in the event of one Siamese twin predeceasing the other" (*U,* 14.1002–3).

But by far the most pervasive theological issue, and the one most directly appropriate to the theme of idolatry, is this question of the very nature of God. The chapter involves, for example, a veritable array of epithets by which God is addressed, calling our attention to the various aspects of God. There are, for instance, references to God the Maker, God the Almighty, God the Wreaker, God the Allruthful, to the Creator, to Bringforth, Phenomenon, Thor, Nobodaddy, Christ, the Author of my Days, the Healer and Herd, the Agenbuyer, Theosophus, and so on. While these epithets obviously reflect man's varied and persistent attempts to discern God's nature, their thematic gist for this episode (and for the whole of *Ulysses*) becomes clearer when we see that they resolve themselves into three "faces" of God: 1) God as creator—as the source of everything that is, physical and spiritual; 2) God as prohibitor, curser, and punisher; and 3) God as reconciler and redeemer. The first aspect of God gets little explicit attention in this episode, but its presence forms a necessary backdrop, for unless we understand that God is the source of matter and of spirit (or of the *prima materia* underlying them) we are likely to fall into denigrating one or the other and thus fail to see the complementariness of matter and spirit, of nature and imagination, that underlies *Ulysses.* But we can fully appreciate the importance of God the creator only after having seen how the other two aspects work in this episode.

The second face of God—that of prohibitor and punisher—is most prominent in this episode. God appears most often and most impressively as one who prohibits, who threatens, or who punishes his creatures for failure to observe his rules. We are told ominously that "the god self was angered" (*U,* 14.411); there is reference to the ambiguous and terrifying "sin against the Holy Ghost" (*U,* 14.226); and we are told that God "was in a very grievous rage that he would presently lift his arm up and spill their souls for their abuses" (*U,* 14.471–72).[28] This face of God is also the one evoked by the Odyssean analogue of this episode. The story of the Oxen of the Sun in Book XII of *The Odyssey* tells of Zeus's interdict against eating the sacred cattle of Helios and of the failure of Odysseus's crew to heed that prohibition. Gnawed by hunger, they are drawn into slaughtering the cows for food. For this offense, Zeus destroys their ship with lightning. Several of the most prominent motifs of this episode derive from this story and take their meaning from it, relating in some way to the punisher aspect of God. Lightning is seen as the tool of God the Wreaker: "Lo, levin leaping lightens in eyeblink Ireland's westward welkin! Full she drad that God the Wreaker all mankind would fordo with water for his evil sins" (*U,* 14.81–83). The omnipresent cow imagery is more variable and more complex, but it is always related to some fetish ("sacred cow") or to some pseudo-authority, generally one acting with purported divine sanction. The Odyssean parallel is a forcible reminder that many cultures have taken cattle as objects of worship and idolatrously endowed them with such sanctity that the people would refuse to eat them even though they might be starving. The papal "Bull" of Pope Adrian IV is an attempt to intimidate and overawe the Irish into accepting as God's will what was in fact the Pope's own wish to see Ireland under the control of England.[29] The cry "Mort aux vaches" (*U,* 14.551) involves a challenge to the supposed authority of king as well as priest when we know that it alludes to Crainquebille's cry "Death to the cops."[30]

Another story involving God the prohibitor is an important source of the imagery, motifs, and themes of this episode—the story of the Garden of Eden. There are repeated direct references to several aspects of this story—the penny pippin for which Eve sold us (*U,* 14.301), the "eating of the tree forbid" (*U,* 14.873), and most notably that "woman should bring forth in pain" (*U,* 14.208–9). The two aspects of Jehovah's curse most important to Joyce's purposes in this episode are death, and woman's bringing forth children in pain. These are important because they form the direct thematic links with the medical, specifically obstetric, setting of the episode, and enable us to see medicine as one of man's attempts to challenge or circumvent God's threatening second face.

Man's attempts to understand God and to placate his more threatening aspects are also suggested by the several references to religious denominations and cults. There are references to a prophetical charm out of Hindustanish (*U,* 14.524), to Madagascar rituals (*U,* 14.345), and to Egyptian priests (*U,* 14.1169). Of particular thematic relevance are two sorts of cults—those that worship the cow, and the phallus. The bovine cults have their paradigm in the Homeric episode, and we have already seen their essence—idolatrous veneration of the cow even at the cost of human life. Worship of the phallus or of physical fertility per se is important here as well. Joyce's comment that the idea of the episode was "the crime committed against fecundity by sterilizing the act of coition" has made many critics wary of speaking against the idea of fertility, no matter how uncomfortable they may have felt about some of the forms it takes in this chapter.[31] But if we approach this theme without preconception, the episode clearly shows that worship of physical fertility easily becomes simplistic and idolatrous.

At best, fertility worship is an acknowledgment of the first face of God, as source and creator of all. But such worship, especially when it venerates an object such as a cow or the phallus, undervalues and betrays the distinctively human, imaginative aspect of the creation and distorts man's proper respect for sexual creativity into sheer idolatry. *Ulysses* does not ask us to worship "yerd our Lord" (*U,* 14.1527), or to approve of Mulligan's fertilization scheme. The ironies seem obvious in Mulligan's proclaiming that as "Fertilizer and Incubator" he plans "to devote himself to the noblest task for which our bodily organism has been framed" (*U,* 14.663). The values Mulligan espouses here are consistent with the simplistic, materialistic values he represents throughout the novel; to take them unironically here would be to invert the underlying values of the novel. This is not to say that there is anything inherently immoral about physical or sexual fertility. There is no idolatry involved in respecting these for the proper place they hold in God's creation.

Furthermore, physical fertility may be seen as a metaphor or a prototype of imaginative creativity, and no idolatry is involved, as long as the metaphor is kept in proper perspective. Idolatry sets in only when we undiscriminatingly regard physical fertility per se as sacred or deific. In this episode, far from espousing sheer physical fertility, Joyce suggests that such veneration is naive to the point of destructiveness, that it is a failure of imagination, that it is tantamount to treating nature, or material things, as sacrosanct. To conceive of material things as objects of worship, to take fertility pure and simple as sacred, is to misconstrue the nature of spirit, of God, and to denigrate the intended roles of man's intelligence and imagination in the creation. Further, such idolatry draws us into regarding nature, the given physical world, as something fixed and absolute, as if it were fully and finally created at one point in time by God, forever after to be worshiped as it is. And such an attitude leads naturally to the conclusion that any attempt on man's part to modify or improve upon nature would be sacrilege and would invite the wrath of the offended deity, of God the prohibitor and punisher.

But if the face of God most prominent in this episode (and perhaps in Judeo-Christian history as well) is that of prohibitor, it is not his only visage. God can, if man is capable of the vision, be seen also as reconciler and redeemer, and this aspect significantly qualifies his darker and more threatening one. This episode suggests that God the redeemer, instead of wishing man to be intimidated by the physical creation or revere it as sacrosanct, wishes him to recognize his distinctive place in it by virtue of being created in God's image, and even to contribute to the creation. This third face of God is suggested in Oxen of the Sun in several ways, among them Stephen's allusion to Christ as our Agenbuyer (*U,* 14.295), the reference to Jesus as "our alther liege lord" (*U,* 14.168), or the suggested power of Christ's rood to placate God the Wreaker (*U,* 14.83). Redemption is also suggested by the several references to rain, which, "please God" (*U,* 14.475), comes after hard drought.

The more open stance toward nature implicit in the redeemer aspect of God is also shown in the dual role attributed to woman in this episode. As Eve she is the "source" of the curse; but as Mary, she is the means of its melioration: "she [Mary] is the second Eve and she won us . . . whereas that other, our grandam, which we are linked up with by successive anastomosis of navelcords sold us all, seed, breed and generation, for a penny pippin" (*U,* 14.298–301). In the context that Joyce develops here, God's willingness to turn to a second woman, Mary—herself a part of the natural creation—as the vehicle by which he presents his redeemer aspect, is a sign of his wish to reconcile himself with his creation and to invite man to join in its extension. As it is presented in this episode, this theme suggests that man, made in the image of God, is himself an agent of God's continuing creation. Nature is not, then (as the Jehovah aspect of God suggests), static and sacrosanct, but is a proto-substance to be given still new forms. As Stephen puts it, "In woman's womb word is made flesh but in the spirit of the maker all flesh that passes becomes the word that shall not pass away. This is the postcreation" (*U,* 14.292–94). The implication is that man's true relationship to God—reflected in his being homo faber—is of the spirit not of the flesh, of Christ not of Adam, and that man is thus obligated to question what may appear to be the prohibitions of Jove or Jehovah, and even to participate in the continuing creation.[32]

In Oxen of the Sun the two main modes of man's extending or remaking of nature—the postcreation—are medicine and literature, the first suggested by the episode's action and setting, the second by its succession of styles (and beneath that, by *Ulysses* itself). As we see medicine here in the maternity hospital, it presents a direct challenge to God's curse in Genesis—through alleviating the pain and danger that Jehovah said childbirth must involve. What medicine attempts to do, then, is in a sense "unnatural," in that it does not accept the status quo of nature—e.g., woman's pain in childbearing—as something immutable or divinely sanctioned. Instead of accepting pain, deformity, and death as parts of some divinely fixed scheme of things, medicine audaciously, imaginatively, and "unnaturally" presumes to ameliorate and correct them. And in doing this, medicine challenges the prohibitor aspect of God and affirms his redeemer aspect.[33]

In one sense, then, just as this episode is about the nature of God, it is also about the nature of nature. One of the many ways this theme surfaces is in the motif of the *lusus naturae*, the freak of nature. In the present context this is a particularly important motif, because the very existence of the freak shows that the "nature" that God the prohibitor would have us revere is itself imperfect and capable of miscarrying. One section of Oxen of the Sun is a veritable catalogue of nature's errors, with particular attention drawn to deformed or monstrous births—miscarriages, acardiac *foetus in foetu*, agnathia, *Sturzgeburt*, "multiseminal, twikindled and monstrous births," harelip, supernumerary digits, swineheaded and doghaired infants (*U*, 14.961–88). These are relevant here because medicine regards such instances of nature's errors not as immutable givens, but as challenges to man's intellect and imagination to amend nature's errors. The point is that nature cannot be left to its own devices; certain aspects of nature need complementing and correcting through the agency of human intelligence, which (we should not forget) also comes from God the creator. For God the creator is after all responsible not only for the material cosmos but for the human mind as well; it too is a part of "nature" in the larger sense.

Approaching the episode through these themes enables us to see the appropriateness, even the brilliance, of Joyce's use of medicine and the setting of the maternity hospital in this episode. Medicine has throughout its history been accused of impiety and unnaturalness in its methods and in its aims. Consider, for example, the struggle that was involved in making it acceptable to study anatomy through the dissection of human corpses (medicine dared to ask, Is man made for the corpse or the corpse for man?), and today medicine continues to present us with trenchant questions about what is and is not "natural" for man to do. The issues of abortion (see p. 256, above), of the artificial prolongation of life, and of *in vitro* fertilization are but three of the most complex current examples. When we debate such issues, we go to the very core of man's inclination to alter or extend God's natural creation. Medicine, then, as Joyce saw, is a perfect subject through which to dramatize the issues of idolatry—the proper relation between matter and spirit—in that it continually involves us in the question of whether physical nature is inviolable and sacrosanct. Joyce, it appears, is sympathetic with young Dr. Dixon's description of medicine as "an ennobling profession which, *saving the reverence due to the Deity*, is the greatest power for happiness upon the earth" (*U*, 14.824–26; emphasis added). Seen in this light, medicine becomes one of man's most noble efforts, and one that materialist Mulligan neither comprehends nor is worthy of.

But if medicine is an important example of man's remaking and extending of nature, language and the literature expressed through it are for the purposes of this episode even more important. God the creator is the source of nature and of "human nature," which means that he is at another remove responsible for language and for those aspects of human nature expressed through it. A. N. Whitehead acknowledges this idea when he says, "it is not going too far to say that the souls of men are the gift from language to mankind. The account of the sixth day should be written, He gave them speech, and they became souls."[34] But the uses or misuses man makes of language, this most powerful tool, while indirectly attributable to God, are ultimately a matter of human judgment and human imagination.

Language, then, as this episode and *Ulysses* suggest, is man's most powerful means for continuing and extending the creation, for "redeeming" it from sheer materiality and randomness. This is true both in the sense that all distinctively human enterprises (including medicine) are enabled by language, and in the sense suggested by Whitehead, that the human spirit, the soul, is dependent upon language for its emergence. The powerful capacities in language can, however, be abused or perverted. Language is in some respects a tool, like fire or atomic energy, and like any other tool, it can be misused; its power for good if used properly and responsibly is matched by its power for harm if used improperly or irresponsibly. And this observation leads us once again to an important point about *Ulysses* that has not sufficiently been appreciated, a point developed in the first half of this essay, that in the various stylistic excursions in the later episodes of the novel, *Ulysses* is to some extent about the various abuses and misunderstandings of language and of literature that our age is subject to.[35]

Within the context of these claims about Joyce's aims and the episode's themes, I wish to reemphasize two points about the style of Oxen of the Sun. First, I do not believe that the narrative voice here reflects Joyce's own attitudes toward language, especially in its attempts to pattern the structure of the episode upon gestation or evolution. Undeniably such an attempt is being made here, but it expresses the intention of some "fallible" narrator or of some Arranger or Presenter—in any event of some persona whose views on literary form Joyce does not share. Second, underlying the stylistic tour de force of this narrator is a theory about literary form that can properly be called idolatry and is thus the appropriate stylistic counterpart of the motifs and themes we have just examined.

The apparent purpose of the narrator here is to present the "evolution" of English prose, based on an analogy with "faunal evolution" and with the development of the fetus in the womb. But there are several reasons to doubt that this program is directly, seriously expressive of Joyce's own attitudes. For one, the style of the exemplary passages is frequently turgid and almost impossible to understand, and does not involve skillful representations of the various writers and periods, though Joyce could certainly have done so. Rather, there is a simplistic, almost parodic, tendency to signal a style through tags, excesses, and superficial, quickly recognized traits. David Hayman notes these qualities when he speaks of the "rigidly stylized prose pastiches" (*Ulysses: The Mechanics of Meaning*, rev. ed., 100).[36]

Another problem is the difficulty, perhaps impossibility, of following with any precision the purported analogies with fetal development and with evolution, and the greater difficulty of seeing what these are supposed to mean. If it can be established that references to Alec Bannon's "cut bob" (*U*, 14.497) and to Mrs Purefoy's biting off "her last chick's nails" (*U*, 14.516) correspond to the fifth month of fetal development, where hair and nails first appear, what is the meaning of having this occur in a passage reflecting the style of Defoe? What is the connection between Defoe, or the eighteenth century generally, and the fifth month of fetal development? More pointedly, if we are to take the purported gestative form of the episode seriously, we must ask where the culminating event of birth occurs and what the thematic implications are of its occurring where it does: When was English style finally "born"?

Critics who have faced this question have come up with differing answers, which is itself disconcerting, considering how obvious and tangible an event birth is. J. S. Atherton says that the birth has begun by *U*, 14.1026, when we are told that "his head appeared," and it is still in progress on *U*, 14.1380. But what an intolerable gestative disproportion is involved in devoting ten pages of the episode's forty-five to the birth! And even in this Atherton has to distinguish between birth "on the literary level," and the birth of Mrs Purefoy's child. Atherton then makes some apologetic claims for justifying the idea that "English prose has apparently reached its full growth with the style of Ruskin."[37] Even allowing for the significant difference between "birth" and Atherton's term "full growth," I cannot believe that Joyce felt any such statement could be made about English prose style. If we think about it carefully, we know that while the literary style of any culture may be said to "develop," in that writers are influenced by what has gone before, we simply cannot use such terms as "birth" or "full growth," or "evolution" to describe literary style.[38] On the basis of the critical efforts I have read, I conclude that anyone who attempts to take this narrator's plan seriously is doomed to failure. The underlying reason for this failure is crucial to the underlying point of this episode—that language and the literature cast in it are one kind of reality (psychological and spiritual, rooted in meaning), while the fetus, or "faunal evolution" is another (physical), and no attempt to ground literary form upon physical process can succeed. When applied to literary style, such physically grounded analogies are necessarily metaphorical, and to lose sight of that is to invite chaos, or, in the terms of this episode, to indulge in idolatry.[39]

Kenneth Burke, in *The Rhetoric of Religion,* makes an axiomatic point:

> Language, to be used properly, must be "discounted." We must remind ourselves that, whatever *correspondence* there is between a word and the thing it names, the word is *not* the thing. The *word* "tree" is not a tree. And just as effects that can be got with the thing can't be got with the word, so effects that can be got with the word can't be got with the thing. But because these two realms coincide so usefully at certain points, we tend to overlook the areas where they radically diverge. We gravitate spontaneously toward naive verbal realism.[40]

My claim is that the narrator of this episode manifests an attitude toward language that involves "naive verbal realism," and is a stylistic equivalent to the simplistic totemism of cow worship or phallus worship, and I believe that Joyce is here taking the measure of the theory of imitative form, as he did in Sirens of an attempt to ground literature in music. For all his attempts—often amazingly successful attempts—to suggest or evoke nonliterary structures through the written word, Joyce knew that literature has its own nature and its own forms, and for a writer literally to take a physical process as a basis for literary form would reveal his deep confusion about the nature of literature. J. S. Atherton in the opening sentence of his essay on this episode puts his finger on an essential point—a point adumbrated years earlier by Harry Levin (see p. 254, above). Atherton says, "This chapter is an exercise in imitative form. Joyce is trying to make words reproduce objects and processes."[41] While I agree with Atherton's first assertion, I attribute this intention to the narrator of the episode rather than to Joyce. On one level Joyce is of course responsible for this, but just as in Nausicaa or Sirens or Eumaeus, Joyce is presenting a mode of language that he does not sanction, so here he dramatizes imitative form, but he does not stand behind it.[42] Why do it then? Because *Ulysses* takes seriously the powers and responsibilities of language, and Joyce wished to incorporate into his novel some of the major current misconceptions about this soul-giving, reality-creating medium. Joyce was aware of attempts to translate one art into another, or to see literature as imitating music or painting, or to use some physical object or event as the basis for literary structure. But for Joyce all such theorizing was mistaken in its failure to recognize the true nature of literary form. We might clarify this important point by distinguishing between two different meanings that have been given to the term "organic form." If by that term we mean that a work should have a form appropriate to its own nature and aims, then Joyce would sanction the idea. If by that term we mean that a literary work should take its form from any object or any process in physical nature, then Joyce would see in this metaphysical confusion and idolatry.[43] The point quite simply is that literature has a "nature" of its own, quite different from the nature of music or painting or of the growth of a fetus or a tree. Literary form is inextricably linked with tone and mood, with character and theme, with meaning; its proper inherent forms are psychological and aesthetic and spiritual rather than physical. Earlier I said that physical fertility may serve as a metaphor for imaginative fertility, but man must not regard physical fertility as his appropriate *telos,* or as sacrosanct. Similarly, critics and writers may use metaphors from the physical world to suggest literary form, but if they lose sight of the fact that these are metaphors, and come to expect literature to imitate physical structures, they commit a failure of discrimination tantamount to idolatry. What Levin and Atherton have said of this episode is true—the style here is an attempt to reproduce in words a physical process. But such an attempt in imitative form is doomed to failure because it mistakes the nature of language and the kind of reality it deals in. That, I contend, is what Joyce has dramatized here.

Notes

1. Among the more important discussions of this issue are the following (these are listed chronologically; most of them will subsequently be cited parenthetically in the body of my essay, by short title): Arnold Goldman, *The Joyce Paradox: Form and Freedom in his Fiction* (Evanston, Ill.: Northwestern University Press, 1966); David Hayman, Ulysses: *The Mechanics of Meaning* (Englewood Cliffs, N.J.: Prentice-Hall, 1970; rev. ed., Madison: University of Wisconsin Press, 1982); Erwin R. Steinberg, *The Stream of Consciousness and Beyond in* Ulysses (Pittsburgh: University of Pittsburgh Press, 1973); Wolfgang Iser, *The Implied Reader: Patterns of Communication in Prose Fiction from Bunyan to Beckett* (Baltimore: Johns Hopkins University Press, 1974); Richard Ellmann, *Ulysses on the Liffey* (Oxford: Oxford University Press, 1975); Ben D. Kimpel, "The Voices of *Ulysses,*" *Style* 9 (Summer 1975): 283–319; Marilyn French, *The Book as World: James Joyce's* Ulysses (Cambridge: Harvard University Press, 1977); William B. Warner, "The Play of Fictions and Succession of Styles in *Ulysses,*" *James Joyce Quarterly* 15 (Fall 1977): 18–35; Hugh Kenner, *Joyce's Voices* (Berkeley and Los Angeles: University of California Press, 1978); "Narrative in *Ulysses,*" in *Joyce & Paris 1902 . . . 1920–40 . . . 1975,* ed. J. Aubert and M. Jolas (Publications de l'Université de Lille, 1979), 33–58; Shari Benstock, "Who Killed Cock Robin? The Sources of Free Indirect Style in *Ulysses,*" *Style* 14 (Summer 1980); 259–73; Roy K. Gottfried, *The Art of Joyce's Syntax in* Ulysses (Athens: University of Georgia Press, 1980); Hugh Kenner, *Ulysses* (London: Allen and Unwin, 1980); Karen Lawrence, *The Odyssey of Style in* Ulysses (Princeton: Princeton University Press, 1981); Marilyn French, "Joyce and Language," *James Joyce Quarterly* 19 (Spring 1982): 239–55; Brook Thomas, *James Joyce's Ulysses: A Book of Many Happy Returns* (Baton Rouge: Louisiana State University Press, 1982); Shari Benstock and Bernard Benstock, "The Benstock Principle," in *The Seventh of Joyce,* ed. Bernard Benstock (Bloomington: Indiana University Press, 1982), 10–21; John Paul Riquelme, *Teller and Tale in Joyce's Fiction: Oscillating Perspectives* (Baltimore: Johns Hopkins University Press, 1983); Erwin R. Steinberg, "Author! Author!", *James Joyce Quarterly* 22 (Summer 1985): 419–24; Monica Fludernik, "Narrative and Its Development in *Ulysses,*" *Journal of Narrative Technique* 16 (Winter 1986): 15–40.

2. For a fuller discussion of this dichotomy among critics of *Ulysses,* see Stanley Sultan's essay in this volume. In recent years several critics of *Ulysses* have treated its style, or its depiction of its own narrative processes, as its subject matter. These include Michael Groden, Ulysses *in Progress* (Princeton: Princeton University Press, 1977); Karen Lawrence, *The Odyssey of Style in* Ulysses; and John Paul Riquelme, *Teller and Tale in James Joyce's* Ulysses. Wolfgang Iser has said pointblank: "In spectacular fashion, *Ulysses* puts an end to representation" (*James Joyce Broadsheet,* no. 9 [October 1982]: 1).

3. The term "initial style" derives from Joyce's letter to Harriet Shaw Weaver of 6 August 1919. After explaining some of the vagaries of the style of Sirens, he says, "I understand that you may begin to regard the various styles of the episodes with dismay and prefer the initial style much as the wanderer did who longed for the rock of Ithaca" (*Letters,* I, 129).

4. Other critics have felt it necessary to remind us of Joyce's pervasive presence. Marilyn French says "Whatever role he momentarily plays, Joyce, in *Ulysses,* is probably the most intrusive author ever to write a piece of fiction" (*Book as World,* 267); and Hugh Kenner says, "Joyce, let us make no mistake, is always present in *Ulysses,* and no talk of that dyad of technicians, the self-effacing narrator and the mischievous Arranger, should permit us wholly to forget that fact" (*Ulysses,* 68–69). And John Paul Riquelme argues similarly in "Enjoying Invisibility: The Myth of Joyce's Impersonal Narrator," in *The Seventh of Joyce,* ed. B. Benstock, 22–24. But even these critics seem subsequently to forget, or to ignore, the implication of this point. One critic has sidestepped this issue by talking as if the novel produced itself. Shari Benstock says, "The technical devices that collectively become the means for rendering plot and establishing tone and point of view are generated from subject matter and context rather than imposed from above (or behind) by an authorial presence hovering close to the narrative product," and more specifically of Aeolus, "These headlines arise in the text of *Ulysses* as they do in most newspapers, from the context of the day's news" ("Who Killed Cock Robin?", 261, 271). This same idea of a book that in effect writes itself is also pursued in Shari and Bernard Benstock, "The Benstock Principle," in *The Seventh of Joyce* (see n. 1).

5. See, for example, Phillip Herring's claim, in a discussion of Cyclops, that Joyce's aim was "to maintain a consistent moral neutrality in his novel" (*Joyce's* Ulysses *Notesheets in the British Museum* [Charlottesville: University Press of Virginia, 1972], 15).

6. A move in this direction is evident as early as Arnold Goldman's *The Joyce Paradox* in 1966. He notes that norms are established for Stephen and Bloom in the first six chapters, and only then does Joyce begin "systematic exploitation of technical experimentation" (81). Goldman says, "We begin, in Chapter Seven, to grasp that the words (and techniques) of *Ulysses* stand between us and the Dublin action" (83). In 1970, David Hayman coined the term "Arranger" to indicate some intervening presence (Ulysses: *The Mechanics of Meaning,* rev. ed. [1982], 84ff.)

Other critics as well have sensed a discrepancy between Joyce and his narrator. Richard Ellmann, speaking of the headlines in Aeolus, says that "their authorship is unclear. . . . By whomever composed, the headlines serve as a warning that the view of reality so far presented may not suffice indefinitely, the world may move less reliably in later chapters than it has so far." And later Ellmann says, "In Aeolus the narrative framework was agitated by the strange, unexplained headlines, which seemed almost composed by another author for purposes at variance with Joyce's" (*Ulysses on the Liffey,* 73, 92). Ben D. Kimpel agrees with Hayman and Ellmann: "As for the various narrators, they are generally reliable as to matters of fact but either clearly prejudiced (as in Oxen of the Sun) or non-committal (as in Ithaca)" ("The Voices of *Ulysses,"* 311).

7. My terminology here obviously owes something to David Hayman's "Arranger" (see the preceding footnote), but I prefer "Presenter" because "Arranger" implies that the persona has some authority over the disposition of the events in the novel, whereas "Presenter" implies that his authority extends only to form, not to content.

8. In a letter to Frank Budgen of 3 January 1920, Joyce said, "*Nausikaa* is written in a namby-pamby jammy marmalady drawersy (alto la!) style with effects of incense, mariolatry, masturbation, stewed cockles, painter's palette, chitchat, circumlocutions, etc. etc." (*Letters* I, 135).

9. Interestingly, this episode poses an interpretative problem for Karen Lawrence. Because she assumes that Joyce aims equally to damn all styles (because all are arbitrary), she finds the more explicit judgment against Nausicaa to involve a double standard on Joyce's part: "The succession of styles in 'Cyclops' and the different styles in the book as a whole imply that all language is, in a sense, inherently stupid, that all styles are arbitrary. But by choosing a member of the 'submerged population' as the object of his parody and by allowing his prose to 'formulate her in a phrase,' Joyce allowed the reader and the writer to be exempt from the indictment of Gerty. If the book has demonstrated that all styles are, in a sense,

equal, the parody here seems to say that some are more equal than others" (*Odyssey of Style,* 122).

10. Pater makes this famous assertion in "The School of Giorgione" in *The Renaissance*. In the first paragraph of that essay, however, he makes exactly the point I shall insist on later in this essay: "Each art, therefore, having its own peculiar and untranslatable sensuous charm, has its own special mode of reaching the imagination, its own responsibilities to its material. One of the functions of aesthetic criticism is to define these limitations; to estimate the degree in which a given work of art fulfills its responsibilities to its special material." But when Pater comes to what this involves for literature, he says it is "to define in a poem that true poetical quality, which is neither descriptive nor meditative merely, but comes of an inventive handling of rhythmical language, the elements of song in the singing." For Joyce, who saw literature as the queen of the arts because it involves meaning, such a focus upon rhythm is dangerously distortive. Richard Ellmann says, "For [Joyce] all music aspires to the condition of language, and being brought to that condition in the *Sirens* episode, reveals itself as less than supreme. After he had completed this episode, Joyce told a friend that he no longer cared for music, having seen through all its tricks" (*Ulysses on the Liffey,* 104).

11. For example, Harry Levin says of Sirens: "Joyce's premise, that any given physical effect can be exactly duplicated by means of language, lures him into a confusing melange des genres" (op. cit., 98). Among others who abjure what they presume to be Joyce's intention are L. A. G. Strong in *The Sacred River: An Approach to James Joyce* (London: Methuen, 1949), esp. 37, and S. L. Goldberg in *The Classical Temper: A Study of James Joyce's* Ulysses (New York: Barnes & Noble, 1961), esp. 281.

12. For example, Karen Lawrence says, "A crucial component of the chapter's irony is its revelation of the way in which writing is not music" (*Odyssey of Style,* 92).

13. In Circe, for example, Joyce criticizes both a literary genre and a psychological theory—expressionistic drama, and its frequent counterpart, Freudian psychology. The Presenter of the Circe episode seems equally committed to various devices of expressionistic drama and to the dark psychological assumptions that drama often embodied. But in my view these psychological mechanisms and their implications for human nature are not borne out by the rest of the novel: if the Presenter of Circe offers us a Freudian view of man and especially of the unconscious, the novel as a whole—involving the Odyssean and Shakespearean and other mythic analogies—is more consistent with Jung's theories. I develop this idea in an unpublished essay on "Some Modes of Allusion in Joyce's Works."

14. A major thesis of Michael Groden's Ulysses *in Progress* is that Joyce's interest shifted away from the "novelistic" elements of plot and character during the composition of *Ulysses,* but this thesis is by no means demonstrated. As his account of the composition of *Ulysses* progresses, Groden continually defers the time when Joyce supposedly lost interest in these elements, and in fact Groden himself detects such an interest into the very last phase of composition. See, e.g., pp. 195 and 196–97 of Groden's book. But Monica Fludernik, in her "*Ulysses* and Joyce's Change of Artistic Aims: External and Internal Evidence," (*James Joyce Quarterly* 23 [Winter 1986]: 173–88) focuses directly upon this question and comes to the opposite conclusion, "that Joyce did not abruptly change his intentions at any point during the writing of *Ulysses,* but that he gradually elaborated a plan, which had existed from the start" (186). Fludernik reexplores this issue from another angle in her article cited in n. 1, again concluding that there is "not sufficient evidence for postulating a major change of aims on Joyce's part" ("Narrative and Its Development in *Ulysses,"* 36).

15. Marilyn French says, "Since the initial style is virtually the only one used in the first six chapters, it sets the decorum of the novel; the reader experiences the advent of any new style as a violation of decorum, a breaking of ground rules. And since no other style occurs more than once in the novel, no other ground rules supplant the original decorum. The reader is left, as it were, with no footing at all, no comprehension of the space he is in. To assure this dislocation, Joyce returns to the initial style on occasion throughout the novel, thus providing the psychologically potent effect of 'intermittent reinforcement' " (*Book as World,* 54). And more recently French has said: "The novel is written in many styles, and from many points of view, none stamped with the author's guarantee of certitude. The ground is shifted under the reader's feet so frequently and extremely that one does not know where one is" ("Joyce and

Language," 251). Hugh Kenner describes the book's strategy as "to clown through various systems of local presentation, all cohesive, hence Styles, and all wrong" (*Joyce's Voices,* 84). Shari Benstock says, "The facade of objective norm, against which the behavior of characters and the method of narration is retroactively judged in *Ulysses,* is pretense from the outset. The narrative equivocates, never establishing models against which its later incarnations can be measured or restructured. The authority assumed behind the narrative voice is no more present on the first page of Telemachus than it is on the last page of Penelope" ("Who Killed Cock Robin?", 264). And a major thesis of Karen Lawrence's book is the relativism of all styles: "As the narrative norm is abandoned during the course of the book and is replaced by a series of styles, we see the arbitrariness of all styles. We see styles as different but not definitive ways of filtering and ordering experience" (*Odyssey of Style,* 9; see also 121, 122). But Monica Fludernik, in her "Narrative and Its Development in *Ulysses,*" emphasizes the variation and development of the style, even within the first six episodes, and argues for a more gradual progression of style throughout *Ulysses* (see n. 1 for citation).

16. Marilyn French says of Sirens, "By using language that is for the most part recognizable English and recognizable syntactic units, yet arranging those units so that they make no sense at all, Joyce is again thrusting in the reader's face the arbitrariness of language, the void at the core" (*Book as World,* 127–28); for a statement of Joyce's change of attitude toward the possibility of a normative style from *Dubliners* to *Ulysses,* see French's "Joyce and Language," 247–48 and 251–52. Karen Lawrence says, "In *Dubliners,* these voices were still consistent with a belief that language could capture reality: each voice of Dublin revealed the precise quality of the life story it told. It is not until *Ulysses* that parody is no longer attached to a specific character and begins to undermine the notion of style as an 'absolute manner of seeing things' " (*Odyssey of Style,* 33).

17. David Hayman says of Oxen of the Sun that "the verbal texture . . . impedes rather than facilitates our attempts to follow the action" (Ulysses: *The Mechanics of Meaning,* rev. ed. [1982], 100). Marilyn French says more generally, "The many styles leave us feeling that we have somehow not seen the real scene at all" (*Book as World,* 182). Hugh Kenner says, again of Oxen of the Sun, "What anyone really says in these paragraphs 'style' keeps us from discerning" (*Ulysses,* 109). Susan Bazargan says of a passage in Oxen that "Joyce's primary intention is not to reveal his character's thoughts but to explore the various ways language can shape and reshape our perception of any situation," and then says, "As prolific symbols words can be used for purposes of enlightenment . . . but they can also be abused in a variety of ways. In 'Oxen,' I think the corruption occurs mainly when discourse draws attention primarily to its own verbal antics, bloats itself and gathers wool as it goes along. Such a use of language often hides or disguises the speaker's undeclared anxieties" ("Oxen of the Sun: Maternity, Language, and History," *James Joyce Quarterly* 22 [Spring 1985]: 276). Karen Lawrence frequently speaks of the style impeding our sense of "events that do occur" and even speaks of "the incongruity between style and object" (*Odyssey of Style,* 124), apparently unaware of how such statements contradict her claim of the true relativity of all style.

18. For an argument that mockery is not the tone *Ulysses* sanctions, see James Maddox's essay in this volume.

19. In a letter to Harriet Shaw Weaver on 25 February 1920, Joyce said "I am now working on the Oxen of the Sun, the most difficult episode in an odyssey, I think, both to interpret and to execute" (*Letters, I, 137*). He had not yet, of course, completed the later episodes.

20. *Letters,* I, 139–40. This corrected version of the letter differs from that given in the earlier edition of the *Letters* (1957) and from that quoted by several critics.

21. Stuart Gilbert, though apparently lacking access to Joyce's letter when he first wrote his *James Joyce's* Ulysses (London: Faber, 1930), did draw on Joyce's schema to discuss the embryological parallels in the episode. Frank Budgen, in his *James Joyce and the Making of* Ulysses (London: Grayson and Grayson, 1934), quotes part of the letter and uses it in his discussion. By far the most determined attempt to read the episode in terms of Joyce's directive was A. M. Klein's 1949 essay, "The Oxen of the Sun," (*Here and Now* 1 [January 1949]: 28–48), in which he posits an extensive number of parallels with the development of the embryo and with geologic evolution, nowhere questioning Joyce's presumed attempt to

ground the literary structure of this episode in these physical processes. Robert Janusko spends several pages showing the wrong-headedness of Klein's article and cites other critics who are skeptical of it; see Janusko's *The Sources and Structures of James Joyce's "Oxen"* (Ann Arbor, Mich.: UMI Research Press, 1983), 3–4 and 41–43.

22. Harry Levin, *James Joyce* (Norfolk, Conn.: New Directions, 1941), 105–6. Levin made no change in this passage in the 1960 revision of his book. S. L. Goldberg expresses similar skepticism, calling this episode a "generally admitted failure" (*Classical Temper,* 284).

23. J. S. Atherton, "The Oxen of the Sun," in *James Joyce's* Ulysses: *Critical Essays,* ed. Clive Hart and David Hayman (Berkeley and Los Angeles: University of California Press, 1974), 320. Atherton modestly adds, "This may, of course, be simply the result of my own lack of perception" (320), but others share his doubts. Anthony Burgess says candidly, "The parallel between the growth of a foetus and the growth of a language does not really work, nor is it maintained consistently" (*Joysprick: An Introduction to the Language of James Joyce,* London: André Deutsch, 1973, 124). Similarly, C. H. Peake repeatedly expresses misgivings about Joyce's purported program; see *James Joyce: The Citizen and the Artist* (Stanford, Calif.: Stanford University Press, 1977), esp. 250–51, 262–63.

24. In the same vein Atherton says that "conscientious objection to contraception appears several times in Joyce's works, but on each occasion the tone of the passage in which the condemnation occurs leaves one in doubt as to its seriousness" ("Oxen," 324). Suzette A. Henke agrees that Joyce's condemnation of contraception must be understood emotionally and spiritually rather than literally (*Joyce's Moraculous Sindbook: A Study of* Ulysses, Columbus: Ohio State University Press, 1978, 174–77).

25. Goldman, *Joyce Paradox,* 95.

We have already noted a more general questioning of the narrator in *Ulysses* by several critics; see n. 6 above, which includes Ben Kimpel's characterization of the narrator of Oxen of the Sun as "clearly prejudiced."

26. Wolfgang Iser says that the central theme is love and even contends that "Each individual style projects a clearly recognizable idea of love, procreation, or birth" (*The Implied Reader,* 190). But general as Iser's central theme is, he fails to substantiate the claims he makes for it. Marilyn French, replacing Iser's broad generality with a trenchant modernity, says, "the episode is a meditation on sex," but then she adds, "the chapter is also about literature" (*Book as World,* 169). Later in her discussion, French attempts to bring these divergent subjects into proximity by referring to "the two main subjects of the chapter, procreation and language" (173), but this still leaves a gap between content and style. Susan Bazargan claims that "the central themes engaging Joyce" in Oxen are "maternity, language, and history" ("Oxen of the Sun: Maternity, Language, and History," *James Joyce Quarterly* 22 [Spring 1985]: 271–80).

27. An interesting parallel argument is Frances L. Restuccia's "Transubstantiating *Ulysses*" (*James Joyce Quarterly* 21 [Summer 1984]: 329–40). Restuccia argues that "in an attempt to establish the correct version—that is to say, the Church version—of the model on which he bases his art, Joyce presents in *Ulysses* erroneous conceptions of this mystery [the Eucharist] by way of contrast. What these false views appear to share (we shall observe) is an overemphasis on matter; they all, it might said, involve what Jacques Maritain has called the 'sin of materialism' " (329).

28. One interesting aspect of the theme of God as prohibitor-punisher is that the "offender" often has no clear sense of what his offense is. The sin against the Holy Ghost is terrible both because it is unforgivable and because we do not know what it is. As a child, Stephen was directed to "apologize" for some offense that is even less clear to him than to the reader (*P,* 8).

29. Etymologically the papal "bull" is quite distinct from the animal, but the context of *U,* 14.625–39 shows that Adrian's bull is to be seen as a sacred cow.

30. In Anatole France's *L'Affaire Crainquebille* (1901)—which Joyce read (see *Letters,* II, 212)—Crainquebille is arrested on the false charge of having said "Mort aux vaches." Later, when he hopes to regain the security of prison life by actually uttering the oath, he is blithely ignored by the police. The allusion is pointed out by Louis Berrone in *James Joyce in Padua* (New York: Random House, 1977), 121–22.

31. Recent critics have shown more temerity; see the comments cited on p. 254 above, and in n. 24.

32. On man as extender of the creation, consider Carl Jung's statement that "man is indispensable for the completion of creation . . . in fact, he himself is the second creator of the world . . ." (*Memories, Dreams, Reflections* [New York: Vintage Books, 1963], 256). And William Blake is even more categorical on this point: "God only Acts and Is, in existing beings, or Men" (*The Marriage of Heaven and Hell).*

33. It also responds to the wishes of the charitable Bloom, who earlier thought with sympathy of Mrs. Purefoy's plight: "Three days imagine groaning on a bed with a vinegared handkerchief round her forehead, her belly swollen out. Phew! Dreadful simply! Child's head too big: forceps. Doubled up inside her trying to butt its way out blindly, groping for the way out. Kill me that would. Lucky Molly got over hers lightly. They ought to invent something to stop that" (*U,* 8.373–78).

34. A. N. Whitehead, *Modes of Thought* (New York: Free Press, 1968), 41.

35. Richard Poirier remarks of *Ulysses* that it expresses Joyce's sense that "it is the responsibility of the novel to remind us of the artificiality of the forms it is taking, and that to do this is to save us somehow from error" (*Book Week* of the Sunday *Herald Tribune,* 14 November 1965, p. 24, in a review of Iris Murdoch's *The Red and the Green).*

36. Atherton too notes the ineptness of several of these passages; Hugh Kenner agrees and devotes several pages to showing how "unMacaulayesque" the passage based on Macaulay is, concluding, "Little is left of Macaulay," and "it is difficult, given Saintsbury's critical pointers, and Joyce's mimetic skill, to account such infidelities inadvertent" (*Joyce's Voices,* 106–9). And in his *Ulysses* (1980), Kenner says of these passages, "The considerable mimetic powers of James Joyce are not at work here" (108).

37. Atherton, op. cit., 328–33.

38. We know from one of his Padua essays of Joyce's disbelief in the applicability of evolution to the development of Western culture: "The theory of evolution, in the light of which our society basks, teaches us that when we were little we were not yet grown up. Hence, if we consider the European Renaissance as a dividing line, we must come to the conclusion that humanity up to that epoch possessed only the soul and body of a youth, and only after that epoch did it develop physically and morally to the point of meriting the name of adult. It is quite a drastic conclusion, and not very convincing. In fact (if I were not afraid to seem a *laudator temporis acti)* I should like to attack it with drawn sword" ("The Universal Literary Influence of the Renaissance," in *James Joyce in Padua,* 19).

39. Among the problems raised by such literalism is the question of what we are to make of that portion of the episode occurring after the presumed birth has been effected—to which A. M. Klein answers, it is the afterbirth! (Klein, op. cit., 31).

40. *The Rhetoric of Religion: Studies in Logology* (Boston: Beacon Press, 1961), 18. Had I space to develop these ideas further, one ally I would invoke is Owen Barfield. In his *History, Guilt, and Habit* (Middletown, Conn.: Wesleyan University Press, 1979), he discusses the dire effects of modern Western man's confusion of physical and spiritual categories. See especially chap. 2, appropriately entitled "Modern Idolatry: The Sin of Literalness."

41. Atherton, op. cit., 313.

42. In this use of imitative form I follow Atherton, who defines it as "trying to make words reproduce objects and processes" ("Oxen," 313). This is different from the meaning given the term by Ivor Winters, for whom "the fallacy of expressive, or imitative, form" involves more generally, "the procedure in which the form succumbs to the raw material of the poem" (*In Defense of Reason* [New York: Swallow Press, 1947], 41), as when a poet writes chaotically to suggest chaos. The two uses of the term are related, but Atherton's is more appropriate here.

43. The first meaning is Coleridge's. Contrasting mechanic and organic form, he says, "The form is mechanic when on any given material we impress a pre-determined form, not necessarily arising out of the properties of the material. . . . The organic form, on the other hand, is innate; it shapes as it develops itself from within, and the fulness of its development is one and the same with the perfection of its outward form. Such is the life, such the form" (*Coleridge's Shakespearean Criticism,* ed. T. M. Raysor [Cambridge: Harvard University

Press, 1930], 1:224). Cleanth Brooks says "The parts of a poem are related as the parts of a growing plant" (*A Handbook to Literature,* 3d ed., ed. C. Hugh Holman [Indianapolis: Bobbs-Merrill, 1972], 312). Coleridge's account stresses the appropriateness of the form to the aim of the work; Brooks's—if taken literally—suggests that literary form is based upon the form of a physical thing. The difference is radical.

The Adventures of *Ulysses* in Our World

STANLEY SULTAN

I

Regarded superficially, the criticism of *Ulysses* seems to reflect literary criticism in general through the middle half of our century, with once-dominant formalist identifying-and-explicating of elements of the WORK—begun in earnest by Gilbert's *James Joyce's* Ulysses—having been more or less succeeded by today's popular rhetorical hermeneutics of Joyce's strategies in his TEXT and our experiences of it. But in actuality, most of the criticism during six decades that superficially seems identified with one or the other of these contrary theories of literature derives from a single—shared—fundamental conception of Joyce's Work/Text itself.

That a single tradition in *Ulysses* criticism has persisted through old-fashioned formalist explication and new-fangled rhetorical hermeneutics can be illustrated with two quotations separated by a half-century. In 1932 Carl Jung wrote:

> *Ulysses* . . . pours along for seven hundred and thirty five pages . . . one single and senseless every day of Everyman . . . a day on which, in all truth, nothing happens. . . .
>
> It not only begins and ends in nothingness, but it consists of nothing but nothingness.

And in 1982 Wolfgang Iser wrote:

> If traditional modes of interpretation are rendered helpless by *Ulysses,* this is because the novel dispenses with a basic concept that was virtually taken for granted throughout the history of interpretation: namely, that the work of art should represent reality. In spectacular fashion, *Ulysses* puts an end to representation.[1]

Although "a novel" (Iser), *Ulysses* "puts an end to representation";[2] it portrays a "senseless every day of Everyman" in which "nothing hap-

© Stanley Sultan, 1985. A different version of this essay is to appear in Stanley Sultan, *Eliot, Joyce and Company* (New York: Oxford University Press, 1987).

pens," for the good reason that "it consists of nothing but nothingness." Both these extreme assertions are accompanied—and belied—by their authors' perceptive observations about what the novel does represent; but both also express the persisting single conception of *Ulysses* fundamental to the dominant tradition of criticism. Two years before Jung wrote, Stuart Gilbert declared that conception, in the formalist idiom of the time, in *James Joyce's* Ulysses:

> The meaning of *Ulysses* . . . is not to be sought in any analysis of the acts of the protagonist or the mental make-up of the characters; it is, rather, implicit in the technique of the various episodes, in nuances of language, in the thousand and one correspondences and allusions with which the book is studded.[3]

Gilbert's formalist concern for "the meaning of *Ulysses*" conceals the fact that he identified precisely elements now being designated important strategies/experiences of a Text, as the primary sources of the *meaning* of a Work. In other words, a conception of *Ulysses* in which "the acts" and "mental make-up of the characters" are literally less meaningful than "technique . . . nuances of language . . . correspondences and allusions," is subordinating elements of the novel that essentially refer to its quasi-reality, to elements of it that essentially are idiolectic ("nothing happens"; "an end to representation"). Today we are more fully conscious than were critics a generation ago of the implications of that subordination: it readily assimilates to the currently popular doctrine of the novel as Text. But the fundamental conception of *Ulysses* shared by most critics throughout the past half-century is the subordination itself.

Hence, despite the theoretical and methodological dissimilarity between characteristic *Ulysses* criticism dating back to the thirties, and *Ulysses* criticism increasingly characteristic of the eighties, most constitutes a single *continuous* tradition that has been the dominant one. Hence, John Paul Riquelme's 1983 *Teller and Tale,* whose concern is "how we may understand our relation and the teller's to the tale" in Joyce's work, echoes Gilbert's general statement in its first words: "This study deals with the styles, techniques, structures, and conceptual implications of narration in Joyce's fiction."[4]

This dominant tradition comprises most criticism, but not all: a tradition of criticism no less continuous, and complementary *because directly antithetical* to this dominant one, comprises the rest.

The year after *James Joyce's* Ulysses, Edmund Wilson published *Axel's Castle*. Its chapter "James Joyce" declares "with 'Ulysses' Joyce has brought into literature a new and unknown beauty," and calls him "really the great poet of a new phase of the human consciousness."[5] But again and again that sympathetic and acute discussion of *Ulysses* qualifies its praise with instances of sharp censure. In the course of the censure Wilson—while echoing Larbaud—reveals implicitly a basic conception of the novel directly opposed to the one that Larbaud had originated and Gilbert had recently articulated. It is best represented in Wilson's own words:

> "Ulysses" . . . must be approached from a different point of view than as if it were merely like [*Dubliners* and *Portrait*], a straight work of Naturalistic fiction.
>
> The key to "Ulysses" is in the title—and this key is indispensable if we are to appreciate the book's real depth and scope. (192)
>
> . . . .
>
> But as we get further along in "Ulysses," we find the realistic setting oddly distorting itself and deliquescing. . . . (206)
>
> . . . .
>
> "Ulysses" suffers from an excess of design rather than from a lack of it. Joyce has drawn up an outline of his novel . . . and from this outline it appears that Joyce has set himself the task of fulfilling the requirements of a most complicated scheme. . . . (211)
>
> . . . .
>
> We had been climbing over these obstacles . . . in our attempts to follow Dedalus and Bloom. The trouble was that . . . beneath the surface of the narrative . . . too many different orders of subjects were being proposed to our attention.
>
> . . . .
>
> And do not the gigantic interpolations of the Cyclops episode defeat their object by making it impossible for us to follow the narrative? (214)
>
> . . . .
>
> The worst example of the capacities for failure of this too synthetic, too systematic, method seems to me the scene in the maternity hospital. . . . Now something important takes place in this episode—the meeting between Dedalus and Bloom—and an important point is being made about it. But we miss the point because it is all we can do to follow what is happening. . . . (214–15)
>
> . . . .
>
> The night-town episode itself and Mrs. Bloom's soliloquy, which closes the book, are, of course, among the best things in it—but the relative proportions of the other three latter chapters and the jarring effect of the pastiche style sandwiched in with the straight Naturalistic seem to me artistically absolutely indefensible. . . . Joyce has here half-buried his story under the virtuosity of his technical devices. (216–17)

Wilson agrees with what I have called the dominant tradition in distinguishing (in his words) "story" from "technical devices"; and he agrees that one is fundamental in *Ulysses;* but he holds the opposite view of which is so. The opposition between his conception of the novel and that of most other early critics is encapsulated in the contrast between the general unquestioning adoption of Joyce's Larbaud-Gilbert "schema," and his impatience with it.

I believe our world evolved, soon after *Ulysses* came into it, the complementary antithetical traditions of criticism I have identified, and that dyad has persisted for six decades: every primarily critical study attaches itself to one or the other. And both have contributed to our understanding of *Ulysses.*

The traditions are complementary because between them they accommodate the compound Joyce achieved in his novel, of idiolectic sign-sequence, and narrative about fictional humans; they are antithetical because they have opposed conceptions of its essence as being one or the other of the two elements. Terms already quoted for one element of Joyce's compound are his and critics' "styles," and critics' "technique(s)" and "telling"; for the other element, critics' "happenings" and "tale." To substitute less general terms used recently in pairs, precisely to specify the two elements: the critics of the dominant tradition implicitly or explicitly conceive *Ulysses* as *essentially* a "symbolic structure" employing its complementary mode of "characters" or "drama" as instrumental adjunct; those of the alternative tradition conceive it as essentially akin to most novels in being a "human drama" employing its (strikingly original) complementary mode of "language" or "surface" as instrumental adjunct.[6]

My subject is not *Ulysses* itself, but those two continuous opposed traditions of its criticism I conceive, and the important consequences of the contrariety for one's appreciation of *Ulysses.*

That some contributors to the canon of criticism emphasized "the tale of the telling," and others contrarily "the naturalistic [*sic*] tale," has been discussed in recent years; and the Wilson-like complaints of a number of the latter—especially S. L. Goldberg, in his nonetheless-praised *Classical Temper*—have been criticized.[7] Although that conception does not dictate the complaints, they derive from the particular (conscious or unconscious) conception of the essential nature of *Ulysses* Wilson also articulated. It has persisted to today—I am among those who conceive *Ulysses* as essentially a "human drama." And so has the contrary conception shared by most *Ulysses* critics—that it is a "symbolic structure"—no matter how much those in that dominant tradition writing today may fail to recognize their kinship with their predecessors of two and more decades ago, or may disagree with them on certain issues in literary theory.

The sensible escape from the dilemma would seem to be a view of *Ulysses* that transcends it by integrating the contraries; and this has been proposed and attempted by a number of critics.[8] However, all of these critics, too, seem fundamentally committed to one conception of *Ulysses* or the other.[9] I shall try to show that the dilemma of alternative conceptions cannot be negotiated: their respective consequences for understanding important elements of the novel are so contrary that the sounder alternative must be identified, if possible.

II

In 1912, shortly before he began work on the novel, Joyce delivered his pair of lectures on two English writers as exemplifying the extremes of *"Verismo ed Idealismo nella letteratura inglese."* Defoe "represent[s] reality" (Veri-similitude) (as Iser says Joyce "dispenses with" doing); and Blake adopts or devises intrinsic formulations (relies on intellect or imagination, *idea* in the root sense). As Walton Litz has written, these lectures "established the twin frontiers of his art and looked forward to *Ulysses.*"[10]

Only a poor reader would claim that the lecturer's extreme example Defoe does not also exploit formal potentialities, or Blake also render experience, in their creations. But Homer, Dante, and Shakespeare, whom Joyce was soon to mine in making his novel (simultaneously claiming for it kinship to all three), were models for syncretizing "storyness" and "textness." And his own syncresis would succeed in emcompassing the two extremes he exemplified in "Daniel De Foe—William Blake." *Ulysses* is, at what seems close to the limit of each, both a veristic "chaffering . . . chronicle" as its own "Carlyle" calls it (*U*, 14.1412), and the idealistic "structure" of "a votary of the way to do a thing that shall make it undergo most doing," as Henry James said of Conrad (in his 1914 essay, "The New Novel"); it is an exquisitely realized symbiosis of fictional quasi-reality embodied, and form of embodiment. A recent critic eschews my temporizing "at what seems close to the limit of each," and declares simply: "No other novel had concerned itself at such length and in such detail with daily life . . . and yet no other novel had been so consciously and even ostentatiously artistic."[11]

In the essay whose comment on Joyce's *"Verismo ed Idealismo"* lectures is quoted above, Litz warns against "the notion—always a reductive one—that the novelistic elements in *Ulysses* can be separated from the *schema* and claimed as the true line of the work's meaning" (405). One must avoid such a reductionist abstraction of one, and neglect of the other, of its two symbiotic elements. And this essay is an attempt to establish the grounds for doing so—by determining their functional relationship in the novel. The practice of critics for more than half a century has documented what I shall try to show: that the relationship is one of means and end. To distinguish—as a *critical* activity—quasi-reality embodied and form of embodiment, no more claims that each exists autonomously in *Ulysses* (no more claims that content and form are separable in art), than to distinguish—as a *scientific* activity—sight from the optic nerve, claims that they are autonomous. Therefore, critics should not be disturbed about making a distinction constantly being made in both the dominant schematist tradition of *Ulysses* criticism and the alternative novel-ist one.

The dismissive generalizations by Jung and Iser to the effect that *Ulysses* does not "represent" anything "happening" simply express the dominant conception they share: that the things represented by the novel's embodying words as happening ultimately are the novelistic action Joyce devised to serve (as its occasion or "subject"), his embodying composition of words itself. An adherent of the alternative tradition, I assert the contrary: that its form of embodiment ultimately—despite Joyce's increasing innovation—serves its created life. Furthermore, my position is radical: today most critics in the dominant tradition would not claim that the textness of *Ulysses* is primary in its first chapters; I claim and shall try to demonstrate that its storyness is its essence even in its last and most stylistically innovative chapters.

III

Having made my declarations and radical assertion, I must now either deal (at least briefly) with certain issues these declarations raise, or fail to do justice to the many critics in the dominant tradition who have helped me read the novel. And to critics like myself as well; for the view of the alternative tradition that, however rich may be the tale of the telling, the telling serves what it tells, can seem simple-minded. The critic who holds that view can seem to be perverting the complex reality of *Ulysses*, seeking—or only able to see—in it a Classics Comics version of itself. (Wilson's "it is all we can do to follow what is happening" was written during the first shock wave.)

No distinction in the novel between Art and Life is implied: all is art by definition, Molly herself as much as the stream of words that embodies her. And it bears repeating that to distinguish manifestations of the two symbiotic modes in the heterocosm *Ulysses*, as I have just done with its last chapter—and as all do who share the current critical concern with its textness—is not a pre-Romantic claim that form and content are separable in art. Someone who did think these separable could not—and probably would not want to—read this book past Stephen on the strand in the third chapter. Only a reader who loves what language can achieve in literature would read a language-structure so rich that reading it and studying it are the same process.

It follows that study of Joyce's Work "for the meaning" is not being opposed to the phenomenalistic experience of reading the words of his Text. Furthermore, in many places its words—or other effects of idiolectic textness—are not primarily serving its quasi-life mode: they are significant in and for themselves. Those idiolectic effects exemplify the dominant critical conception of the whole of *Ulysses* as essentially its textness (and Joycefully express the creative power of this massively egotistical great writer). But its many instances of textness do not make it *essentially* this mode described as "technique . . . correspondences and allusions" yesterday and as "word-world" today. To oppose generalizing from them—to dispute so conceiving of *Ulysses*—no more involves ignoring those instances, than it involves being insensitive to the working of language in the novel.

In his fine recent book in the dominant tradition, which I cite because I have learned from it, Brook Thomas charges: "But despite Joyce's fascination with words, an entire strain of *Ulysses* criticism has chosen to ignore, minimize, or complain about the role of language in the book." (8) He also points out reasonably "that to read the book as book" is "not ruling out the possibility of reading the book as world" (16); and he cites Hugh Kenner (whose "appreciation of the human story," he says shrewdly, "seems to have sharpened over the last twenty years"), in support of the proposition that we must "rid ourselves of the belief that the story exists prior to the book's language."[12] I concur with his positive points and plead innocent to his charge.

Unfortunately, neither plea nor concurrence will save me from the charge of naive empiricism. The alternative critical tradition, to which I adhere—conceiving the quasi-reality it embodies to be the essence of the novel—directly confronts the prevailing current view of both the reader's relationship to language, and the relationship of language to reality. Currently we who so conceive *Ulysses* are said to betray, in Thomas's phrase, "the objectivist-positivist notion of meaning."[13] This local manifestation of today's ubiquitous general debate is the last preliminary matter that must be brought up. But without a long excursion into the familiar field of that debate, little can be accomplished beyond making two points about the nature of narrative.

The thesis (originated by Ferdinand de Saussure) asserts that nothing outside a (hearer's or) reader's mind is implicated in reading. Therefore, the linguistic *signe* has no referential component. Instead, only a response-thought, a *signifié* generated in the mind of a reader, is invoked by the *signifiant* he or she reads; the thesis is neatly expressed in the hermetic autonomy—root *sign* with two conjunctive suffixes—of that "lexicon of signification" (Roland Barthes). In other words, while the author may be referring with his or her written language, the reader's process of apprehending meaning in the language excludes—is isolated from—what the language refers to. The relationship of this thesis to the doctrine of indeterminacy in language is direct. And *Ulysses* lends itself to the doctrine in a number of ways.

However, I propose that the narrated events in the novel—its explicit thoughts, speeches, and actions—give that doctrine no encouragement. Whatever aporias of language may or may not exist in *Ulysses,* even in the language that is necessarily the medium of its events, a sequence of those actions, speeches, and thoughts is specified. To extend the doctrine of indeterminacy to narratives, on the grounds that all apprehended sequences are readers' constructs out of language, ignores the difference between possibly indeterminate signs *put* in a sequence by an author, and events *made to occur* in a sequence by an author.[14] Each event is specified (referred to) by language. But usually only its significance, not the event itself, is debatable. Even in the rare instance when the language saying what has happened is equivocal, the other events in the sequence provide a context for determining it. In other words, the coherent sequence of events occurring in *Ulysses* is a component of narrative that (I propose) constitutes a *metalanguage*. If that is so, it is beyond the reach of the current hot debate between what seem to be alternative myths (each believed, neither provable) about the relationship of language and meaning.

My second point concerns character in a narrative. It is true that Bloom, for example, not only does not exist prior to the language of the novel, but also is, as Thomas vividly describes his textness, "a verbal construct . . . the result of words marching across the pages of *Ulysses*" (15). But how important a statement about the nature of narrative is that? In *Six Characters in Search of an Author,* Pirandello dramatized the paradox involved; and he discussed it in the Preface. The evidence about Bloom the verbal construct is that the statement is as undeniably true as, and little more important than, the observation that his creator was less than a dollar's worth of chemicals at 1922 prices. Recently we have had both a book extrapolating an account of Bloom and Molly from the "defoe-esque or narrative side" of the novel, and a "biography" of Bloom.[15] Every issue of the *James Joyce Broadsheet* contains illustrations from one or two new series of paintings or graphics portraying Bloom and other characters that (who) are just words. Whatever the value of any one series, all are testimony to the impress of the quasi-life in *Ulysses* called Leopold Bloom on the actual lives of the denizens of our world. Writing about Bloom in *A Colder Eye,* Hugh Kenner exemplifies Brook Thomas's observation about him—as much in the ironic tribute to Joyce of "seemingly," as in his positive statement:

> Bloom, though, grows in stature throughout the day. . . . His emergence as a man to care about and ponder is among the greatest of literary miracles, seeing that we encounter it in a book so seemingly insistent on its own indifference to . . . anything but schemes of formal consistency. By less than the halfway point the book seems wholly preoccupied for good with stylistic pastiche, yet already Leopold Bloom is so firmly established we cannot lose sight of him. . . .[16]

While he originates in the words marching across the pages, our Bloom is not meaningfully reducible to them. We know well that character in narrative can have such a quasi-life, unconfined (and unexplained) by the language that constitutes it/her/him. Most true paradox is mystery.

The dominant tradition in *Ulysses* criticism has made and continues to make an indispensable contribution to all our understanding. This must be emphasized in the course of proposing that the alternative tradition has the sounder conception of the novel. Of course, every writing that represents happenings is, to some extent, an idiolectic composition of words as well; and in certain such writings that element is prominent enough to be a joint mode of its ontology, in the philosophical sense. But one of the two modes usually is identifiable as essential, with the other its instrumental adjunct. For example, although both novels repeatedly draw attention reflexively to their own textuality, most critics would agree that the essential mode of *Moby-Dick* and *The Ambassadors* is the quasi-life embodied in the book of words; and most would agree that the book of words is the essential mode in *Tristram Shandy* and *Finnegans Wake*. Critics have been unable to agree about *Ulysses*. Three questions are involved, not one: Is one of its two modes really essential and the other instrumental?; If so, which is which?; Does which is which matter for our criticism? I have indicated my answers to all three and shall try to defend them.

IV

Discussing "The tension in the book between an emphasis on the telling of the story and an emphasis on the story itself," Karen Lawrence, one of the recent critics who express the view (alluded to above) that the "emphasis on the telling" does not occur until after the nine chapters of Joyce's "First Part," specifies that "Beginning in 'Aeolus' . . . and continuing in . . . 'Sirens,' the writing of the text begins to dominate our attention."

> The book does not abandon its interest in the characters and their stories, but one can locate a shift of attention from the dramatic action of the plot to the drama of the writing. . . .[17]

Another, Michael Groden, declares "after 1919 Joyce was no longer writing a novel based primarily on human actions. . . ."[18] Unlike Kenner's "a book so seemingly insistent," these statements are positive answers to the first two questions: they agree with my claim that the modes are never equipoised—that a critic cannot weight them equally, for one is always essential, the other instrumental; and they propose that, after the early chapters, the essential mode is "the telling of the story"/"drama of the writing." I hope to show that even in the three chapters of III (the "Nostos"), the essential mode of the novel is "the story itself."

But first the third question must be addressed. Does it matter for our criticism? Must one mode be shown to have primacy, one conception of the novel prevail, as the critical practice of both traditions suggests? I shall cite one instance of critical generalization and one of specific reading in support of my affirmative answer.

Lawrence makes the valuable point that Joyce employs topoi of classical rhetoric throughout the catechism chapter, and concludes: "The performance of the catechism is really a school performance in the rhetorical classification of facts. . . . Using these topoi for comic purposes, Joyce plays with the idea of the human wish to arrive at truth."[19] This generalization about the form of the catechism chapter does not admit an equipoise of the two modes. If the form is itself its subject—if the essential function of all the pedantic factuality about Stephen, Bloom, Bloom's house, etc., is to implement Joyce's rhetorical performance commenting on a universal human trait—Bloom and Stephen, being quasi-human, are included in that comment. But as a direct consequence, their importance in the chapter and so in the novel is diminished. They have been reduced to two particular examples of the universal humanity. And if so, the tale of their particular quasi-life, carried forward by the rhetorical performance Joyce uses to comment on humanity in general, must be merely the instrument of what the chapter is (essentially) about—the central tale is of the telling.

As with general critical propositions, so with the specific reading process, the two fundamental conceptions of the novel can be irreconcilable. An instance of the tale of the telling cited by Brook Thomas is Stephen's mental sentence in the first chapter about the key to the tower, in which a full stop between two sentences has been ungrammatically elided to a comma: "It is mine, I paid the rent" (*U*, 1.631). Thomas and a number of other critics have proposed recently that Stephen is quoting Mulligan, and so Mulligan paid the rent for the tower.[20] The issue is important not only for subsequent events, but also for our understanding of Stephen. For example, the last paragraph of the chapter, after Stephen has given Mulligan the key, and two-pence "for a pint," is a single word, representing his thought: "Usurper" (*U*, 1:744). Is the accusation the author has emphasized so heavily Stephen's legitimate projection of the incident onto the symbolic plane? If indeed Mulligan paid the rent, *usurper* is inaccurate and a touch whining. Literally illegitimate, it is also symbolically pretentious. Therefore, who paid the rent has no trivial significance for this major character at the beginning of this long novel.

Either of two irreconcilable alternative meanings (Stephen paid/ Mulligan paid) can be inferred from the sentence, by a critic in either tradition. The issue is relevant here because one's understanding of what it says will be directed by whether one reads it primarily as a discrete structure of words, or primarily in its context in the action. In other words, it must be taken *either* as its own textness (conveying by the comma its special status as Stephen's quotation), *or* as functioning essentially for the tale (exposition comma and all of who did pay the rent). And if there is no strict causal connection, there is a manifest correlation between its two irreconcilable meanings on the one hand, and on the other, two irreconcilable conceptions of which mode of the novel is the essential one and so must prevail, that represented by the rhetorical possibilities in Stephen's ungrammatical sentence, or that represented by the place of the thought his sentence conveys in the story of the quasi-life his thought helps compose.

It also is relevant that the recent subtle reading of the language of the passage seems to be simultaneously a limited reading of the nature of human character:

> He wants that key. It is mine, I paid the rent. Now I eat his salt bread. Give him the key too. All. He will ask for it. That was in his eyes. (*U*, 1.630–32)

Three words in the two sentences following the one at issue—"Now," "Give," "too"—and the next sentence—"All."—merit attention.

Stephen's reference to Mulligan's providing his food *now* seems to invoke a time when he supplied their or at least his own food. But if the problematic sentence is really his anticipation of the words of Mulligan's legitimate demand, and so is interrupting the sequence of his thought, a question arises; What has food to do with the key (He wants that key. Now I eat his salt bread)? If Stephen is connecting receiving Mulligan's food *now* (as against the unspoken *then*), with having been receiving lodging all along—if Mulligan indeed "paid the rent"—why does he not make explicit the connection with receiving lodging, and contrast with formerly providing his own food (Now I eat his salt bread too)? To me, what Stephen's *now* signifies in its context is a rueful contrast of his present reliance on Mulligan for his very food with a time when he had enough money to pay the rent on the tower; it is a familiar human sentiment.

Give does not seem the correct word, if Mulligan paid the rent; for then the key is, as Stephen has him say, his. Furthermore, with the connective *too* Stephen does use, he links not accepting lodging from Mulligan, but *giving* Mulligan the key, with taking Mulligan's food. If Mulligan paid the rent, they are not corollary. If Mulligan paid the rent, the action on Stephen's part corresponding to eating Mulligan's food would be retaining Mulligan's key (I eat his food; I'll keep his key *too*). Of course, this would make nonsense of *now*.

The isolated word *all* not only connects the key and the food, but signifies a general resignation. If Mulligan paid the rent, Stephen is not submitting to very much by relinquishing the key to its rightful owner, who also feeds him; and so the sentence "All" joins the final paragraph "Usurper" as a grandiose pose by this major character. If, however, the key is Stephen's because *he* paid the rent; yet *now* he must submit to eating *Mulligan's* bread; and he will submit to *give* Mulligan his key (and, it turns out, twopence) *too;* then indeed he is submitting in *all*—to Mulligan's usurpation. He is no shallow *poseur,* but the depressed and isolated young man we get to know better in the next two chapters and in the National Library. That young man is irreconcilable with the primacy of the textness of the passage; and as with the example of general criticism, either of two alternative novels begins to emerge from each of two irreconcilable conceptions of which is the essential mode of *Ulysses,* and which the mode instrumental to that mode.

Having demonstrated the consequences of inclining to give greater weight either to a comma or to a quasi-live character, I should mention that the issue of whose words Stephen is thinking now has been largely obviated. According to Hans Walter Gabler's *Ulysses: A Synoptic and Critical Edition* (1984), not a comma but a full stop follows "It is mine" (*U,* 1.631). ("Salt bread" replaced "food" on the second proof.)

V

In "Error and Figure in *Ulysses,*" a chapter in his book about "Writing, Textuality, and Understanding," Gerald L. Bruns invokes rhetoric to describe the nighttown chapter: " 'Circe' is really nothing more than this: an episode of contrivances . . . repression . . . and (above all) rhetoric, which is the art of making anything appear to be the case . . . ."[21] Bruns begins his chapter with an explanation of the phrase in its title: "error" and "figure" are alternative interpretations critics make of "misperception or misconstruction" by Bloom, Stephen, and other characters. He cites Hugh Kenner and Fritz Senn as readers of *Ulysses* whose criticism "emphasizes respectively Joyce's naturalism and its consequent irony" (error), and "figural transformation." And he calls these emphases "the two most coherent and satisfying positions on *Ulysses* that Joyce criticism has given us."[22]

My reason for mentioning his instructive distinction is his own emphasis. For these "positions" are restricted to "how things make sense in Joyce's fiction"—to the reader's process of apprehending. The product thereby apprehended, the quasi-life of a character who sometimes is self-deluding (error), sometimes self-ennobling (figure), and sometimes—true of both Stephen and Bloom—the latter by way of the former, is literally dis-regarded.

Yet the concentration of recent critics in the dominant tradition on the process of apprehending the textness of *Ulysses* has expanded all our sensitivity to, and awareness of, the complexity and variety of Joyce's telling in it. For example, when I first wrote about the novel, I believed Joyce was trying to conceal the authorial presence, and his strategies of concealment were unwittingly drawing attention to it.[23] It is this recent criticism that has taught me how mistaken I was—how precisely Joyce meant the personal implications of his simple word *styles* for the varieties of language, pattern, and narrative strategy his telling employed.

Of the six forms of telling I now distinguish, nothing needed to be taught about Joyce's three familiar ones: dialogue; a character-narrator; and the "invisible" nonparticipating narrator of a "dramatic" narrative—the anonymous "voice" that is self-effacing and sometimes adopts the diction of the subject-character (a device also being used by other modernists, such as Conrad and Lawrence). I failed totally to recognize the ubiquity of a fourth: the nonparticipating narrator who, while remaining anonymous like the last mentioned, makes himself "visible," asserts his presence. That fourth form of telling in *Ulysses* is Joyce's modernization of the familiar blatantly authorial voice addressing the "Dear reader," as in "As said before he ate with relish . . ." (*U*, 11:519–20) and, two pages later, "Bloom ate liv as said before." (*Who* said before? It is being "said" again and again for the sake of that word.) A fifth form is the now-familiar convention of arranging words to represent the largely non- or pre-verbal phenomenon, thought—inner monologue, interrupted by other forms of telling except in the last chapter, where it is an uninterrupted "stream." What I realized only recently is how profoundly different inner monologue is *as form of telling* from dialogue, which in other respects it resembles. Dialogue is a printed reproduction, in a narrative, of actual words of the language as they would be spoken; inner monologue is an arranged disposition of words in a narrative to represent something that is not language. And the disposition is arranged by its arranger.

But the arranger is a familiar invisible presence that enables its arrangings to be read through (past) itself: inner monologue is a form of telling employing the *transparent* arranger that (for example) arranges paragraphs for the words of the *self-effacing* narrator. And all five forms of telling were used before *Ulysses.* For example, although he tells things he could not know, the character-narrator himself takes responsibility for the transparent arrangement of such things as the marbled page in *Tristram Shandy;* and the arranger of the facsimile stage directions in late chapters of *Moby Dick* is transparent. *Ulysses* takes the next step. The new sixth form of telling Joyce evolved in it is an arranger different from the traditional transparent one precisely as the blatant authorial "voice"—the "visible" nonparticipating narrator who asserts his presence with "Dear reader" or "As said"—differs from the self-effacing narrator of "dramatic" narrative. The sixth form is the new kind of arranger—that (*who* almost seems more proper) blatantly asserts its opacity.

The "non-human voice" first distinguished by Arnold Goldman in 1966 and named by David Hayman in 1970, *The Arranger,* Hayman describes as "a significant, felt absence in the text" and Kenner designates "perhaps the most radical, the most disconcerting innovation in all of *Ulysses.* It is "something new in fiction," is—though "not a voice at all," as Kenner says—"heard," a "felt absence" because it is a clamorous presence: it is this second, blatant, arranger originated by Joyce that attention to his telling has disclosed to us.[24] Responsible for the headlines in the newspaper chapter, typographical arrangements in the library chapter, interpolated passages, the format of the nighttown and catechism chapters, and so much else, the blatant arranger raises as well as settles questions. For example, when the unnamed narrator of the doings in Barney Kiernan's tells of urinating (*U,* 12. 1561–72), his narrative includes his thoughts and the sounds of his spitting as happening while he speaks, although they happened in the past he is telling about. Is the blatant arranger timewarping?; our Homer nodding? There is no way to know.

The explications, in the early decades of the dominant tradition, of formal and allusive patterns, and of symbolic and tropistic meanings, built bridges to *Ulysses* over which all of us have passed. No less is the current concern with the tale of the telling doing so. Furthermore, this valuable development in *Ulysses* criticism acknowledges the symbiotic presence of the novel's mode of quasi-life, for it considers that mode the instrumental medium of the novel's essential textness. Mine is not a theoretical concern with its conception of which mode is the essential one. I am concerned about the consequences of that conception: an unavoidable methodological bias I detect in critical *practice.*

For decades, Wilson, Goldberg, and others complained about the indifference of their contemporaries in the dominant tradition to the possible *function,* for the *quasi-life* of the novel, of elements of its textness. A general example of the bias is the persistence of that indifference. Hence, early explicators of the Homeric pattern, informed by the Gilbert "schema" that the third chapter is "Proteus," failed to ask what Telemachus had to do with Proteus—and to recognize the *function* for *Stephen's story* of Menelaus's wrestling with Proteus in *The Odyssey.* Hence, critics of today in the dominant tradition study Joyce's dramatically increased emphasis, after the novel's "First Part," on his telling, while neglecting the *function* of that new emphasis for *the story* told by the audacious new tellings. With Bloom's confrontation with his sirens in the Ormond, the tale of the telling begins in earnest. And at precisely that point in the novel—the point at which the changes in Joyce's "style" commence—Bloom commences to change in both attitude and conduct toward the situation that is the major subject of the action.

Whether the change in the tale or the change in the telling is primary—which is the means and which the end—is the subject under consideration. But two points are beyond debate. That its tale and its telling change simultaneously—its quasi-life concurrently with its form—is a relevant fact about *Ulysses,* is self-evident. The other point is that the relevant conjunction is not mentioned in any of the rhetorically-oriented recent criticism I have read. In this case, the bias that causes neglect of the quasi-life in the novel also results in obscuring an accomplishment of its form.

The contrary bias of the alternative to this dominant tradition occasionally expressed itself in a shortsighted impatience with stylistic and formal innovations in *Ulysses;* but my thesis is that its conception of the novel is the sounder one. My thesis is most appropriately tested against its final part, III, conceived and written in the most advanced stage of Joyce's evolution of its textness. In the next three sections I shall try to show that Joyce's telling in each of the three chapters of the "nostos" perpetuates to the end of *Ulysses* the primacy of its complementary mode—that of the quasi-life it embodies.

VI

Most critics in both traditions always have characterized the blatantly arranged narrative of the first chapter of III as "fatigued" or "tired."[25] And recently, some in the dominant tradition—expressing the current rhetorical emphasis of that tradition—have augmented its ostensible function: in addition to "depicting Bloom's or both characters' exhaustion," it embodies the author's comment on the state of discourse, or the state of all language.[26] For example, declaring it "indeed the 'narrative old' that Joyce described to Gilbert," Karen Lawrence writes:

> If the language of "Eumaeus" is enervated, it is not merely to reflect the fatigue of the characters or a narrator but to reveal that language is tired and "old," used and reused so many times that it runs in grooves.[27]

I believe this more general ostensible function must be attributed to the concerns of current critics, not to the narrative style itself. In the version of his "schema" that was embraced *ab initio* by the dominant tradition, the "technic" Joyce specified for the chapter was recorded as "narrative (mature)," and changed to "(old)" in the revised (1952) edition of Gilbert's book. Neither of its (very different) parenthetical epithets makes this designation of "technic" more enlightening than is its corollary/contrary, the "technic" for the chapter that begins the novel: "Narrative (young)." In either case: Who—or What—is young or mature (or old)? Possible answers are embarrassingly silly. "Relaxed prose" ("*Prosa rilassata*"), in the "schema" Joyce gave Carlo Linati, at least has the virtue of being suggestive.

But setting Joyce's *schemae* aside, most demotic discourse always has been "formulaic," "of the tribe," as Gerald Bruns says of the narrative style (367), and most written language as well. Inferring that it functions to make doleful general statements about the language of his time attributes to James Joyce arrogant superficiality and a lack of historical sense; also, his not just breaking off his own work-in-progress in despair of writing vital and original prose contradicts that sort of ostensible statement *prima facie*.

Bruns points toward a more intrinsic function for Joyce's telling than general commentary on discourse, in his remark that the "spirit of ordinary life . . . which dominates the episode" (because of the "collectivity" that is the narrator) is "the spirit of bloom, perhaps" as well. Other critics provide additional guides. Arnold Goldman "assumes" that Bloom specifically is associated with the narrator's mode of discourse, "speak[ing] 'in the style' of the chapter: that is, Bloom did not really say this in this way." Michael Groden makes Bloom more instrumental: Joyce "created . . . a literary equivalent of the state of Bloom's [exhausted] mind at 1:00 A.M." (53). And David Hayman confidently reverses Goldman's assumption by averring that although "Bloom, like his style, is tired," "the voice [of the narrator] . . . is Bloom's": "The technique is parody . . . of a Bloomish mind turned inside out."[28]

The attributions of the narrative mode to Bloom's, or "a Bloomish," mind do two things simultaneously. They invoke the tale to explain the telling. And in doing so they put into relief the unanswered, central, question of the essential function of Joyce's rhetorical performance in the chapter. By this point in his novel, hundreds of pages of inner monologue have portrayed Bloom's mind; why did Joyce employ this singular mode of discourse to portray it here?

The way to the answer is indicated by those few critics, again of both traditions, who characterize the narrative as the very opposite of fatigued: in the words of the most recent of them, Brook Thomas, "the style shows a mind gushing forth."[29] The same critics all specify more precisely the association, noticed by Hayman, of the narrative style with Bloom's "voice." They identify the style as the exact correspondence *in written narrative* to Bloom's way of speaking to Stephen: even cursory comparison of a narrative passage with Bloom's adjacent dialogue indicates that were he in fact "to pen something out of the common groove . . . *My Experiences,* let us say, *in a Cabman's Shelter*" (*U,* 16.1229–31) in the way he has taken to speaking to Stephen, it would have the periphrastic and otherwise pretentious, cliché-ridden, style of the narrative.[30] Hence, when the narrator gives Bloom's thoughts, his/its idiom is more or less indistinguishable from Bloom's

A (limited) function for the narrative style might be clear at this point, did Joyce not insist that the arranged narrator is distinct from "The irrepressible Bloom" (*U,* 16.929) he/it tells of—as when his/its heavy jocularity extends to the mistaken name in the *Evening Telegraph* report of Dignam's funeral: "Boom (to give him for the nonce his new misnomer) whiled away a few odd leisure moments in fits and starts with the account of the third event at Ascot" (*U,* 16.1274–6). The subject of Bloom's "fits and starts" warrants attention, because it is central to the actual function of the narrator's egregious style; but the phrase itself separates narrator from character as much as his/its prior jocularity at Bloom's expense.

Thomas describes the mind "gushing forth" in the narrative as "trying to express sophisticated ideas": "The style of 'Eumaeus' approximates the style Bloom would like to adopt to impress his companion in intellect." And here, too, Bruns's account of a "collective" narrator is enlightening: he/it "speaks not to the reader—not to Joyce's audience—but to an imaginary audience of his peers."[31] These perceptions bear on the function of the chapter's bizarre mode of telling. Their needed increment—and corrective—is supplied by proper attention to *the tale.* For its chief character is speaking—*literally* speaks—in the oral style equivalent to the narrative, and is doing so to impress his *actual* "companion"/"audience."

In other words, to explain the narrative style as strictly a model *Bloom* would like to *adopt,* is to abstract both Bloom and it from the tale. Bloom cannot know the narrator, while he/it must know Bloom; and his/its style is arranged prose *corresponding to* Bloom's actual way of speaking to Stephen in the chapter. Hence, its radical status is the reverse of Bloom's model. For Bloom's speech is the quasi-reality reported by the narrator;

and having the elementary priority of (fictional) prior existence, his speech is the informing context of the narrative style employed by the *persona:* if reported speech and reporting prose correspond, Bloom's way of speaking must be *the narrator's* model.

In addition to its radical priority as utterance reported, the style of oral discourse by way of which Bloom tries to impress Stephen has the primary significance because of the role of his endeavor—which constitutes the chapter's central action—in the novel. It and his reasons for it are important in the development of his story, and crucial to Stephen's story.

The rest of this section will be devoted to presenting my grounds for that assertion, because doing so will establish for the present chapter my thesis that the quasi-life *Ulysses* embodies is primary to its end. The chapter's telling does serve its tale if the style of telling, which is modeled on Bloom's way of speaking, *thereby* functions to emphasize a double crux in the plot of the novel whose locus is Bloom's pretentious table talk.

Bloom's sordid endeavor fails, of course: Stephen will not become a son/lover and so supplant Boylan. But the relationship he simultaneously—and unknowingly—establishes with Stephen results in the conclusion of Stephen's story in *Ulysses.*

Joyce made instrumental both in that story, of his Telemachus's search for the father who would provide rescue from the predicament that held the young man helpless, and in the no less but differently ironic and comic story of his Odysseus's efforts to return home, the two elaborate sets of coincidences involving Bloom he worked into the novel. It is possible to do no more here than recapitulate these coincidences briefly; but both sets bear directly on the developments in the chapter. The more elaborate is the set of coincidences originating in "the third event at Ascot," the *Telegraph* "account" of which occasioned Bloom's "fits and starts": the Gold Cup race run there on 16 June 1904. The race is the single public event of that day in history made crucial to the novel; and being crucial, it is a legitimate *intrinsic* reason why that is the day of *Ulysses.* The other is the set of coincidences originating in Stephen's dream of deliverance ("I flew") the night before, which he recalls first on the strand in the presence of the three intentionally misnamed "crosstrees" (*U,* 3:365; 3.504), then twice in Bloom's presence (*U,* 9.1207; 15.3922). The first set is instrumental in the story of Bloom's exile, both in that of Stephen's predicament.

Following Stephen's third recollection of his dream, in the parlor of Bella Cohen's brothel—he had recalled "street of harlots" the other two times (*U,* 3.366; 9.1207)—Bloom (characteristically) identifies himself unwittingly as the agent of delivery dreamed about. Stephen says, "It was here. Street of harlots. . . . a fubsy widow. Where's the red carpet spread?" (*U,* 15.3930–1). Unlike Bloom, Stephen (characteristically) understands the literal significance of Bloom's repeated "Look," and rejects the agent of the *dio boia* ("Break my spirit, will he?"), for he believes it was "Beelzebub showed me her" (*U,* 15.3931). He then has a fantasy involving his earthly father and a race run by the Ascot horses. The *"favourite,"* a *"stumbling"* and *"brokenwinded . . . nag"* ridden by the anti-Semite Deasy, comes in last, while the winner is *"A dark horse, riderless"* (*U,* 15.3974). Stephen's fantasy-race contrasts significantly with Lenehan's (nevertheless inaccurate) account, in his presence at the maternity hospital, of Throwaway's close win of the Ascot race from Sceptre (*U,* 14:1131–3); and it reflects Lenehan's (equally inaccurate) statement, at Burke's, that the "sheeny" knowingly predicted the unexpected winner (*U,* 14.1526).

Immediately after Stephen's rejection of—and elucidatory fantasy about—God's prophetic Jewish agent, an *integrated* sequence of events begins: he identifies "Our friend, noise in the street!" in the singing of Private Carr and his companions "beneath the windows," and is moved by it to begin his frenzied dancing (*U,* 15.3995); he is stopped "dead" by the advent of "The Mother" (*U,* 15.4153–4); she tells him to repent and prays for him (*U,* 15.4212; 4232–3); he strikes the chandelier, invoking Siegfried's successful attack on the supreme god Wotan (*U,* 15.4242); and he runs out to the altercation that ends in Carr's striking *him*—ends in exact retribution for his blow, exacted by the "noise in the street" Who initiated the sequence (*U,* 15.4370–4748). In other words, a metalanguage of linked events associates Stephen's dream, Bloom, the Ascot race whose "prophet" Bloom was, and the central elements in Stephen's story—and does so at the dramatic climax of that story.

The elaborate set of coincidences by which the Ascot race figures in Bloom's story associates him with Throwaway and with Elijah, in the complex: Bloom / the "throwaway" announcing "Elijah" Dowie / the "dark horse" / the Jewish prophet-agent of deliverance.[32] In the catechism chapter, he himself recapitulates the essential elements of this instrumental conceit: during his "Reminiscences of coincidences, truth stranger than fiction, preindicative of the result of the Gold Cup flat handicap," stimulated by sight of the torn tickets for Boylan's bet on Sceptre, he connects his inadvertent tip to Bantam Lyons with the "throwaway (subsequently thrown away), advertising Elijah" and with prophecy (*U,* 17:332; 17.339–41).

The association of him with Elijah and Throwaway that the novel effects, by way of the set of coincidences relating to the Ascot race, serves as a vital element in each of the exiled Bloom's major relationships: not only that with Stephen, and that with Molly, but even that with his fellow Dubliners. On the very page after the set of coincidences is initiated by his "I was just going to throw [the *Freeman's Journal*] away" and Bantam Lyons's excited response (*U,* 5.534–41), the sixth chapter, portraying the first overt anti-Semitic treatment of him, begins with "—Come on, Simon. . . .—Are we all here now? Martin Cunningham asked. Come along, Bloom" (*U,* 6.8). Subsequent coincidences which involve his relationship with his society—and with Molly—include: his passing by *while* Lyons tells companions in Davy Byrne's of the tip, and so being identified as its source (the only response is "scorn," [*U,* 8.1024]); and the sequence in which he is seen by Lenehan and M'Coy *seconds after* Lenehan tells of meeting Lyons "going to back a bloody horse . . . that hasn't an earthly," whereupon Lenehan identifies the source of Lyons's tip, then launches into his anecdote about pawing Molly after the Glencree reformatory dinner (*U,* 10.530–77).

These two coincidence-filled rejections of Bloom's coincidence-based unconscious prophetic act prefigure the interpolated "trial" of the bumbling messiah "ben Bloom Elijah" by an Irish "sinhedrim" (*U,* 12.1125), and the corresponding trial by the twelve Irishmen actually in Barney Kiernan's. Their verdict, executed by the citizen's attempt to "crucify" him "By Jesus" (*U,* 12.1812), is the direct consequence of Lenehan's allegation that his errand on the widow Dignam's behalf "is a blind. He had a few bob on *Throwaway* and he's gone to gather in the shekels" (*U,* 12.1550–51).

During this chapter, the set of coincidences figures in Bloom's relationship with Molly as well; and appropriately, Lenehan again is the agent. Although Bloom is arguing with the citizen at the time, and may have missed Lenehan's news that Throwaway won the Ascot gold cup with "the rest nowhere" and "Bass's mare" "still running," he overhears Lenehan's disclosure that on his advice Boylan bet on Sceptre "for himself and a lady friend" (*U,* 12.1223). This is revealed in the maternity hospital (*U,* 14.1185–90), immediately after Lenehan gives his directly contrary (and less inaccurate) account of the relative performance of the two horses, again—coincidentally—in Bloom's (as well as Stephen's) presence. Between that instance and Bloom's shabbily-motivated endeavor to impress Stephen in the cab shelter, Throwaway's victory, and the twenty to one "dark horse" odds he paid, are mentioned in nighttown by Bloom's fantasms of "Bello" (*U,* 15.2935–36) and Corny Kelleher (*U,* 15.4813–15).

This review of the working in the novel of coincidences originating in the Gold Cup race at Ascot on Bloomsday, and in Stephen's dream of deliverance the night before, is necessarily sketchy; it is intended only to help establish my thesis that the telling of the first chapter of the "nostos" functions to serve the tale. I have proposed that these intertwined sets of coincidences bear directly on a crucial development of Stephen's story in *Ulysses,* whose locus is Bloom's endeavor to impress him across the cab shelter table. Their function in the novel actually culminates in that development.

Significantly, it commences immediately after the words pointing up the kinship between Bloom's pretentious table talk and the narrative style:

> . . . suppose he were to pen something out of the common groove . . . *My Experiences,* let us say, *in a Cabman's Shelter.*
> The pink edition . . . of the *Telegraph* . . . lay, as luck would have it [!], beside his elbow . . . (*U,* 16.1229–33)

Before the "fits and starts" proper, Bloom has "a bit of a start" as "his eyes went aimlessly over the respective captions": but its cause "turned out to be only" the name "H. du Boyes." There are articles about an earlier "dark horse" that "Throwaway recalls" and "Lovemaking . . . damages"; Deasy's letter on "Foot and mouth"; and the account of Dignam's funeral, which he reads aloud. Then, while Stephen reads Deasy's letter, he begins his "fits and starts with the account of the third event at Ascot on page three" (*U,* 16.1275–76).

Given what he already knows about the race and Boylan's bet, their initial cause can only be the news that Throwaway did not just barely beat out "Mr. W. Bass's bay filly Sceptre," which came in third, but "Secured the verdict cleverly by a length": "so that Lenehan's version of the business was all pure buncombe. . . . Different ways of bringing off a coup. Lovemaking damages."[33] And—perhaps even more—his "fits and starts" mark a sudden understanding, recorded in the remainder of the paragraph. It is of the connection between his inadvertent tip to "that halfbaked Lyons"—who, he believes, stayed with Throwaway and had "positive gain" (*U,* 17.352)—and his brutal treatment in Barney Kiernan's pub. He correctly infers that Lenehan misconstrued, and so misrepresented to the others in his absence (*U,* 12.1548), his "light to the gentile": "—There was every indication they would arrive at that, he, Bloom, said" aloud to Stephen, when the paragraph ends.

Bloom's "Different ways of bringing off a coup. Lovemaking damages" just before it ends, adapting one of the headlines, does little for his exile. But he has commented to Stephen on the consequence, for his relations with his fellow Dubliners, of the set of coincidences involving Throwaway and invoking Elijah. And *immediately* after his comment, the portrayal of the consequence for Stephen—and the consequence as well of the set of coincidences about Stephen's dream intertwined with it—begins.

Stephen understandably responds "—Who?"; the cabman (who had originally "laid aside" the *Telegraph* at Bloom's elbow, (*U,* 16.709), says that "One morning . . . the paper" would announce *"Return of Parnell";* and Kitty O'Shea and her cuckolded husband are discussed (*U,* 16.1352). Bloom reflects that she "also was Spanish or half so," announces this to Stephen, and produces his photo of Molly with the disingenuous question, "—Do you consider by the by . . . that a Spanish type?" (*U,* 16.1425–26).

Of his deliverer, Stephen had dreamed "A creamfruit melon he held to me" (*U,* 9.1208). He knows nothing about the set of coincidences associating Bloom with Throwaway and Elijah, which Joyce has intertwined with the set relating to his own dream; but he had identified Bloom as the Jewish-prophet/agent of the God he condemns and resists. Now Bloom has, as Stephen put it in his first recollection of his dream, "held against my face" Molly, "The melon he had" (*U,* 3.367–68). And so unknowingly (of course), he has revealed that God's emissary is simultaneously the deliverer Stephen dreamed of. The coincidence of, respectively, three-mastered schooner, first full encounter with Bloom, and intercession by Bloom, with Stephen's three recollections of his dream, now falls into place for him: it is not "Beelzebub" but God's agent whom the dream portrayed showing him "a fubsy [grass] widow" (*U,* 15.3931). The God Stephen rejected as cruel announced His ministration in a dream, and has provided it promptly the next day.

When Bloom next speaks, it is to ask Stephen when he ate last (*U,* 16.1572); and next after that, to "propose . . . while prudently pocketing her photo," that "you just come home with me and talk things over" (*U,* 16.1643–45). Stephen not only goes with him ("That man led me, spoke. I was not afraid. . . . said. In. Come. Red carpet spread. You will see who," [*U,* 3.367–69]), but begins to sing.[34] Telemachus failed in his quest to find his father, but Odysseus returned to reunite them; and transformed in appearance by divine agency, he made himself known to his son in Eumaeus's hut. The same has happened with Stephen and his Father—appropriately, by comic inversion.

Less significant than the major crux in Stephen's story is the role of Bloom's table talk in his own. His shabby endeavor to end his exile by using Stephen to displace Boylan ultimately—ironically—succeeds, at least in Molly's thought: after thinking of Stephen as a potential lover, she dismisses "the ignoramus that doesnt know poetry from a cabbage" from her mind and the novel (*U,* 18.1370–71); then she thinks of Stephen as a son instead, and decides to "just give him one more chance" and make Bloom's breakfast (*U,* 18.1442–98).

I have tried to show in the chapter, and in the intertwined sets of coincidences culminating in it, a metalanguage of events so purposeful, and so elaborate, as to mock any proposal to ignore elements of it, or attempt to explain it away piecemeal. It is insisted on—by coincidence compounded, conjunction, sequence, and juxtaposition.

A juxtaposition as gratuitous as the narrator's reference to Bloom's "penning" his experiences in a cabman's shelter just when the crucial sequence described above begins, and therefore as eloquent a declaration of the function of the narrative style, occurs earlier, "at commons in Manse of Mothers," where the Ascot race is mentioned (coincidentally) in both Bloom's and Stephen's presence. There, in Joyce's parody of Landor, Lenehan gives the one account of the race Bloom apparently has heard (reading the *Telegraph* story, he refers to a single "version" as "buncombe"), and the company notice that Bloom is staring at a bottle of Bass's ale—brewed not by Sceptre's owner, as Lenehan says, but his uncle (*U,* 14.1165). Then a paragraph praises Bloom's "astuteness" and presents his thoughts, which concern "two or three private transactions of his own" related to "the turf" (*U,* 14.1179–89). He is "astute" enough to have become aware that Boylan lost the bet he placed for himself and Molly, and probably also that Bantam Lyons "ran off at a tangent" in the morning because he had inadvertently named the "dark horse" who won. (In the "Light to the gentiles" catechism passage, he lists Davy Byrne's, where Lyons identified him as the source of the tip, as one place where "previous intimations" had "been received by him" [*U,* 17.327].) This paragraph, interrupting the roughly chronological sequence between the Landor parody and the next one (of Macaulay), is in a style that the first-time reader meets again after the interval of the nighttown chapter. Devoted to "The individual . . . as astute if not astuter than any man living" and his thoughts about "the turf," it begins: "However, as a matter of fact though, the preposterous surmise about him being in some description of a doldrums or other . . . ." (*U,* 14.1174–89).

Against the sequence of parodied classic English prose stylists, Joyce has juxtaposed a specimen of the egregious narrative style that will tell of Bloom's perceptions, thoughts, and table talk in the cab shelter. What his striking juxtaposition does is identify that style with Bloom and the set of Throwaway/prophecy coincidences. He has announced, before the chapter begins, the connection that stylistic ineptitude has to the two chief agents of its vital plot developments: Bloom's endeavor in it, and the interwined sets of coincidences whose function in *Ulysses* culminates there.

In the first chapter of III: Bloom's endeavor to impress Stephen is the vehicle of the important developments; an inept pseudo-eloquence is the means he employs; and the style of the narrative corresponds to his oral style—and so emphasizes the endeavor of which it is the instrument. Joyce's prior announcement reaffirms the abundant evidence in the chapter itself that its telling functions to serve its tale.

VII

The disrespectful narrator of the first chapter of III derides "woolgathering" by his/its model (*U,* 16.626). But his/its account of a vagrant thought, "Sulphate of copper poison SO_4 or something" (*U,* 16.801–2), does not—presumably cannot—amend Bloom's defective knowledge by completing the formula $CuSO_4$, or even comment on it. Although exhaustively informative, the catechetical respondent of the next chapter is—like that narrator—less than adequately informed; and he/it is error-prone as well. For example, when Bloom boils water for cocoa, the description of "the phenomenon of ebullition" concludes "an expenditure of 72 thermal units [is] needed to raise 1 pound of water from 50° to 212° Fahrenheit" (*U,* 17.257–71), although the correct figure is 162 British Thermal Units. The error may be a miscalculation, but the more likely cause is defective knowledge, which is to say, ignorance. The "Unit" is specifically the amount of heat "needed to raise 1 pound of water" *one* Fahrenheit degree. All the respondent needed to do was subtract correctly the lower temperature from the higher: the point of the misinformation he/it provides is its egregiousness.

Furthermore, the defective knowledge cannot be reasonably attributed to Joyce. The respondent's phrasing insists on the precise definition of a B.T.U., which uses water, by weight, specifically one pound avoirdupois; and any dictionary would have aided Joyce's uncertain or partial memory, from elementary physics, of the equation. But he most likely thought to use it because its sensible neatness (1 unit: 1 pound/degree)—allowing easy computation, and so the display of ignorance (or bizarre error)—was fully familiar. Not the author outside the chapter, or even the blatant arranger of both the queries and the responses by which it proceeds, but its arranged quasi-narrator, the encyclopedically knowledgeable catechetical respondent, has defective knowledge, unreliable (exhaustive) information.

Only attention to the textness of the novel can reveal this characteristic of the second chapter of III. And it is because of recent critics in the dominant tradition that I perceived the respondent's misinformation about "ebullition"; for their work has augmented our understanding of the chapter greatly. Writing about its form in a passage part of which was quoted earlier, Karen Lawrence simultaneously throws light on the ignorance and errors:

> In "Ithaca," Joyce employs the rhetorical topoi of "inventio," the first part of classical rhetoric. The narrative proceeds by ingenious "arguments" from analogy, difference, cause and effect, example. . . . The . . . catechism is really a school performance in the rhetorical classification of facts. . . . Using these topoi for comic purposes, Joyce plays with the human wish to arrive at truth.[35]

Furthermore, the coldly objective "aridities," in Joyce's word, of the respondent's endeavor to embody truth, are subverted not only by the instances of ignorance and error, but also by his/its ambitious tropes, romantic phrasing, and other manifestations of a totally incongruous human subjectivity. Lawrence points out that this occurs even in the relentless scientism itself:

> we try to understand the relationship among characters and encounter mathematical tangents and algebraic equations.
>
> There seems to be a mechanism of avoidance in the narrative . . . . [It] sometimes dovetails with Blooms's own mechanism of avoidance . . . Bloom's strategy for dealing with his domestic situation merges with the narrative strategy.[36]

Another recent critic, James Maddox, observes the psychological trait and relates it to the respondent's errors—by extending his/its similarity to Bloom:

> the style loses sight of the human significance of the question and becomes absorbed in a purely mathematical calculation.
>
> Now this kind of thinking is not unlike Bloom's. Repeatedly throughout the day Bloom mentally approaches some thought of major emotional import but then shies away from it—frequently by substituting some mathematical or scientific speculation . . . . For example:
>
> > A million pounds, wait a moment . . . . Yes, exactly. Fifteen millions of barrels of porter.
> >
> > What am I saying barrels? Gallons. . . . (*U*, 5.307–11)
>
> This is Bloom's mind, sharp, active, calculating—and always tending toward errors of computation. . . . There is, in fact, enough error in "Ithaca" to at least suggest the use of error as a motif—as if the style itself were committing Bloomisms.
>
> The "Ithaca" style, then, partakes of certain very definite qualities of Bloom's mind.[37]

The egregious style of the previous chapter, resulting from attempted eloquence, was attributed to "a Bloomish mind"; in this one, egregious errors result from attempted omniscience—and are "as if the style itself were committing Bloomisms."

David Hayman draws a more definite—and positive—conclusion:

> In a sense this chapter . . . is the warmest of them all. This is largely because, despite his elaborate pose, the speaker is . . . after all a projection of Bloom's scientific mentality rather than of the spirit of inquiry pure and simple.[38]

And using a phrase from Joyce's *Letters* (I, 173), Walton Litz makes the general statement that "the 'dry rock pages of Ithaca' are supersaturated with Bloom's humanity"[39]

"Bloom's humanity" is in the catechetical respondent's "habit of mind

. . . in its displacement," as Lawrence puts it;[40] in his/its ambitious tropes and romantic phrasing; in response after response throughout the catechism, to the sleepy wordplay at its end. Not just the respondent's errors, but his/its defective knowledge as well, and all these "very definite qualities of Bloom's mind" so incongruous with even a flawed scientific objectivity, have the same provenance as the prose style of the previous chapter's narrator. Hence, as the *narrative* of that chapter focusses on Bloom, even when Stephen is present, so does *what is divulged* in this one.

This chapter's pedantic catechism is even more outlandish and arbitrary than that one's garrulous narrative style. And it more insistently raises the question of its reason for being. I am among those readers for whom the ugly ducking gradually grew into a swan; but the unfailing ineptitude of the cab shelter narrative is no less beguiling to me because Joyce makes it accomplish the work of the novel by way of its connection with Bloom. This chapter too functions in the novel—the striking and arbitrary telling of the catechism serves the tale—by way of its connection with him.

To begin with, the catechism is fully as revealing of Bloom's inner life as are the early inner monologues and his fantasies in nighttown. The respondent portrays the way Bloom's mind works, and expounds the things he generally treasures, aspires to and craves. Most instrumentally for the novel, the respondent divulges Bloom's remembrances, reflections, deliberations—and conduct—in his unended exile. But as with the previous chapter, so with this, what is disclosed about Bloom does not itself explain the form of disclosure.

The explanation is the salient—indeed, dramatic—fact about the form that one distinctly cannot (as D. H. Lawrence put it) "trust . . . the teller": that the exhaustively informative catechetical respondent not only fails to be consistently objective, but also proffers unreliable information. For example, directed to "Compile the budget for 16 June 1904" (*U,* 17.1455), the Bloomian respondent produces a minor inaccuracy—Bloom did return one pound seven (*U,* 17.956–59), but Stephen had given him only one pound six and eleven (*U,* 15.3613)—and a major omission. The money Bloom gave Bella Cohen for Stephen's damage to the ceiling light had to come from his own pocket, and is not listed. As Hugh Kenner has pointed out, "This is not the budget *an sich,* but such a version as Bloom might let Molly inspect."[41]

Like his/its scientism, "shie[ing] away," and the rest, the unreliable statements of fact reflect the respondent's defining "Bloomism." As in the preceding chapter the narrative was formally distinct from Bloom but essentially identified with him, so is the catechism in this one. And the purpose of the singular telling is—as in that chapter—to emphasize happenings significant in the tale.

The unreliable budget, Bloom's in every sense, is unreliable as misrepresentation. Other ostensible facts about Bloom and his story are unreliable as error and as ignorance. An example of the latter, most significant for Bloom's and Molly's story, is the ostensible "preceding series" of Molly's lovers the respondent provides when Bloom joins Molly in the marriage bed (*U,* 17.2132–42), a list lacking the name of Boylan's most likely predecessor in that bed, of whose very existence Bloom is ignorant.

The ostensible catalogue of her lovers is best discussed with the help Molly gives in the last chapter of III and of the novel. That in proffering it the respondent—characteristically —represents Bloom's ignorance without amendment or comment, is additional evidence of the nature of the telling in this chapter; that the shared ignorance is significant, indicates the function of the telling for the tale.

VIII

The two traditions in *Ulysses* criticism have tended to disagree about whether or not the major action of the novel has any prospect for success when it ends. A complication is that the ultimate issue of Bloom's belated effort to return home does not depend solely on his quasi-heroic conduct and Molly's willing response: his story must end in ironic failure if meaningful return is foredoomed by the nature of the deeply-loved wife with whom he strives to reunite. What the proffered list of (exactly) twenty-five other occupants of her bed, almost every one during their marriage, does or does not signify about his Penelope, is crucial for the novel.

James Maddox has called "Molly's sexual history" "the most hotly debated question in recent Joyce criticism." That in his/its "series" the catechetical respondent may be expressing not only Bloomian ignorance, but—as in the budget—misrepresentation as well, is suggested *prima facie* by such unlikely lovers as two priests, an organ grinder, a bootblack. As long ago as the first edition of *James Joyce,* Richard Ellmann perceptively discounted the list because of unlikely inclusions. and for two other reasons: it is Bloom's catalogue (its source is ambiguous but also, given the Bloomian nature of the respondent, immaterial); and "the book" contradicts it:

> But on examination the list contains some extraordinary names: there are two priests, a lord mayor, an alderman, a gynecologist . . . . In the book it is clear that she has confessed to the priests, consulted the gynecologist, and coquetted with the rest . . . .
>
> The two lovers Molly has had since her marriage are Bartell D'Arcy and Boylan.[42]

The opposing position in the debate has a much longer history. On the basis of the list, the equally reliable gossip of Bloom's fellow Dubliners, and her sensual reflections, Molly was relatively benignly called "the compliant body" with "animal placidity" in 1941, but more recently such things as "a great lust-lump," "at heart a thirty-shilling whore," and (elegantly) "a swine."[43] One critic cites Ellmann's discrediting of the list in the course of a detailed discussion of "The Twenty-five Lovers of Molly Bloom," and remarks that "a really skeptical scrutiny" by "a really determined doubter" would remove every name but Boylan's. Nevertheless, "her sexual appetites are literally insatiable"; and in a second book published four years later—in which "She is a slut, a sloven, and a voracious sexual animal"—the list is implicitly rehabilitated:

> She is made for men, all men, indiscriminately, tramps, bootblacks, lord mayors, Boylan, Poldy, Mulvey—so that "he" and "him" come to refer, in the course of her soliloquy, to an almost limitless array of lovers.[44]

The belief that *Ulysses* depicts a grossly promiscuous Penelope has continued into this decade.[45] Nevertheless, today most critics are aware of extensive evidence contradicting it. In fact, it is a grotesque distortion of the novel's third principal character.

The list itself is discredited above all by its exclusion of "Gardner Lieut Stanley G" (*U,* 18.389; also 18.313; 18.366–67), the one person in addition to Bloom, Boylan, and her girlhood lover Mulvey, with whom Molly's reverie reveals a serious erotic involvement; it also is discredited by specific information Joyce provided—both in the chapter and elsewhere in the novel—about the others it catalogues. More than a dozen of the twenty-three men come up in the chapter itself; and of these only Bartell D'Arcy, who "commenced kissing me" on the single occasion "after I sang Gounods *Ave Maria*" (*U,* 18.274–75), she both knew and thinks of without scorn.[46]

From her thoughts, we learn that she kept her virginity with her premarital lover, Mulvey (*U,* 18.821–22), and (besides those of Bloom and Boylan) has felt and/or seen the phallus of Gardner (*U,* 18.313)—and those of two "disgusting" exhibitionist Scots soldiers in kilts (*U,* 18.544). We learn also that, despite more than a decade of erotic frustration, degradation, and neglect by her husband, she just committed adultery for the first time. When the chapter has barely begun, she thinks of Bloom's perverse physical activities with her and their mutually degrading oral accompaniment:

> question and answer would you do this that and the other with the coalman yes with a bishop yes . . . who are you thinking of . . . the german Emperor is it yes imagine Im him think of him can you feel him

> trying to make a whore of me . . . simply ruination for any women and no satisfaction in it pretending to like it till he comes and then finish it off myself anyway and it makes your lips pale anyhow its done now once and for all with all the talk of the world about it people make (*U*, 18.89–101)

The unlikely partners aside, that which Bloom's masochistic and provoking questions propose his wife "would . . . do" is the obvious alternative (the only feasible one for an Irish Catholic bourgeois wife) to the situation he has imposed on her for the past "10 years, 5 months and 18 days" (*U*, 17.2282). It is because only "now" she has finally "done" it that her very long and very sensual reverie includes thoughts about actual sexual intercourse with only Bloom and Boylan: as the day of the novel is a singular one for Stephen and Bloom, so it is for Molly as well. Critics have "hotly debated" the character of Molly with much less reason than in the strikingly similar case of Chaucer's Criseyde, because Joyce has been much less equivocal—although no less subtle—in his portrayal. That Molly was so stubbornly misrepresented—a fictional character ("words") calumniated as though living, in despite of the evidence—has interesting implications for the recent past of our culture; but its only relevance to novel or character is the support it gives her low estimation of men.

Certain recent critics, unimpeded by a negative misconception of Molly, have increased all our understanding of what Joyce wrought in her. About her thoughts on one of her confessors, "Father [Bernard] Corrigan" (*U*, 18.107)—they occur just ten pages after he is listed in the "series"—David Hayman writes:

> It is worth noting that Molly's yearning is more appropriate to an adolescent than to a hardened woman. Still, she has had no relations with a priest, and she will go on to disprove most of the list in detail and to show herself to be even less worldly than Bloom. . . .[47]

This is quoted not for the central point, first made by Ellmann, but for the comments about Molly herself at either side of it. Father Robert Boyle's essay "Penelope" describes her attitude "toward sex" as "often naive," and observes shrewdly from "Her somewhat adolescent musings on the details of genitalia and of coition" that "Molly's actual sexual experience is indeed limited." Marilyn French notes certain reticences. Most recently, James Maddox, whose comment on the debate about Molly was quoted at the beginning of this section, has examined the nature of her eroticism in extensive and persuasive detail. He demonstrates that it is not only "appropriate to an adolescent" emotionally, "naive" in attitude, and "limited" in experience, but also extremely conventional. His evidence shows Molly to be—behind her "roving eye" and "obscene tongue"—"actually tentative and conservative about sexual acts themselves even as she is curious about variations from the sexual norm." And he concludes:

> She likes to imagine herself as sexually daring and adventurous, but she is adept at finding excuses for refraining from anything very far from ordinary . . . beneath Molly's image of herself as a sexual dynamo, there is reticence and a girlish curiosity.[48]

This fuller understanding of the character Joyce has created in Molly Bloom redirects attention to other details in the novel. One recognizes the equivocation edging toward reluctance behind her "anyhow its done now once and for all." There is the genuine guilt about having "done" "it" in her fear (shades of Stephen) that the thunderstorm was "the heavens . . . coming down about us to punish when I blessed myself and said a Hail Mary" (*U,* 18.135–36). Both equivocation and guilt are reinforced, when she is planning in the final pages of the novel to "just give him one more chance" (*U,* 18.1497–98), and serve Bloom breakfast in bed, by the self-conscious but indignant protest, "its all his own fault if I am an adulteress as the thing in the gallery said" (*U,* 18.1516–17)—especially by its key term. And reflecting back to the pages that introduce her and her husband to the novel, one appreciates how thoroughly inexperienced is the supposed career adulteress. After bringing her the card from Milly and a letter he has guessed is from Boylan, Bloom "waited till she laid the card aside" and then "delayed" further, before going for her breakfast; but she refrains from opening the letter (*U,* 4.256–57). When he returns, the letter he delivered is—incompletely—hidden under the pillow, and she admits Boylan sent it (*U,* 4.308–12). This Molly Bloom very well could have done as Hugh Kenner suggests in "Molly's Masterstroke": caused Boylan to move the parlor furniture in an attempt to tire him and so avoid sexual relations.

Maddox quotes Molly's wish "to be embraced 20 times a day almost . . . to be in love or loved by somebody if the fellow you want isnt there" (*U,* 18.1408–10), and comments:

> The combination of sexual indiscriminateness ["at a safe distance"] with the phrase "if the fellow you want isnt there" brings Molly's eroticism into clear focus. Molly has a roving eye ["imagined promiscuity"] because she is unwilling to set her sights exclusively on one man beyond Bloom, the fellow she wants who isn't there.

And following his point about her conventional eroticism, quoted above, Maddox writes: "Molly's combination of bravado and reticence makes her in some ways the ideal partner in Bloom's sexual fantasies."[49]

The ingenuous conduct toward Boylan's letter of both distressed husband and desperate wife, simultaneously comic and poignant, shows them to be ideal partners in a more touching way as well. That occurs with their very introduction to *Ulysses:* Molly's final chapter completes the novel's abundant documentation of their relationship with the surprising revelation of its mutuality. This wife and husband show reciprocal: doting admiration—hence, each considers collecting the other's sayings: solicitude—hers for him repeatedly punctuates expressions of her justified resentment; and most important, profound commitment. French observes, "Given the view of her held by Dublin males, it seems unlikely that it would take Molly all these years in sex-starved Dublin to find a lover," likens Molly's commitment to her husband to Penelope's as "a little unbelievable," and declares: "Molly is finally faithful to Bloom: fairly faithful physically and totally so emotionally. That is, her emotional commitment is to him above any other man." The final qualifying phrase is explained by her next and concluding paragraph on Molly: "Her deepest commitment, of course, is to . . . hearing the voice of her own body and merging it with the voices of nature . . . she embodies the life force."[50]

The character of Molly Bloom in *Ulysses* takes on symbolic meaning more insistently than does that of either Leopold Bloom or Stephen Dedalus. This is not only explained but also warranted by her nature, by her subordinate but instrumental role in the novel, suggestive of a dea ex machina, and above all by Joyce's way of presenting her—first in sketchy details and indirections, then with repeated overt symbolic suggestiveness in the catechism chapter, and finally in her uninterrupted recumbent memories and reflections. The hyperbolic sensualist so presented is symbolic enough to anticipate the archetypal sleeping giant of Joyce's next book.

But Molly's eventual symbolic meaning emerges principally out of specific structural relations and precise information that are functional story. Her chapter is a shaped sequence of (mental) events prepared for, and required by, the preceding action. And even more distracting for her role in the novel's story than according primacy to her undoubted symbolic suggestiveness, is the recent preoccupation of the dominant tradition with "the tale of the telling," as when John Paul Riquelme writes about her chapter solely as the last installment in that tale: "The substance of the episode is and will remain beyond the horizon of writing and reading . . . because ["unwritten"] it is inaccessible to writing."[51]

That thought is not written language is beyond dispute; however, neither is physical action written language, or situation/scene. To limit one's attention to an abstracted model of the telling itself in "this last style, which presses the mimesis of consciousness toward the nonlinguistic," is precisely to *place* "the substance of the episode" simplistically "beyond the horizon of . . . reading." For abstracting a single telling from the told obscures *Joyce's* telling of Molly's telling, an eight-part written composition initiating, developing and concluding the action that is its subject's psychomachia.

Although our increasing understanding of her nature, based on her true testimony, shows that much of her own telling was for long beyond the horizon of our reading, the chapter representing Molly's mental acts as language manifestly portrays that nature. But in addition, the chapter provides the specific dual revelation instrumental at its final position in the novel: of her patiently enduring more than a decade of neglect and perversity; and of the abiding commitment to Bloom that implies.

The texture of the chapter alone—the verbally rendered mental acts that are Molly's telling—reveals her patient self-denial. But the structure by which Joyce tells her telling is the necessary vehicle of her attitude to the husband who exacted the self-denial. That attitude is the dénouement of narrated (mental) action, a decision she arrives at. And her thought process may continue until sleep, but as the landscape beyond the margins of a landscape painting; the novel concludes with her decision. Although the texture of the chapter is reverie, almost totally passive stream of consciousness, its structure is auto-debate, recording the process by which she resolves her psychomachia about both her general attitude toward her husband and its specific index. Of course, the index is his final action in the novel, his specific initiative to alter the routine in—and mark of—their usual relationship that normally would occur next, when they awake, and with which their story in the novel began. What both Molly and Joyce make of Bloom's initiative transforms its apparent triviality.

The eight sections, or "sentences" as Joyce repeatedly called them (*Letters,* I, 168, 169, 170), present roughly symmetrical stages in the parabolic evolution of Molly's initially and ultimately favorable general attitude toward Bloom.[52] That structural pattern probably is the covert meaning of Joyce's reference to "the final amplitudinously curvilinear episode Penelope" (*Letters,* I, 164).

Placement in the chapter, and sequence, indicate how she will respond to the initiative that is Bloom's final action, revealed only in its plot consequence—her initial reaction, "Yes because he never did a thing like that before as ask to get his breakfast in bed. . . ." (*U,* 18.1–2). After her surprised reaction, she ignores Bloom's request until almost the last third of the chapter; then she thinks about it four times, in a sequence first of scorn (*U,* 18.929–32), then plaintive resentment (*U,* 18.1243–44), then bluster (*U,* 18.1431–32), and finally, two pages later and at almost the end of the chapter and novel, with the decision to "give him one more chance" (*U,* 18.1498).

The structure is elaborately articulate when she reaches this specific conclusion. Her decision coincides with a desire to dress as Bloom had dreamed of her the night before; the key references are to "red slippers" and "Turkish" / "Turks." As with Stephen's dream of delivery, the sentence "Wait." occurs when he first remembers the dream (*U,* 13.1240)—which is of return: in the hospital chapter, the mode of dress Joyce has him dream of, and her now want to wear, is said to signify "a change" (*U,* 14.510). Her decision also promptly precipitates: the complaint "its all his own fault if I am an adulteress"; an extensive and vehement expression of her resentment of him; and plans to tempt him, "make his micky stand for him," and even "put him into me." Then on the next page she plans to "make him want me thats the only way" (*U,* 18.1539–40), and begins her final rhapsody, which ends in her conflation of Mulvey with her husband at the beginning of their relationship. In *Characters of Joyce,* David G. Wright proposes that the issue "may be" whether or not "the Blooms [will] . . . break their 'fast' in bed";[53] and Joyce is fully capable of having decided on the specific subject of Molly's auto-debate partly to play on the original meaning of the key word of "breakfast in bed."

It is impossible to recount here the details of Joyce's integration and resolution of significant elements of Bloom's story in its final chapter.[54] It also is unnecessary for indicating the use to which he put the relatively familiar form of telling he caused to follow a sequence of strikingly innovative ones. The chapter's apparent simplicity of texture subtly portrays Molly's true nature, and is disposed in a purposive structure.

Apparently not circumstances but story explains why Joyce worked on the two last chapters simultaneously.[55] After attending Stephen's departure from his home and the novel, Bloom returns by way of the parlor—and promptly bumps his head against the sideboard moved by Boylan. Although the narrative technique of the ostensibly objective catechism chapter contrasts strikingly with that of the ostensibly subjective stream of consciousness chapter, from that point of Bloom's abrupt confrontation with his marital situation, it is the final chapter's functional complement.

The sequence of proffering in the one, and ironic and significant discrediting in the other, of the list of lovers, is an obvious example of their complementary function. A no less significant inter-chapter peripeteia is the list's sequel, Bloom's tortuous rationalizing to indifference his distress over Molly's infidelity ("slaying the suitors"), and her obviating his sophistry by revealing her commitment to him. Following his process of rationalizing, four pages after the respondent proffers the list and less than two before the chapter ends, a third peripeteia occurs. The catechist asks, "What limitations of activity and inhibitions of conjugal rights were perceived by listener and narrator concerning themselves" (*U,* 17.1171–72); and using the first phrase, the respondent reveals the decade of limited "activity" suffered by the listener, and the nine months' limitation of "mental intercourse" "perceived" by the narrator—but never addresses the second part of the question. The peripeteia consists of Molly's revelation that until the day of the novel the "limitations of activity" involved not just her husband, but all men.

However, the respondent's suppression of the second phrase exemplifies another use to which Joyce puts the Bloomian catechism: emphasis. Hence, the chapters also are complementary in that it is precisely what he / it has suppressed, Molly's emphatically articulated "perception" of Bloom's "inhibition of conjugal *rights*" (emphasis added), that motivated her resentful imperious treatment of "the fellow [she] want[s]," and justifies her response to Boylan's desire for her. After all, Bloom was not taken off to war against his will. It is in the suppressed phrase the suitors are slain, if anywhere in the catechism chapter, for Molly really wants not lovers but her conjugal rights.

Revealing her true nature, her compatibility with and commitment to Bloom, and even her specific response to his specific final initiative to alter their relationship, Molly's chapter of mental acts is no less significant for what it reveals about Bloom himself. The author's gentle mockery in his total ignorance of Gardner is the same tone as informs his Jewishness, as when he declares to Stephen, "so I . . . told [the citizen] his God, I mean Christ, was a jew too . . . like me though in reality I'm not" (*U,* 16.1083–85). Eclipsing Joyce's fun with him is Molly's confirmation of his stature. The novel does not mock his emotional commitment to her as the degrading and foolish yearning for a frivolous slut. It discloses that she deserves and desires his cherishing her and wanting her back. The soundness of his commitment is the key to Bloom's stature, as his folly would be if Molly were as his fellow Dubliners, and the Bloomian respondent, believe. Of course, if he does actually believe—even momentarily—the respondent's list, organgrinder, bootblack and all, it is another example of how silly his ephemeral ideas can be, and how grand his abiding instincts; and Joyce has, once again, had it both ways.

The respondent's list of lovers received so much attention in the critical debate about Molly because its significance is far greater than as a detail in a rhetorical gambit—because it is implicated in the novel's quasi-life. The debate concerned not telling, but tale—not "words marching across a page," but the quasi-person unconsciously acknowledged in the metaphor of Brook Thomas's vivid phrase. As at any point in life, so at the end of *Ulysses,* there is no closure. But the complementary tellings of its two final chapters have concluded Joyce's tale of Bloom's desire and endeavor to return to Molly: they have told her willingness to alter the destructive pattern of the marriage, and completed the novel's subtle revelation of the extent of both mates' commitment, and suitability, to each other. Strikingly different as they are, Joyce used those two singular forms of embodiment together in the service of the quasi-life they embody.

IX

Almost simultaneously with the publication of *Ulysses,* Larbaud initiated the attention early critics in the dominant tradition gave to its Homeric pattern and other elements of "design." That same year, Eliot noted its "singular" achievement of totally eliminating a recognizable style;[56] and the attention now being given to the extreme innovation and resourcefulness of Joyce's telling, by critics in our world working in that tradition, is increasing our understanding of the elegant artistry of his novel. I have put and have been trying to answer a three-part question about the relationship in *Ulysses* between the composition of telling words they conceive as (or assume to be) its essential mode, and its essential mode as conceived (or assumed) by the alternative tradition: the things told by its telling words. The three-part question is: do its symbiotic modes of a quasi-life embodied, and a book of words constituting the form of embodiment, relate as end and means?; if so, which is the essential mode, and which the mode instrumental to it?; and finally, does their relationship matter?

Joyce's first new creative initiative during his odyssey of composition culminated in the ultimate parody-pastiche of the hospital chapter; and he began his second and more radical initiative with the stunning tour de force of the nighttown chapter. Each of the three chapters of the "nostos" contributes to a dramatic sequence of innovative narrative strategies. Yet all three radical forms of telling serve the quasi-life told—and the same is true of the nighttown chapter that began his final adventure in creative telling. It is no accident that the quasi-life the four chapters tell is continuous—an uninterrupted narrative—throughout. For each of the four innovative narrative strategies was tailored to function in the service of the story.

This is most apparent, perhaps, in the last chapter. Instead of being some final, transcendent, tour de force of the previously dominant blatant arranger, it is self-effacing, transparent arrangement, a direct verbal rendition of a character's thoughts. It is really a subtle telling, of course—in both texture and structure. But its form is only an extreme version of the inner monologue that characterizes the familiar "initial style." And Joyce's reason for the apparent regression recent critics have noted, from his sequence of radical new blatant arrangings, cannot be unrelated to the fact that the representation of thought was required to tell what needs to be told: that Molly is qualified, and intends, to provide "the countersign to Bloom's passport to eternity" (*Letters,* I, 160). The requirement that the telling serve the tale also explains why both Molly's final chapter, and the catechism chapter written simultaneously with it, "which [David Hayman writes], as though in an afterthought, carries so much of the book's exposition,"[57] contain immense amounts of—and are such apt vehicles of—sheer information. A book of words can disdain such extreme claims upon it by information about the lives and stories of characters.

Most of the information in the two chapters is about Bloom and Molly. The role of their complementary elements in the completing of Bloom's story has been discussed; but the corrective revelations about Molly's character and attitudes that complete it, are part of a pattern Joyce created in the "nostos" as a whole, in which once again telling is to tale as means to end. The narrative strategies of all three chapters are effective instruments of characterization, and they comprise a portrayal of the two principal persons of Bloom's odyssey in its last phase. The "Bloomian" first two chapters render, respectively, Bloom's public idiom *in extremis* (hundreds of pages have given his private idiom), and his aspirations, values, mental habits, and deliberations about those things he values and craves. Molly's soliloquy renders her private idiom and her aspirations, values, and the rest.

The emphasis on characterization in the "nostos" is no more than a persistence to its end of that emphasis in *Ulysses*—generally in the form of a direct representation of mental events. Only one of its eighteen chapters, that in which Bloom contends with the citizen in Barney Kiernan's, involves little psychological portrayal; the nameless narrator reveals himself, but it is incidental to his gospel of Bloom. Of the remainder, the tenth, Joyce's analogue to the non-episode in the *Odyssey* of the wandering rocks, and three others, are partly psychological portrayal; those three present Bloom's thoughts on the strand (after his encounter with Gerty MacDowell), in the hospital, and in the cab shelter. And thirteen chapters—including three of the final four, and numbering more than three-fourths of the pages in the novel—primarily portray the principal characters' mental events.

Throughout his novel, Joyce the early modernist emphasizes the inner lives of his characters. Perhaps more than anything else, his consistent emphasis establishes the primacy for him of the quasi-life he was creating. *Ulysses* portrays situations crucial to the destinies of three Dubliners; and the resolution of the situation confronting each of them requires no more—though demonstrably no less—than a change of attitude. The portrayal of a crucial conflict or crisis by way of a character's consciousness was not new in literature and drama. But what was new with *Ulysses*—and with Eliot's "Prufrock," *The Waste Land,* and *Murder in the Cathedral*—is that the crucial situation is portrayed in an *action* that has, as its significant *arena,* the mind itself in which the attitude must change, and, as its significant *outcome,* the change of attitude itself—only that mental event—or in the case of "Prufrock," the thwarting of it. In *Ulysses:* the story of Stephen resolves in his mind in nighttown and in the cab shelter; that of Bloom (and Molly), in his own mind in nighttown and in the portion of the catechism following his collision with the sideboard, and in her mental "countersign." In none of the four works are the consequences of the mental event important; and in *Ulysses* they are not even portrayed.

In the interplay between the novel's form and its life, textness and storyness, idiolexis and mimesis, Joyce increased the idiolexis brilliantly as he worked. And there is no doubt that he encourages us to admire and vicariously reproduce his creative odyssey: one need only recall his exultant "How's that for High?" in the letter to Budgen describing the hospital chapter (*Letters,* I, 139). Furthermore, the study of literature in our world causes us to conspire with him by emphasizing technique, allusive pattern, irony and/or indeterminacy, rhetorical and stylistic strategies of narration and/or equivocation. But we would be doing his grand achievement a disservice if we thereby failed to appreciate the end of those means. And because in the reality that is a work of art, means and end are dancer dancing dance, we would simultaneously be partly denigrating the means as well.

The evolution of *Ulysses* enlightens for our world the relationship of telling and tale in it. Joyce's two dramatic creative departures evolved not out of ingenuity, or colored pencils, but out of a felt necessity to change direction. Paradoxically, his increasing emphasis on the formal mode of his book was achieved by the source of its quasi-life—his capacity for experiencing, and using creatively for it, his feelings about it. Able to feel his own life as artist so well, he could feel and create the life—and so, the world—of his characters. Even the tale of the telling is a tale of human experience—of a seven-year lived artistic odyssey.

Notes

1. C. G. Jung, "'Ulysses'—A Monologue," trans. W. Stanley Dell, *Nimbus* 2 (1953); 7–20, 7–8; Wolfgang Iser, "*Ulysses* and the Reader," *James Joyce Broadsheet,* no. 9 (October 1982): 1.

2. My own use of *novel* in the following pages may seem like question-begging; but those pages themselves should supply the grounds of it. For the view that *Ulysses* is best not called a novel, see, e.g.: A. Walton Litz, "The Genre of *Ulysses,*" in *The Theory of the Novel,* ed. John Halperin (New York: Oxford University Press, 1974), 109–20; and Brook Thomas, *James Joyce's* Ulysses: *A Book of Many Happy Returns* (Baton Rouge: Louisiana State University Press, 1982), 141–42. An alternative would be to regard the term as designating, like *tragedy,* the sort of humanistic concept the late aesthetician Morris Weitz called "open": an "open concept" changes, and cannot be defined precisely; but it does not consequently fail to exist.

3. Stuart Gilbert, *James Joyce's* Ulysses (New York: 1930), 8–9; 2d ed., 22.

4. John Paul Riquelme, *Teller and Tale in Joyce's Fiction* (Baltimore: Johns Hopkins University Press, 1983), xv, xiv.

5. Edmund Wilson, *Axel's Castle* (New York: Charles Scribner's Sons, 1931), 220, 221.
6. The terms "symbolic structure" and "human drama" are from Michael Groden's *Ulysses in Progress* (Princeton: Princeton University Press, 1977), 21; the terms "characters" and "language" are from Hugh Kenner's *Joyce's Voices* (Berkeley and Los Angeles: University of California Press, 1978), 41, and "drama" and "surface" from David Hayman's *Ulysses: The Mechanics of Meaning*, 2d ed. (Madison: University of Wisconsin Press, 1982), 88.
7. S. L. Goldberg, *The Classical Temper: A Study of James Joyce's Ulysses* (London: Chatto and Windus, 1961). See Groden, 18–20 and Thomas, 8–16. The parallel phrases recur in Thomas.
8. Among the authors of book-length studies, Marilyn French, Arnold Goldman, David Hayman, James H. Maddox, Jr., to an extent Brook Thomas (see, e.g., 18).
9. The inability of these critics to integrate the alternative conceptions of the novel's essential mode can be illustrated neatly by two valuable discussions of the relationsip of the two modes themselves: Barbara Hardy, "Form as End and Means in 'Ulysses,'" *Orbis Litterarum* 19 (1964): 194–200; and the relevant parts of Peter K. Garrett, "JAMES JOYCE: The Artifice of Reality," *Scene and Symbol from George Eliot to James Joyce* (New Haven: Yale University Press, 1969): 214–17, 245–71. Garrett uses "mode" as I do: his subject is Joyce's "progress from a realistic . . . toward a more symbolic mode" (214) through *Ulysses*. Hardy's title refers to the three purposes served by "form" (197); and two correspond to the two modes.

Garrett finds an increasing "conflict of modes" in the course of the novel; Hardy proposes instead that the two functions of "form" achieve throughout "a human complexity" eliciting "the admission of paradox" (199). What is to the point here is not their contrary views of the relationship of the modes of *Ulysses*, but their own shared implicit conception of the novel. While granting due acknowledgment to the presence of gratuitous idiolectic play—"free play," "form as end rather than means" as Hardy puts it (196)—both critics are concerned with, in Garrett's words, "the respective roles ["of symbolism and realism in *Ulysses*"] in the creation of meaning" (256). Hence, both subvert their common intention by conceiving the novel as essentially "tale"—the "meaning" created.

10. Walton Litz, "Ithaca," in Clive Hart and David Hayman, eds., *James Joyce's Ulysses* (Berkeley and Los Angeles; University of California Press, 1974); 385–405, 387.
11. C. H. Peake, *James Joyce: The Citizen and the Artist* (Stanford, Calif.: Stanford University Press, 1977), 347.
12. Thomas, op. cit. 16–17.
13. Ibid., 23.
14. A similar flaw seems to me true of attempts, such as that by Roger Fowler, in *Linguistics and the Novel* (London: Methuen, 1977), to liken the elements of a novel to those of a linguistic structure. For example, lexical items may be paradigmatically exchangeable, but narrative "items" are not. A character is what he or she has done and been as plot since the opening paragraph; hence, to substitute a different character is not to change meaning within the (syntagmatic) action of the novel, but to subvert that action.
15. John Henry Raleigh, *The Chronicle of Leopold and Molly Bloom: Ulysses as Narrative* (Berkeley and Los Angeles: University of California Press, 1977); Peter Costello, *Leopold Bloom: A Biography* (Dublin: Gill and Macmillan, 1981). The quoted phrase is from Raleigh, 6.
16. Hugh Kenner, *A Colder Eye* (New York: Alfred A. Knopf, 1983), 195–96.
17. All quotations from Karen Lawrence, *The Odyssey of Style in Ulysses* (Princeton: Princeton University Press, 1981), 12.
18. Groden, 21. He characterizes the two modes as "balanced" in the novel's "middle stage" (from the end of the "First Part" to the nighttown chapter), which "serv[es] as a bridge" 94. See also, e.g., Kenner, *Joyce's Voices*, 41, 45; and Riquelme, 217.
19. Lawrence, 196.
20. Thomas, 158; Hugh Kenner, *Ulysses* (London: Allen and Unwin, 1980), 55. Thomas cites Fritz Senn, and Kenner, Arnold Goldman, as suggesting the reading to them. It should be mentioned that Kenner invokes the quasi-life in support: Stephen is too poor and profligate to have been able to pay the twelve pounds rent.

21. Gerald L. Bruns, *Inventions: Writing, Textuality, and Understanding in Literary History* (New Haven: Yale University Press, 1982), 160–74; quotation from 171–72.
22. Ibid., 160–61, 194 n.3.
23. Stanley Sultan, *The Argument of Ulysses* (Columbus: Ohio State University Press, 1964), 144.
24. Arnold Goldman, *The Joyce Paradox: Form and Freedom in His Fiction* (Evanston, Ill.: Northwestern University Press, 1966), 82; Hayman, 1st ed. (Englewood Cliffs, N.J.: Prentice-Hall, 1970, 70 (the quotation is from the 2 ed., 123); Kenner, *Ulysses,* 64–65.
25. See e.g., Wilson, 208 and Gilbert, 351; among recent critics, see, e.g., Groden, 53 and Lawrence, 168.
26. See respectively, e.g.: Gerald L. Bruns, "Eumaeus," 363–83 in Hart and Hayman, 363–67; and Lawrence, 168. The quoted phrase is Groden's.
27. Lawrence, 168.
28. Bruns, in Hart and Hayman, 364, 366; Goldman, 101; Groden, 53; Hayman, 2d ed., 102–3.
29. Thomas, 134. Also Kenner, *Joyce's Voices,* 38; and Sultan, 364. The energy of the style is a bit more apparent in the *Critical Edition,* because of the removal of about six hundred spurious commas.
30. Sultan and Thomas, ibid; Kenner, ibid., 35–38.
31. Thomas, 134; Bruns, 367.
32. For details of the associative pattern, see, e.g., Sultan 252–53, 256–57, 434–35.
33. Joyce seems to have copied much of the actual *Evening Telegraph* phrasing in the passage (e.g., "Throwaway . . . won cleverly at the finish by a length"); but his insertion of "bay filly," and having characters call Sceptre a mare, seems to be subverting the phallic significance of the name of the horse backed by Boylan and favored to defeat the "rank outsider." For the *Telegraph* article, see Don Gifford and Robert J. Seidman, *Notes for Joyce: An Annotation of James Joyce's Ulysses* (New York: E. P. Dutton, 1974), 357, 451.
34. For a discussion of the details of Stephen's realization and response, see, e.g., Sultan, 378–82.
35. Lawrence, 196.
36. Ibid., 182–83.
37. James H. Maddox, Jr., *Joyce's Ulysses and the Assault upon Character* (New Brunswick, N.J.: Rutgers University Press, 1978), 188–89.
38. Hayman, 2d ed., 103.
39. Litz, "Ithaca," in Hart and Hayman, 393.
40. Lawrence, 184.
41. Hugh Kenner, "Molly's Masterstroke," *James Joyce Quarterly,* 10 (1972): 19–28, 23.
42. Maddox, 221; Ellman, *James Joyce* (New York: Oxford University Press, 1959), 388.
43. The first phrases are from Harry Levin, *James Joyce: A Critical Introduction* (Norfolk, Conn: New Directions, 1941; rev. ed., 1960), 125. For the sources of the others, see Maddox, p. 222 n.5. In the course of a functional explanation it proposes for "her most salient characteristic—marital infidelity" (50), Philip F. Herring, "The Bedsteadfastness of Molly Bloom," *Modern Fiction Studies* 15 (1969); 49–61, gives a detailed account of such appraisals of Molly's character (57–59).
44. Robert M. Adams, *Surface and Symbol: The Consistency of James Joyce's Ulysses* (New York: Oxford University Press, 1962), 35–43, 37, 40; and *James Joyce: Common Sense and Beyond* (New York: Random House, 1966), 166.
45. For example, Costello perpetuates it in his 1981 "biography"; and a paper read at the English Institute the same year accepted it without question. Gilbert and other critics have discussed the possible relevance to *Ulysses* of post-Homeric accounts of Penelope as adulterous—most often the lover of the god Hermes and mother of Pan, although Joyce also may have recalled Vico's statement in *La Scienza Nuova* that "In other versions Penelope prostitutes herself to the suitors." For details see Herring, 53–55.
46. For a detailed exposition, see Sultan, 431–33. See, also: Hayman, 2d ed., 23–24, 117–118 n. 5, p. 154 (which records an exchange in print about the list); Robert Boyle, S. J., "Penelope," Hart and Hayman, 407–33, 413–15; Marilyn French, *The Book as World: James Joyce's Ulysses* (Cambridge: Harvard University Press, 1976), 252–56; Maddox, 221.

47. Hayman, 2d ed., 118.
48. Boyle, 411, 413–14; French 255–56; Maddox, 223, 224.
49. Maddox, 222, 224.
50. French, 257, 260, 260–61.
51. Riquelme, 228.
52. See Sultan, 422–25.
53. David G. Wright, *Characters of Joyce* (Totowa, N.J.: Barnes and Noble, 1983), 97.
54. For a discussion, see Sultan, 425–49.
55. See, e.g., Groden, 187.
56. "Ulysse n'est . . . que le gigantesque aboutissement d'une époque révolue. Avec ce livre Joyce atteint à un résultat . . . singuliérement distingué . . . elle ne possède aucun des signes qui permettent de diagnostiquer la présence d'un style." T. S. Eliot, "Lettre d'Angleterre: Le Style Dans La Prose Anglaise Contemporaine," *La Nouvelle Revue Francaise* 19 (1922): 751–56, 754.
57. Hayman, 103.